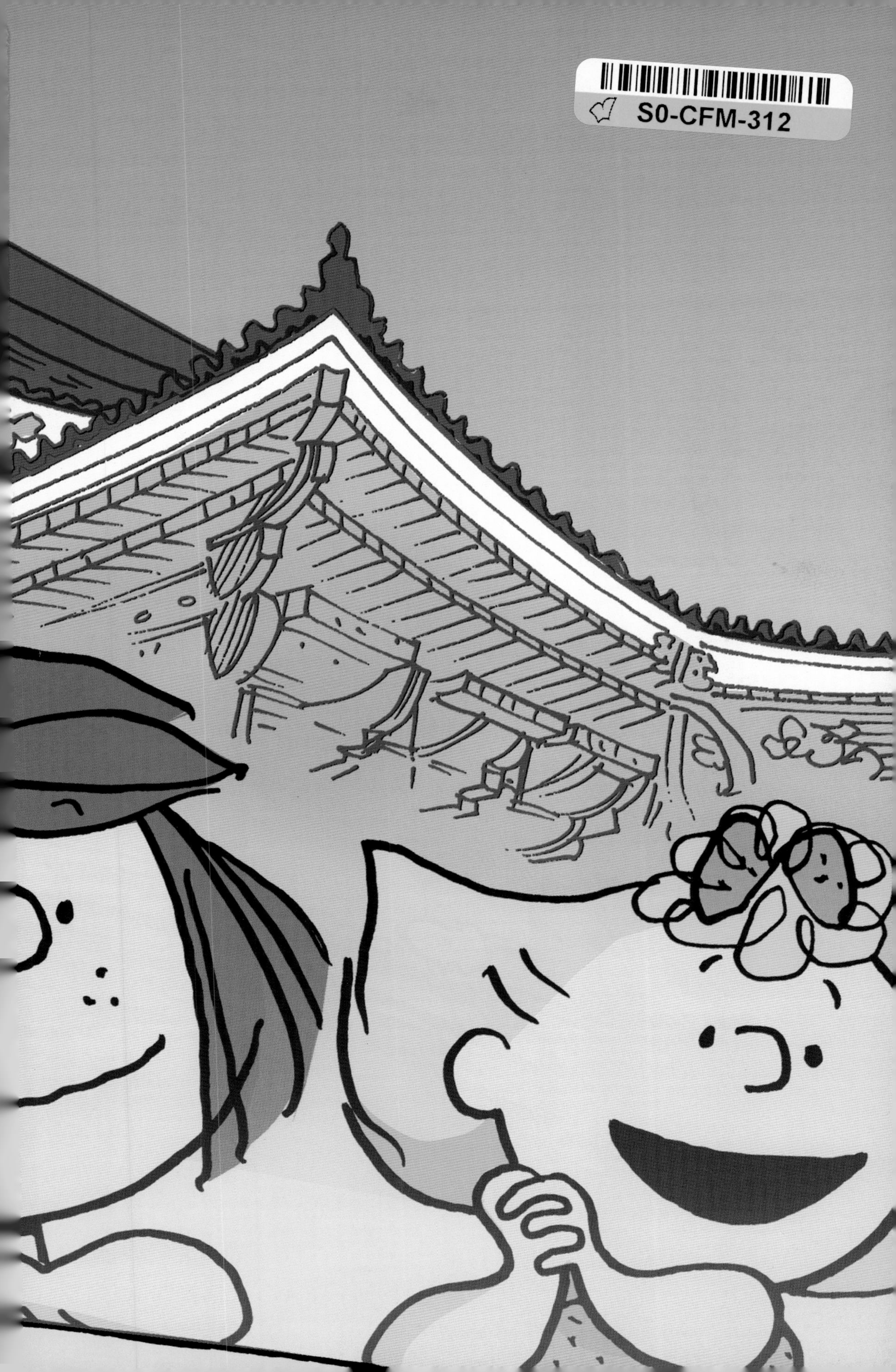

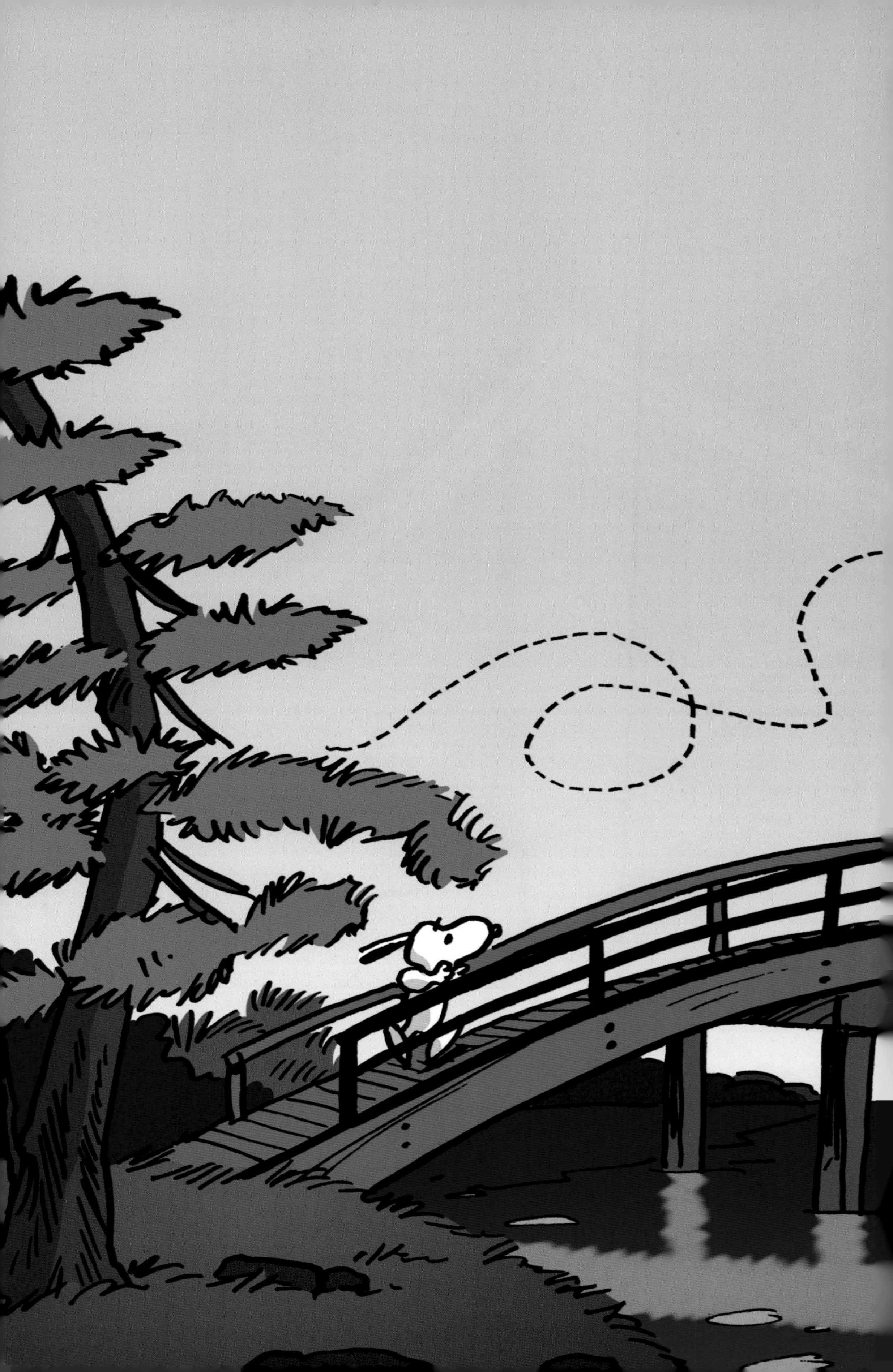

Charles M. Schulz

PEANUTS

IT'S TOKYO, CHARLIE BROWN!

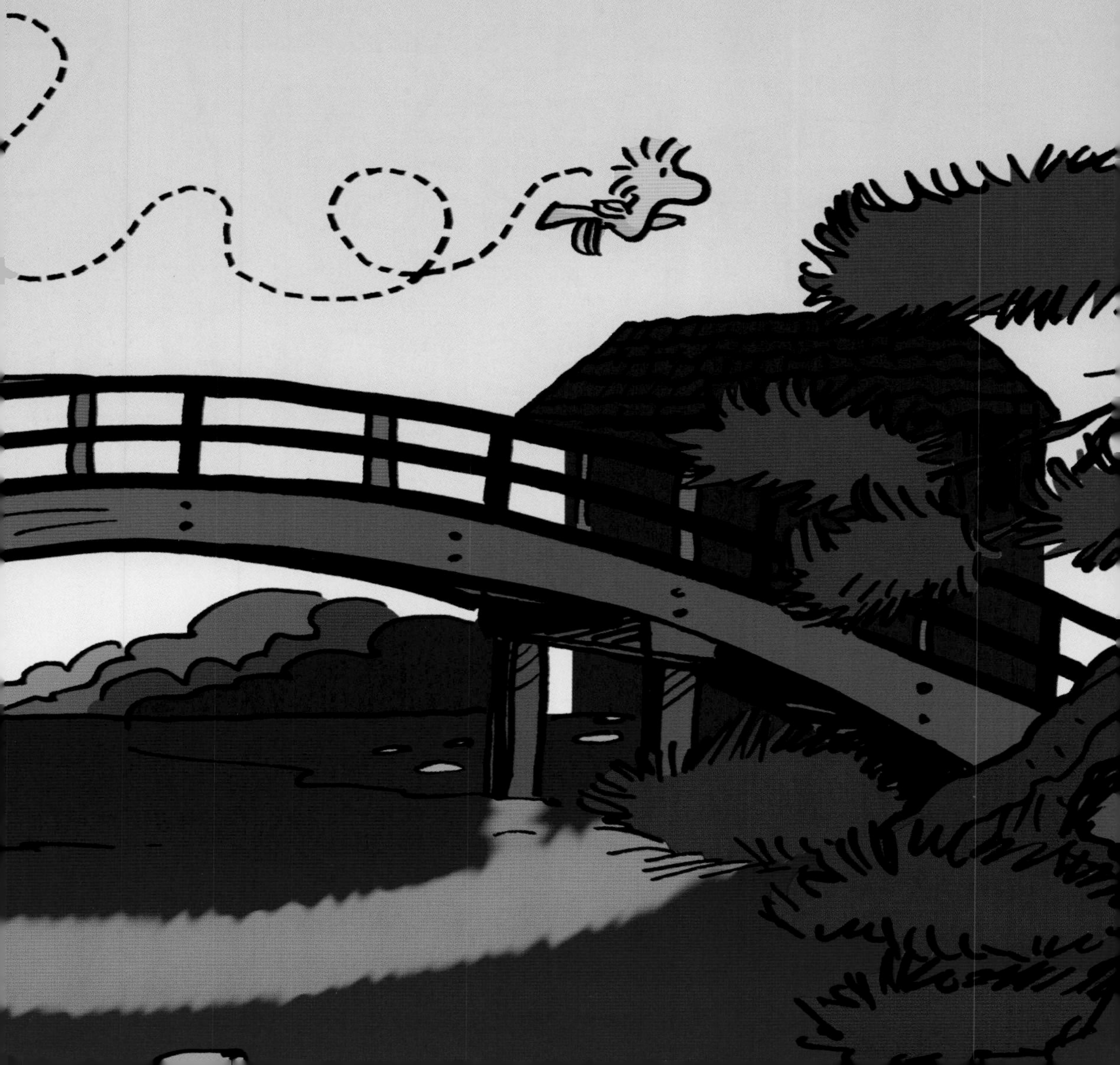

ROSS RICHIE CEO & Founder • JACK CUMMINS President • MARK SMYLIE Founder of Archaia • MATT GAGNON Editor-in-Chief • FILIP SABLIK VP of Publishing & Marketing • STEPHEN CHRISTY VP of Development
LANCE KREITER VP of Licensing & Merchandising • PHIL BARBARO VP of Finance • BRYCE CARLSON Managing Editor • MEL CAYLO Marketing Manager • SCOTT NEWMAN Production Design Manager • IRENE BRADISH Operations Manager
DAFNA PLEBAN Editor • SHANNON WATTERS Editor • ERIC HARBURN Editor • REBECCA TAYLOR Editor • IAN BRILL Editor • CHRIS ROSA Assistant Editor • ALEX GALER Assistant Editor • WHITNEY LEOPARD Assistant Editor
JASMINE AMIRI Assistant Editor • CAMERON CHITTOCK Assistant Editor • HANNAH NANCE PARTLOW Production Designer • KELSEY DIETERICH Production Designer • EMI YONEMURA BROWN Production Designer
DEVIN FUNCHES E-Commerce & Inventory Coordinator • ANDY LIEGL Event Coordinator • BRIANNA HART Executive Assistant • AARON FERRARA Operations Assistant • JOSÉ MEZA Sales Assistant • ELIZABETH LOUGHRIDGE Accounting Assistant

PEANUTS: IT'S TOKYO, CHARLIE BROWN, May 2014. Published by KaBOOM!, a division of Boom Entertainment, Inc. All contents, unless otherwise specified, Copyright © 2014 Peanuts Worldwide, LLC. All rights reserved. KaBOOM!™ and the KaBOOM! logo are trademarks of Boom Entertainment, Inc., registered in various countries and categories. All characters, events, and institutions depicted herein are fictional. Any similarity between any of the names, characters, persons, events, and/or institutions in this publication to actual names, characters, and persons, whether living or dead, events, and/or institutions is unintended and purely coincidental. KaBOOM! does not read or accept unsolicited submissions of ideas, stories, or artwork.

A catalog record of this book is available from OCLC and from the KaBOOM! website, www.kaboom-studios.com, on the Librarians Page.

BOOM! Studios, 5670 Wilshire Boulevard, Suite 450, Los Angeles, CA 90036-5679. Printed in China. Second Printing.

ISBN: 978-1-60886-270-2, eISBN: 978-1-61398-113-9

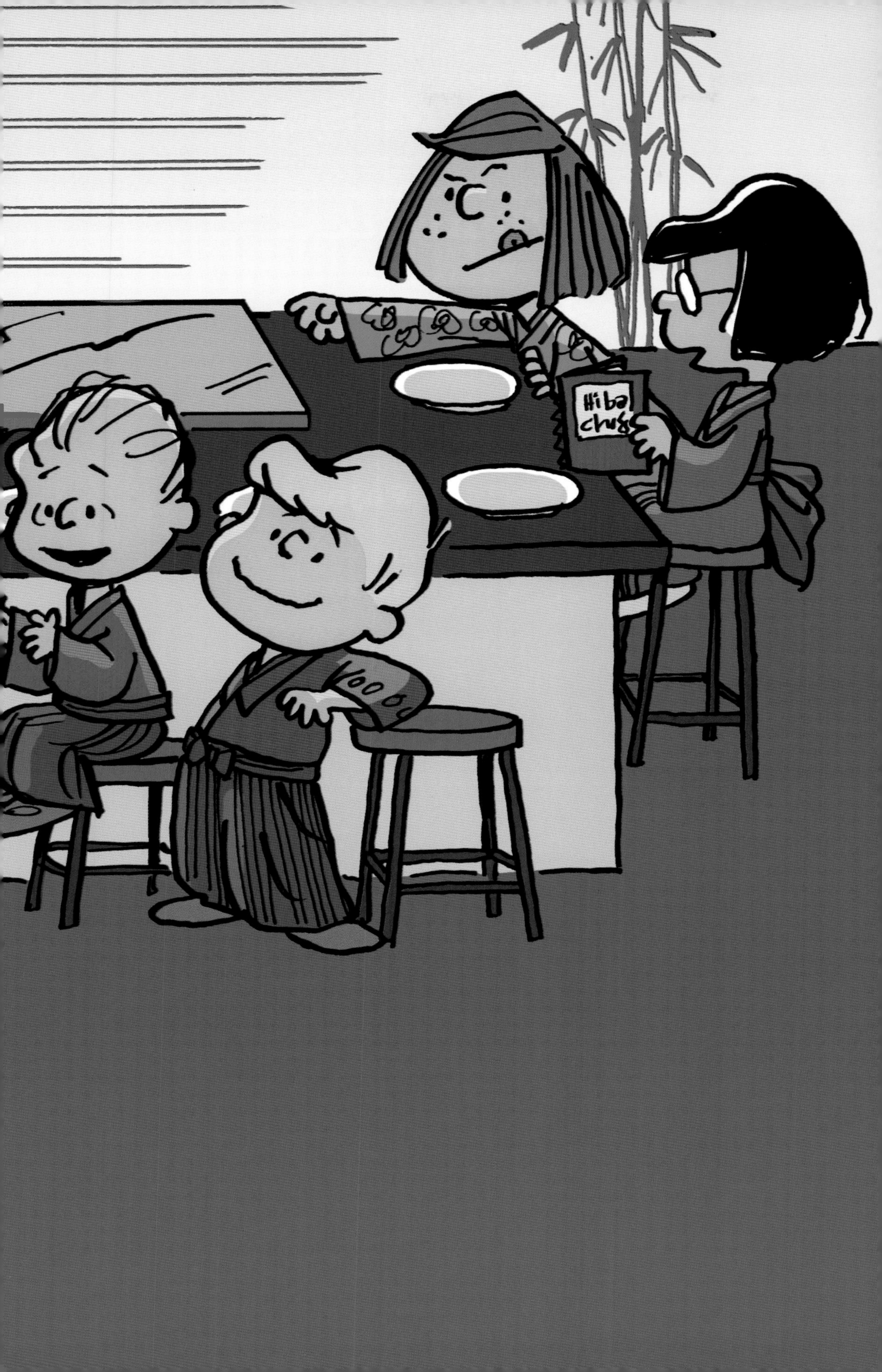

Based on the comic strip, Peanuts, by
Charles M. Schulz

STORY AND PENCILS:
Vicki Scott

INKS:
Paige Braddock

COLORS:
Nina Kester with Mirka Andolfo

LETTERS:
Alexis E. Fajardo

COVER:
Vicki Scott

COVER DESIGN:
Iain R. Morris

ASSISTANT EDITOR:
Adam Staffaroni

EDITOR:
Matt Gagnon

TRADE DESIGN:
Stephanie Gonzaga

FOR CHARLES M. SCHULZ CREATIVE ASSOCIATES:
Creative Director: Paige Braddock
Mananging Editor: Alexis E. Fajardo

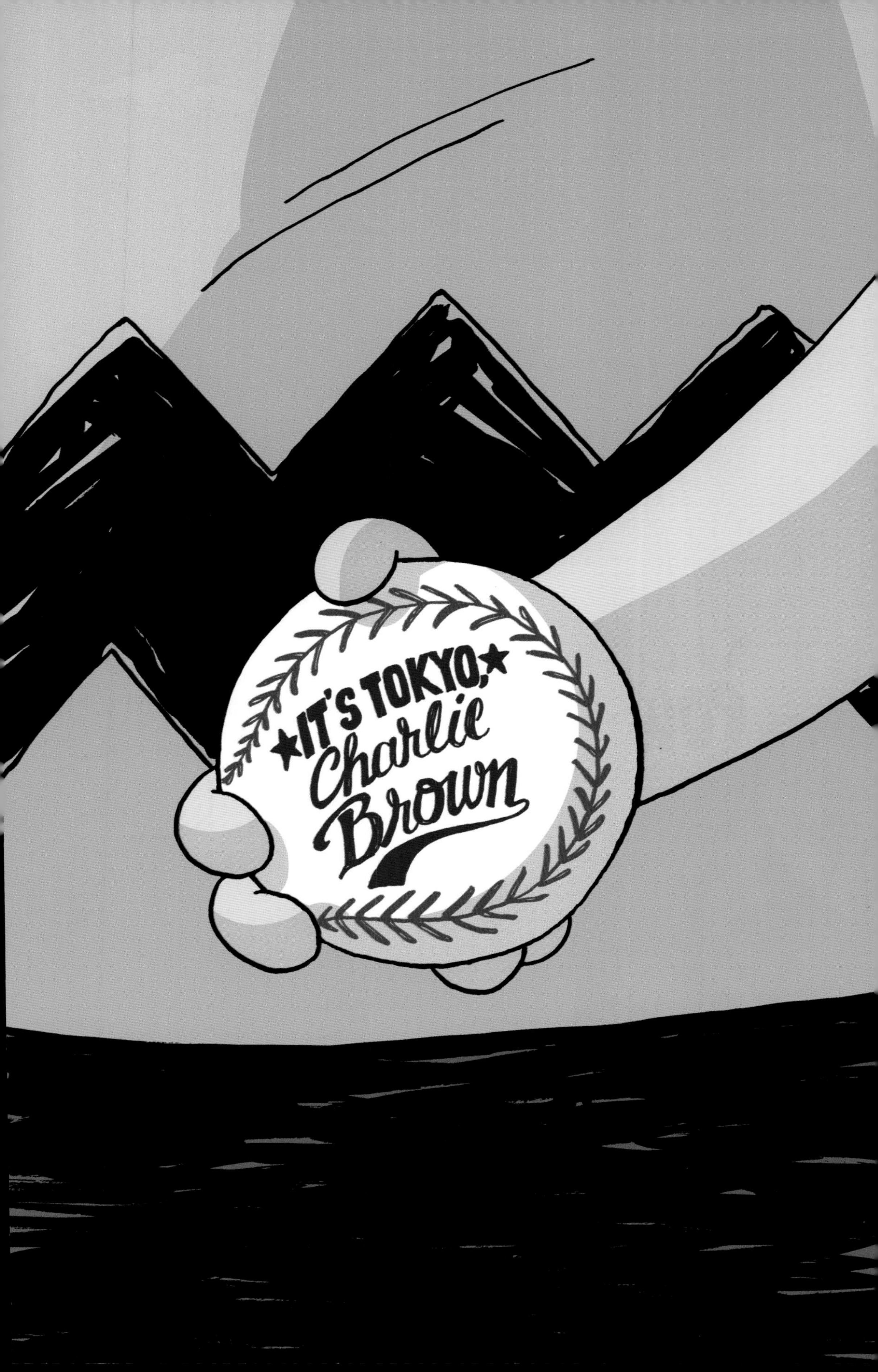
★IT'S TOKYO,★
Charlie
Brown

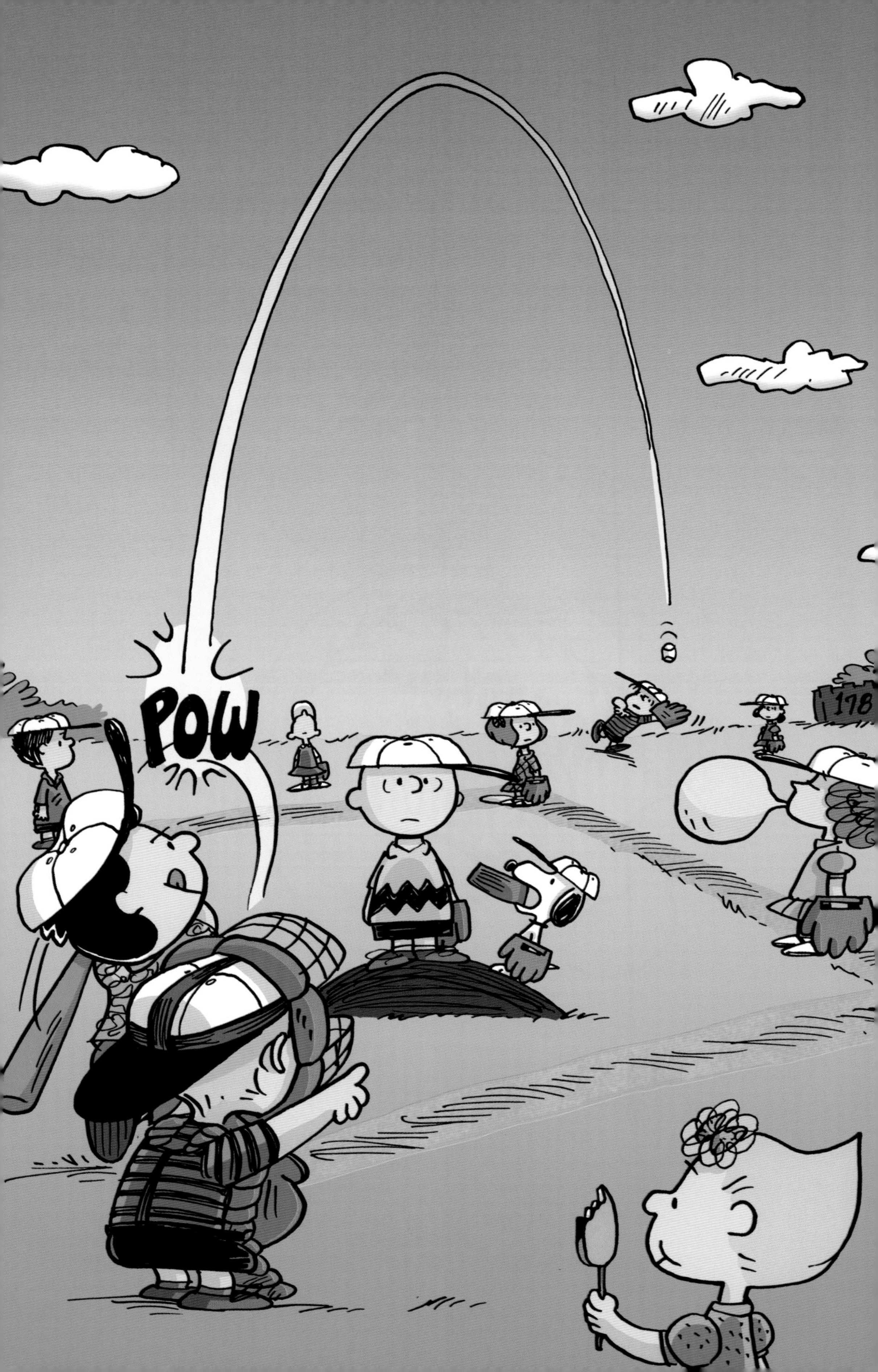
POW
178

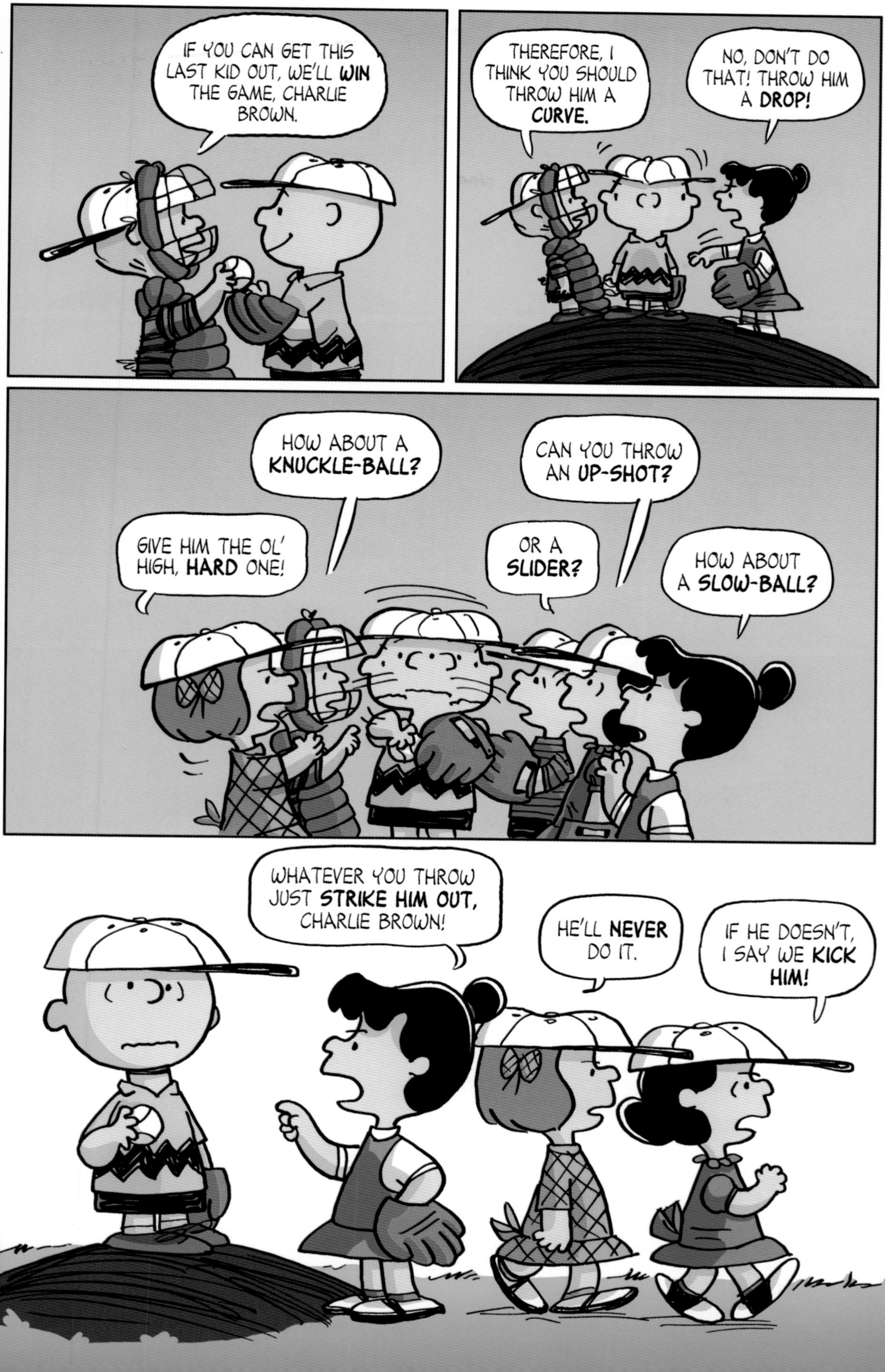
IF YOU CAN GET THIS LAST KID OUT, WE'LL WIN THE GAME, CHARLIE BROWN.
THEREFORE, I THINK YOU SHOULD THROW HIM A CURVE.
NO, DON'T DO THAT! THROW HIM A DROP!
GIVE HIM THE OL' HIGH, HARD ONE!
HOW ABOUT A KNUCKLE-BALL?
OR A SLIDER?
CAN YOU THROW AN UP-SHOT?
HOW ABOUT A SLOW-BALL?
WHATEVER YOU THROW JUST STRIKE HIM OUT, CHARLIE BROWN!
HE'LL NEVER DO IT.
IF HE DOESN'T, I SAY WE KICK HIM!

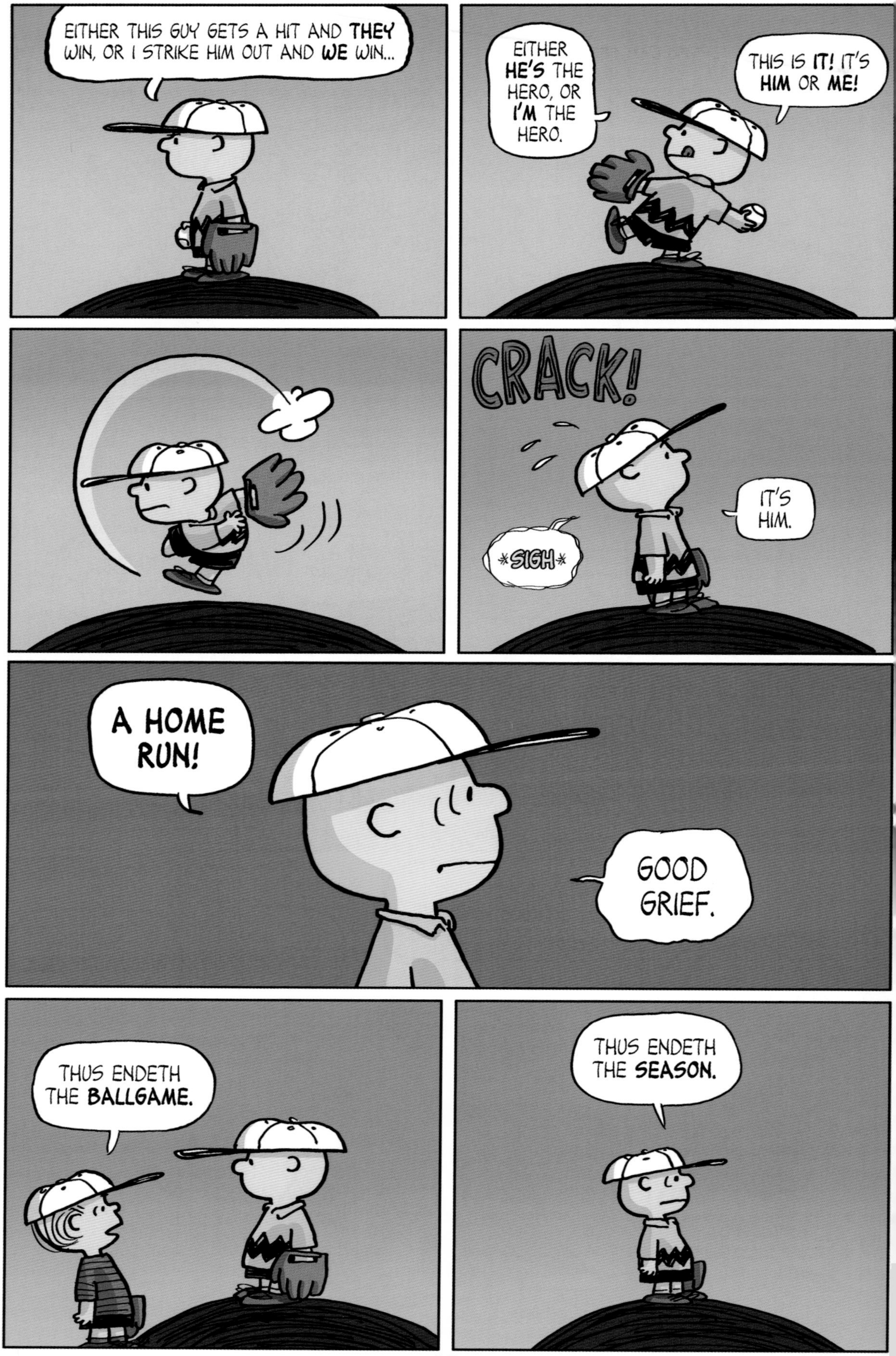
EITHER THIS GUY GETS A HIT AND THEY WIN, OR I STRIKE HIM OUT AND WE WIN...
EITHER HE'S THE HERO, OR I'M THE HERO.
THIS IS IT! IT'S HIM OR ME!
CRACK!
SIGH
IT'S HIM.
A HOME RUN!
GOOD GRIEF.
THUS ENDETH THE BALLGAME.
THUS ENDETH THE SEASON.

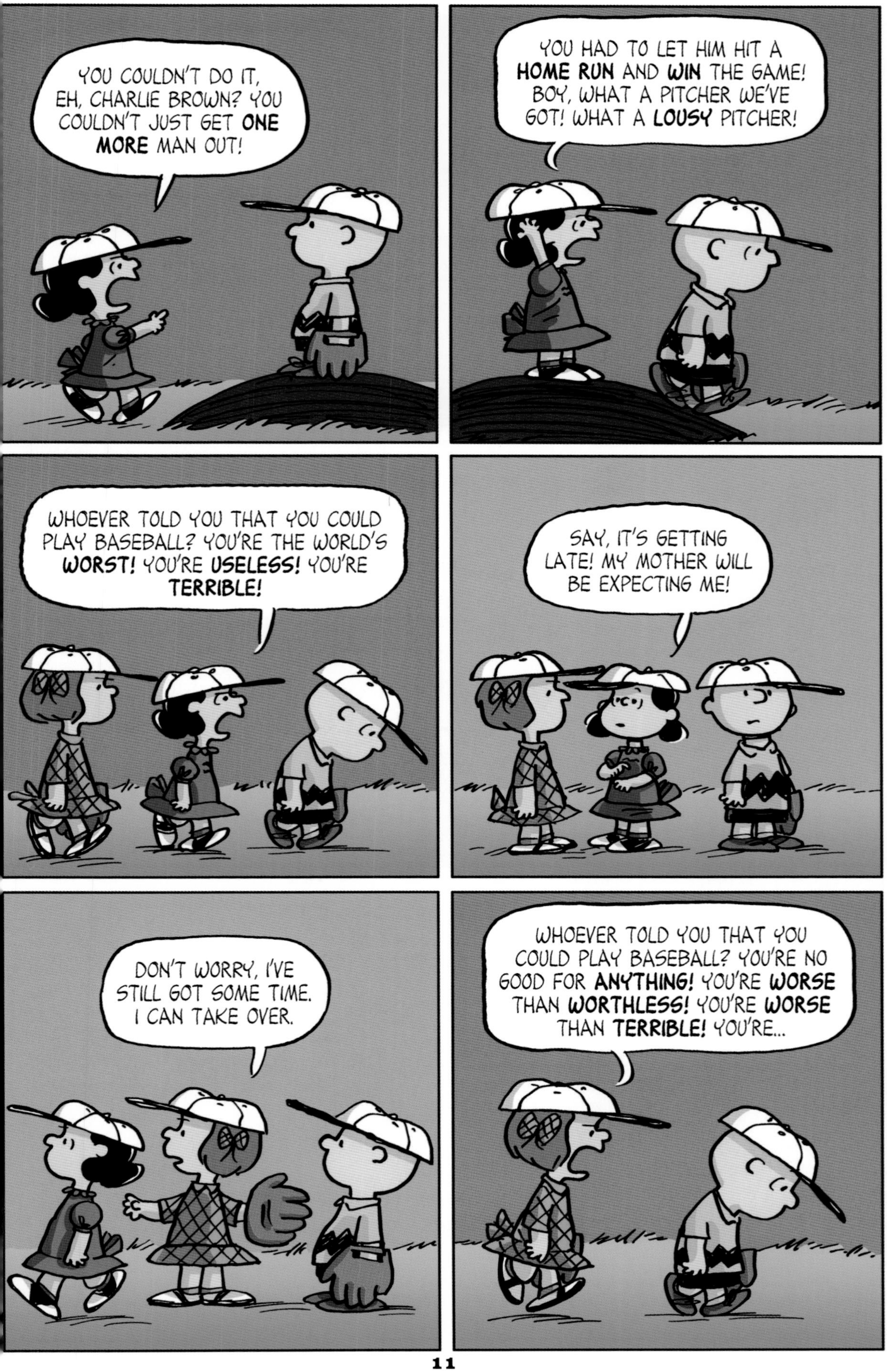
YOU COULDN'T DO IT, EH, CHARLIE BROWN? YOU COULDN'T JUST GET **ONE MORE** MAN OUT!
YOU HAD TO LET HIM HIT A **HOME RUN** AND **WIN** THE GAME! BOY, WHAT A PITCHER WE'VE GOT! WHAT A **LOUSY** PITCHER!
WHOEVER TOLD YOU THAT YOU COULD PLAY BASEBALL? YOU'RE THE WORLD'S **WORST!** YOU'RE **USELESS!** YOU'RE **TERRIBLE!**
SAY, IT'S GETTING LATE! MY MOTHER WILL BE EXPECTING ME!
DON'T WORRY, I'VE STILL GOT SOME TIME. I CAN TAKE OVER.
WHOEVER TOLD YOU THAT YOU COULD PLAY BASEBALL? YOU'RE NO GOOD FOR **ANYTHING!** YOU'RE **WORSE** THAN **WORTHLESS!** YOU'RE **WORSE** THAN **TERRIBLE!** YOU'RE...

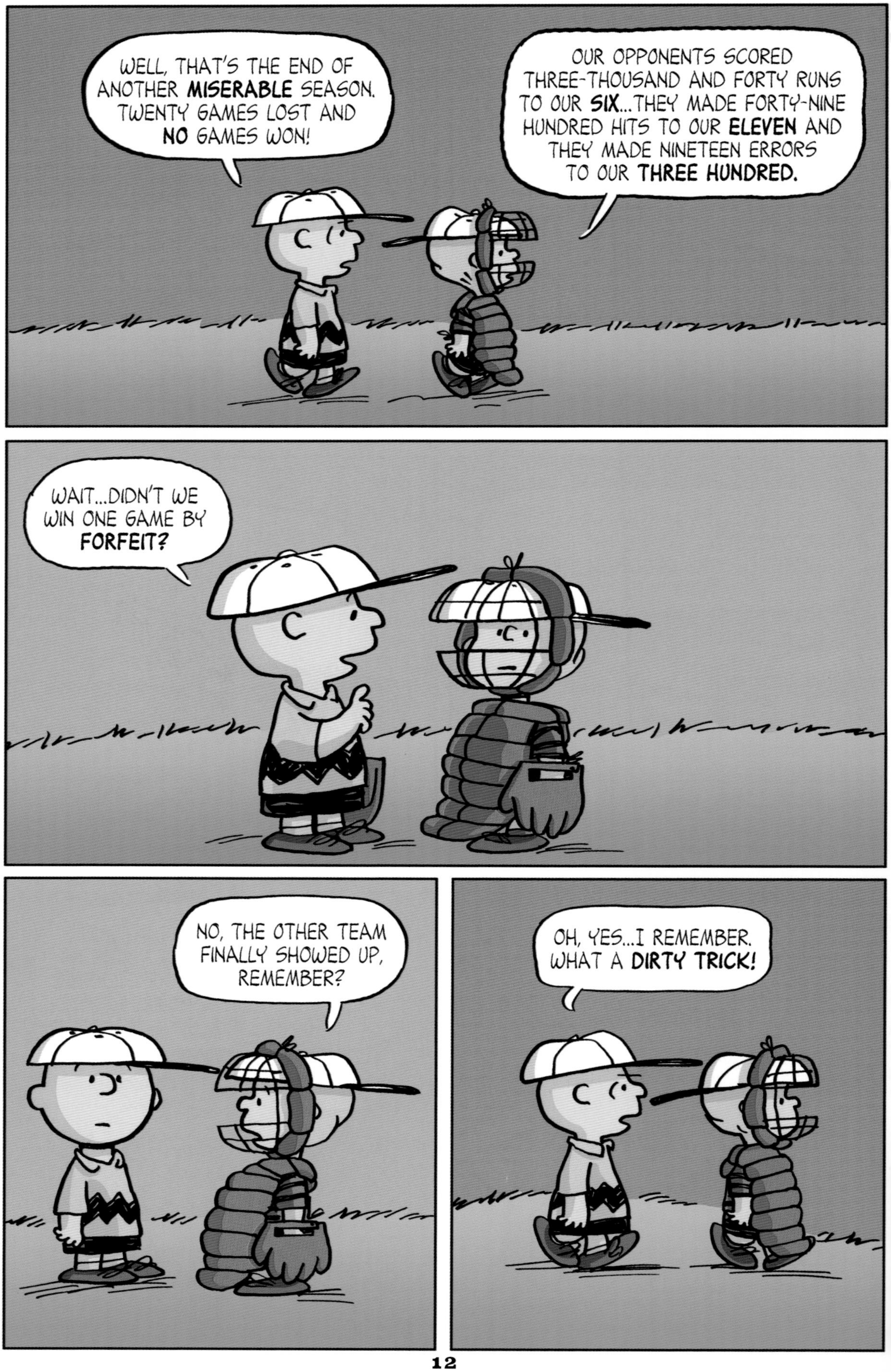
WELL, THAT'S THE END OF ANOTHER **MISERABLE** SEASON. TWENTY GAMES LOST AND **NO** GAMES WON!
OUR OPPONENTS SCORED THREE-THOUSAND AND FORTY RUNS TO OUR **SIX**...THEY MADE FORTY-NINE HUNDRED HITS TO OUR **ELEVEN** AND THEY MADE NINETEEN ERRORS TO OUR **THREE HUNDRED.**
WAIT...DIDN'T WE WIN ONE GAME BY **FORFEIT?**
NO, THE OTHER TEAM FINALLY SHOWED UP, REMEMBER?
OH, YES...I REMEMBER. WHAT A **DIRTY TRICK!**

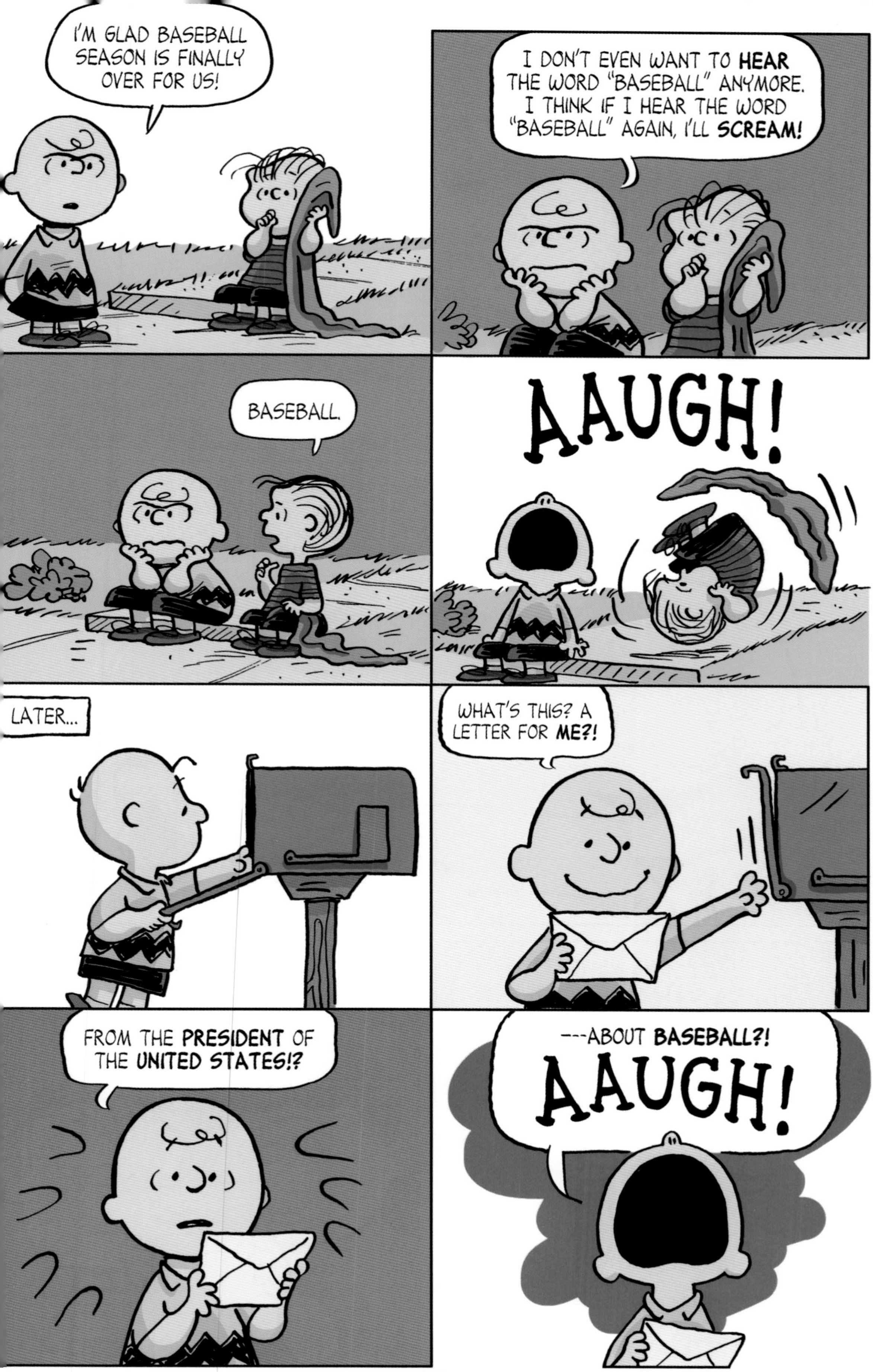

I'M GLAD BASEBALL SEASON IS FINALLY OVER FOR US!
I DON'T EVEN WANT TO HEAR THE WORD "BASEBALL" ANYMORE. I THINK IF I HEAR THE WORD "BASEBALL" AGAIN, I'LL SCREAM!
BASEBALL.
AAUGH!
LATER...
WHAT'S THIS? A LETTER FOR ME?!
FROM THE PRESIDENT OF THE UNITED STATES!?
---ABOUT BASEBALL?! AAUGH!

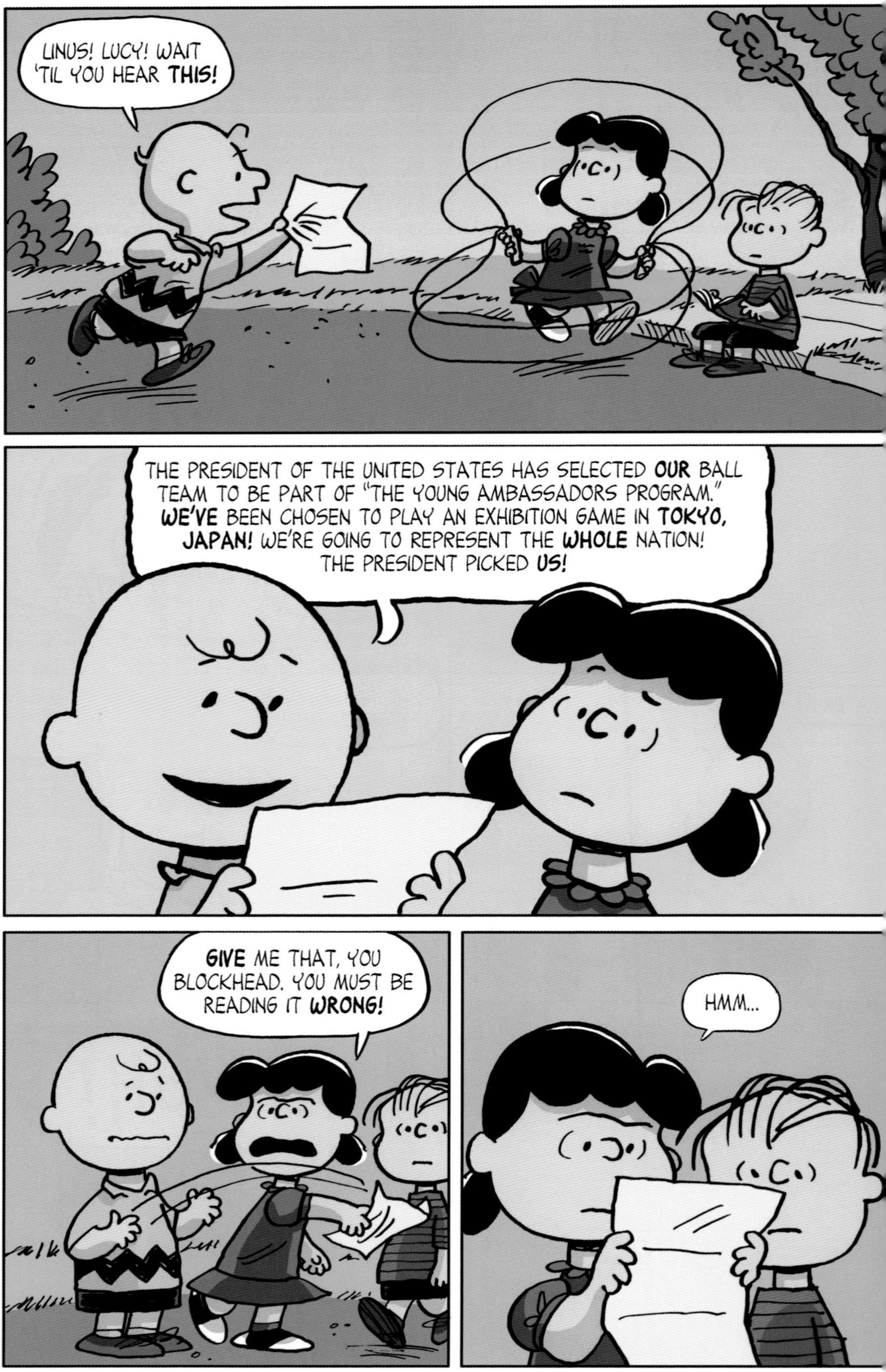
LINUS! LUCY! WAIT 'TIL YOU HEAR **THIS!**
THE PRESIDENT OF THE UNITED STATES HAS SELECTED **OUR** BALL TEAM TO BE PART OF "THE YOUNG AMBASSADORS PROGRAM." **WE'VE** BEEN CHOSEN TO PLAY AN EXHIBITION GAME IN **TOKYO, JAPAN!** WE'RE GOING TO REPRESENT THE **WHOLE** NATION! THE PRESIDENT PICKED **US!**
GIVE ME THAT, YOU BLOCKHEAD. YOU MUST BE READING IT **WRONG!**
HMM...

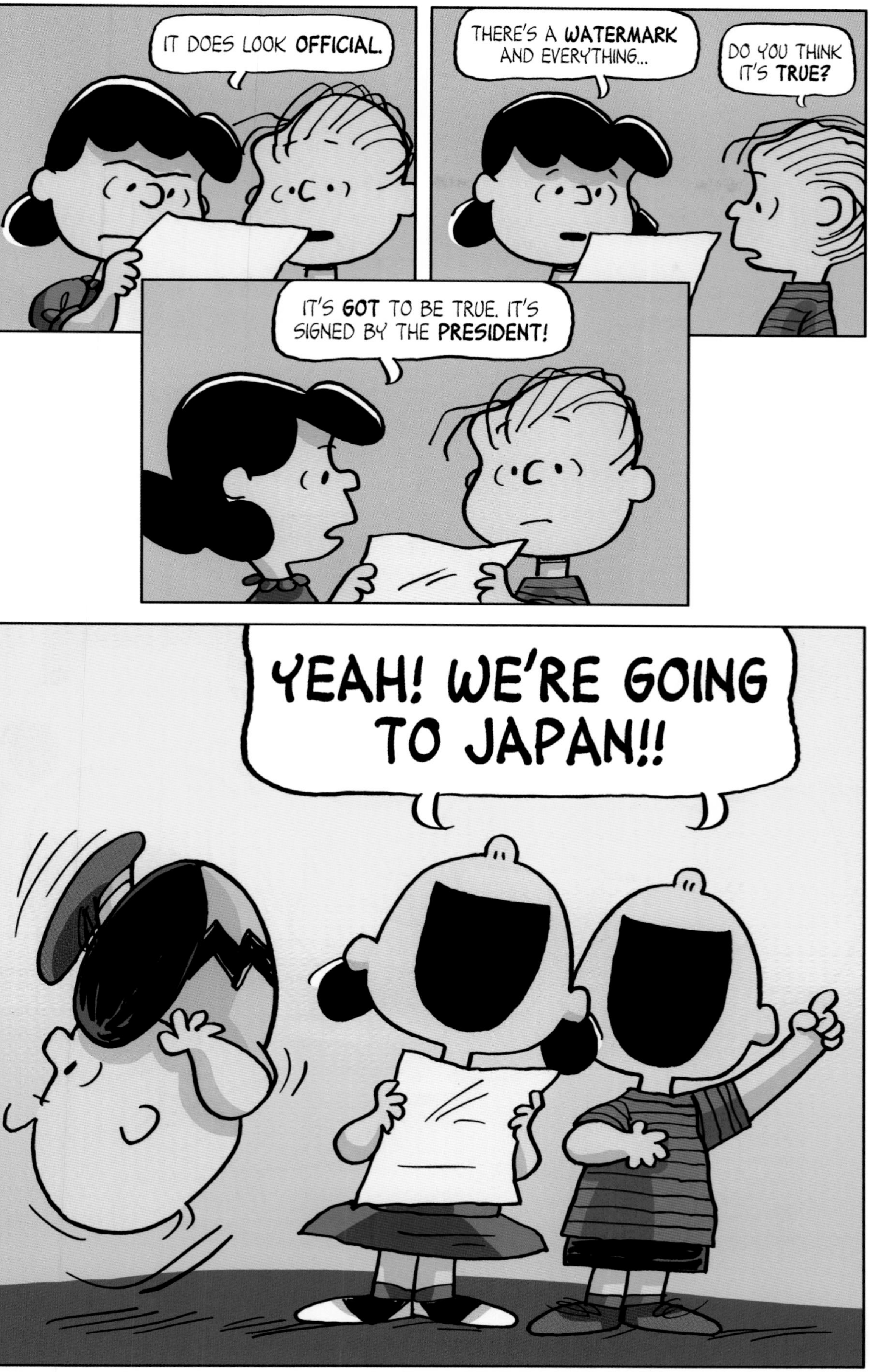
IT DOES LOOK OFFICIAL.
THERE'S A WATERMARK AND EVERYTHING...
DO YOU THINK IT'S TRUE?
IT'S GOT TO BE TRUE. IT'S SIGNED BY THE PRESIDENT!
YEAH! WE'RE GOING TO JAPAN!!

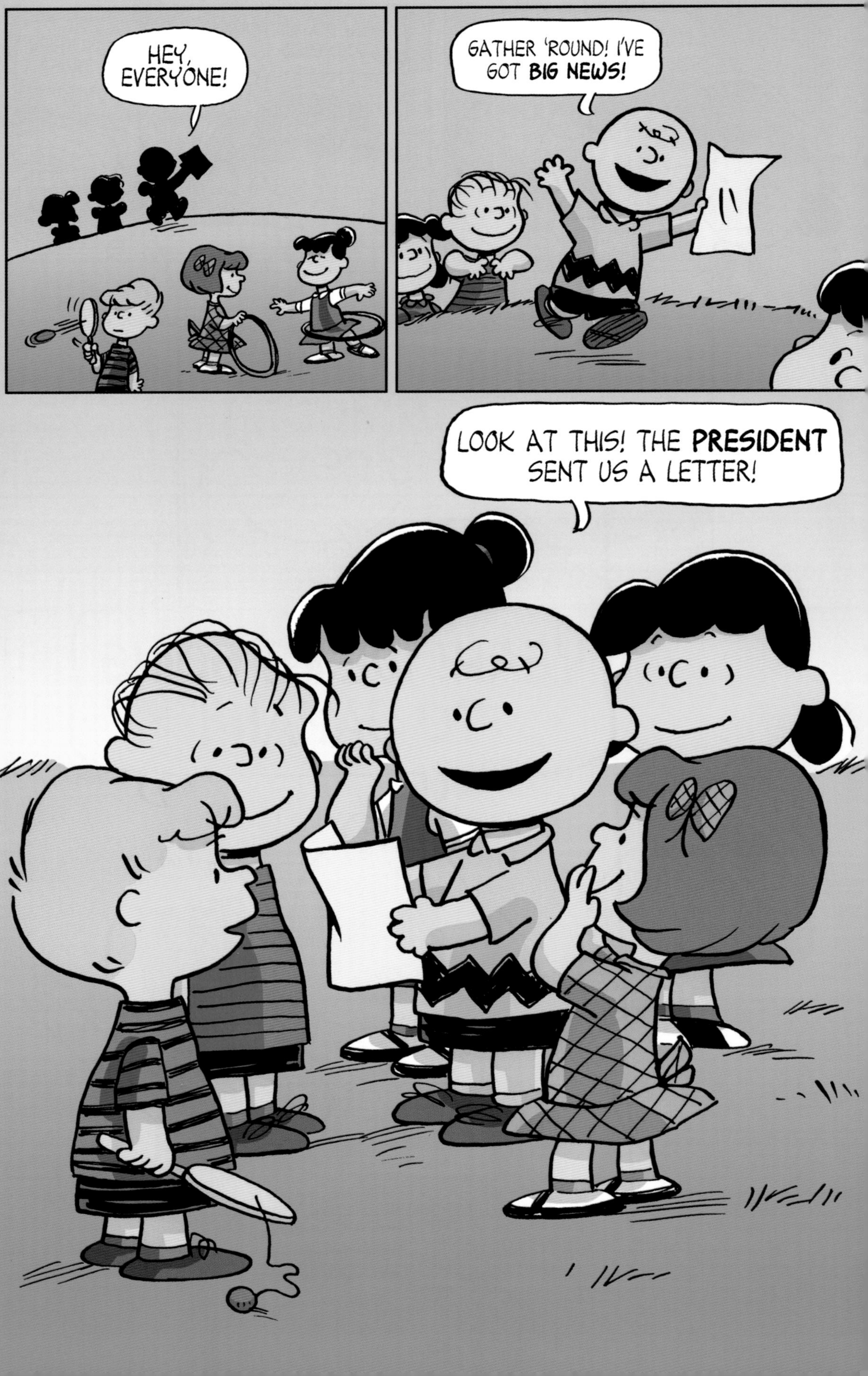
HEY, EVERYONE!
GATHER 'ROUND! I'VE GOT BIG NEWS!
LOOK AT THIS! THE PRESIDENT SENT US A LETTER!

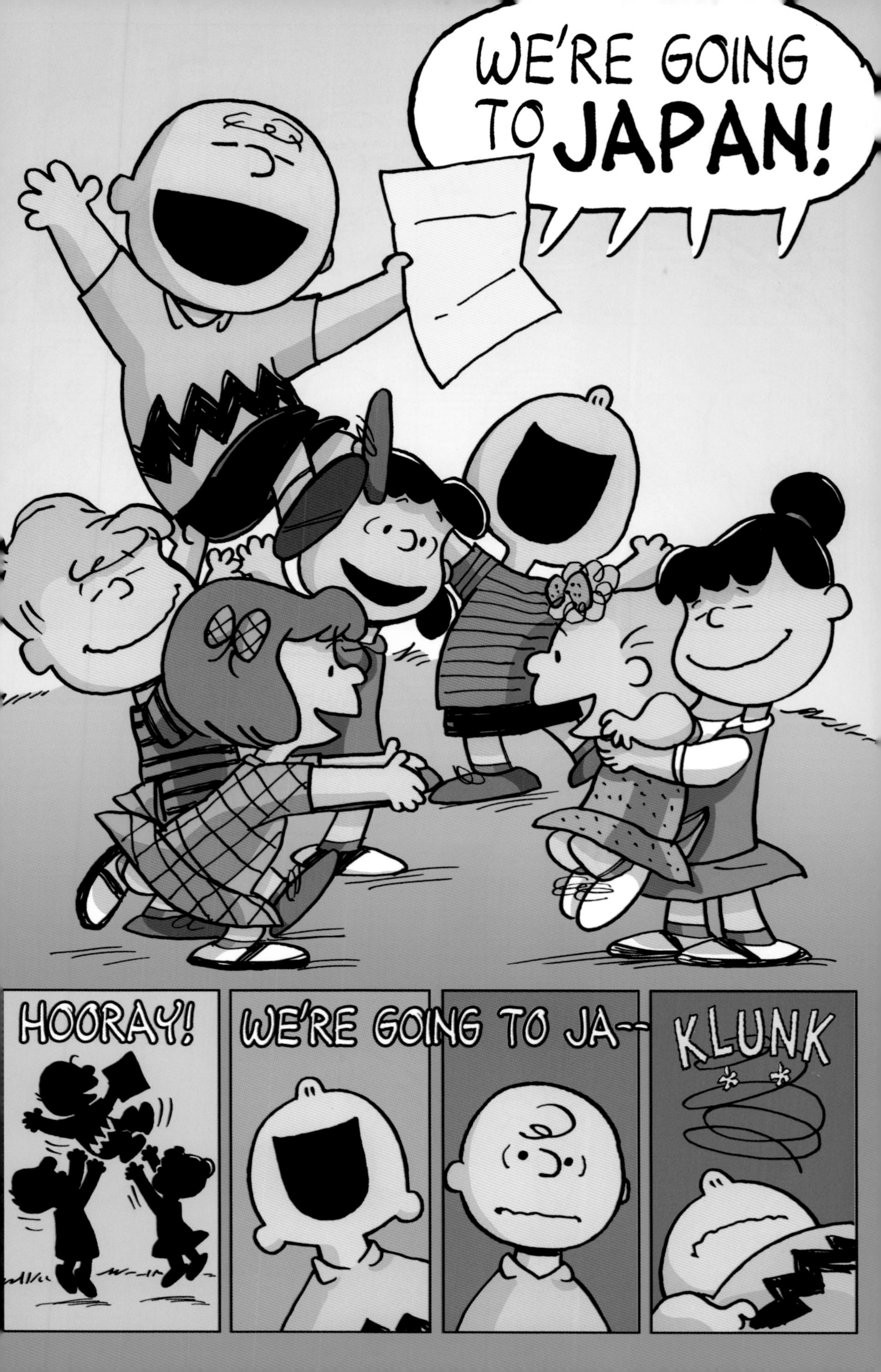
WE'RE GOING TO JAPAN!
HOORAY!
WE'RE GOING TO JA--
KLUNK

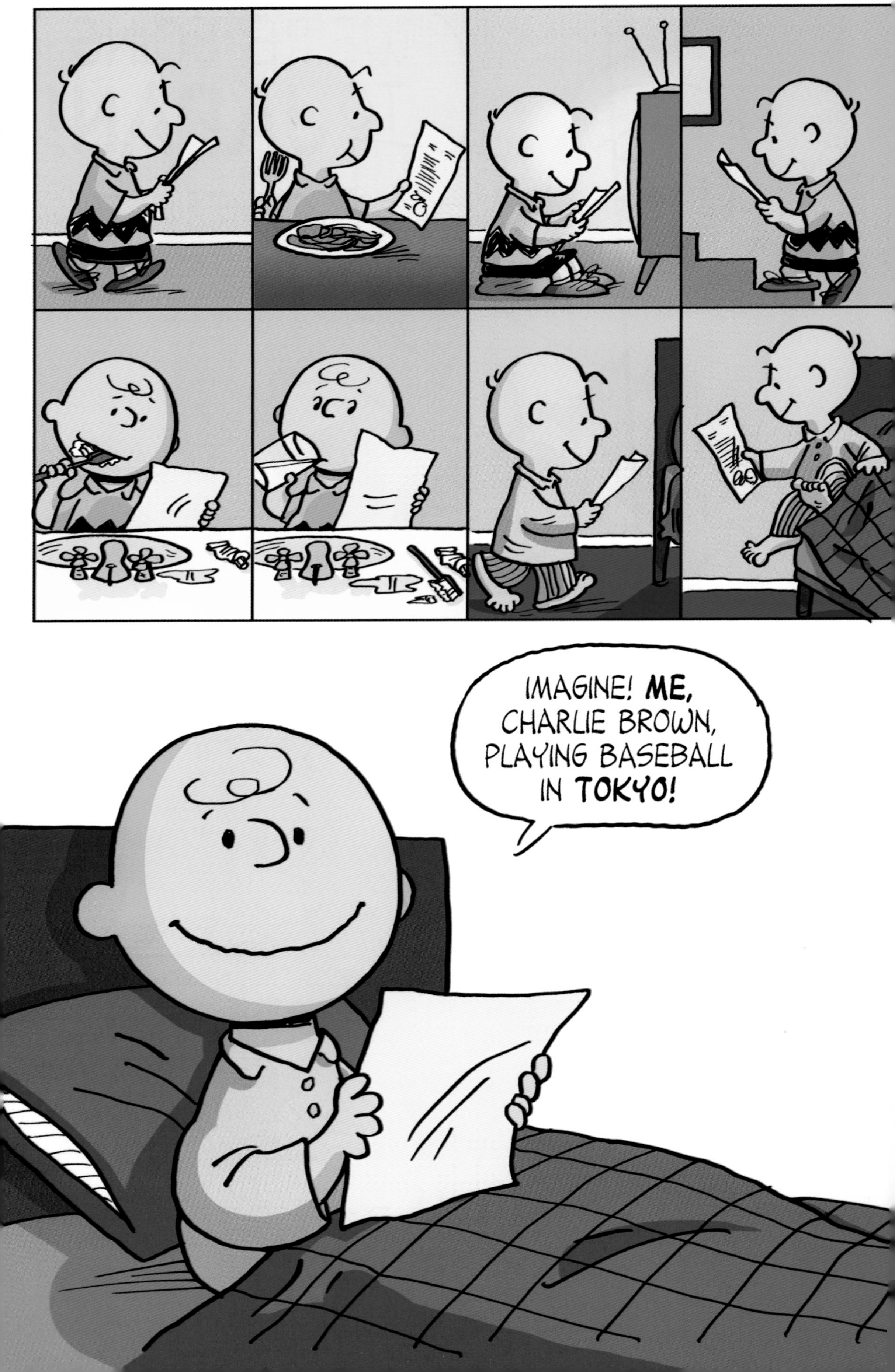
IMAGINE! ME, CHARLIE BROWN, PLAYING BASEBALL IN TOKYO!

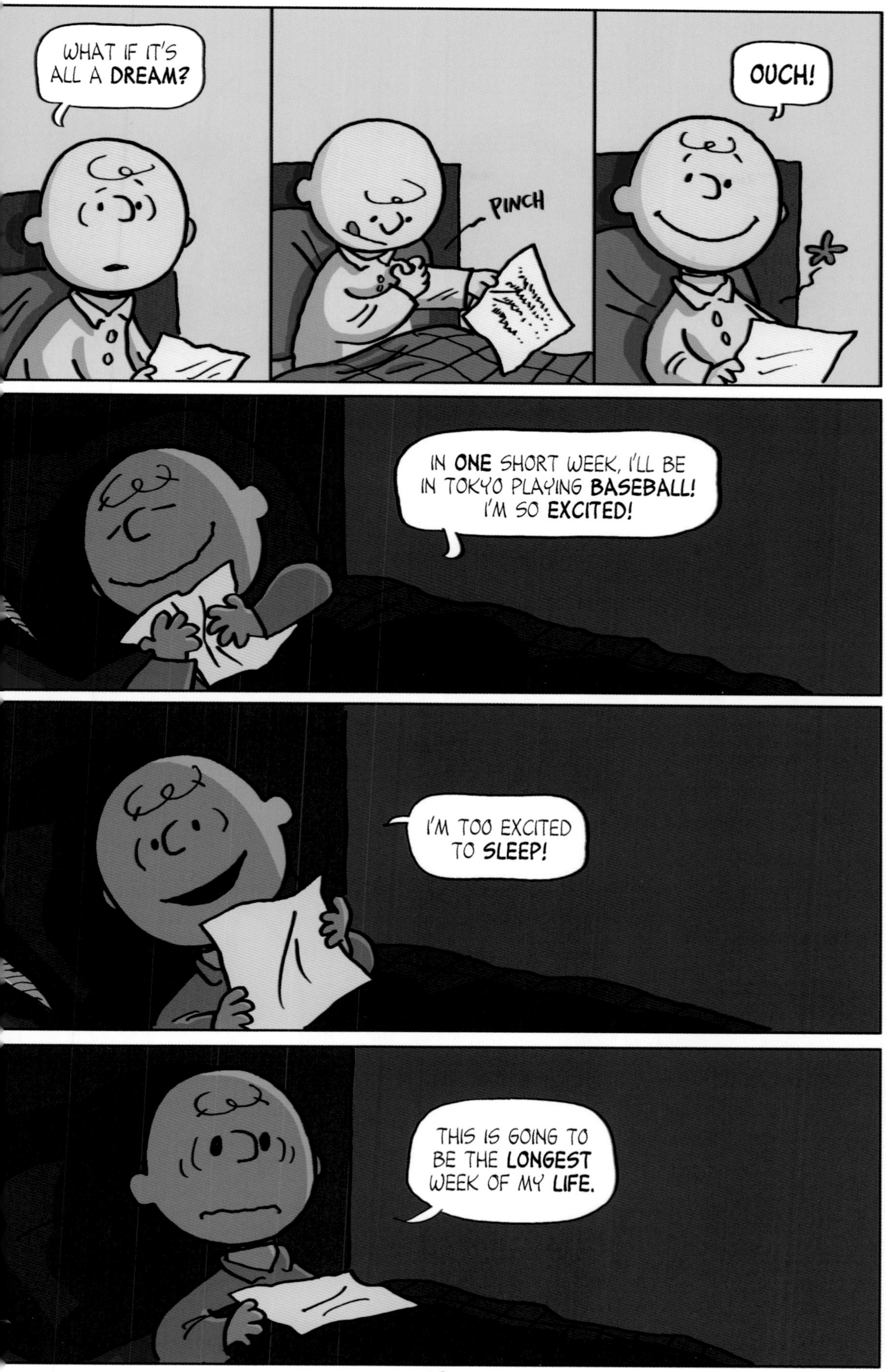
WHAT IF IT'S ALL A DREAM?
PINCH
OUCH!
IN ONE SHORT WEEK, I'LL BE IN TOKYO PLAYING BASEBALL! I'M SO EXCITED!
I'M TOO EXCITED TO SLEEP!
THIS IS GOING TO BE THE LONGEST WEEK OF MY LIFE.

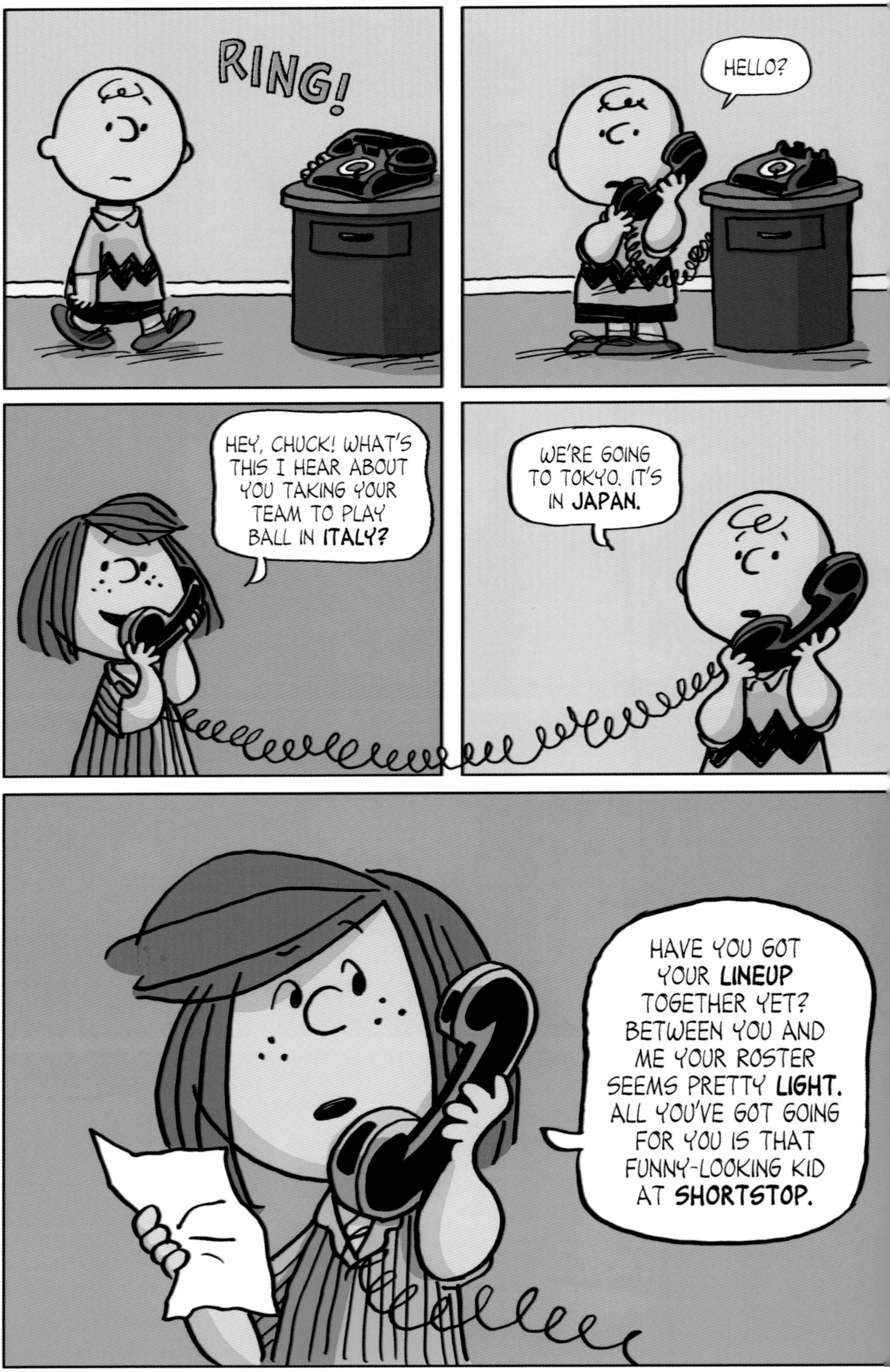
RING!
HELLO?
HEY, CHUCK! WHAT'S THIS I HEAR ABOUT YOU TAKING YOUR TEAM TO PLAY BALL IN ITALY?
WE'RE GOING TO TOKYO. IT'S IN JAPAN.
HAVE YOU GOT YOUR LINEUP TOGETHER YET? BETWEEN YOU AND ME YOUR ROSTER SEEMS PRETTY LIGHT. ALL YOU'VE GOT GOING FOR YOU IS THAT FUNNY-LOOKING KID AT SHORTSTOP.

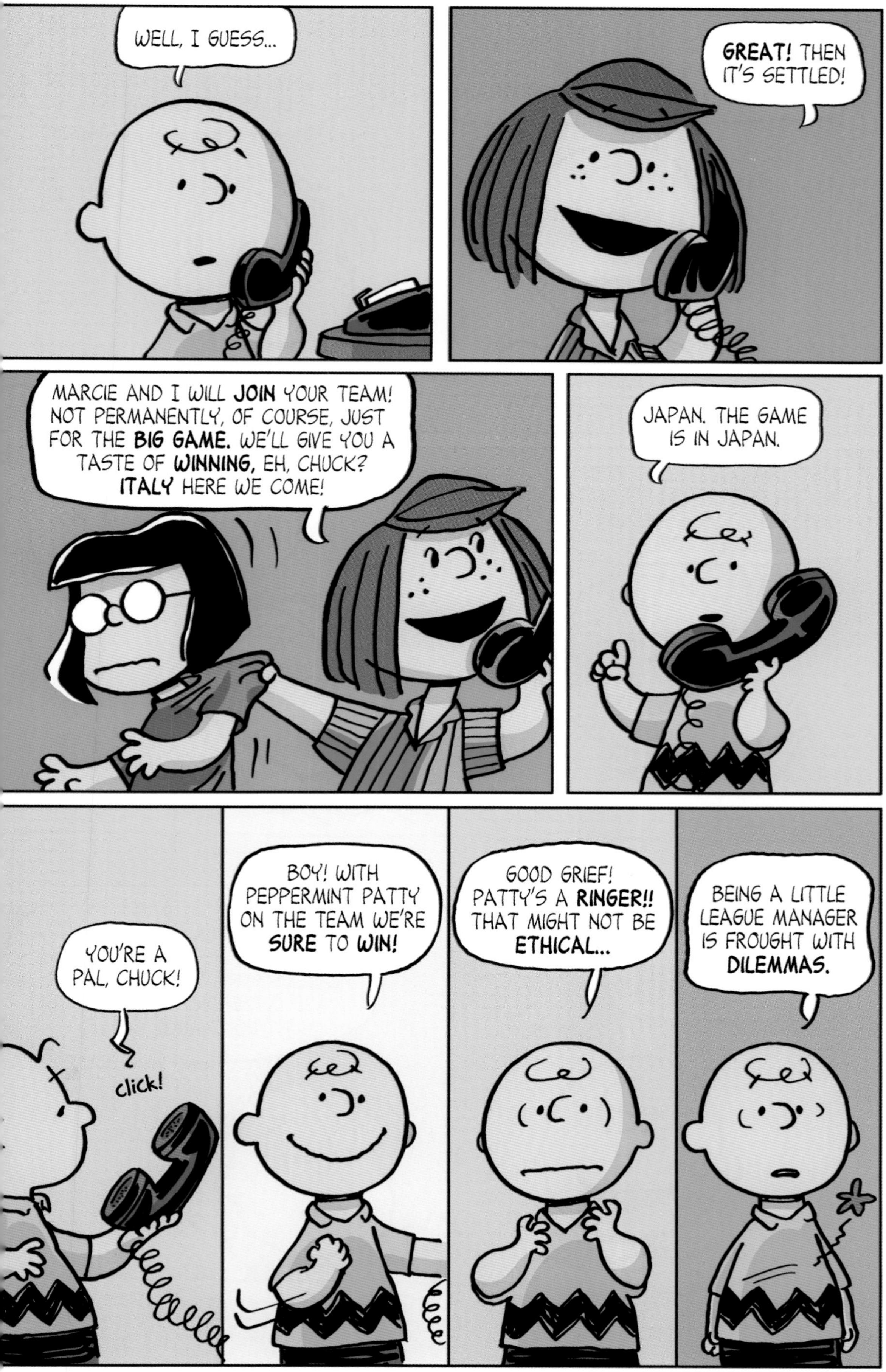
WELL, I GUESS...
GREAT! THEN IT'S SETTLED!
MARCIE AND I WILL JOIN YOUR TEAM! NOT PERMANENTLY, OF COURSE, JUST FOR THE BIG GAME. WE'LL GIVE YOU A TASTE OF WINNING, EH, CHUCK? ITALY HERE WE COME!
JAPAN. THE GAME IS IN JAPAN.
YOU'RE A PAL, CHUCK!
click!
BOY! WITH PEPPERMINT PATTY ON THE TEAM WE'RE SURE TO WIN!
GOOD GRIEF! PATTY'S A RINGER!! THAT MIGHT NOT BE ETHICAL...
BEING A LITTLE LEAGUE MANAGER IS FROUGHT WITH DILEMMAS.

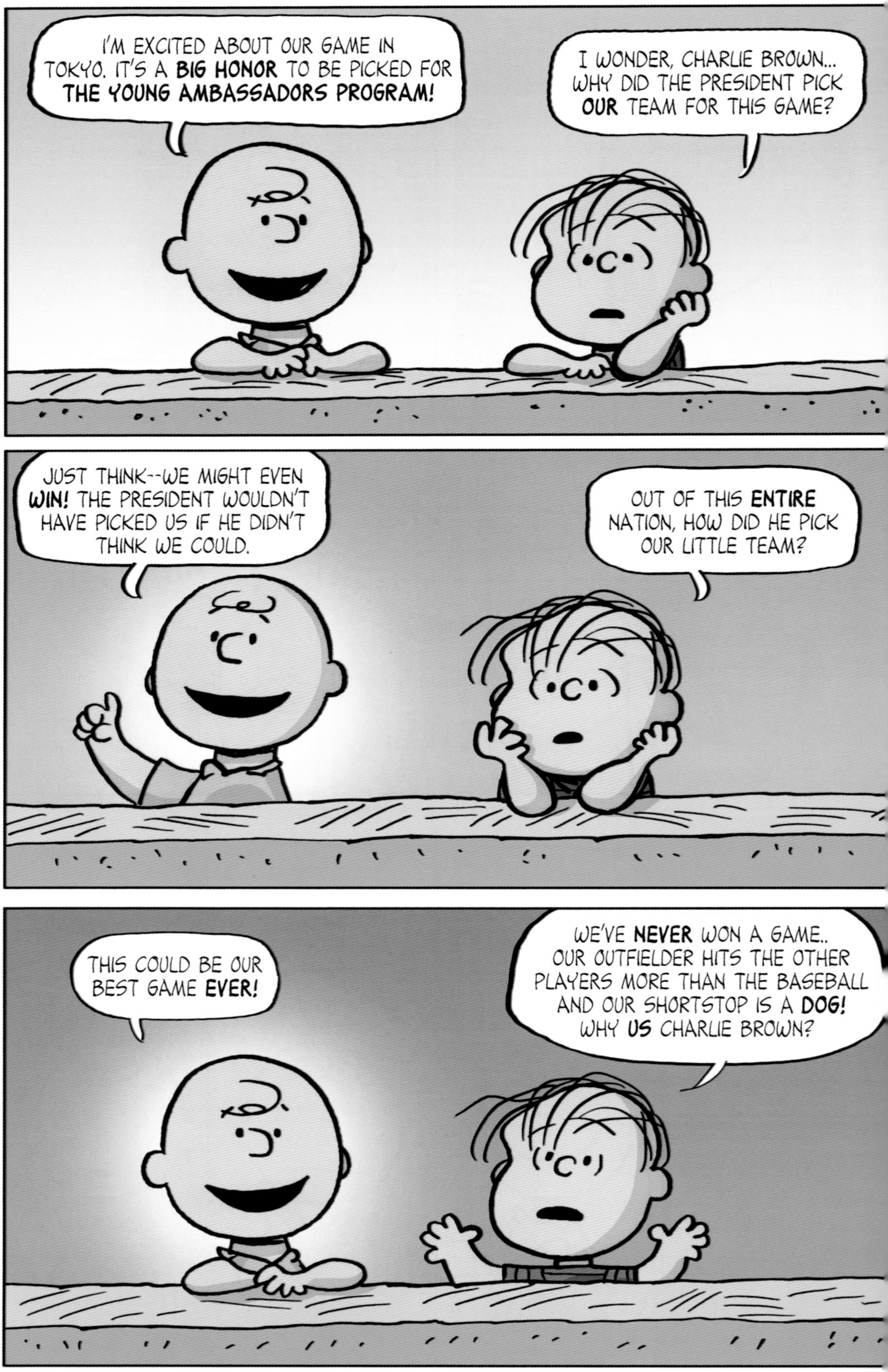
I'M EXCITED ABOUT OUR GAME IN TOKYO. IT'S A **BIG HONOR** TO BE PICKED FOR **THE YOUNG AMBASSADORS PROGRAM!**
I WONDER, CHARLIE BROWN... WHY DID THE PRESIDENT PICK **OUR** TEAM FOR THIS GAME?
JUST THINK--WE MIGHT EVEN **WIN!** THE PRESIDENT WOULDN'T HAVE PICKED US IF HE DIDN'T THINK WE COULD.
OUT OF THIS **ENTIRE** NATION, HOW DID HE PICK OUR LITTLE TEAM?
THIS COULD BE OUR BEST GAME **EVER!**
WE'VE **NEVER** WON A GAME.. OUR OUTFIELDER HITS THE OTHER PLAYERS MORE THAN THE BASEBALL AND OUR SHORTSTOP IS A **DOG!** WHY **US** CHARLIE BROWN?

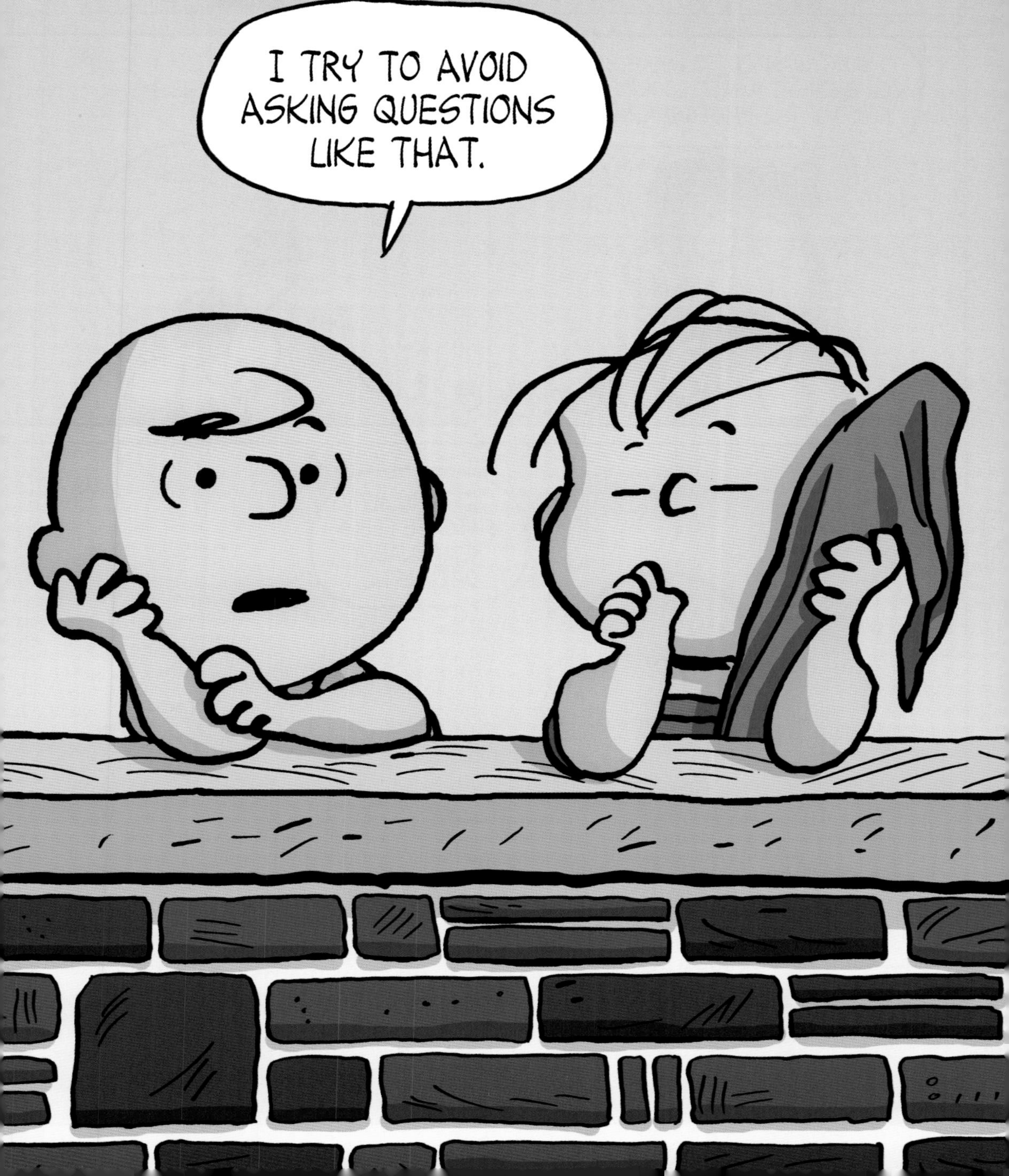
I TRY TO AVOID ASKING QUESTIONS LIKE THAT.

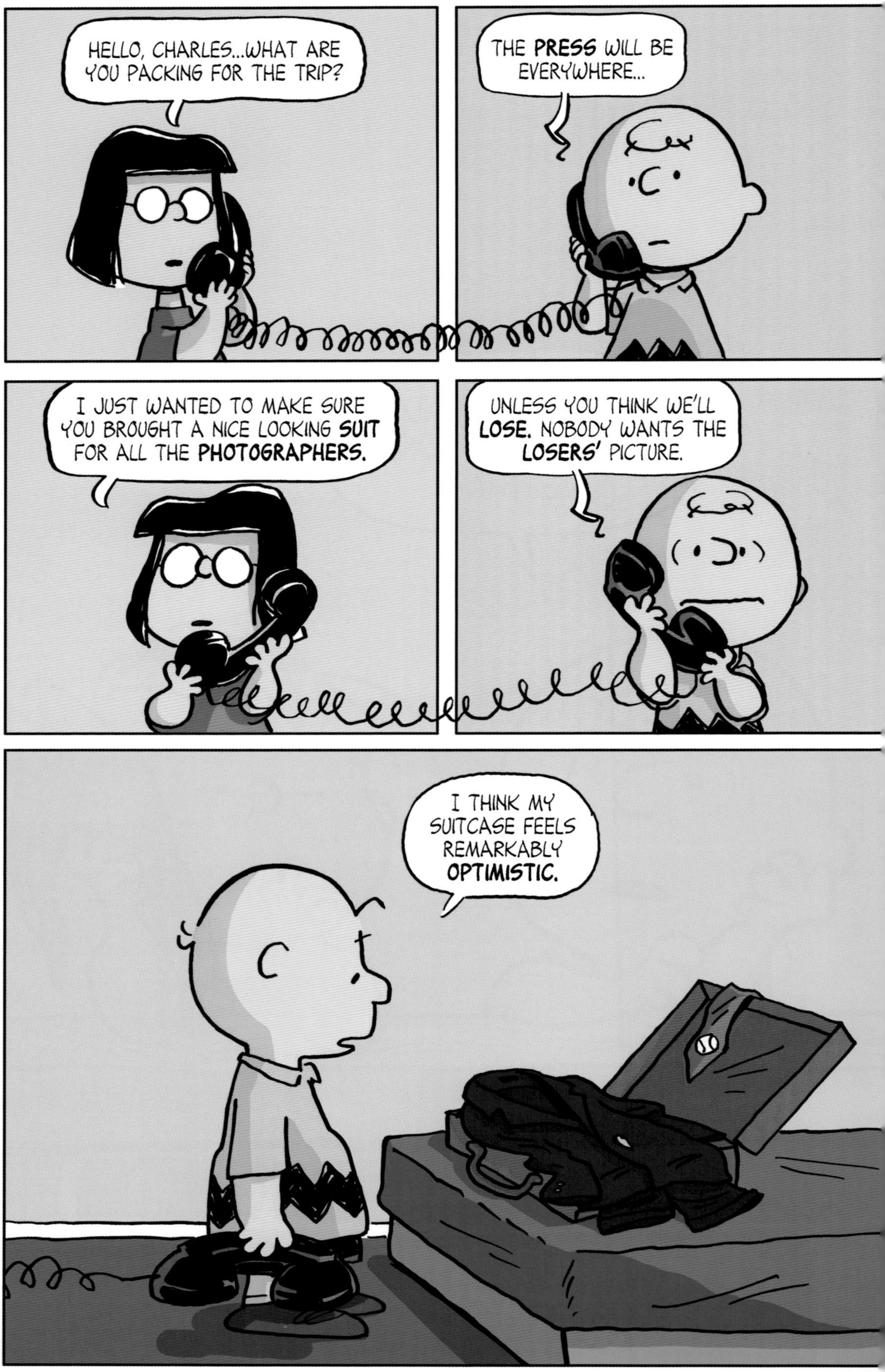
HELLO, CHARLES...WHAT ARE YOU PACKING FOR THE TRIP?
THE PRESS WILL BE EVERYWHERE...
I JUST WANTED TO MAKE SURE YOU BROUGHT A NICE LOOKING SUIT FOR ALL THE PHOTOGRAPHERS.
UNLESS YOU THINK WE'LL LOSE. NOBODY WANTS THE LOSERS' PICTURE.
I THINK MY SUITCASE FEELS REMARKABLY OPTIMISTIC.

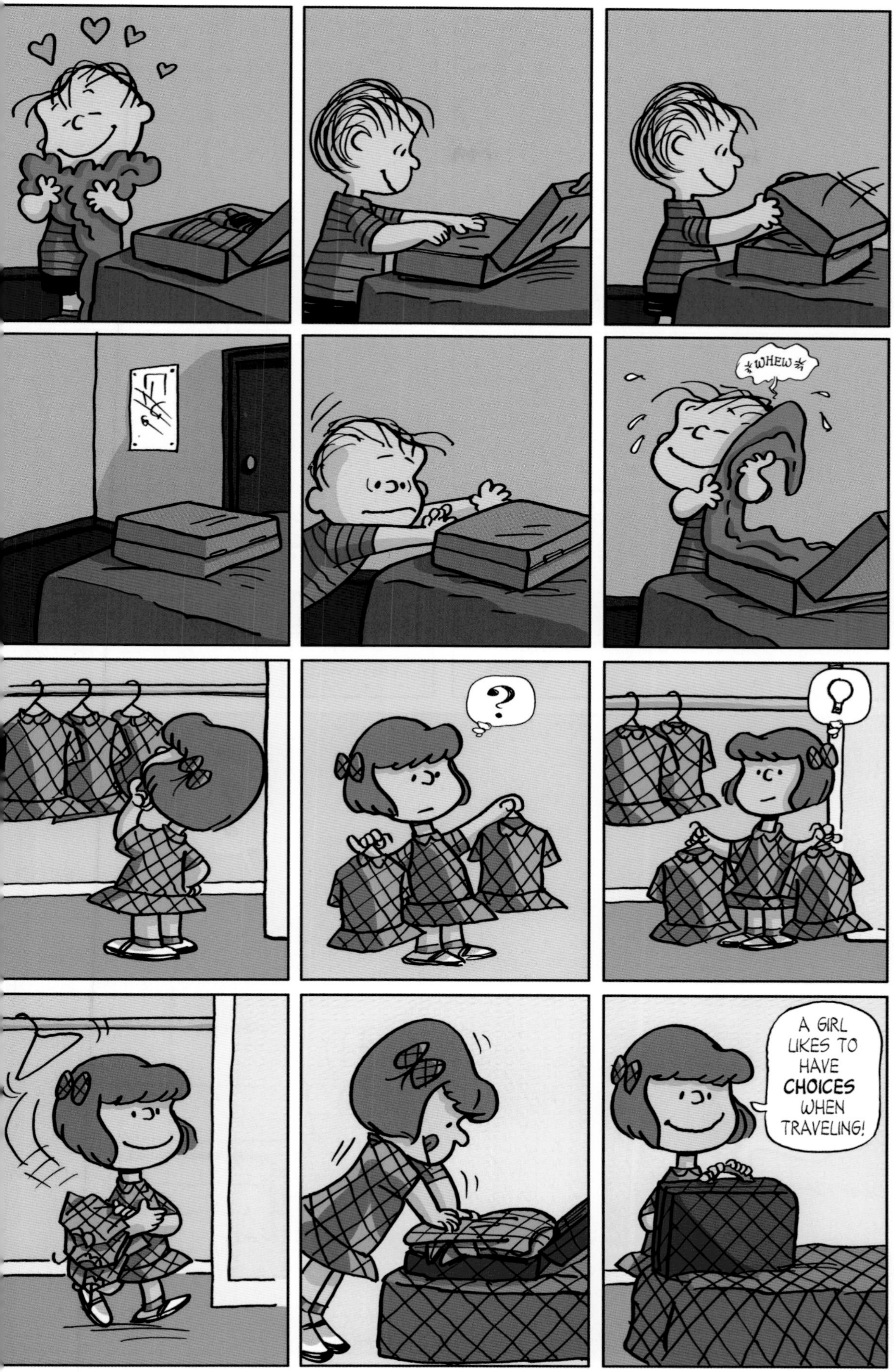
WHEW
?
A GIRL LIKES TO HAVE **CHOICES** WHEN TRAVELING!

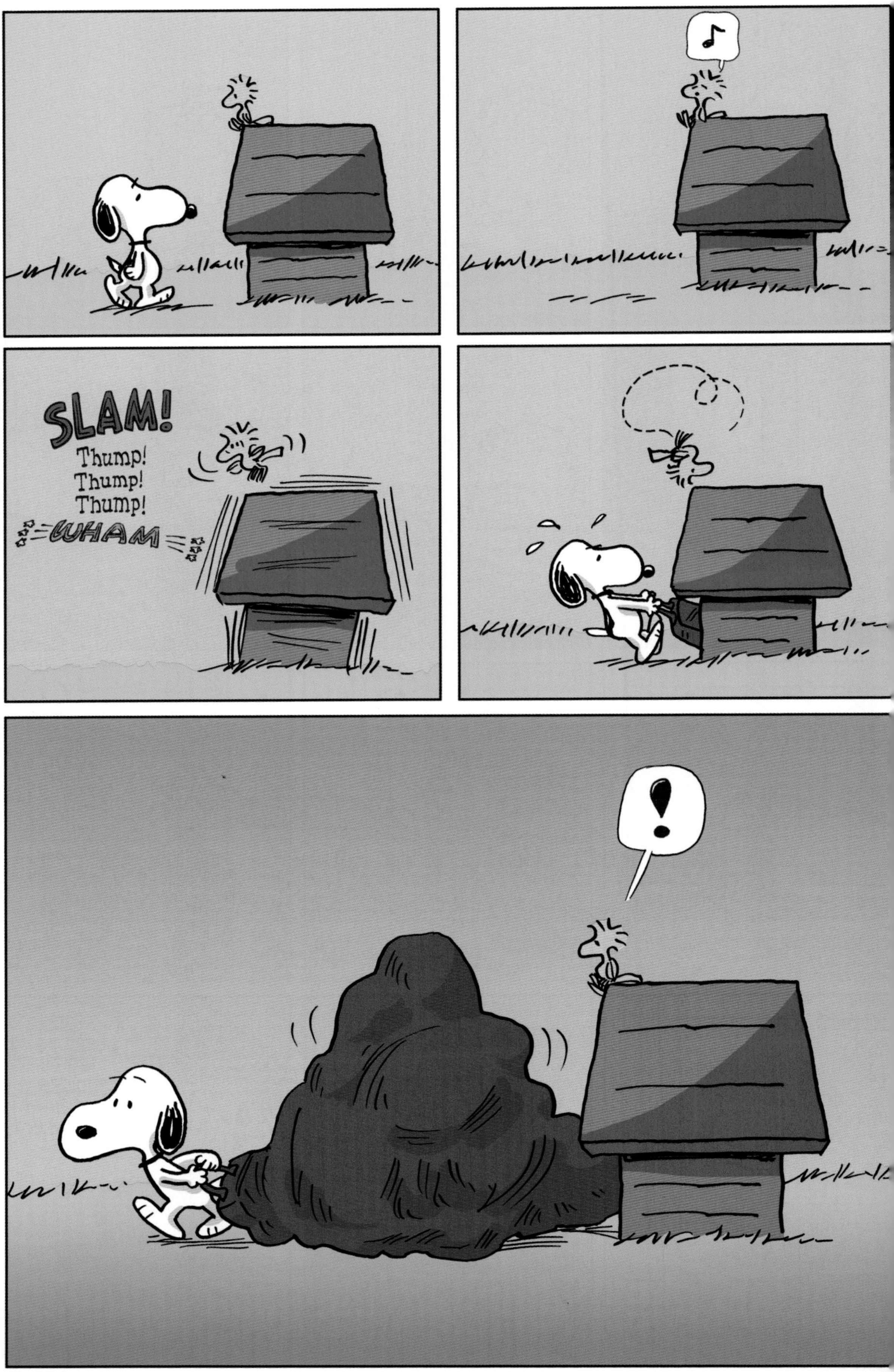

♪
SLAM!
Thump!
Thump!
Thump!
WHAM
!

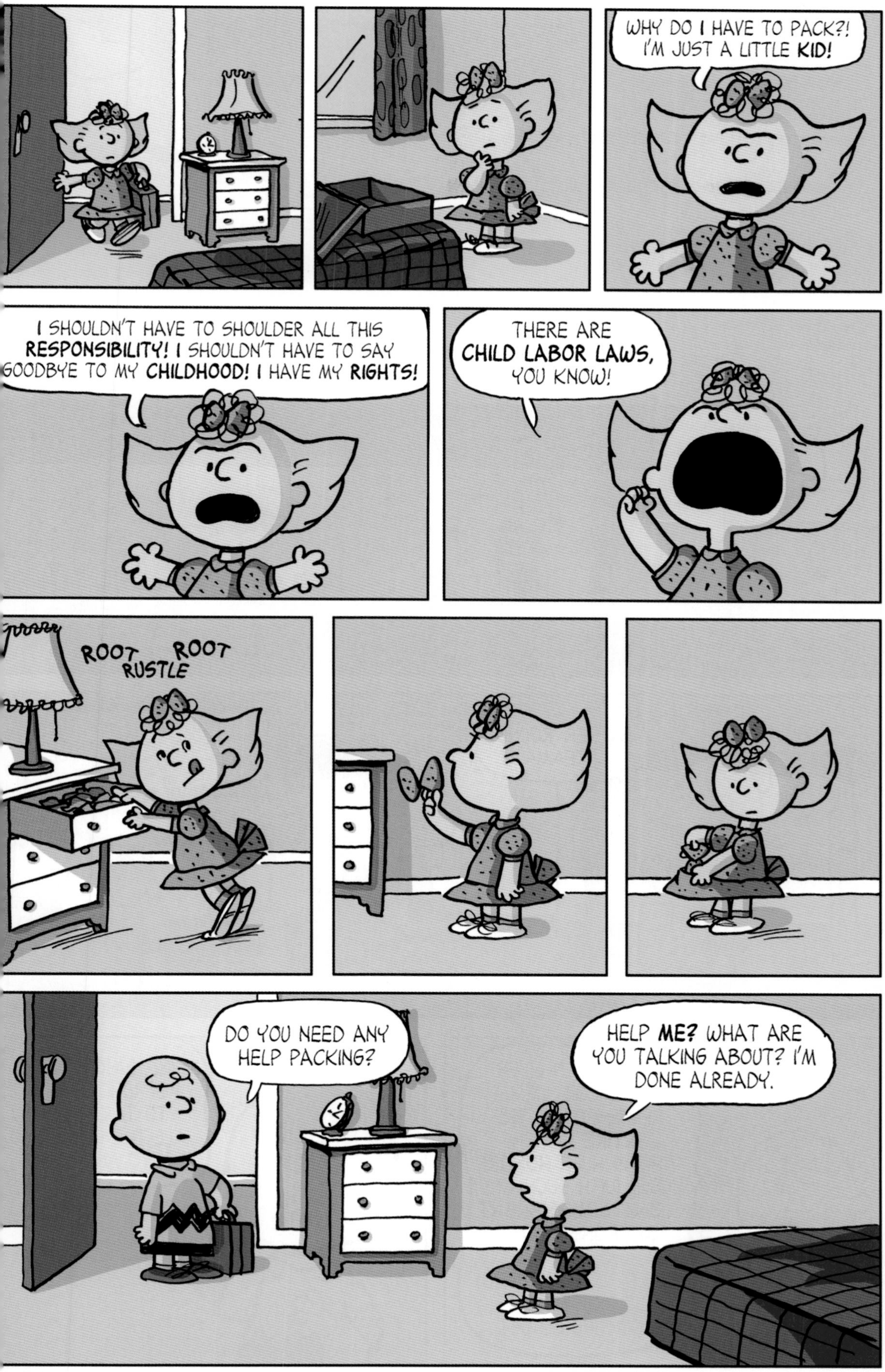

WHY DO I HAVE TO PACK?! I'M JUST A LITTLE **KID!**
I SHOULDN'T HAVE TO SHOULDER ALL THIS **RESPONSIBILITY!** I SHOULDN'T HAVE TO SAY GOODBYE TO MY **CHILDHOOD!** I HAVE MY **RIGHTS!**
THERE ARE **CHILD LABOR LAWS,** YOU KNOW!
ROOT RUSTLE ROOT
DO YOU NEED ANY HELP PACKING?
HELP **ME?** WHAT ARE YOU TALKING ABOUT? I'M DONE ALREADY.

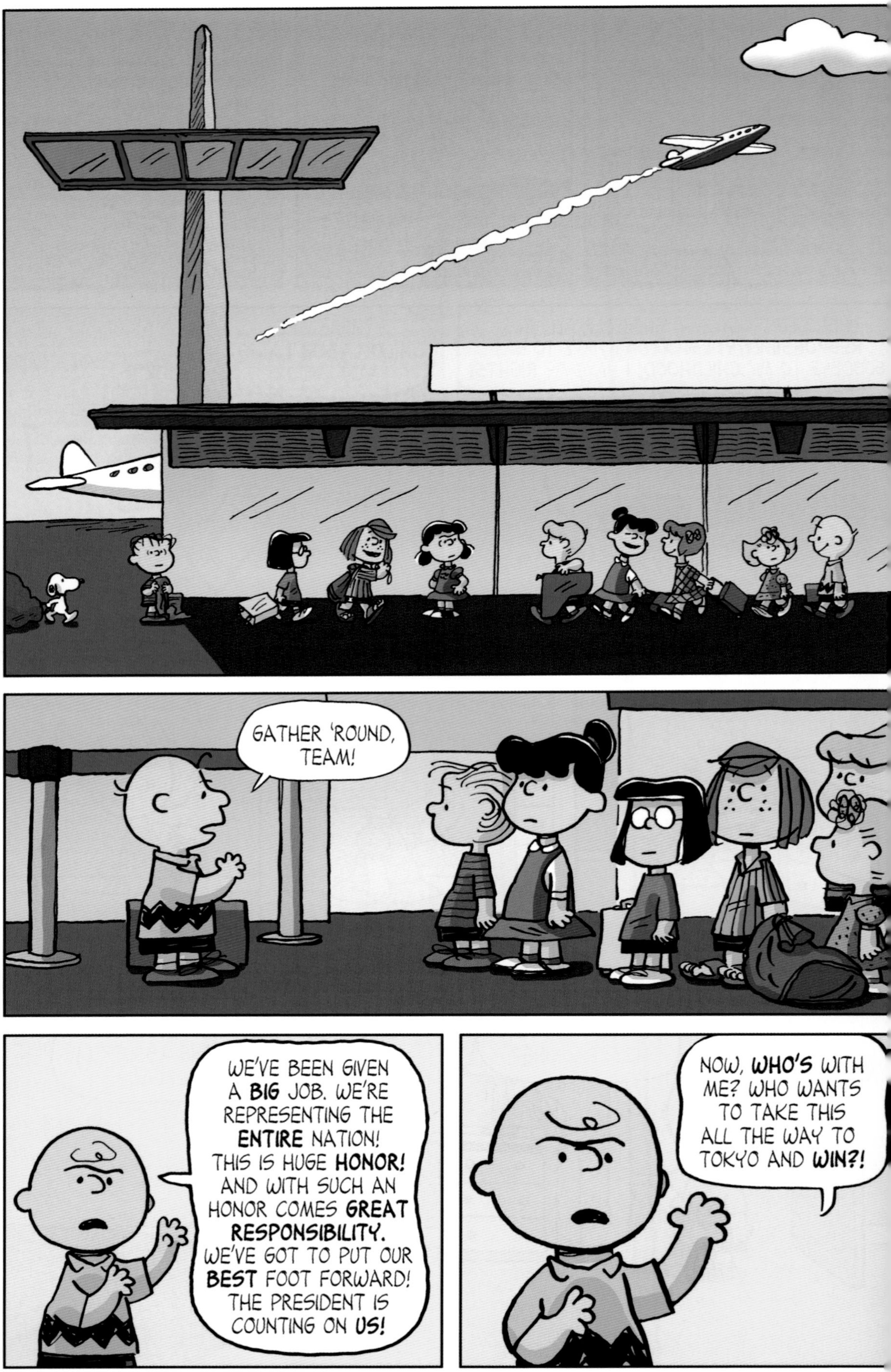
GATHER 'ROUND, TEAM!
WE'VE BEEN GIVEN A BIG JOB. WE'RE REPRESENTING THE ENTIRE NATION! THIS IS HUGE HONOR! AND WITH SUCH AN HONOR COMES GREAT RESPONSIBILITY. WE'VE GOT TO PUT OUR BEST FOOT FORWARD! THE PRESIDENT IS COUNTING ON US!
NOW, WHO'S WITH ME? WHO WANTS TO TAKE THIS ALL THE WAY TO TOKYO AND WIN?!

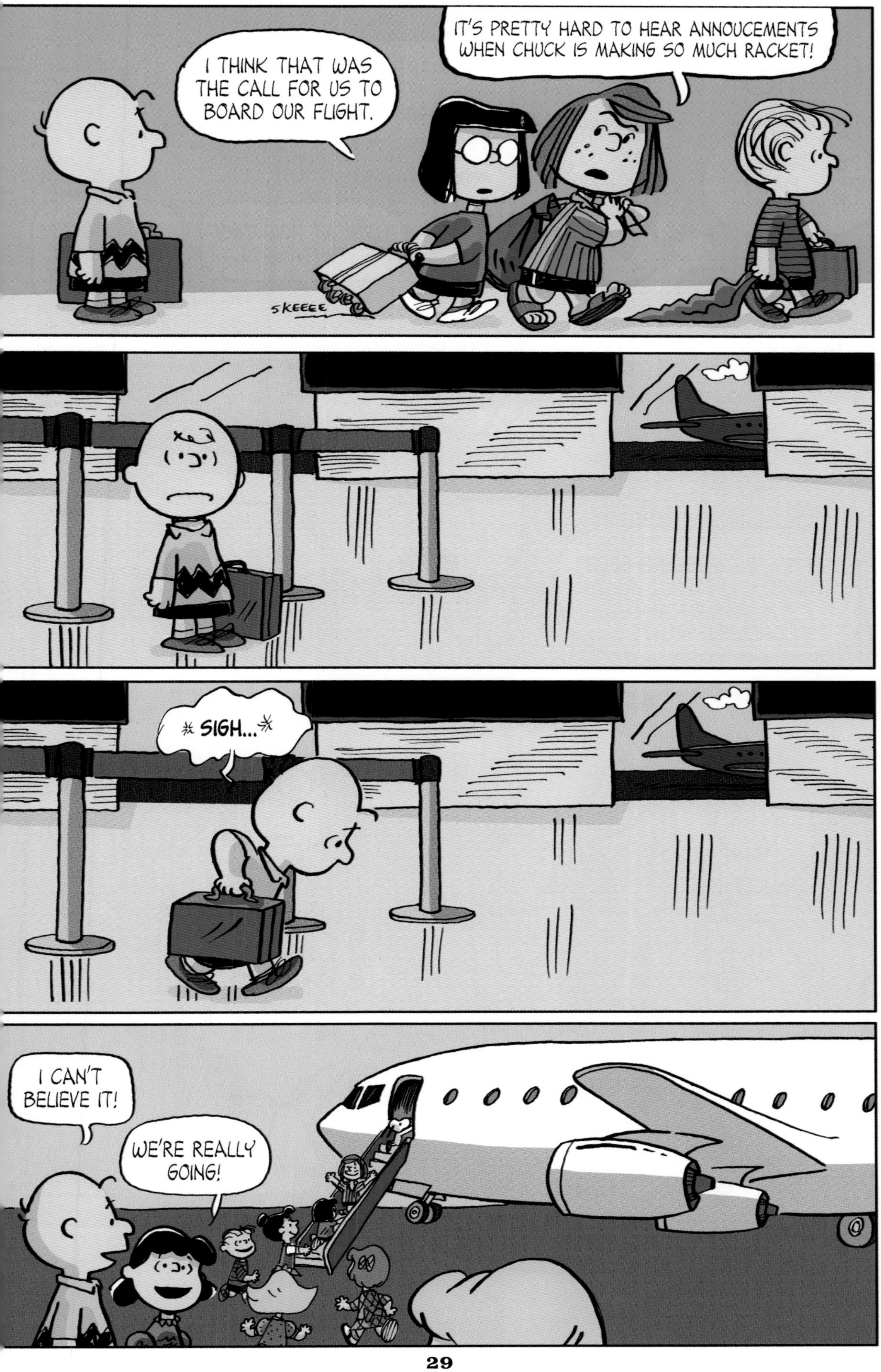
I THINK THAT WAS THE CALL FOR US TO BOARD OUR FLIGHT.
IT'S PRETTY HARD TO HEAR ANNOUCEMENTS WHEN CHUCK IS MAKING SO MUCH RACKET!
SKEEEE
SIGH...
I CAN'T BELIEVE IT!
WE'RE REALLY GOING!

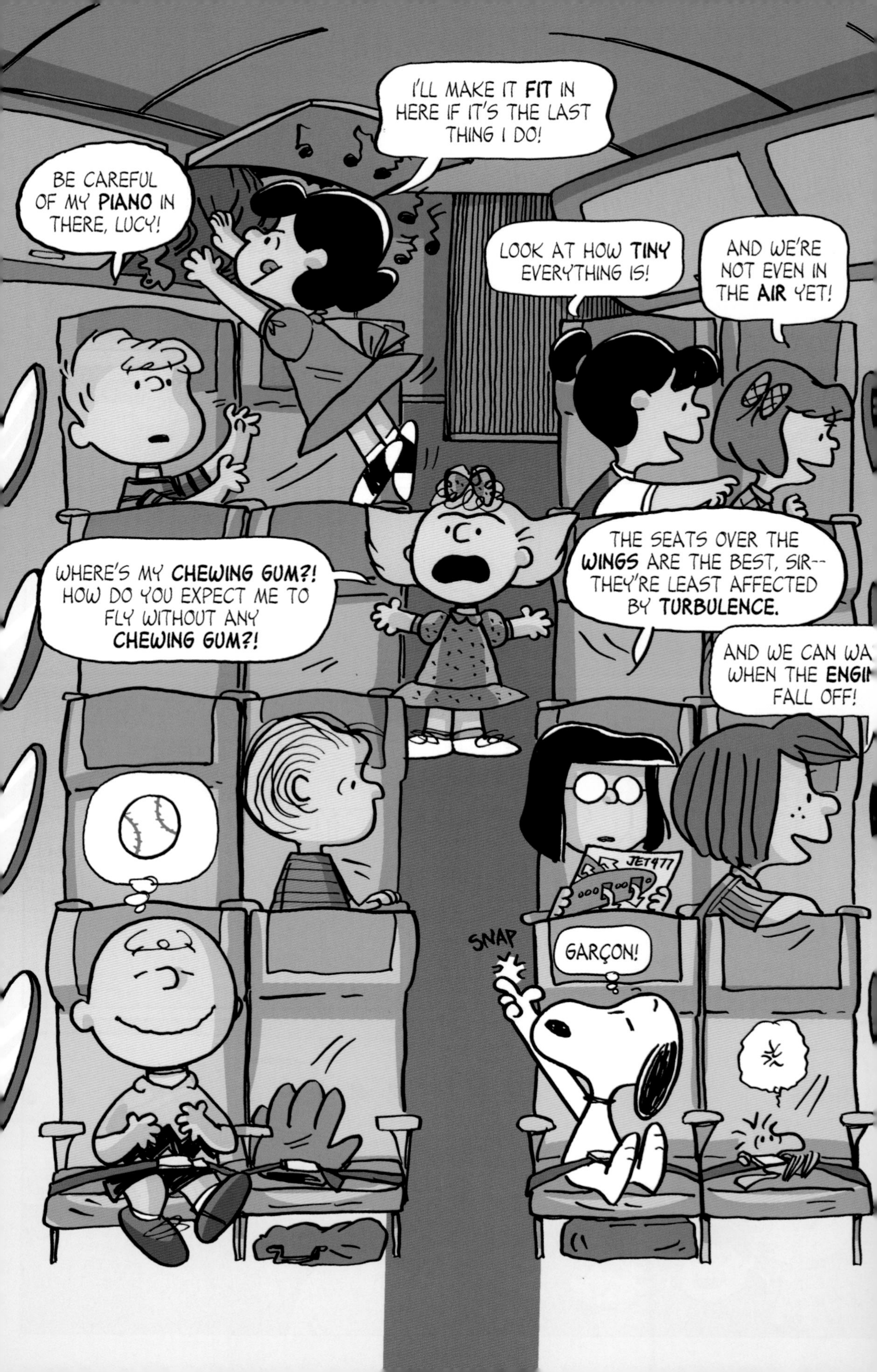
BE CAREFUL OF MY PIANO IN THERE, LUCY!
I'LL MAKE IT FIT IN HERE IF IT'S THE LAST THING I DO!
LOOK AT HOW TINY EVERYTHING IS!
AND WE'RE NOT EVEN IN THE AIR YET!
WHERE'S MY CHEWING GUM?! HOW DO YOU EXPECT ME TO FLY WITHOUT ANY CHEWING GUM?!
THE SEATS OVER THE WINGS ARE THE BEST, SIR-- THEY'RE LEAST AFFECTED BY TURBULENCE.
AND WE CAN WA WHEN THE ENGI FALL OFF!
JET 477
SNAP
GARÇON!

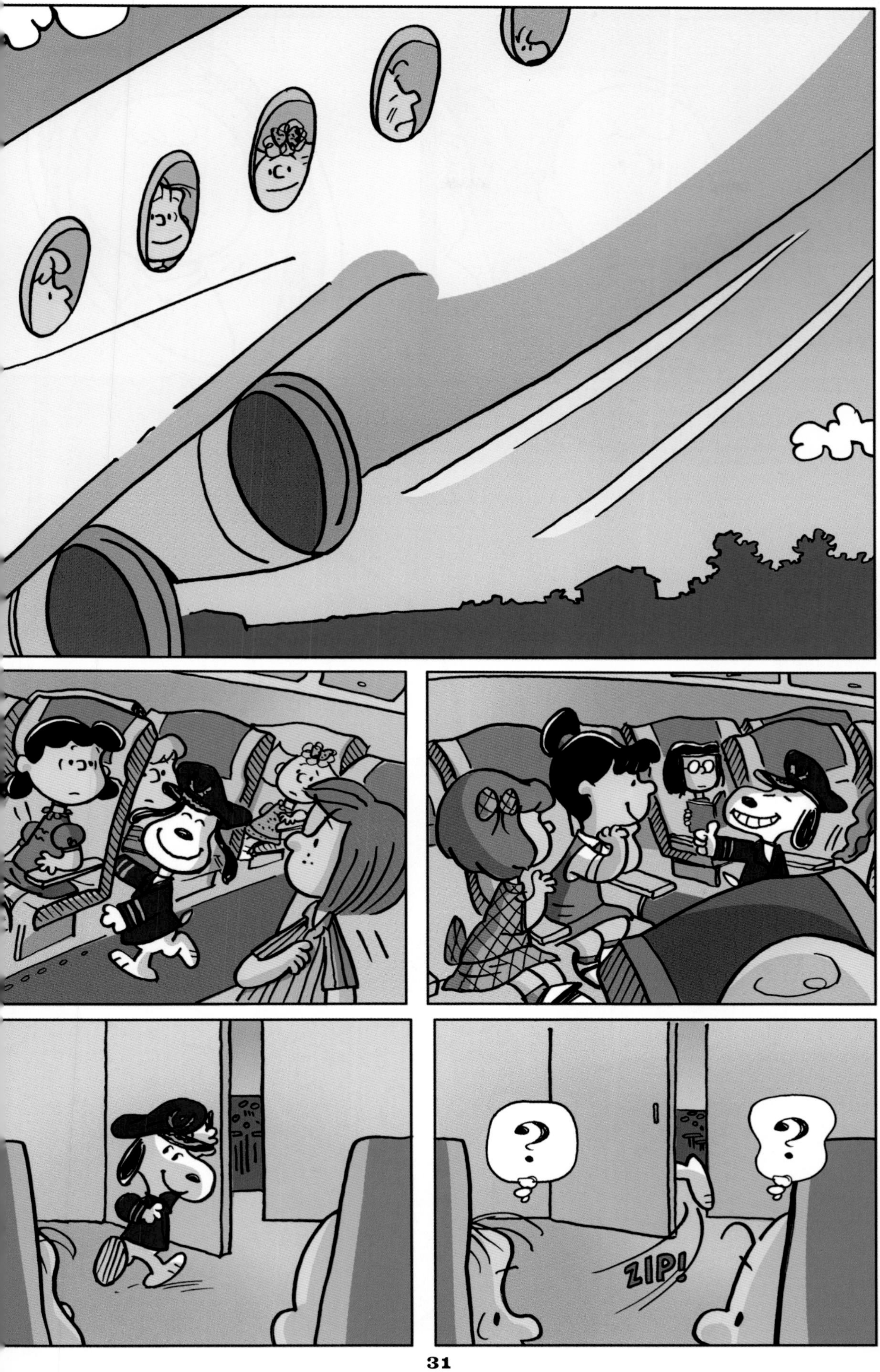
?
?
ZIP!

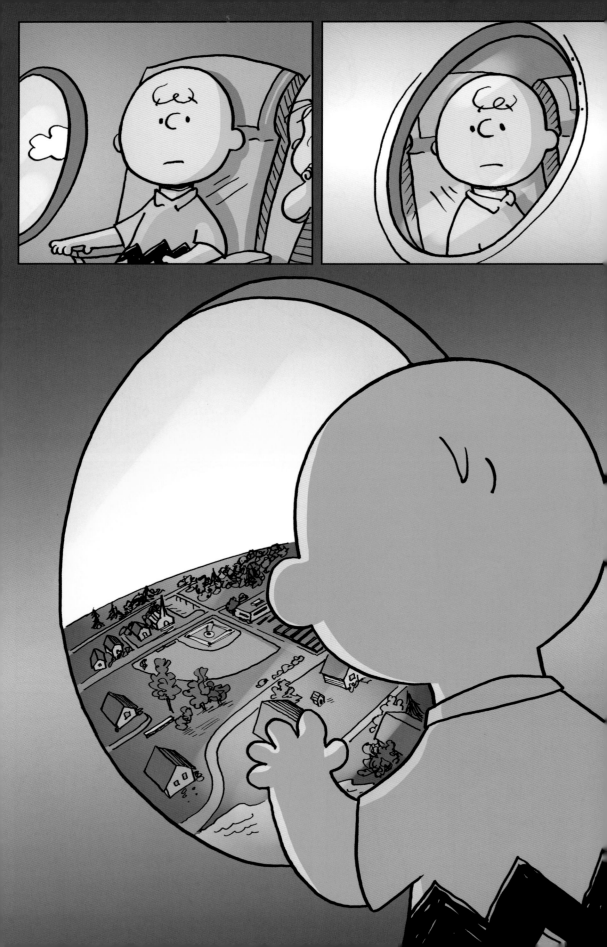

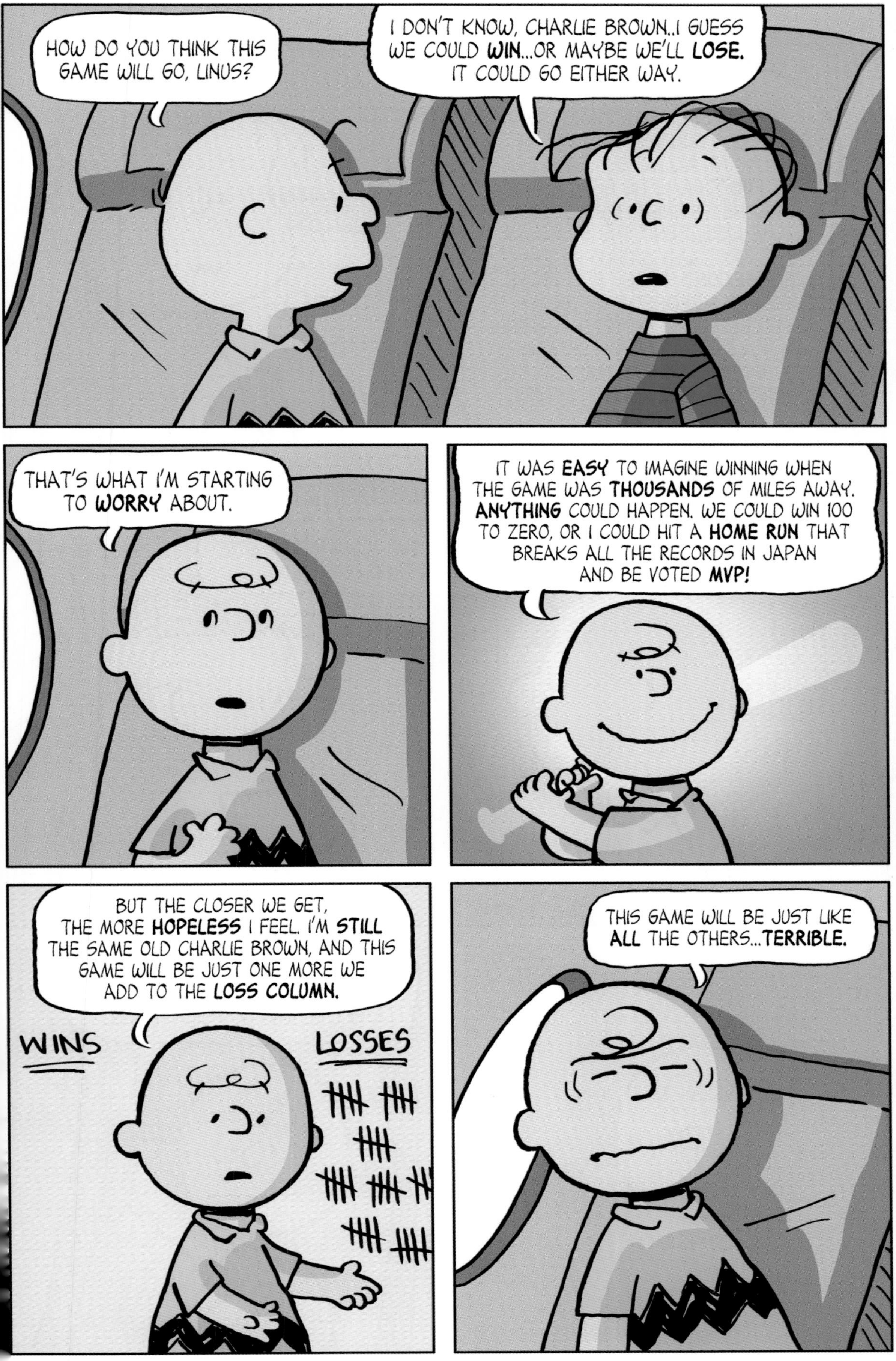
HOW DO YOU THINK THIS GAME WILL GO, LINUS?
I DON'T KNOW, CHARLIE BROWN..I GUESS WE COULD **WIN**...OR MAYBE WE'LL **LOSE.** IT COULD GO EITHER WAY.
THAT'S WHAT I'M STARTING TO **WORRY** ABOUT.
IT WAS **EASY** TO IMAGINE WINNING WHEN THE GAME WAS **THOUSANDS** OF MILES AWAY. **ANYTHING** COULD HAPPEN. WE COULD WIN 100 TO ZERO, OR I COULD HIT A **HOME RUN** THAT BREAKS ALL THE RECORDS IN JAPAN AND BE VOTED **MVP!**
BUT THE CLOSER WE GET, THE MORE **HOPELESS** I FEEL. I'M **STILL** THE SAME OLD CHARLIE BROWN, AND THIS GAME WILL BE JUST ONE MORE WE ADD TO THE **LOSS COLUMN.**
WINS
LOSSES
THIS GAME WILL BE JUST LIKE **ALL** THE OTHERS...**TERRIBLE.**

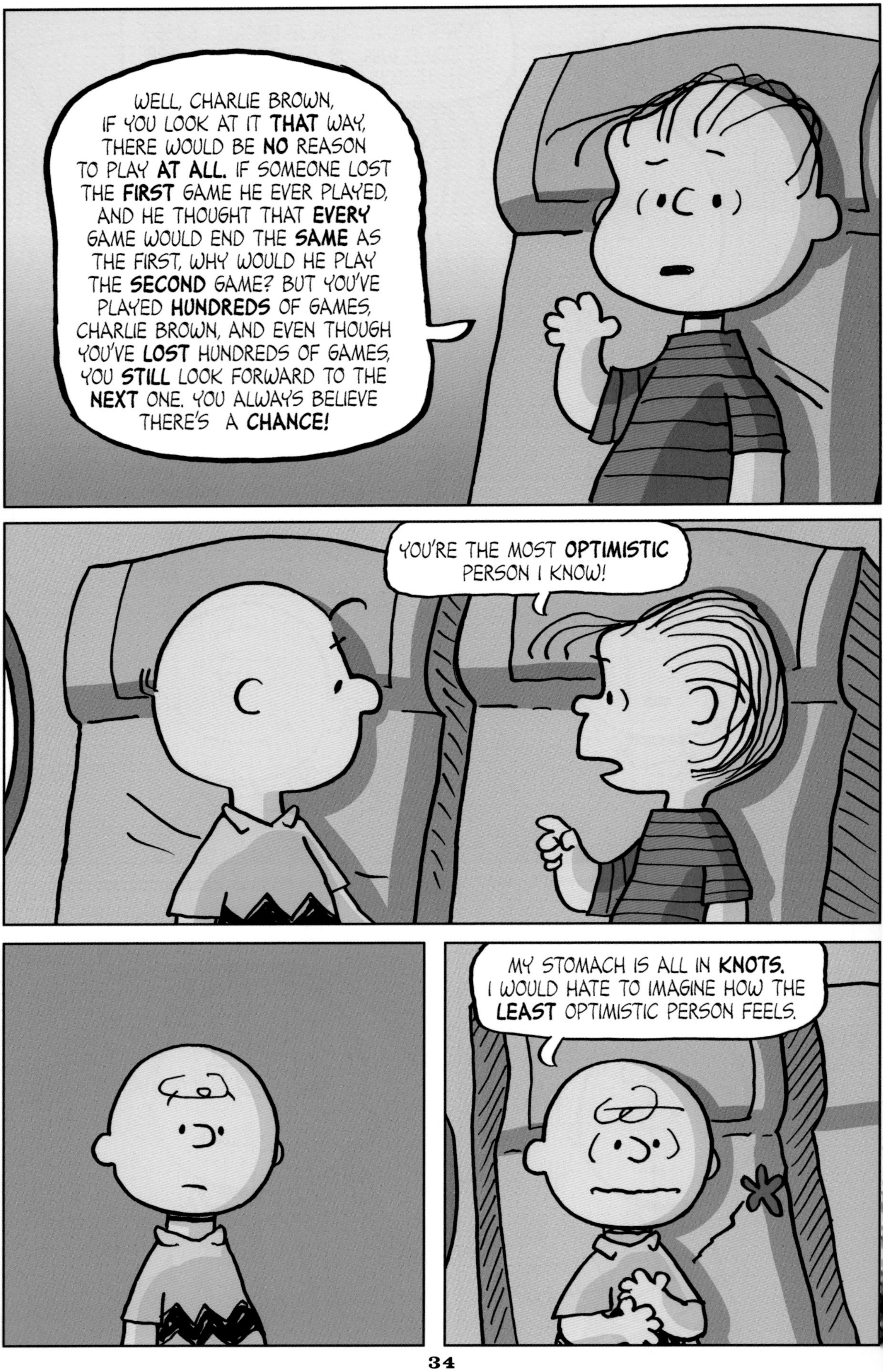
WELL, CHARLIE BROWN, IF YOU LOOK AT IT THAT WAY, THERE WOULD BE NO REASON TO PLAY AT ALL. IF SOMEONE LOST THE FIRST GAME HE EVER PLAYED, AND HE THOUGHT THAT EVERY GAME WOULD END THE SAME AS THE FIRST, WHY WOULD HE PLAY THE SECOND GAME? BUT YOU'VE PLAYED HUNDREDS OF GAMES, CHARLIE BROWN, AND EVEN THOUGH YOU'VE LOST HUNDREDS OF GAMES, YOU STILL LOOK FORWARD TO THE NEXT ONE. YOU ALWAYS BELIEVE THERE'S A CHANCE!
YOU'RE THE MOST OPTIMISTIC PERSON I KNOW!
MY STOMACH IS ALL IN KNOTS. I WOULD HATE TO IMAGINE HOW THE LEAST OPTIMISTIC PERSON FEELS.

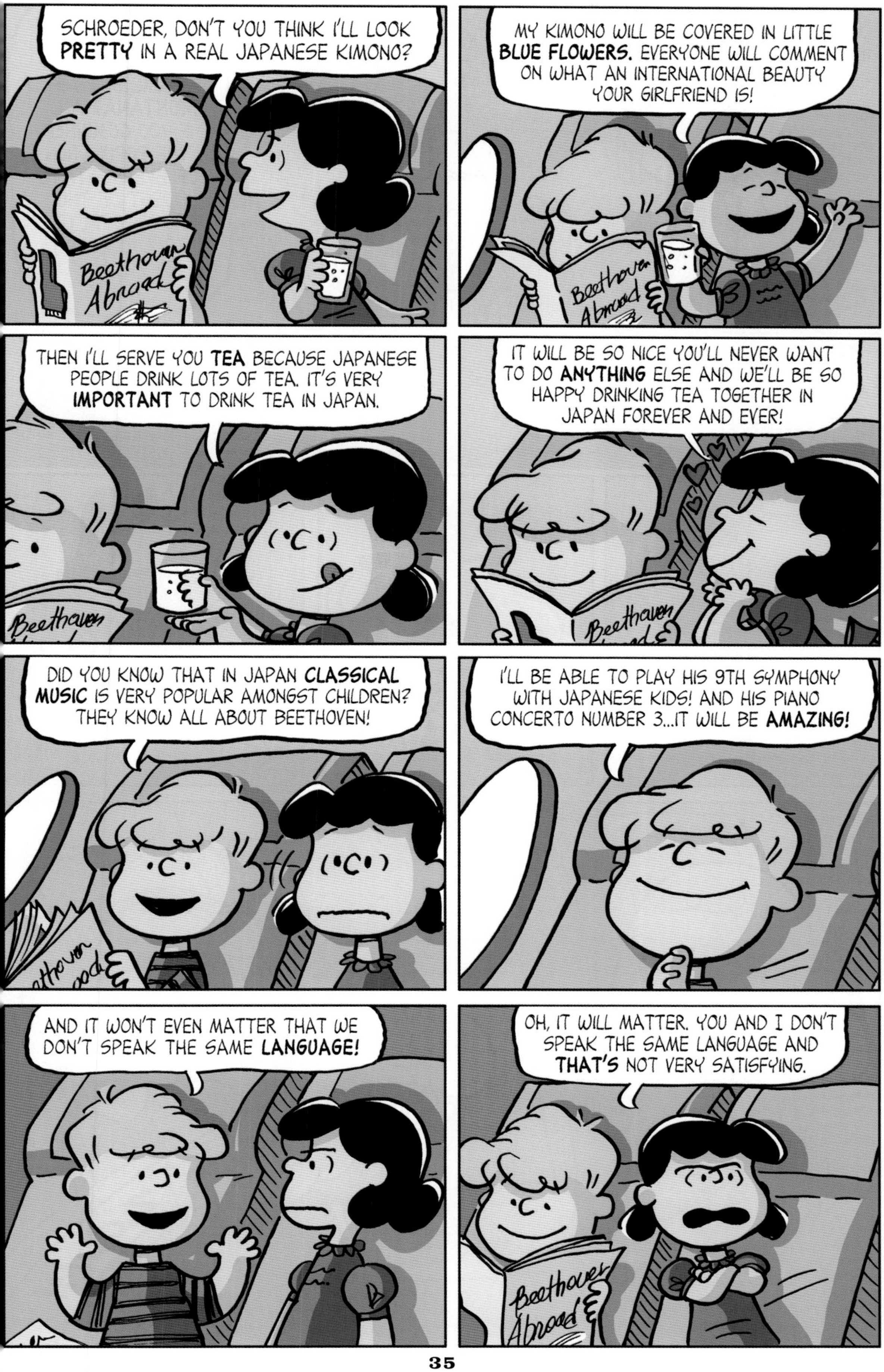
SCHROEDER, DON'T YOU THINK I'LL LOOK PRETTY IN A REAL JAPANESE KIMONO?
Beethoven Abroad
MY KIMONO WILL BE COVERED IN LITTLE BLUE FLOWERS. EVERYONE WILL COMMENT ON WHAT AN INTERNATIONAL BEAUTY YOUR GIRLFRIEND IS!
Beethoven Abroad
THEN I'LL SERVE YOU TEA BECAUSE JAPANESE PEOPLE DRINK LOTS OF TEA. IT'S VERY IMPORTANT TO DRINK TEA IN JAPAN.
IT WILL BE SO NICE YOU'LL NEVER WANT TO DO ANYTHING ELSE AND WE'LL BE SO HAPPY DRINKING TEA TOGETHER IN JAPAN FOREVER AND EVER!
DID YOU KNOW THAT IN JAPAN CLASSICAL MUSIC IS VERY POPULAR AMONGST CHILDREN? THEY KNOW ALL ABOUT BEETHOVEN!
I'LL BE ABLE TO PLAY HIS 9TH SYMPHONY WITH JAPANESE KIDS! AND HIS PIANO CONCERTO NUMBER 3...IT WILL BE AMAZING!
AND IT WON'T EVEN MATTER THAT WE DON'T SPEAK THE SAME LANGUAGE!
OH, IT WILL MATTER. YOU AND I DON'T SPEAK THE SAME LANGUAGE AND THAT'S NOT VERY SATISFYING.
Beethoven Abroad

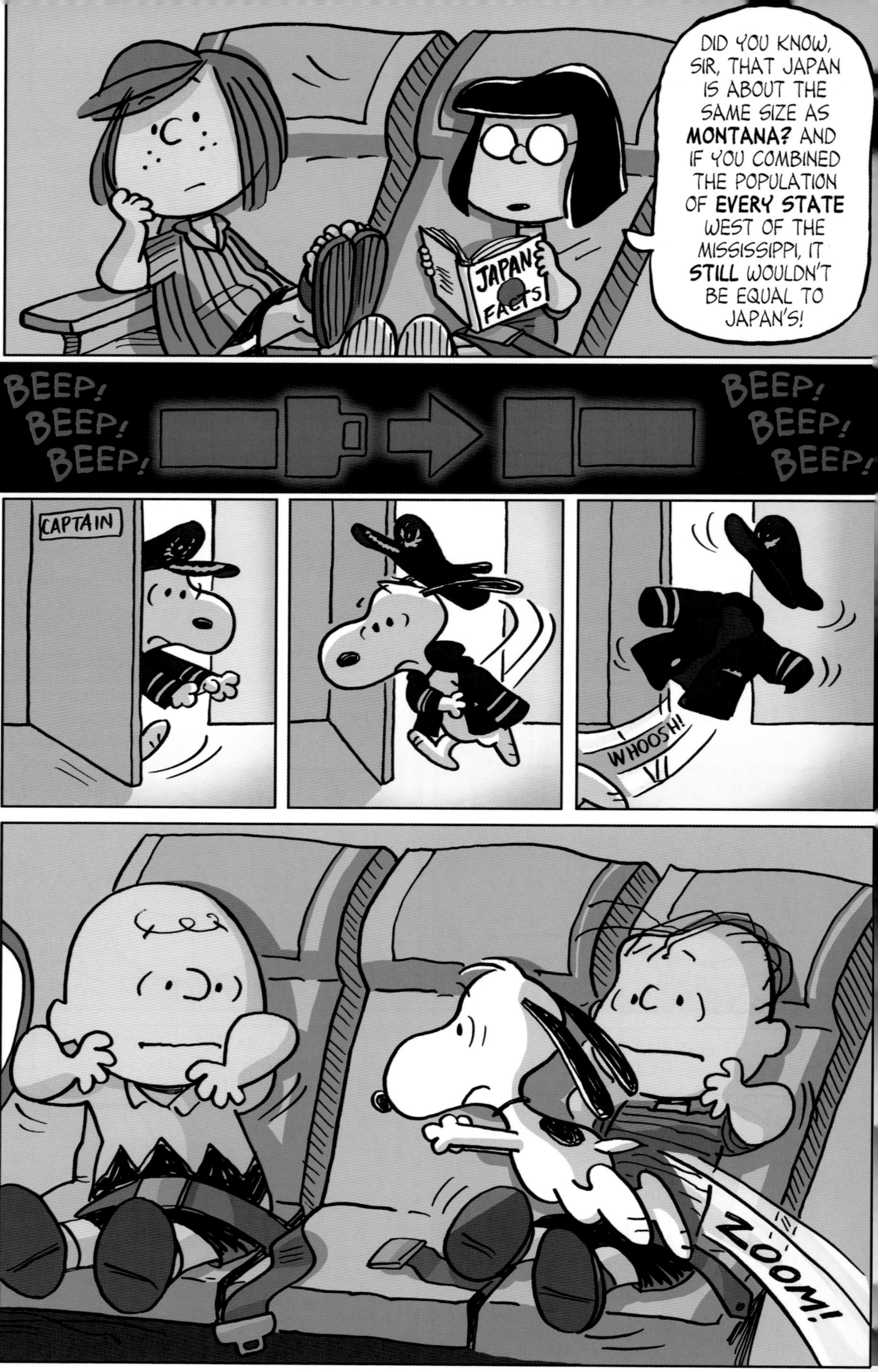
DID YOU KNOW, SIR, THAT JAPAN IS ABOUT THE SAME SIZE AS MONTANA? AND IF YOU COMBINED THE POPULATION OF EVERY STATE WEST OF THE MISSISSIPPI, IT STILL WOULDN'T BE EQUAL TO JAPAN'S!
JAPAN FACTS
BEEP! BEEP! BEEP!
BEEP! BEEP! BEEP!
CAPTAIN
WHOOSH!
ZOOM!

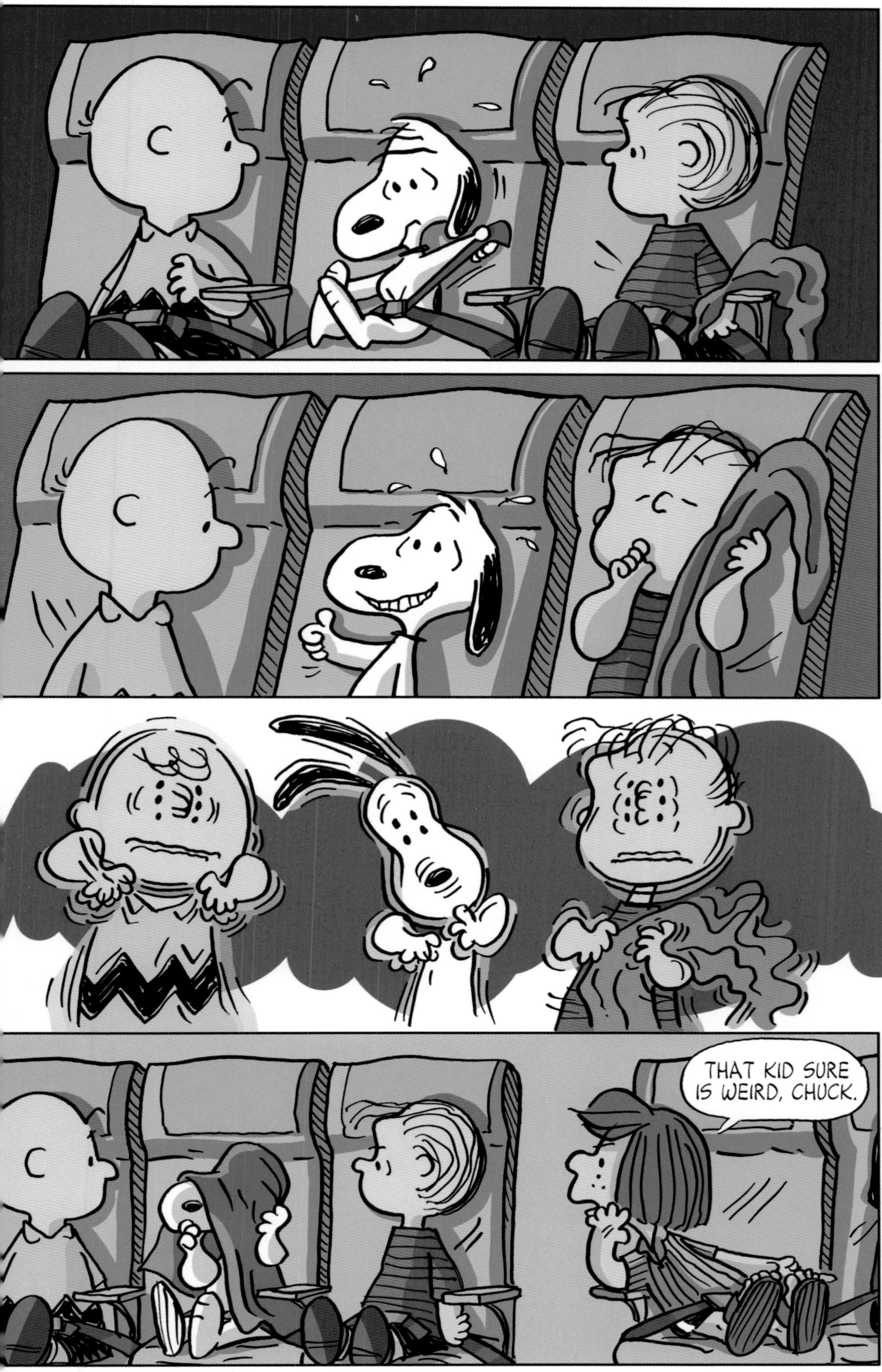
THAT KID SURE
IS WEIRD, CHUCK.

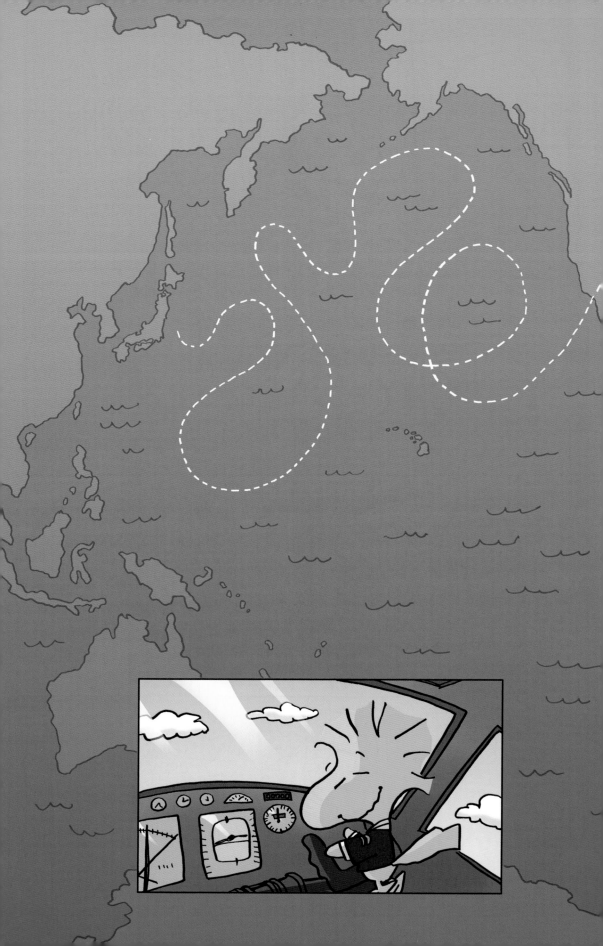

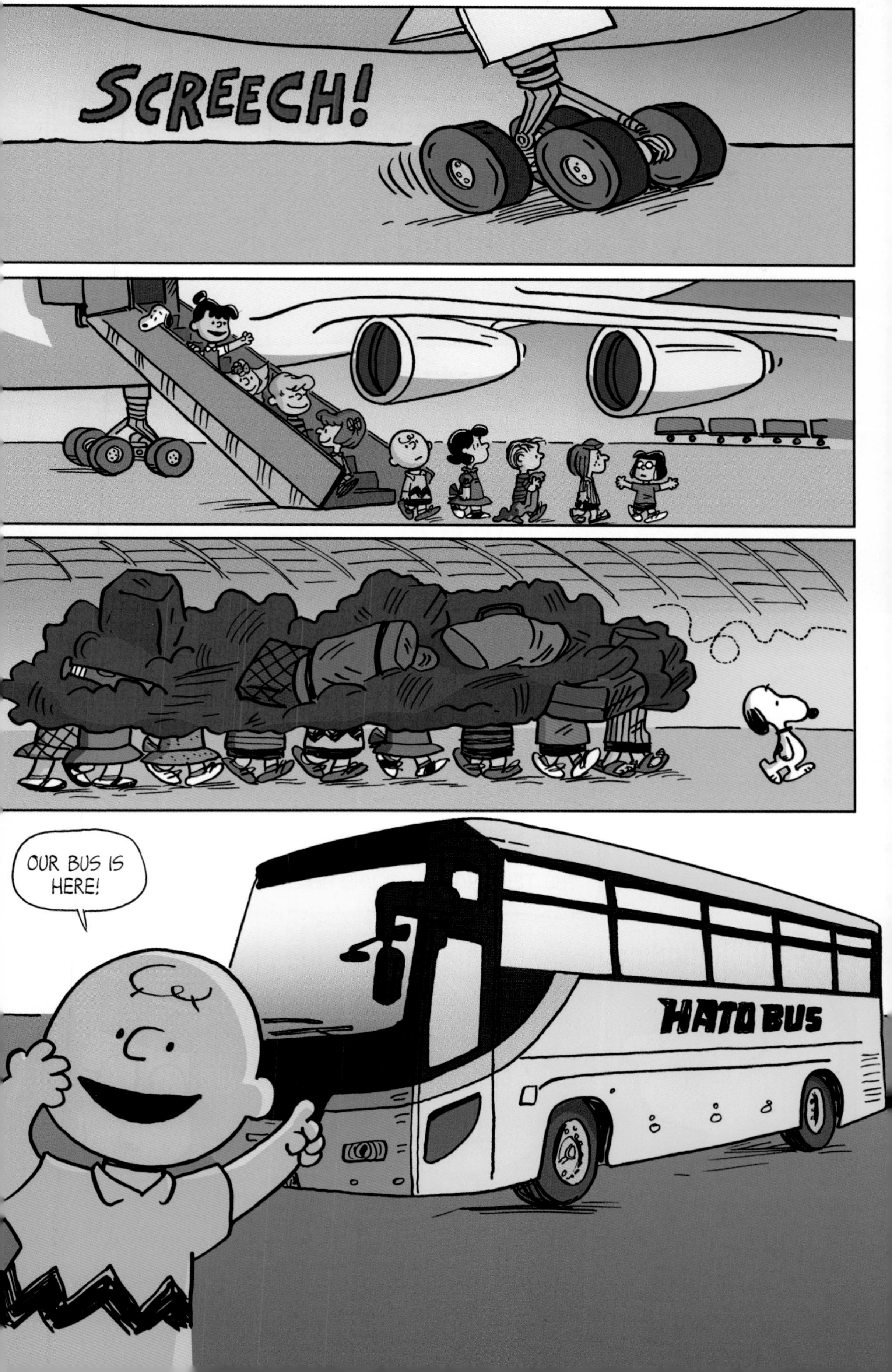
SCREECH!
OUR BUS IS HERE!
HATO BUS

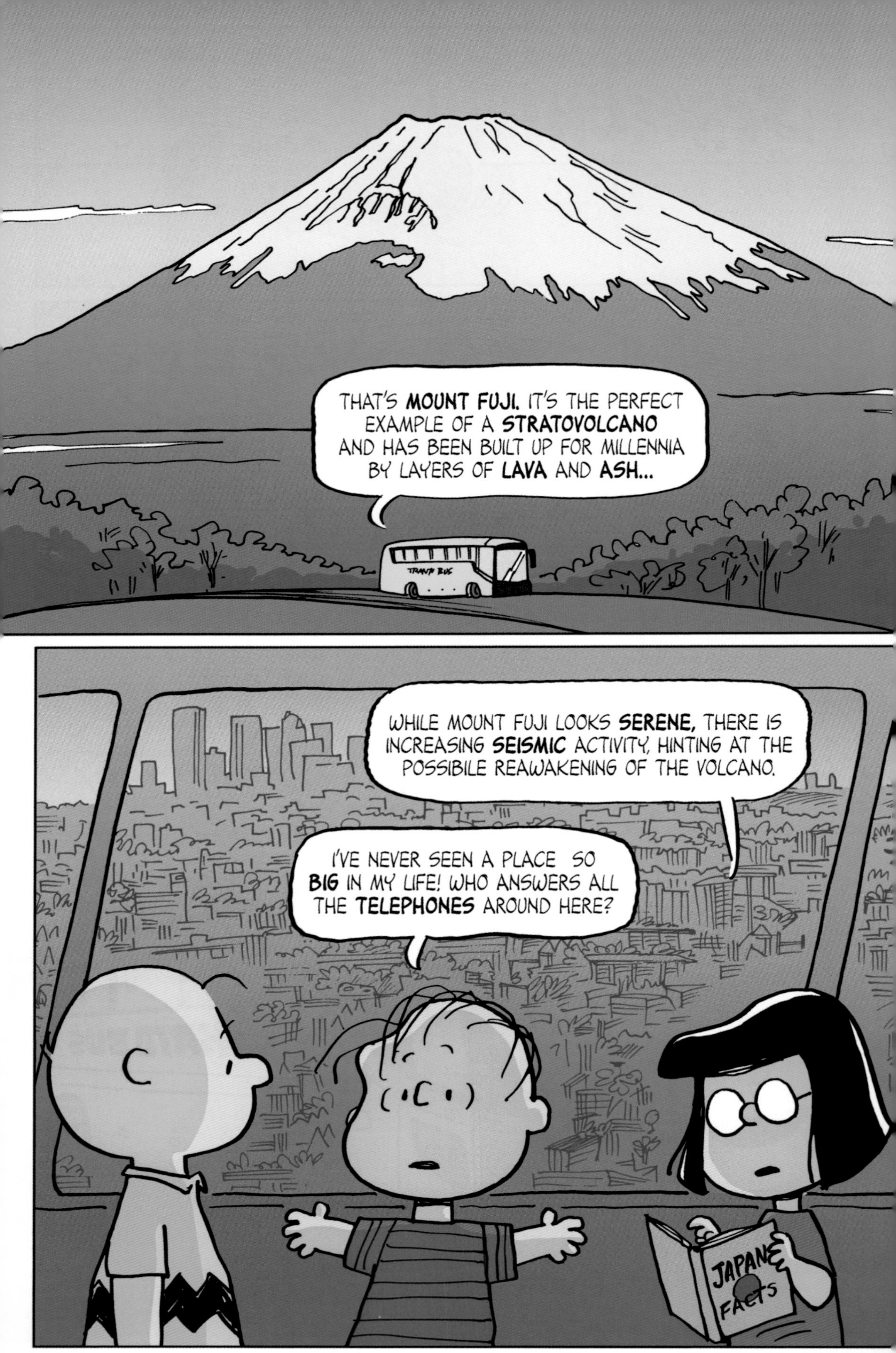
THAT'S MOUNT FUJI. IT'S THE PERFECT EXAMPLE OF A STRATOVOLCANO AND HAS BEEN BUILT UP FOR MILLENNIA BY LAYERS OF LAVA AND ASH...
WHILE MOUNT FUJI LOOKS SERENE, THERE IS INCREASING SEISMIC ACTIVITY, HINTING AT THE POSSIBILE REAWAKENING OF THE VOLCANO.
I'VE NEVER SEEN A PLACE SO BIG IN MY LIFE! WHO ANSWERS ALL THE TELEPHONES AROUND HERE?
JAPAN FACTS

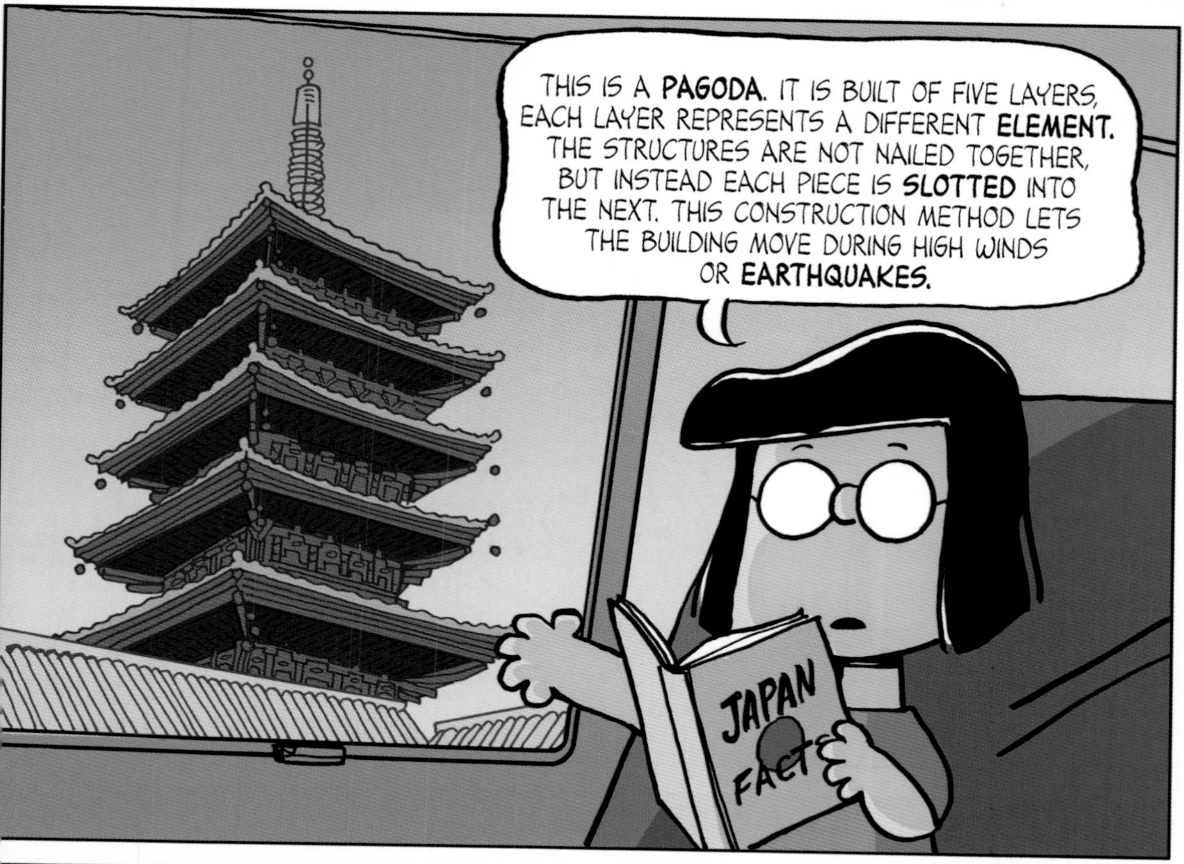
THIS IS A PAGODA. IT IS BUILT OF FIVE LAYERS, EACH LAYER REPRESENTS A DIFFERENT ELEMENT. THE STRUCTURES ARE NOT NAILED TOGETHER, BUT INSTEAD EACH PIECE IS SLOTTED INTO THE NEXT. THIS CONSTRUCTION METHOD LETS THE BUILDING MOVE DURING HIGH WINDS OR EARTHQUAKES.
JAPAN FACTS

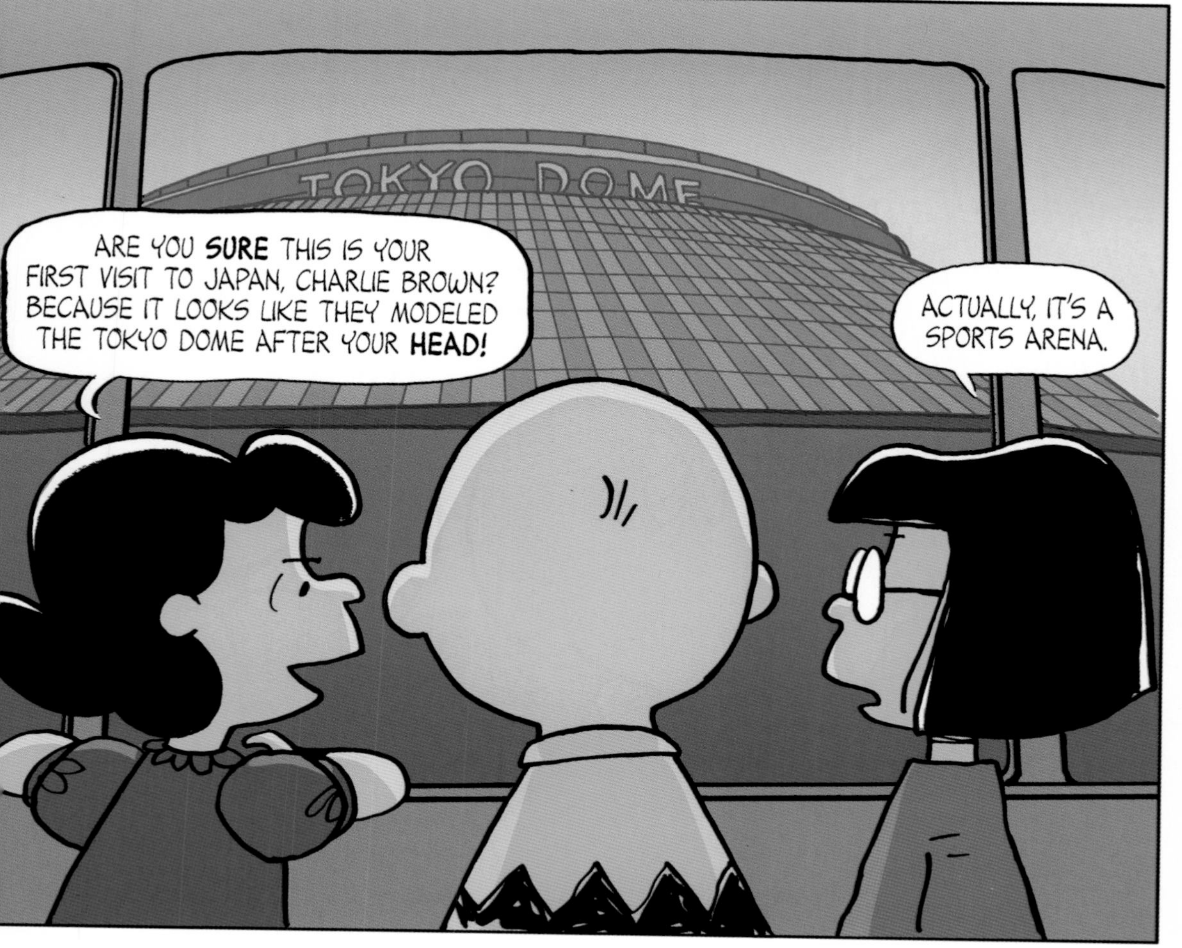
TOKYO DOME
ARE YOU SURE THIS IS YOUR FIRST VISIT TO JAPAN, CHARLIE BROWN? BECAUSE IT LOOKS LIKE THEY MODELED THE TOKYO DOME AFTER YOUR HEAD!
ACTUALLY, IT'S A SPORTS ARENA.

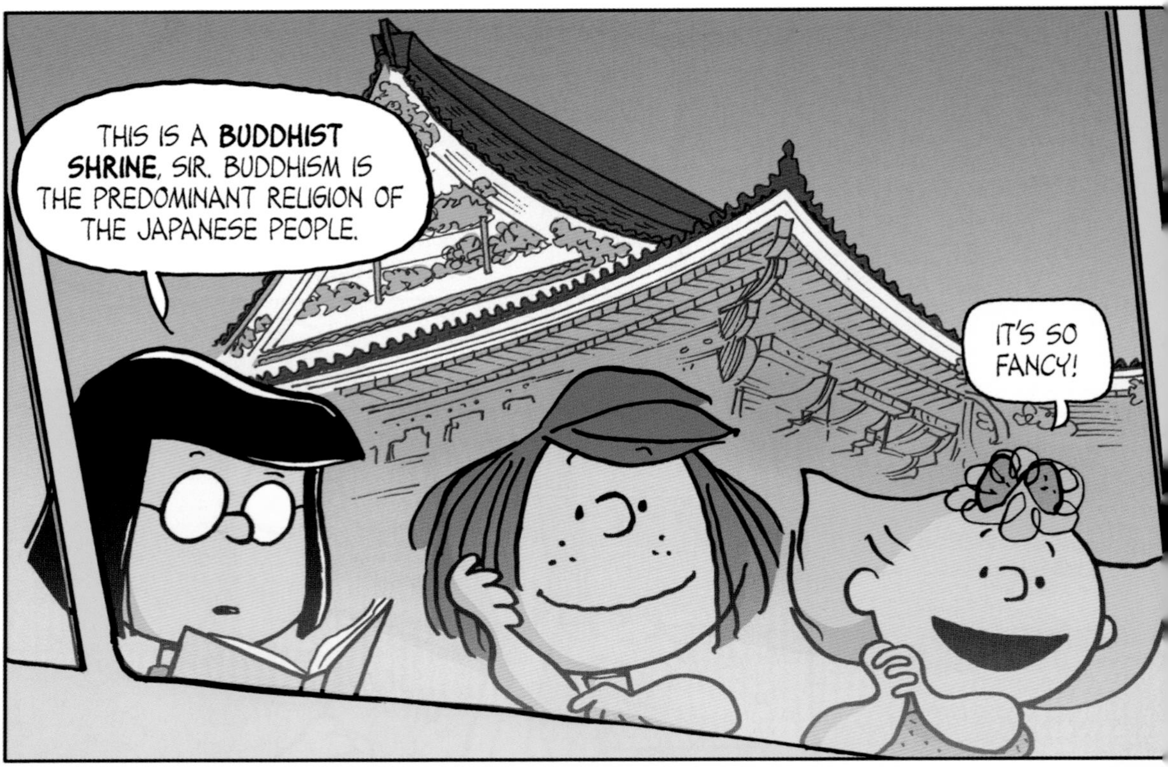
THIS IS A **BUDDHIST SHRINE**, SIR. BUDDHISM IS THE PREDOMINANT RELIGION OF THE JAPANESE PEOPLE.
IT'S SO FANCY!

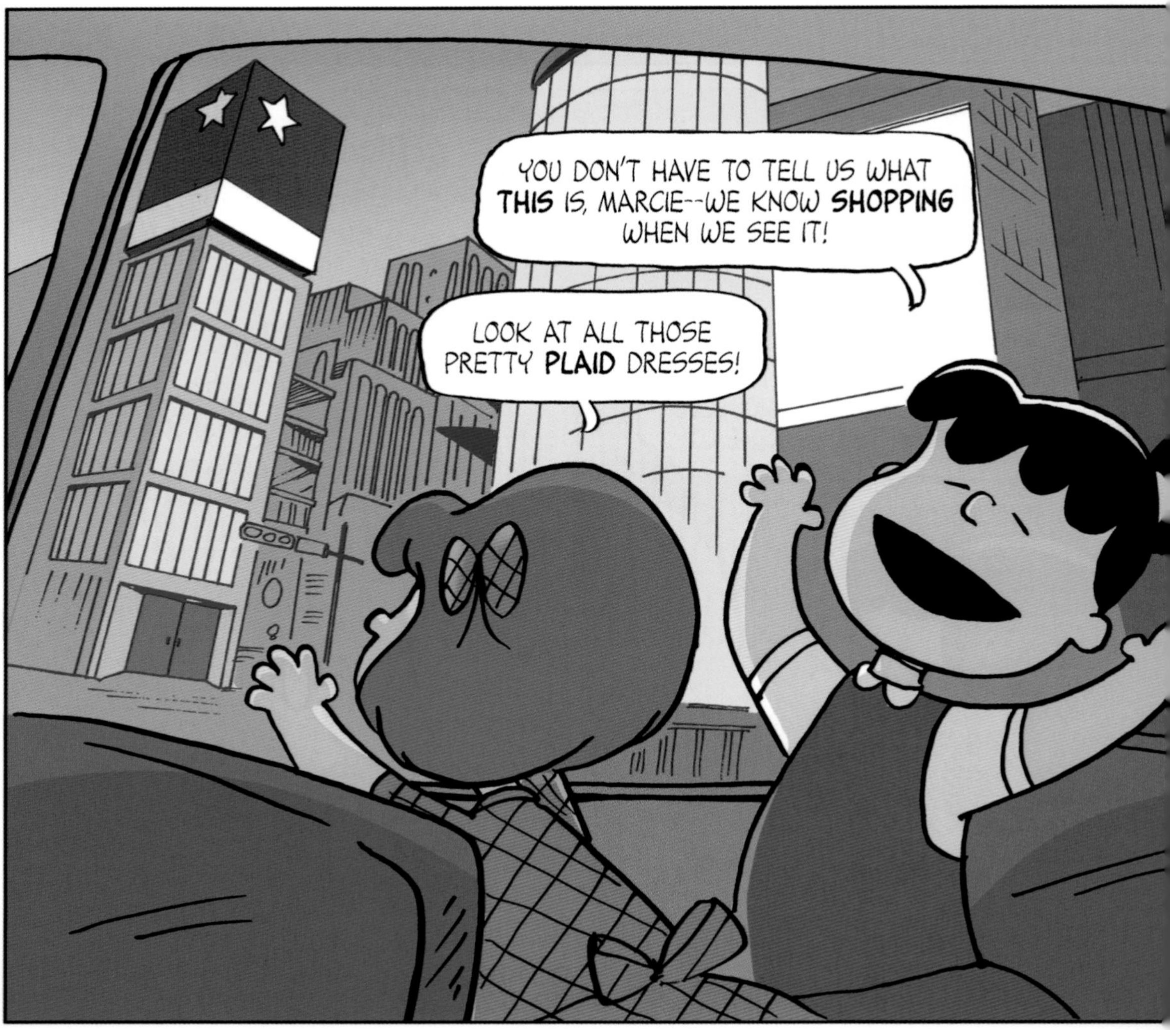
YOU DON'T HAVE TO TELL US WHAT **THIS** IS, MARCIE--WE KNOW **SHOPPING** WHEN WE SEE IT!
LOOK AT ALL THOSE PRETTY **PLAID** DRESSES!

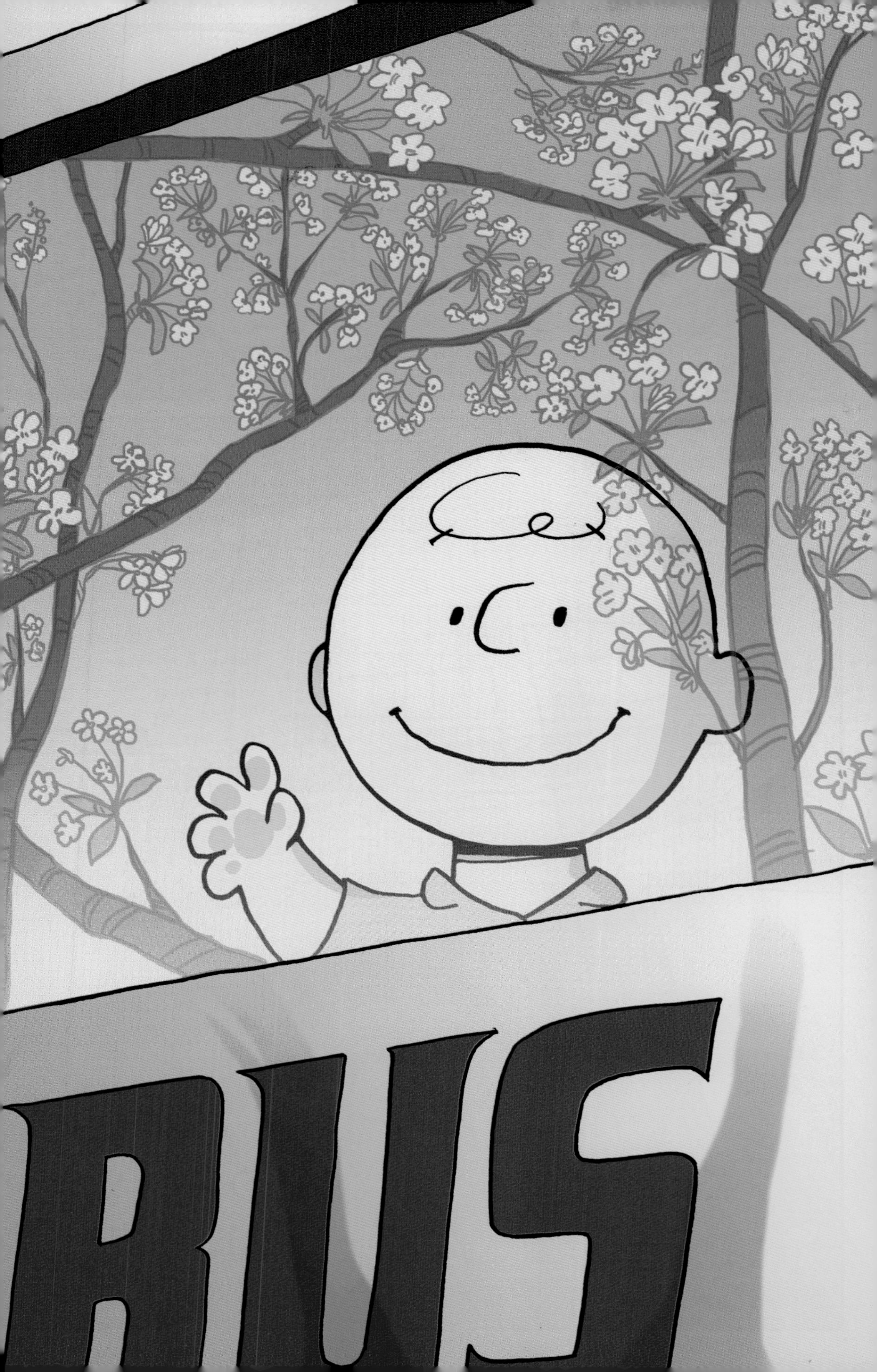

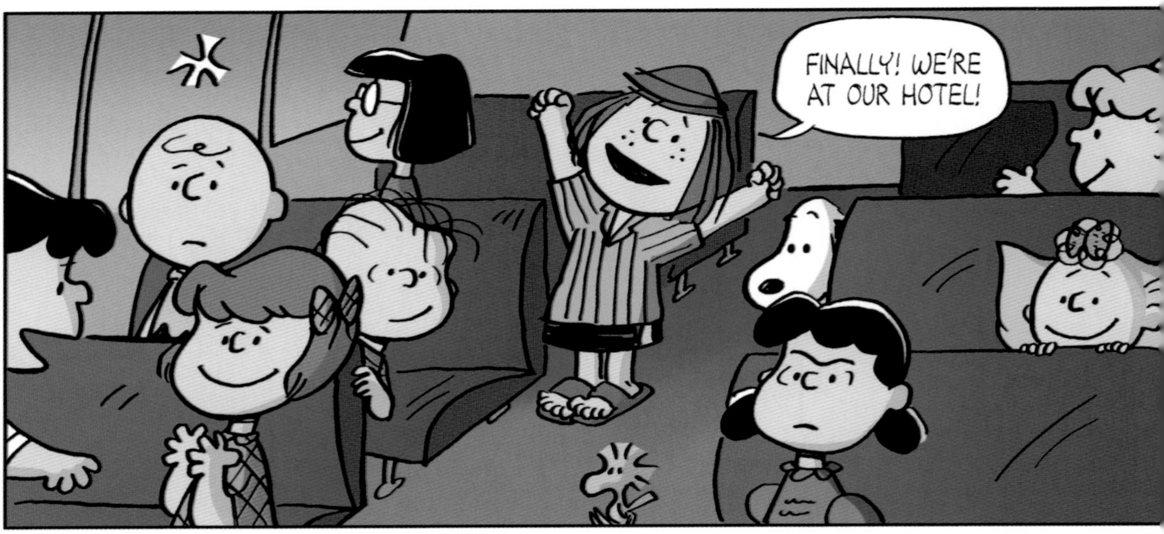
FINALLY! WE'RE AT OUR HOTEL!

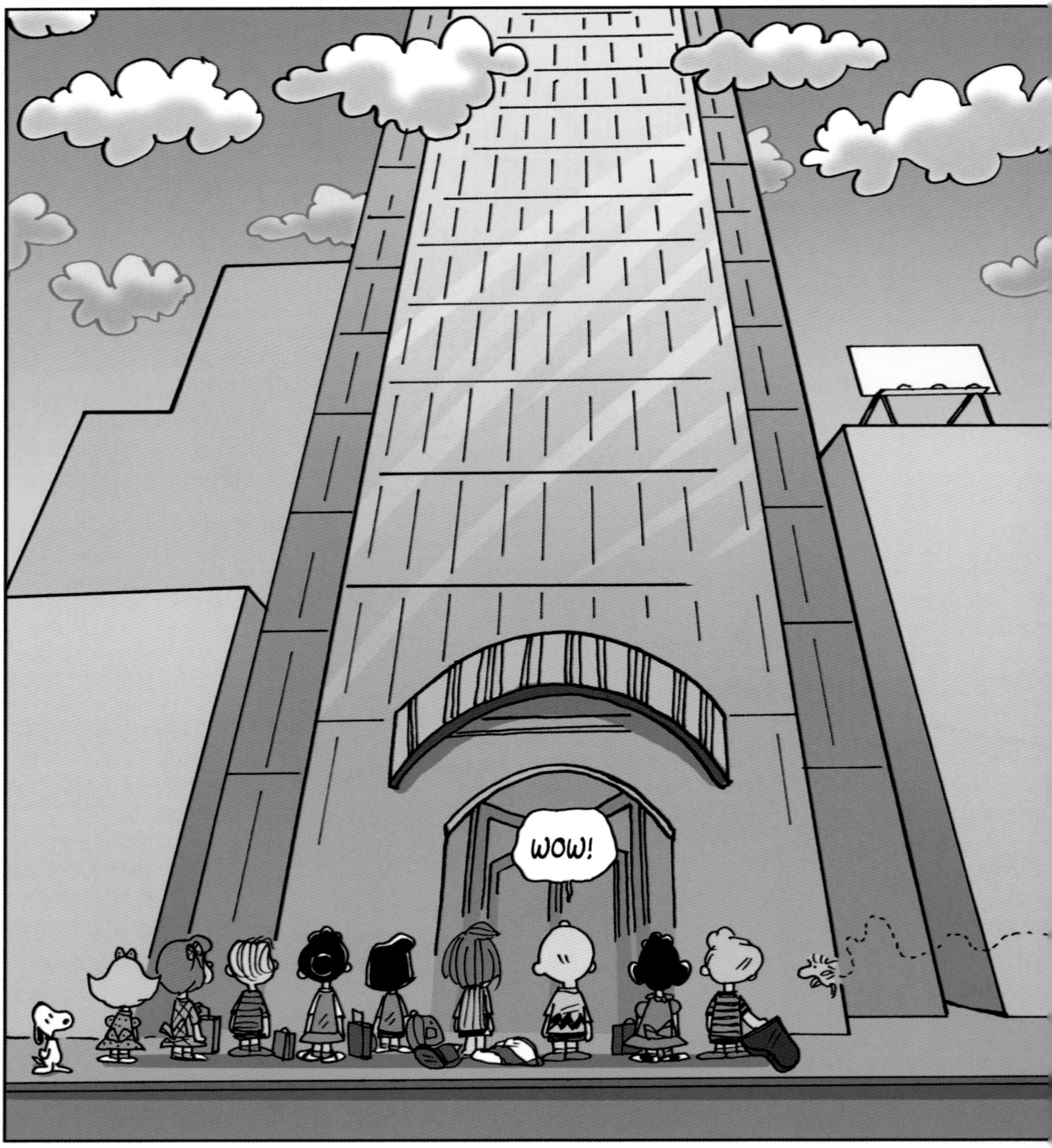
WOW!

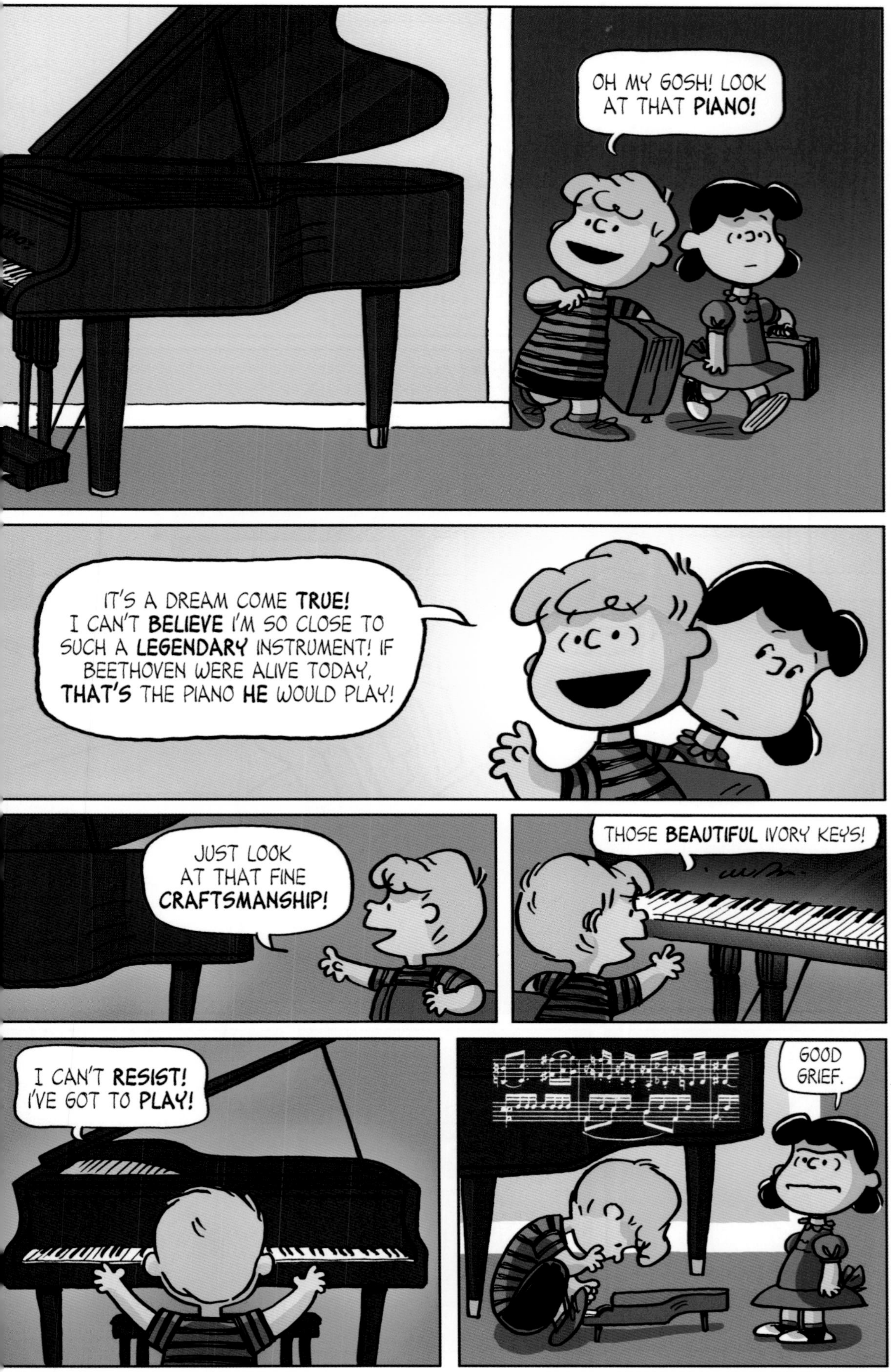
OH MY GOSH! LOOK AT THAT PIANO!
IT'S A DREAM COME TRUE! I CAN'T BELIEVE I'M SO CLOSE TO SUCH A LEGENDARY INSTRUMENT! IF BEETHOVEN WERE ALIVE TODAY, THAT'S THE PIANO HE WOULD PLAY!
JUST LOOK AT THAT FINE CRAFTSMANSHIP!
THOSE BEAUTIFUL IVORY KEYS!
I CAN'T RESIST! I'VE GOT TO PLAY!
GOOD GRIEF.

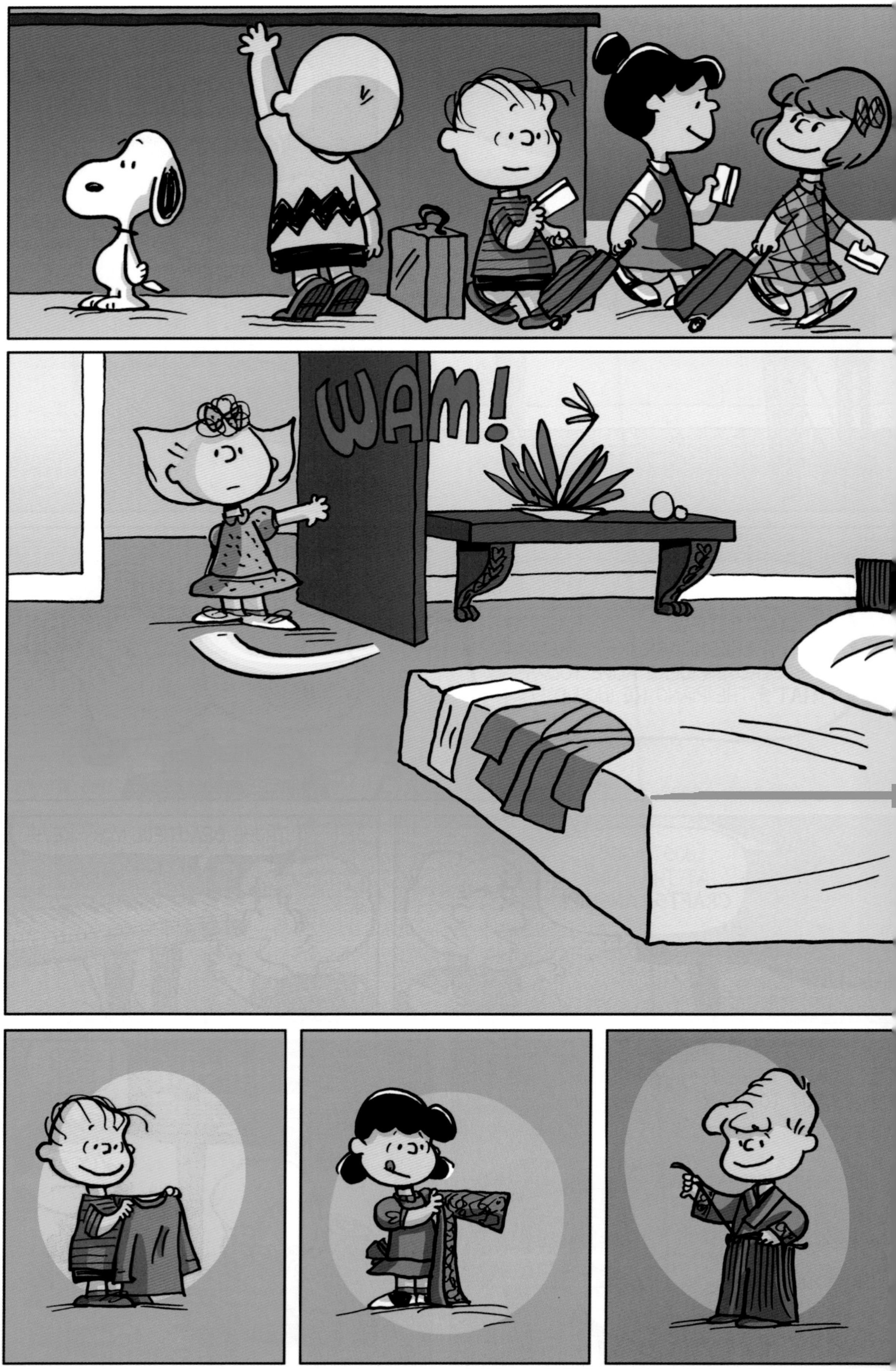
WAM!

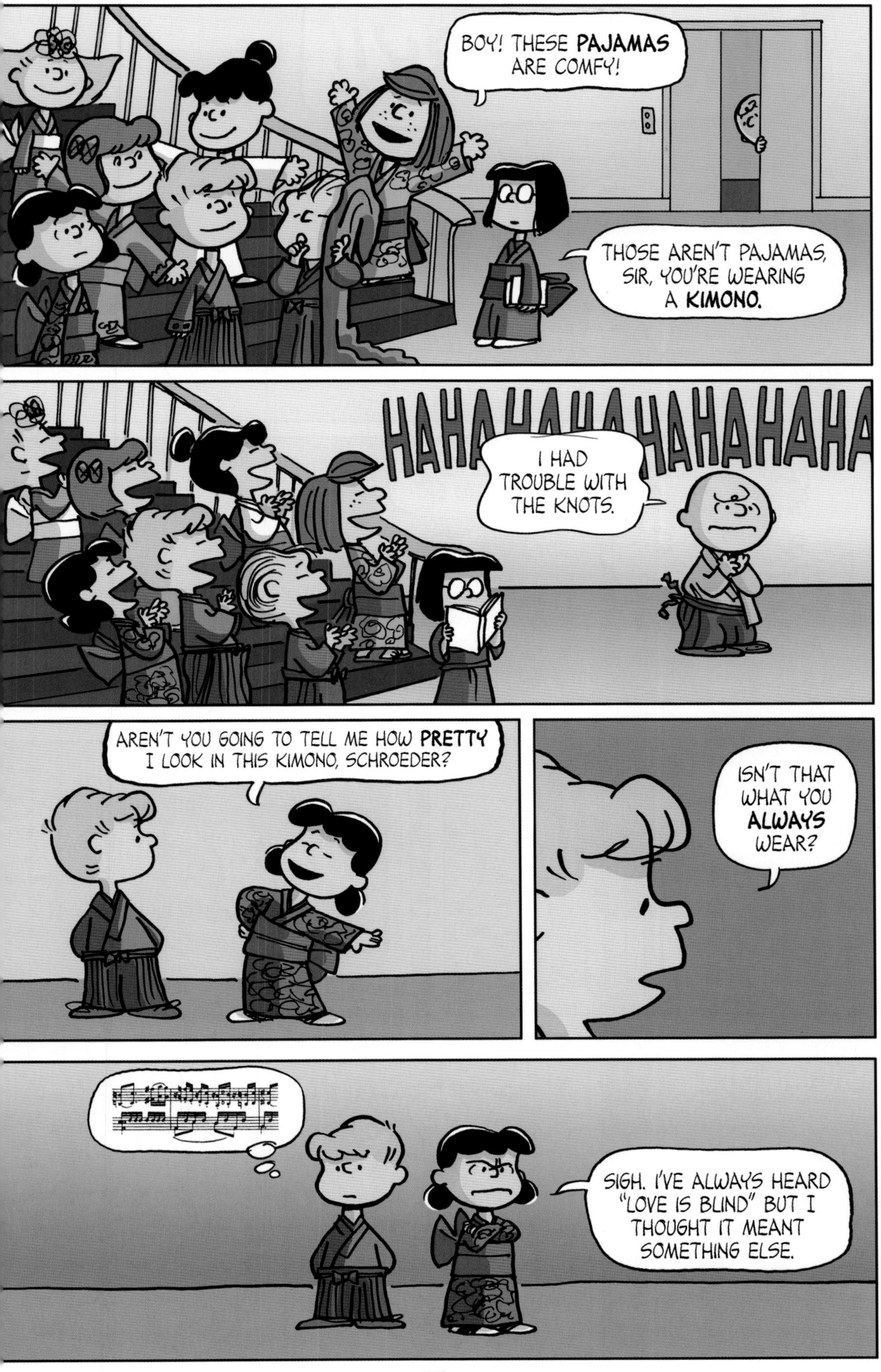
BOY! THESE PAJAMAS ARE COMFY!
THOSE AREN'T PAJAMAS, SIR, YOU'RE WEARING A KIMONO.
HAHAHAHAHAHAHAHAHA
I HAD TROUBLE WITH THE KNOTS.
AREN'T YOU GOING TO TELL ME HOW PRETTY I LOOK IN THIS KIMONO, SCHROEDER?
ISN'T THAT WHAT YOU ALWAYS WEAR?
SIGH. I'VE ALWAYS HEARD "LOVE IS BLIND" BUT I THOUGHT IT MEANT SOMETHING ELSE.

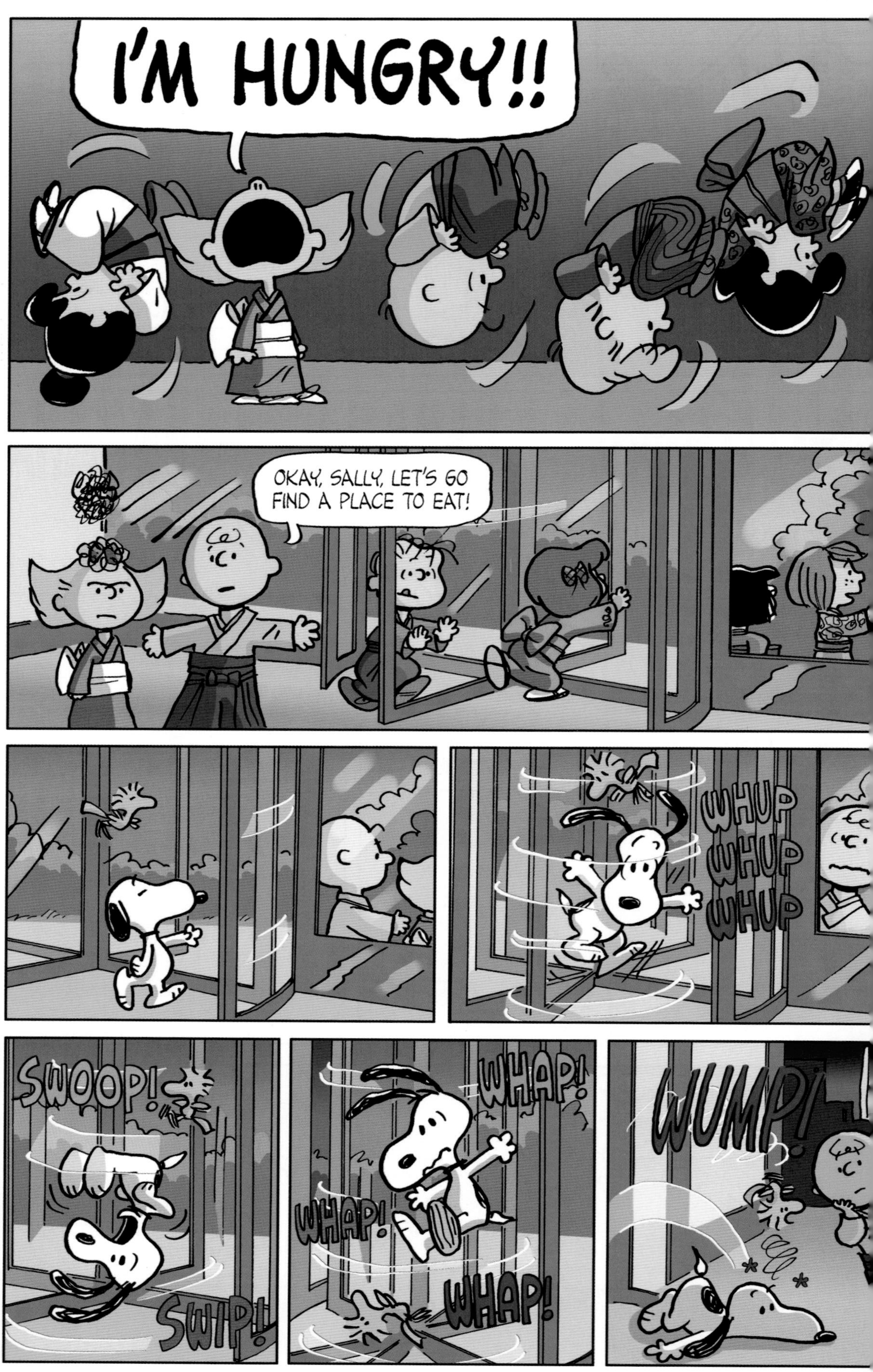
I'M HUNGRY!!
OKAY, SALLY, LET'S GO FIND A PLACE TO EAT!
WHUP
WHUP
WHUP
SWOOP!
SWIP!!
WHAP!
WHAP!
WHAP!
WUMP!

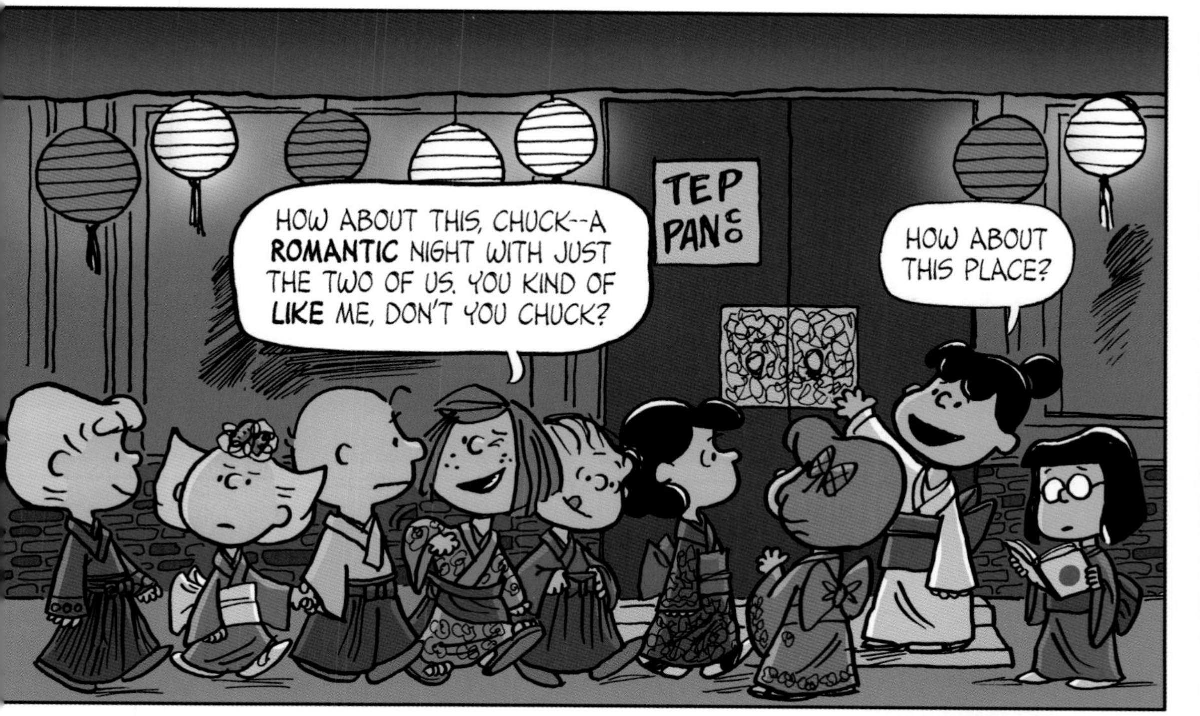
TEP PAN CO
HOW ABOUT THIS, CHUCK--A ROMANTIC NIGHT WITH JUST THE TWO OF US. YOU KIND OF LIKE ME, DON'T YOU CHUCK?
HOW ABOUT THIS PLACE?

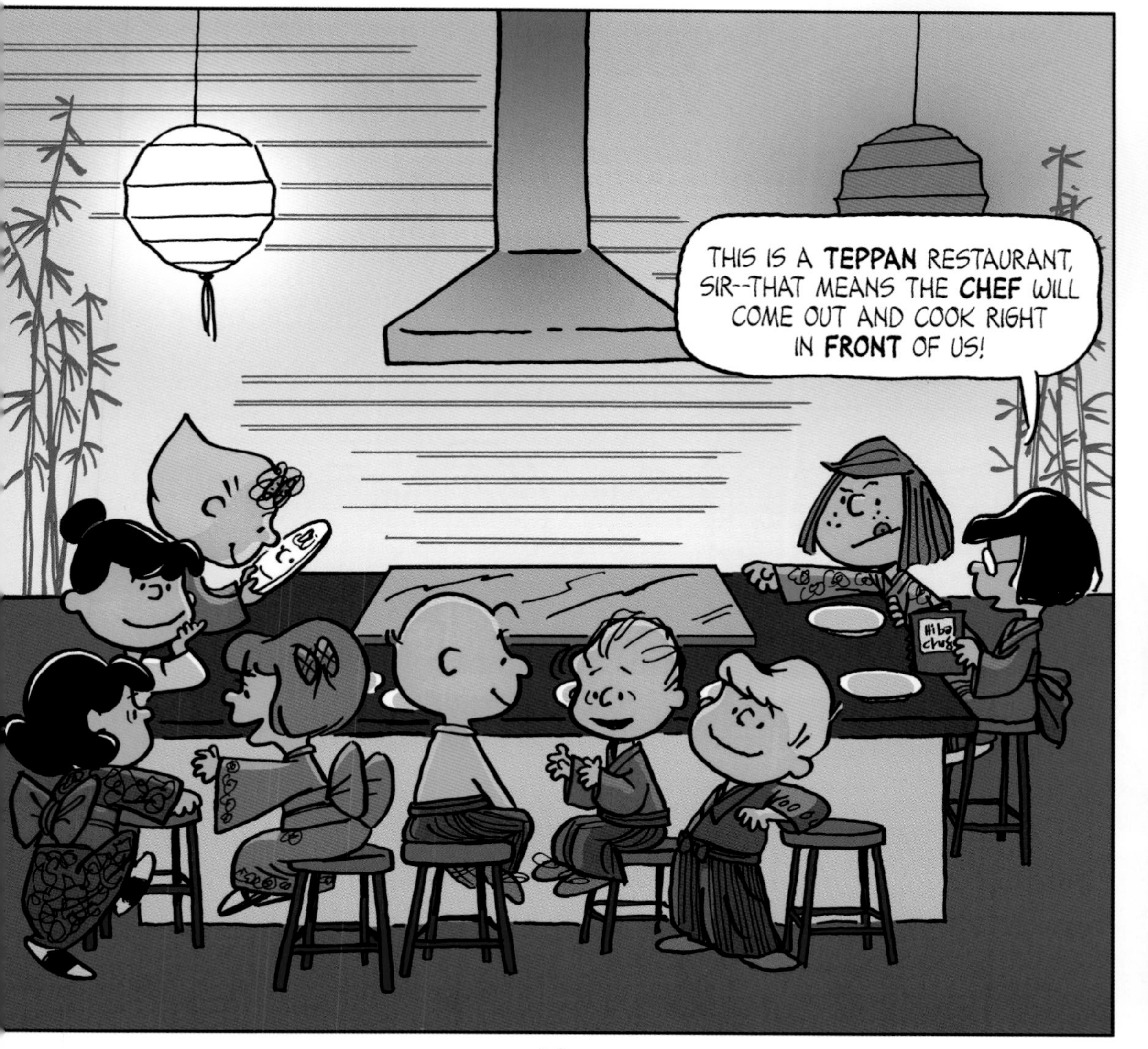
THIS IS A TEPPAN RESTAURANT, SIR--THAT MEANS THE CHEF WILL COME OUT AND COOK RIGHT IN FRONT OF US!

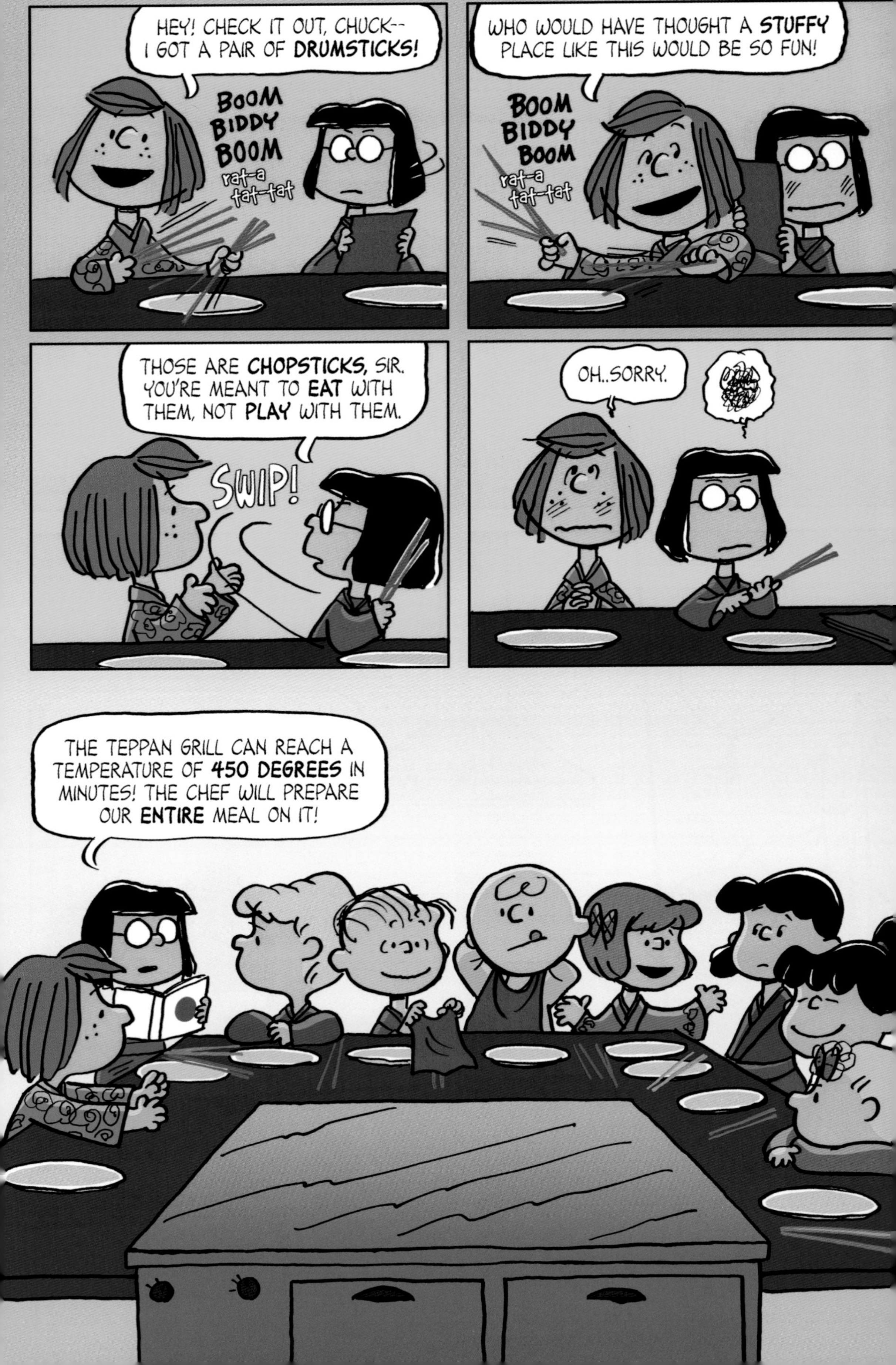

HEY! CHECK IT OUT, CHUCK-- I GOT A PAIR OF **DRUMSTICKS!**
BOOM BIDDY BOOM
rat-a tat-tat
WHO WOULD HAVE THOUGHT A **STUFFY** PLACE LIKE THIS WOULD BE SO FUN!
BOOM BIDDY BOOM
rat-a tat-tat
THOSE ARE **CHOPSTICKS,** SIR. YOU'RE MEANT TO **EAT** WITH THEM, NOT **PLAY** WITH THEM.
SWIP!
OH..SORRY.
THE TEPPAN GRILL CAN REACH A TEMPERATURE OF **450 DEGREES** IN MINUTES! THE CHEF WILL PREPARE OUR **ENTIRE** MEAL ON IT!

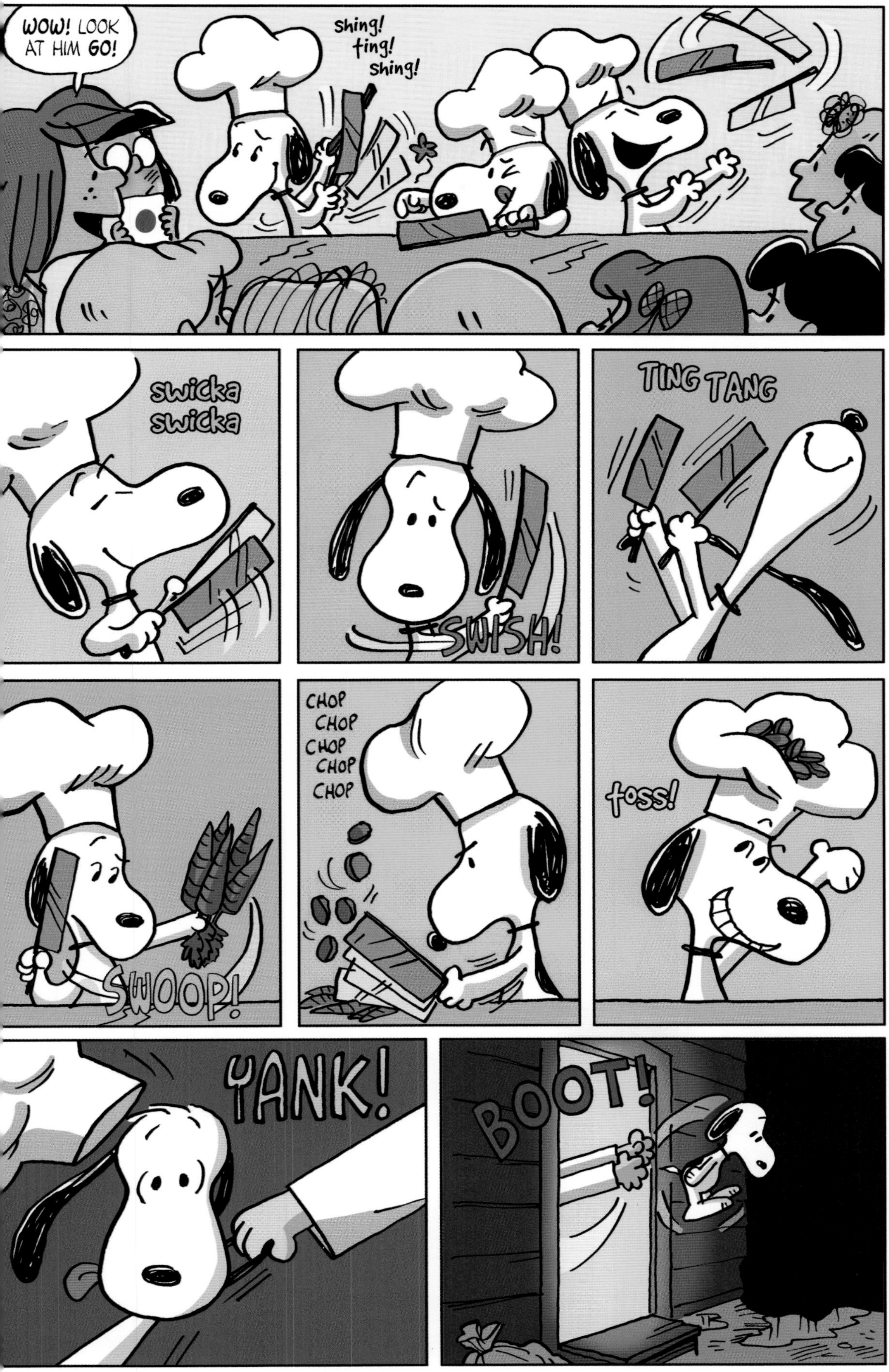
WOW! LOOK AT HIM GO!
shing! ting! shing!
swicka swicka
SWISH!
TING TANG
SWOOP!
CHOP CHOP CHOP CHOP CHOP
toss!
YANK!
BOOT!

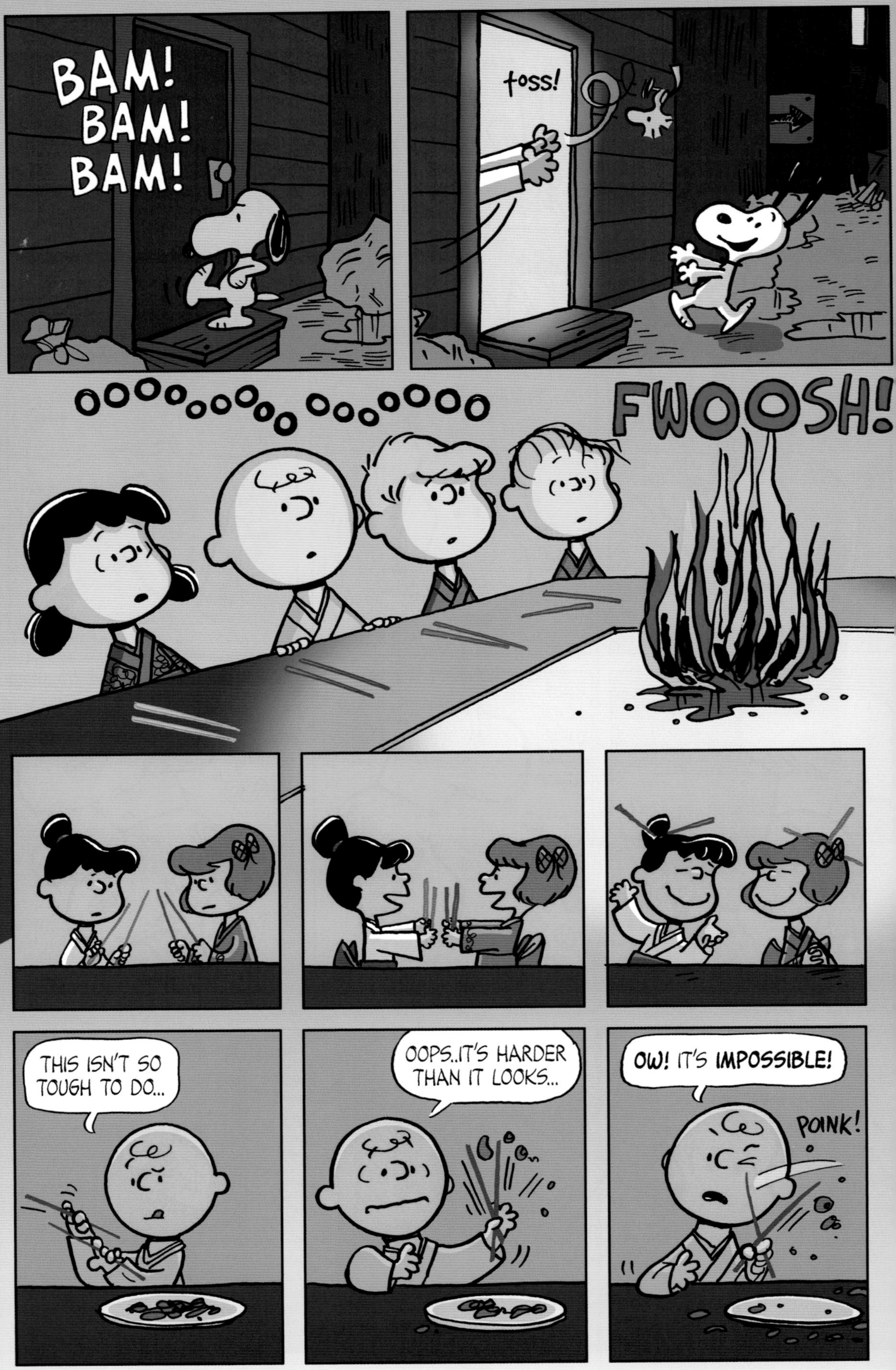
BAM! BAM! BAM!
toss!
OOOOOOOOOO OOOOOOOO
FWOOSH!
THIS ISN'T SO TOUGH TO DO...
OOPS..IT'S HARDER THAN IT LOOKS...
OW! IT'S IMPOSSIBLE!
POINK!

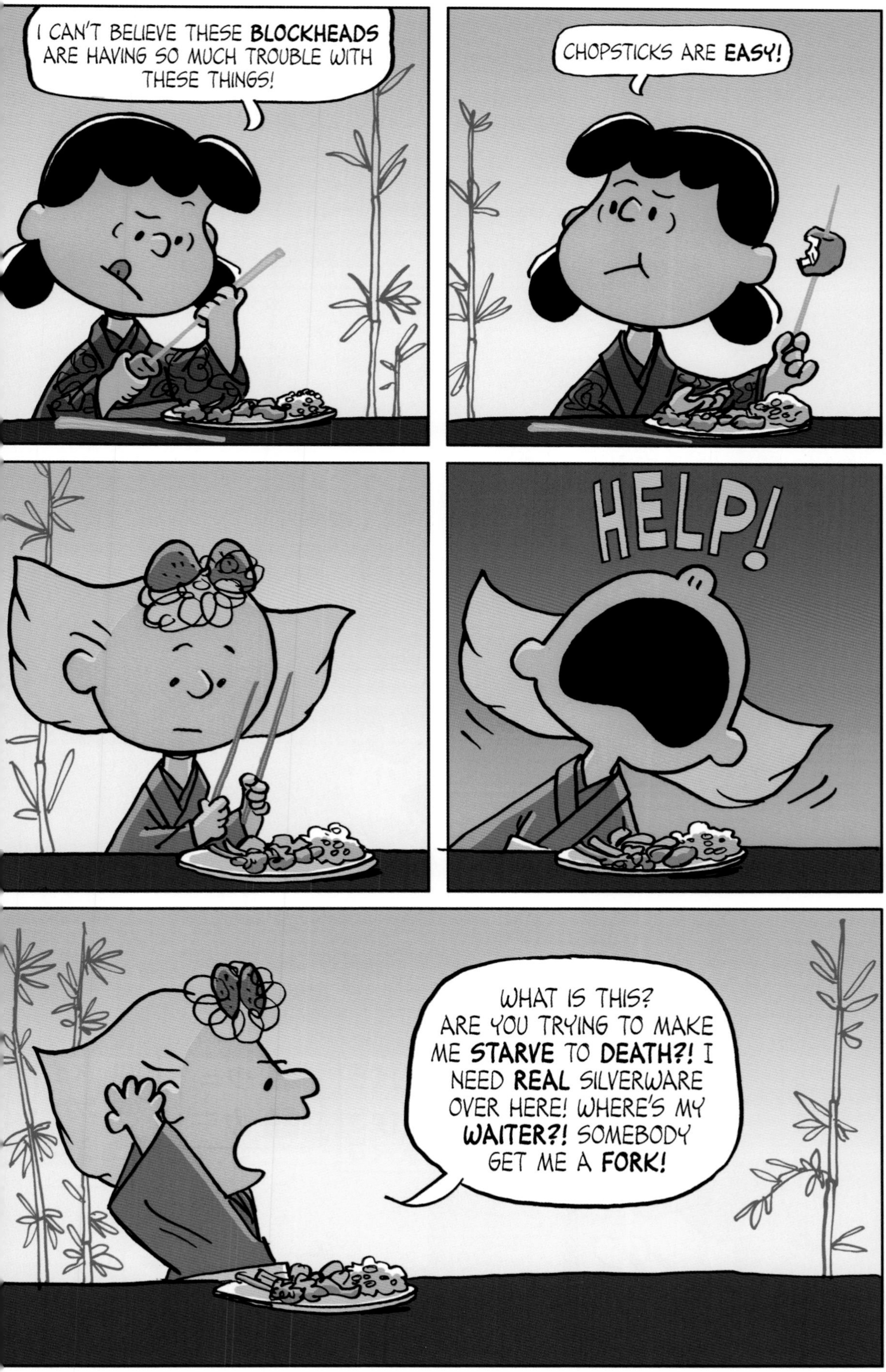
I CAN'T BELIEVE THESE BLOCKHEADS ARE HAVING SO MUCH TROUBLE WITH THESE THINGS!
CHOPSTICKS ARE EASY!
HELP!
WHAT IS THIS? ARE YOU TRYING TO MAKE ME STARVE TO DEATH?! I NEED REAL SILVERWARE OVER HERE! WHERE'S MY WAITER?! SOMEBODY GET ME A FORK!

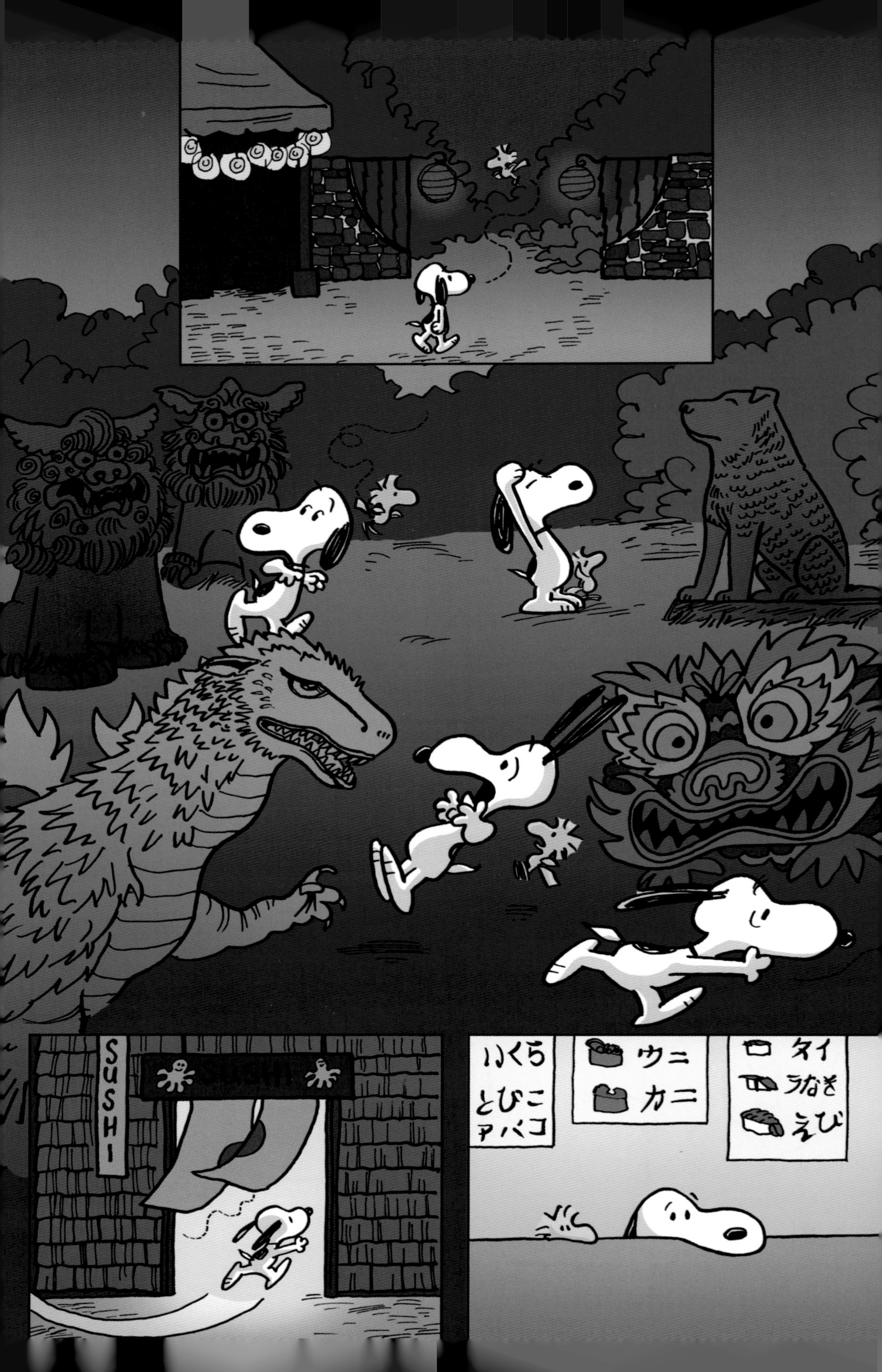
SUSHI
SUSHI
いくら
とびこ
ウニ
カニ
タイ
うなぎ
えび

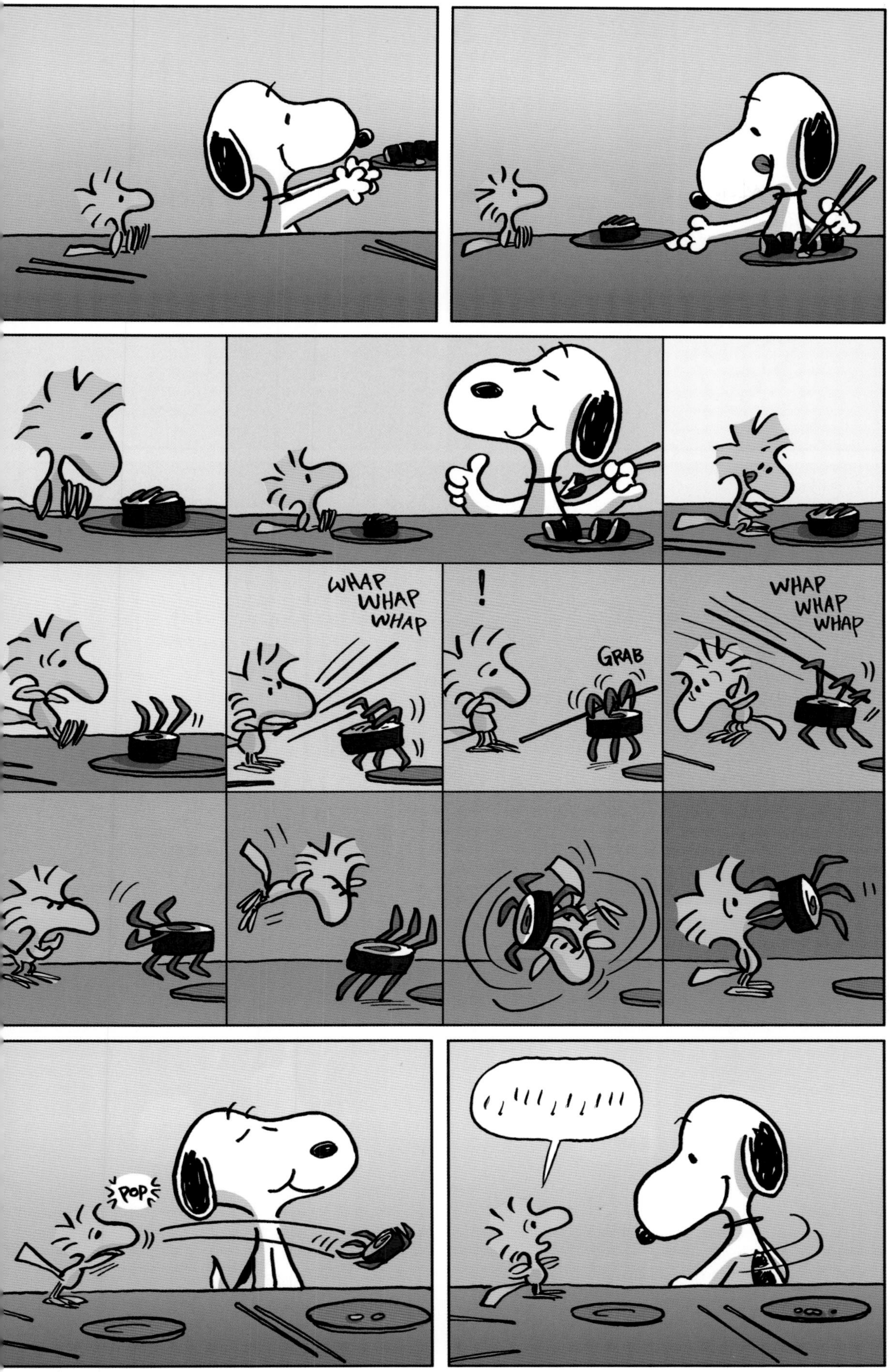
WHAP
WHAP
WHAP
!
GRAB
WHAP
WHAP
WHAP
POP

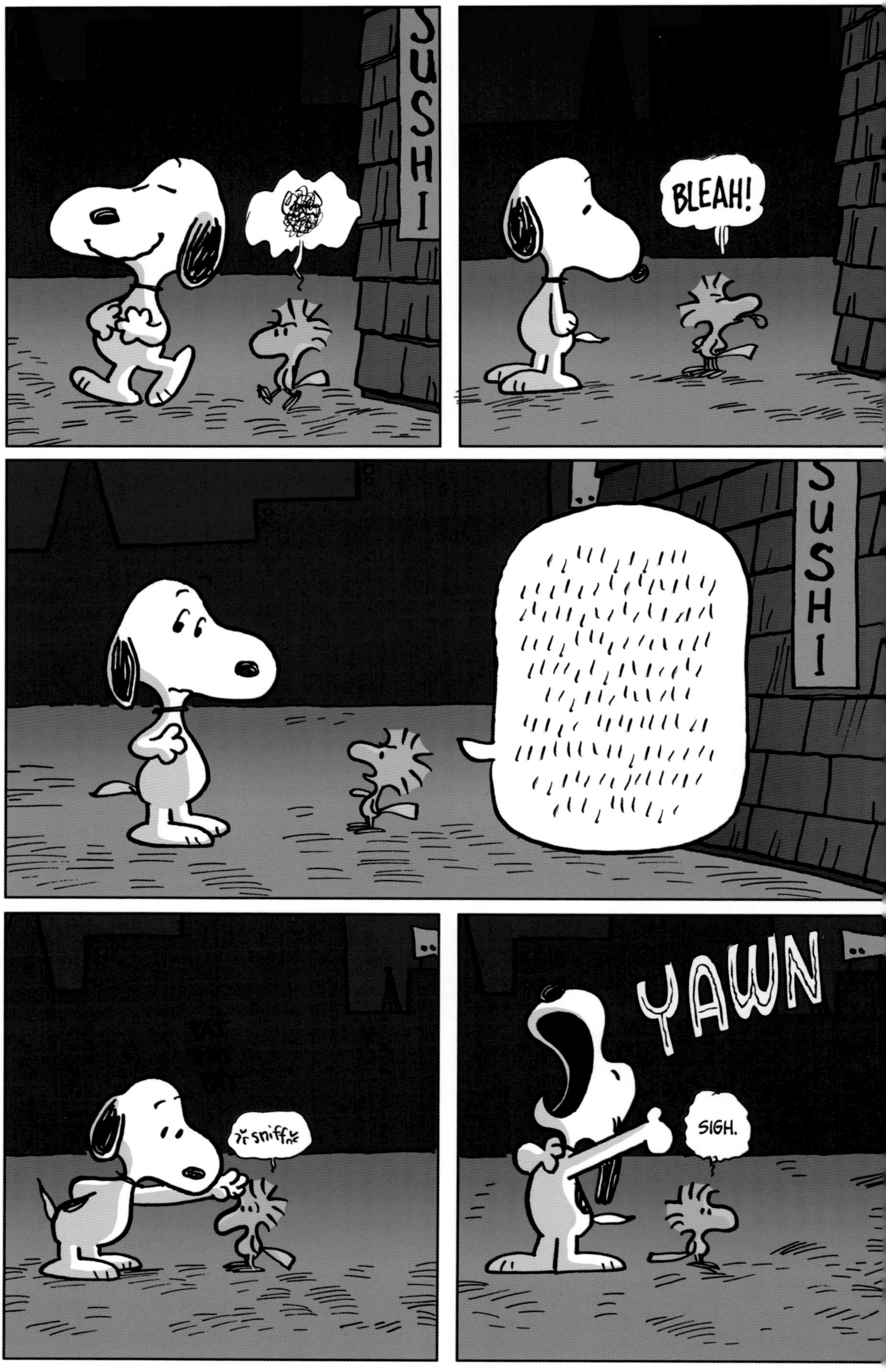
SUSHI
BLEAH!
SUSHI
sniff
YAWN
SIGH.

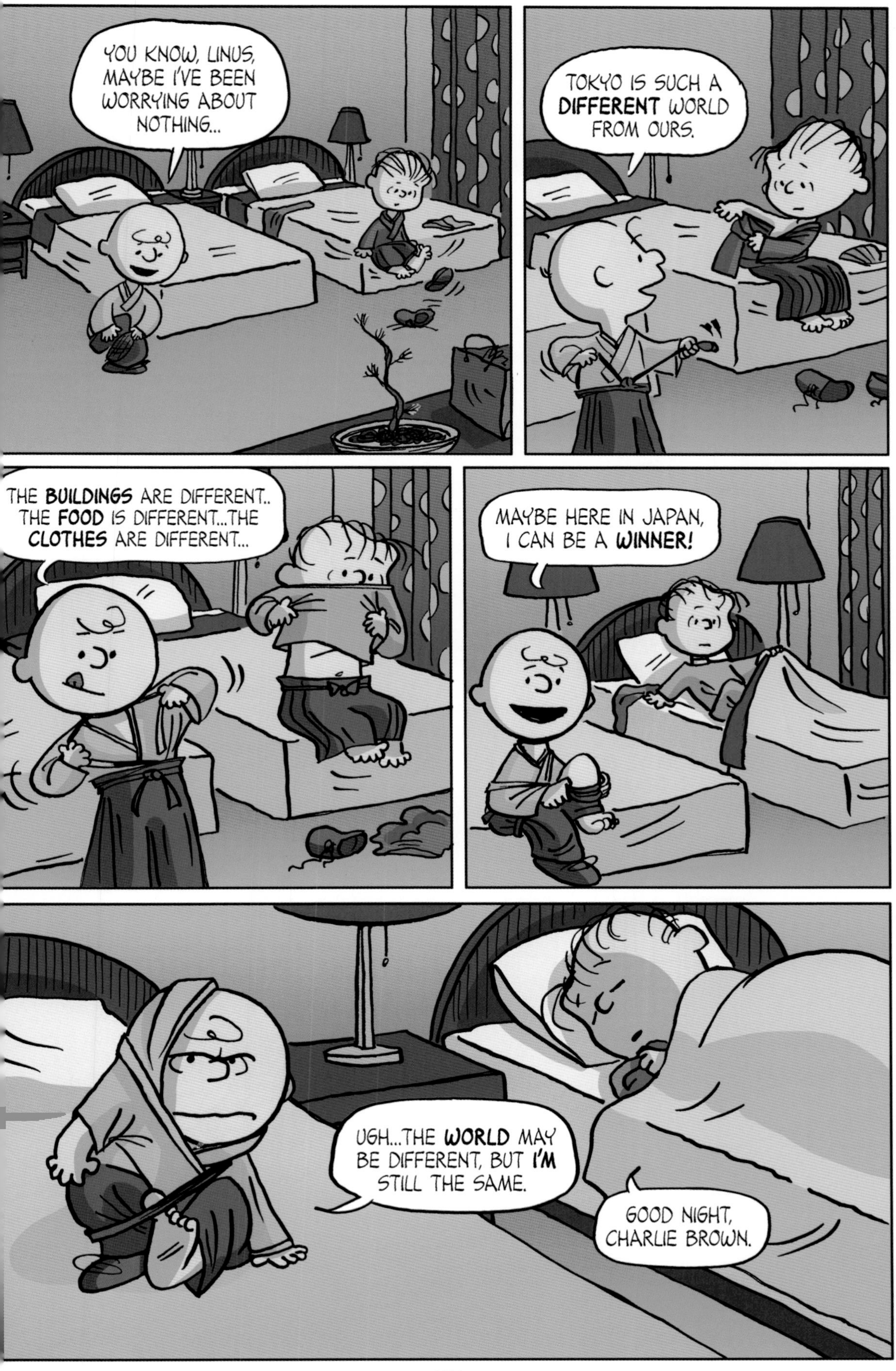
YOU KNOW, LINUS, MAYBE I'VE BEEN WORRYING ABOUT NOTHING...
TOKYO IS SUCH A **DIFFERENT** WORLD FROM OURS.
THE **BUILDINGS** ARE DIFFERENT.. THE **FOOD** IS DIFFERENT...THE **CLOTHES** ARE DIFFERENT...
MAYBE HERE IN JAPAN, I CAN BE A **WINNER!**
UGH...THE **WORLD** MAY BE DIFFERENT, BUT **I'M** STILL THE SAME.
GOOD NIGHT, CHARLIE BROWN.

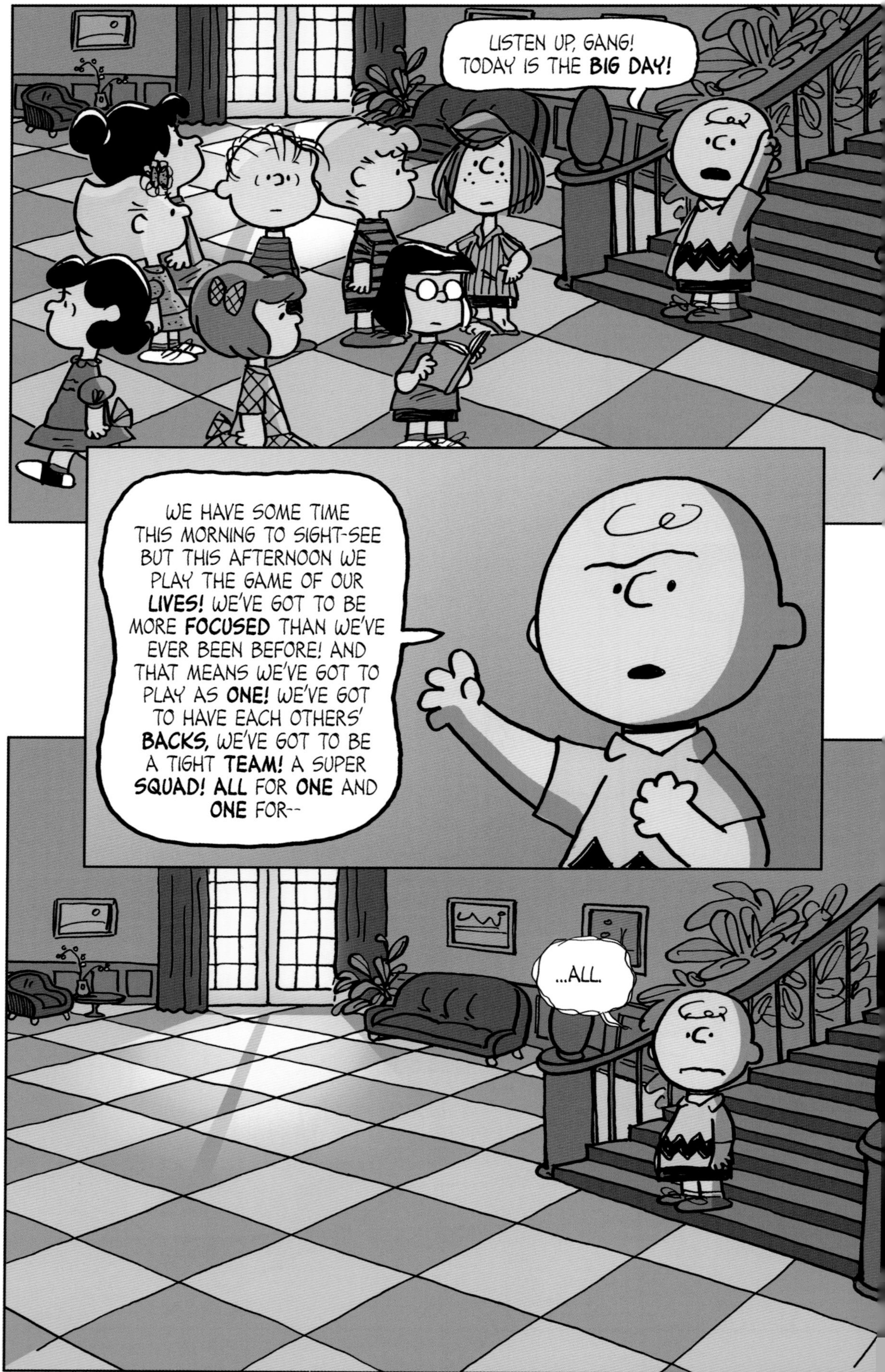
LISTEN UP, GANG! TODAY IS THE **BIG DAY!**
WE HAVE SOME TIME THIS MORNING TO SIGHT-SEE BUT THIS AFTERNOON WE PLAY THE GAME OF OUR **LIVES!** WE'VE GOT TO BE MORE **FOCUSED** THAN WE'VE EVER BEEN BEFORE! AND THAT MEANS WE'VE GOT TO PLAY AS **ONE!** WE'VE GOT TO HAVE EACH OTHERS' **BACKS,** WE'VE GOT TO BE A TIGHT **TEAM!** A SUPER **SQUAD! ALL** FOR **ONE** AND **ONE** FOR--
...ALL.

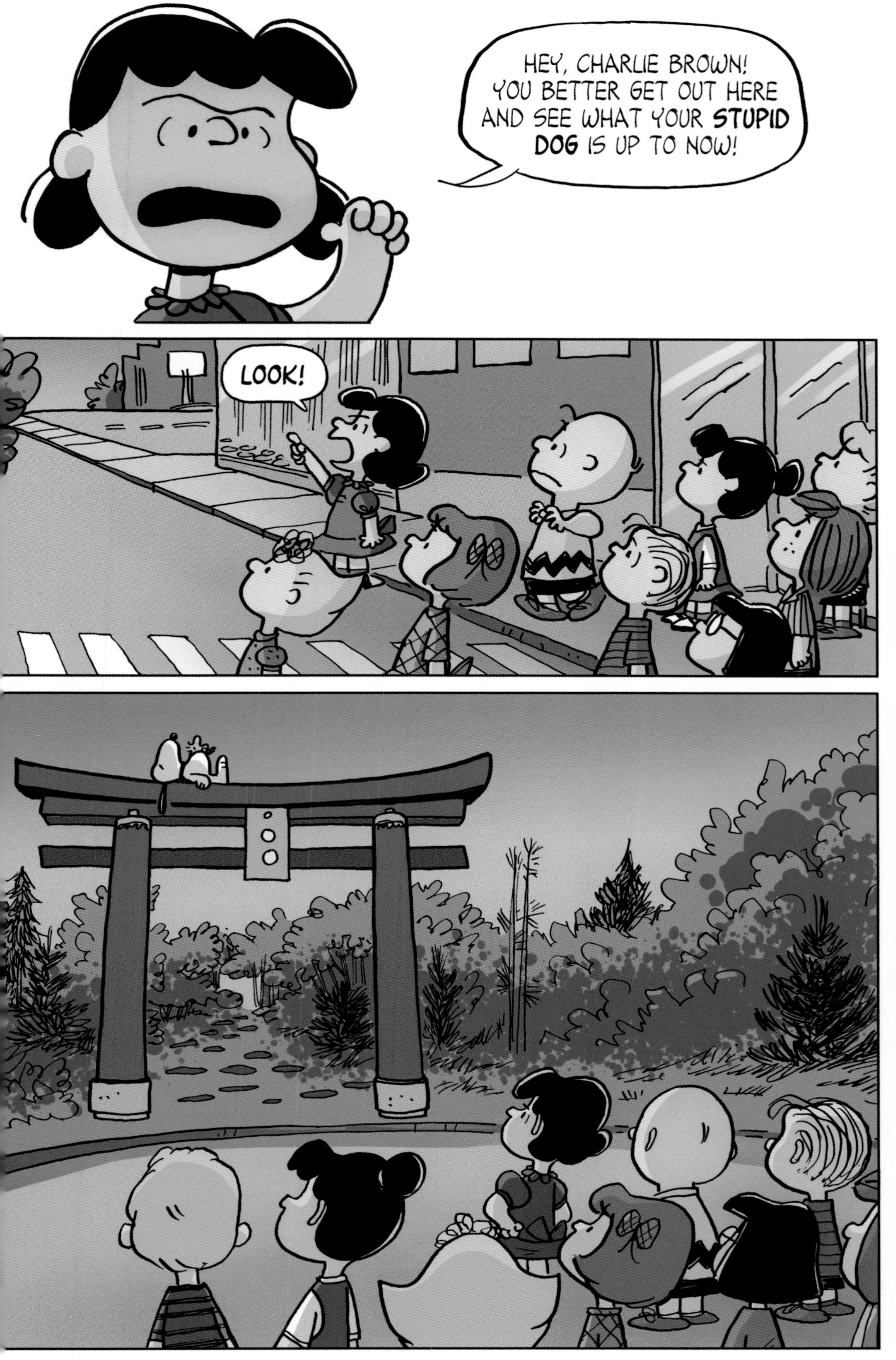
HEY, CHARLIE BROWN! YOU BETTER GET OUT HERE AND SEE WHAT YOUR **STUPID DOG** IS UP TO NOW!
LOOK!

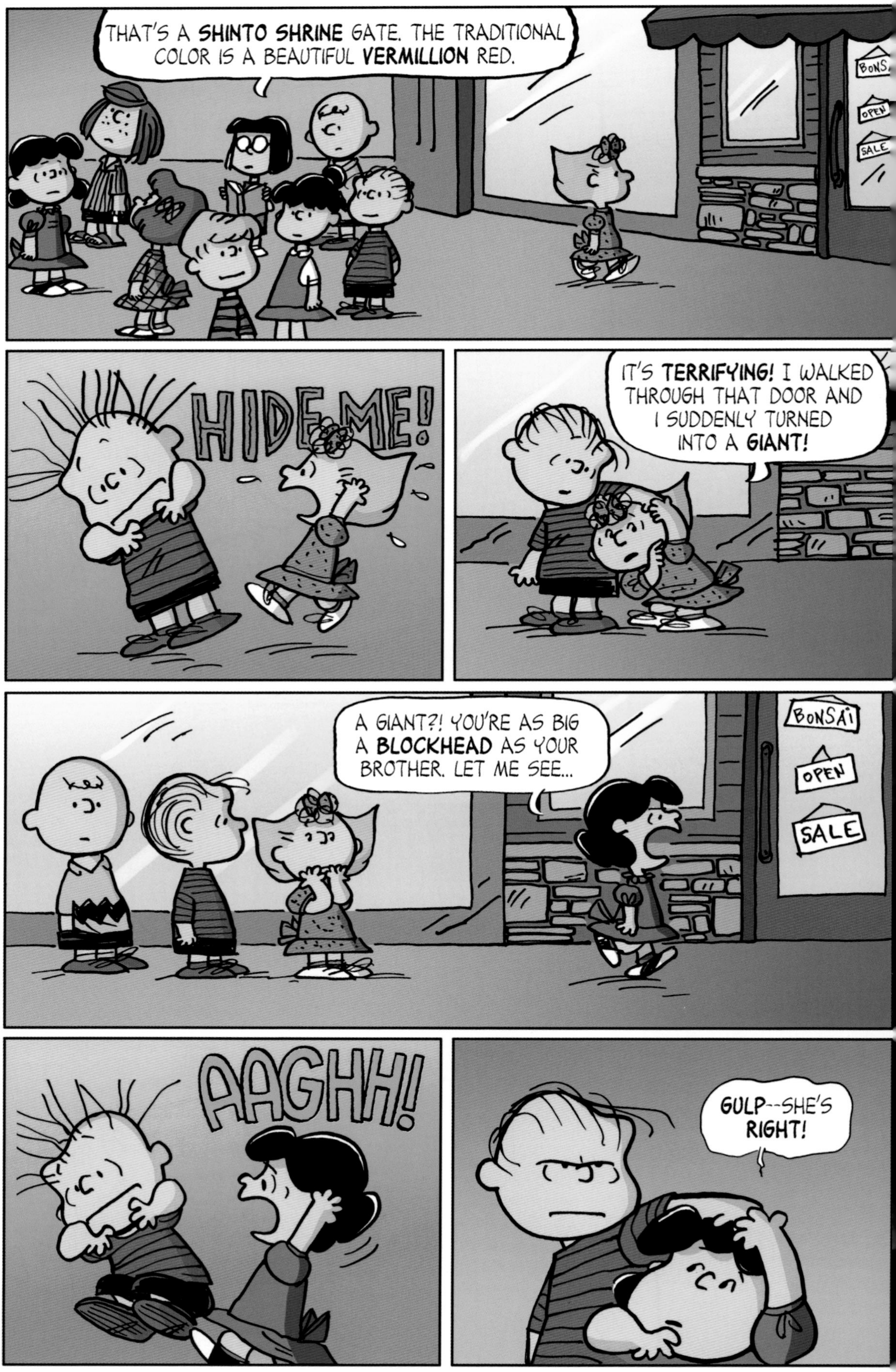
THAT'S A SHINTO SHRINE GATE. THE TRADITIONAL COLOR IS A BEAUTIFUL VERMILLION RED.
BONS
OPEN
SALE
HIDE ME!
IT'S TERRIFYING! I WALKED THROUGH THAT DOOR AND I SUDDENLY TURNED INTO A GIANT!
A GIANT?! YOU'RE AS BIG A BLOCKHEAD AS YOUR BROTHER. LET ME SEE...
BONSAI
OPEN
SALE
AAGHH!
GULP--SHE'S RIGHT!

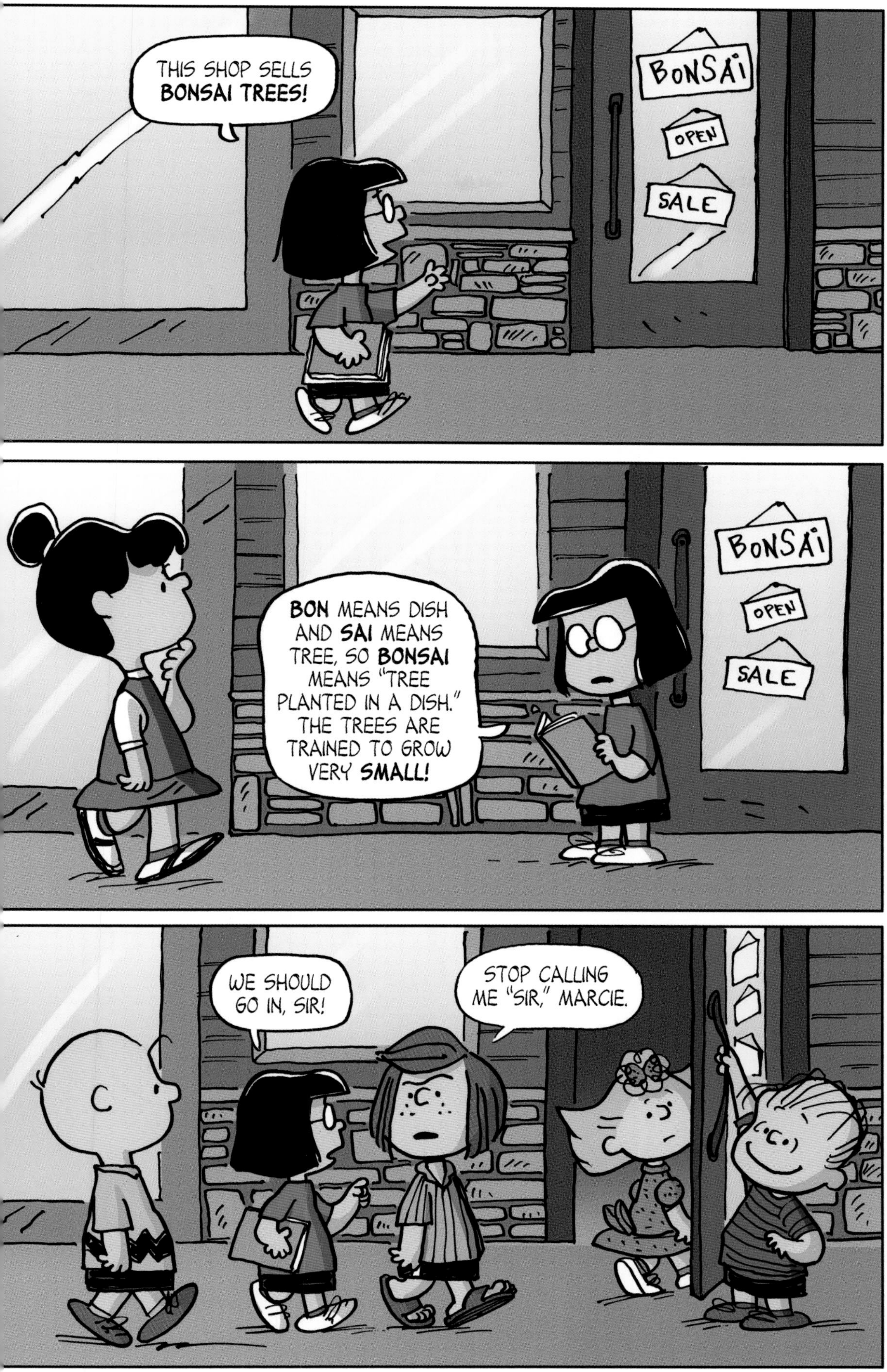

THIS SHOP SELLS **BONSAI TREES!**
BONSAI
OPEN
SALE
BON MEANS DISH AND **SAI** MEANS TREE, SO **BONSAI** MEANS "TREE PLANTED IN A DISH." THE TREES ARE TRAINED TO GROW VERY **SMALL!**
WE SHOULD GO IN, SIR!
STOP CALLING ME "SIR," MARCIE.

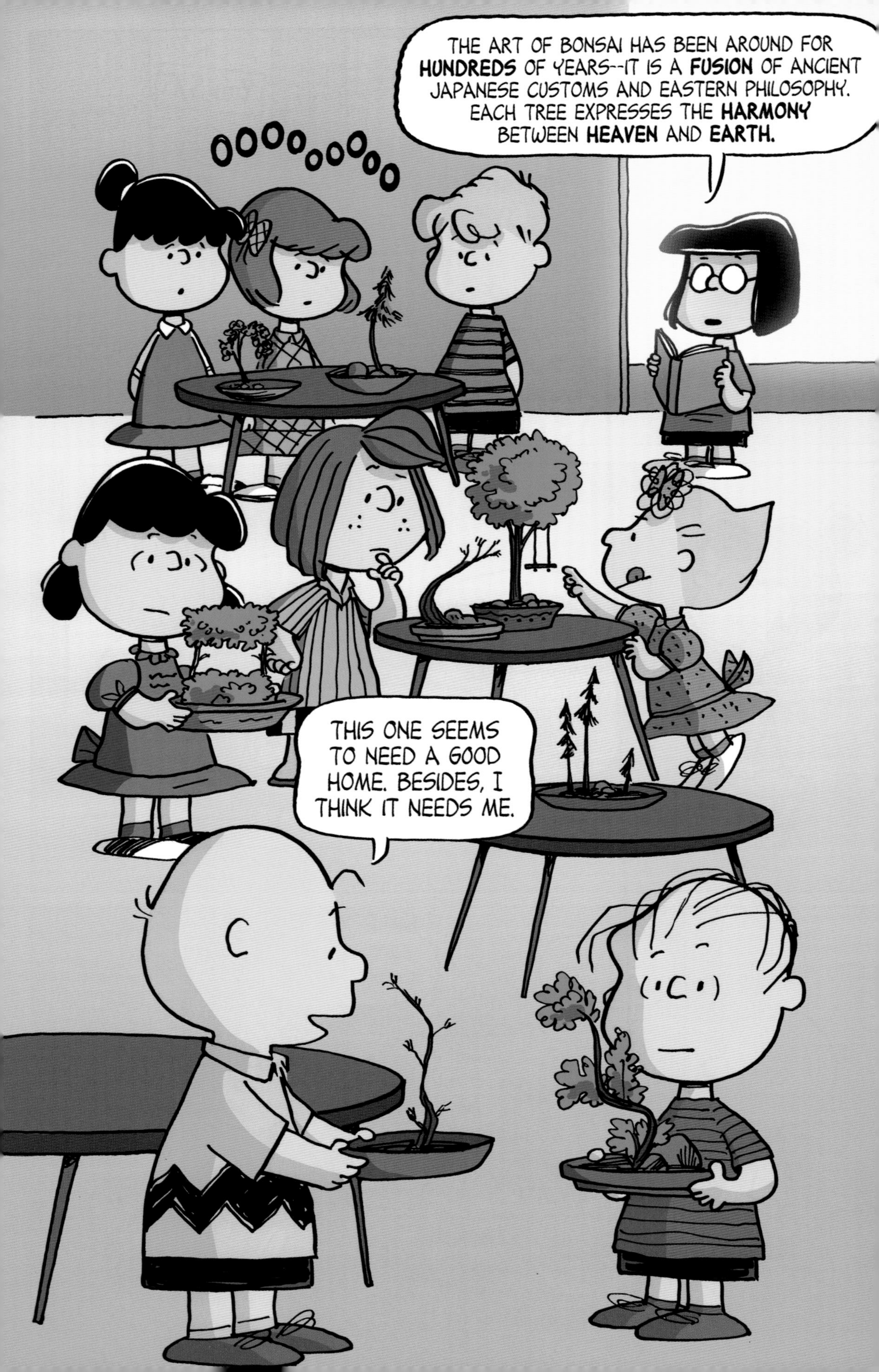
THE ART OF BONSAI HAS BEEN AROUND FOR **HUNDREDS** OF YEARS--IT IS A **FUSION** OF ANCIENT JAPANESE CUSTOMS AND EASTERN PHILOSOPHY. EACH TREE EXPRESSES THE **HARMONY** BETWEEN **HEAVEN** AND **EARTH.**
OOOOooOOOO
THIS ONE SEEMS TO NEED A GOOD HOME. BESIDES, I THINK IT NEEDS ME.

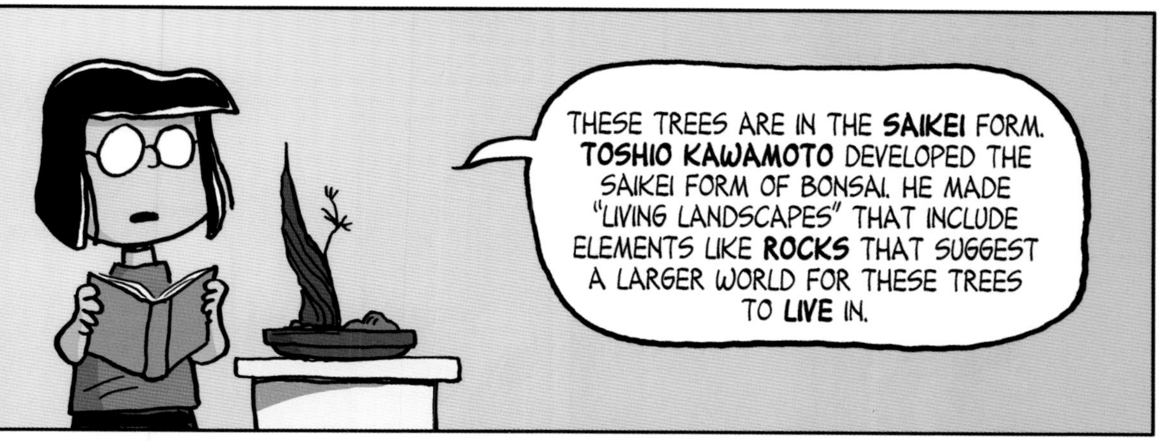
THESE TREES ARE IN THE **SAIKEI** FORM. **TOSHIO KAWAMOTO** DEVELOPED THE SAIKEI FORM OF BONSAI. HE MADE "LIVING LANDSCAPES" THAT INCLUDE ELEMENTS LIKE **ROCKS** THAT SUGGEST A LARGER WORLD FOR THESE TREES TO **LIVE** IN.

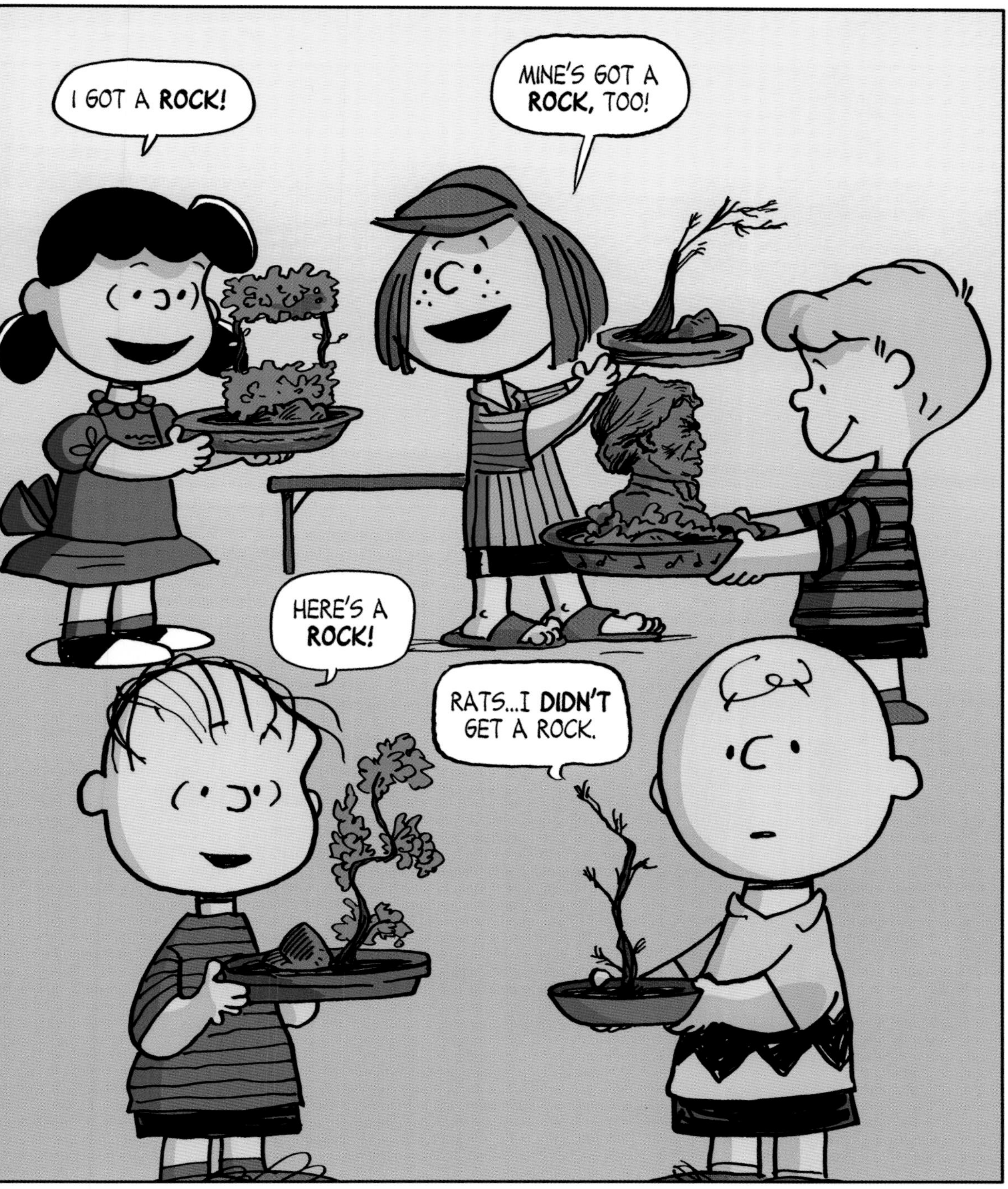
I GOT A **ROCK!**
MINE'S GOT A **ROCK,** TOO!
HERE'S A **ROCK!**
RATS...I **DIDN'T** GET A ROCK.

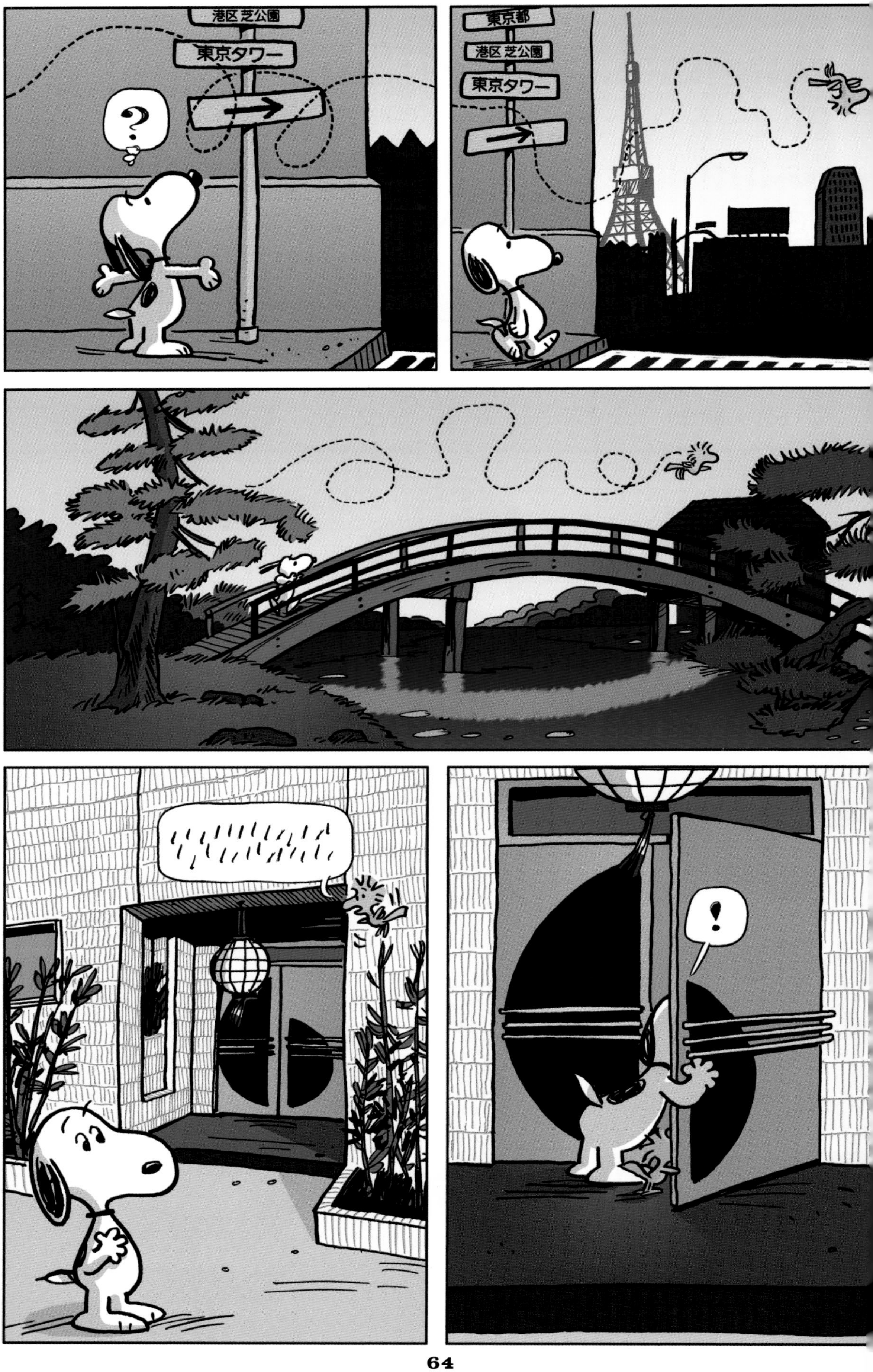
港区 芝公園
東京タワー
?
東京都
港区 芝公園
東京タワー
!

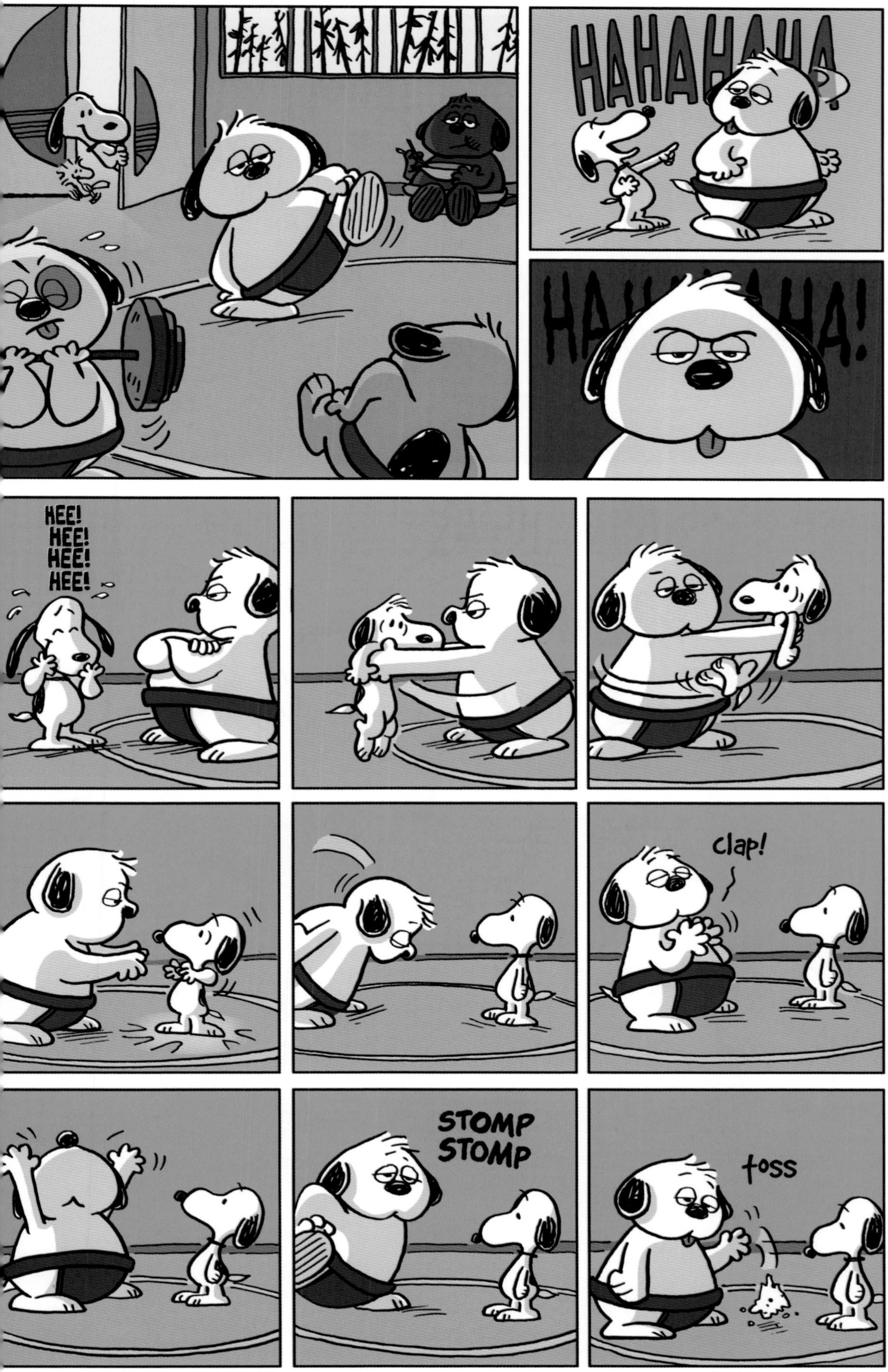
HAHAHAHAHA
HAHAHAHA!
HEE!
HEE!
HEE!
HEE!
clap!
STOMP
STOMP
toss

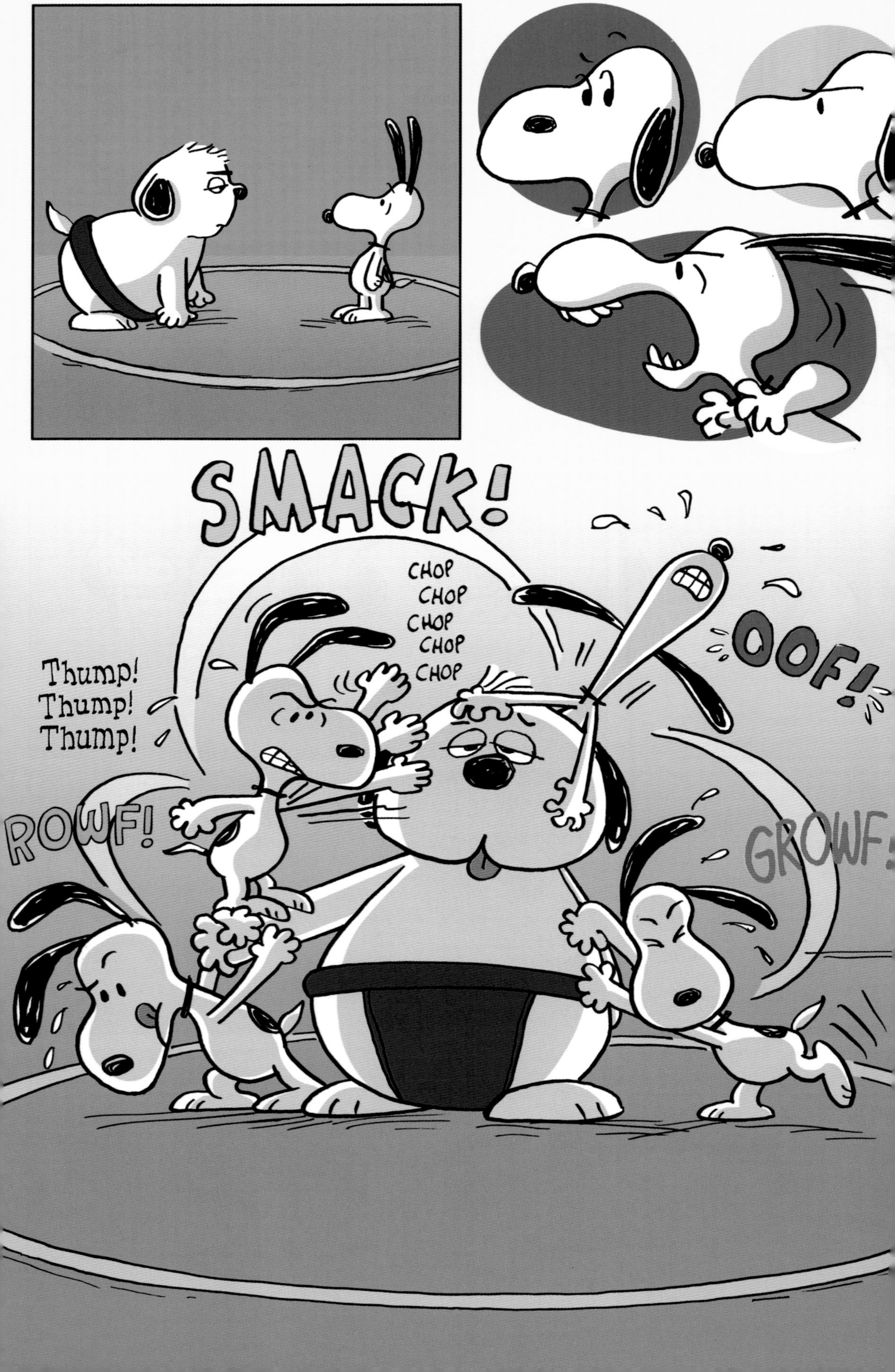
SMACK!
CHOP
CHOP
CHOP
CHOP
CHOP
Thump!
Thump!
Thump!
OOF!
ROWF!
GROWF!

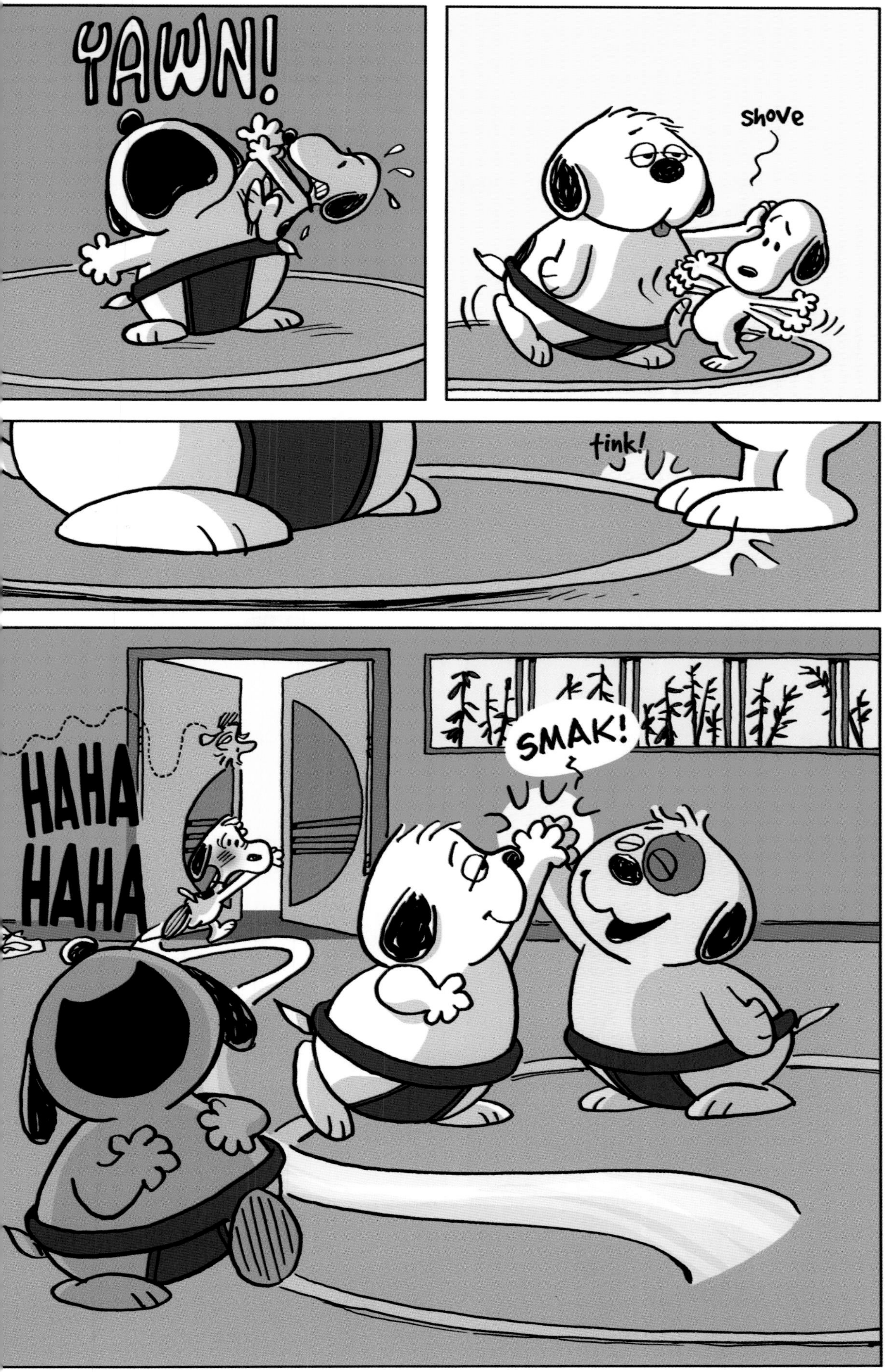
YAWN!
shove
tink!
HAHA
HAHA
SMAK!

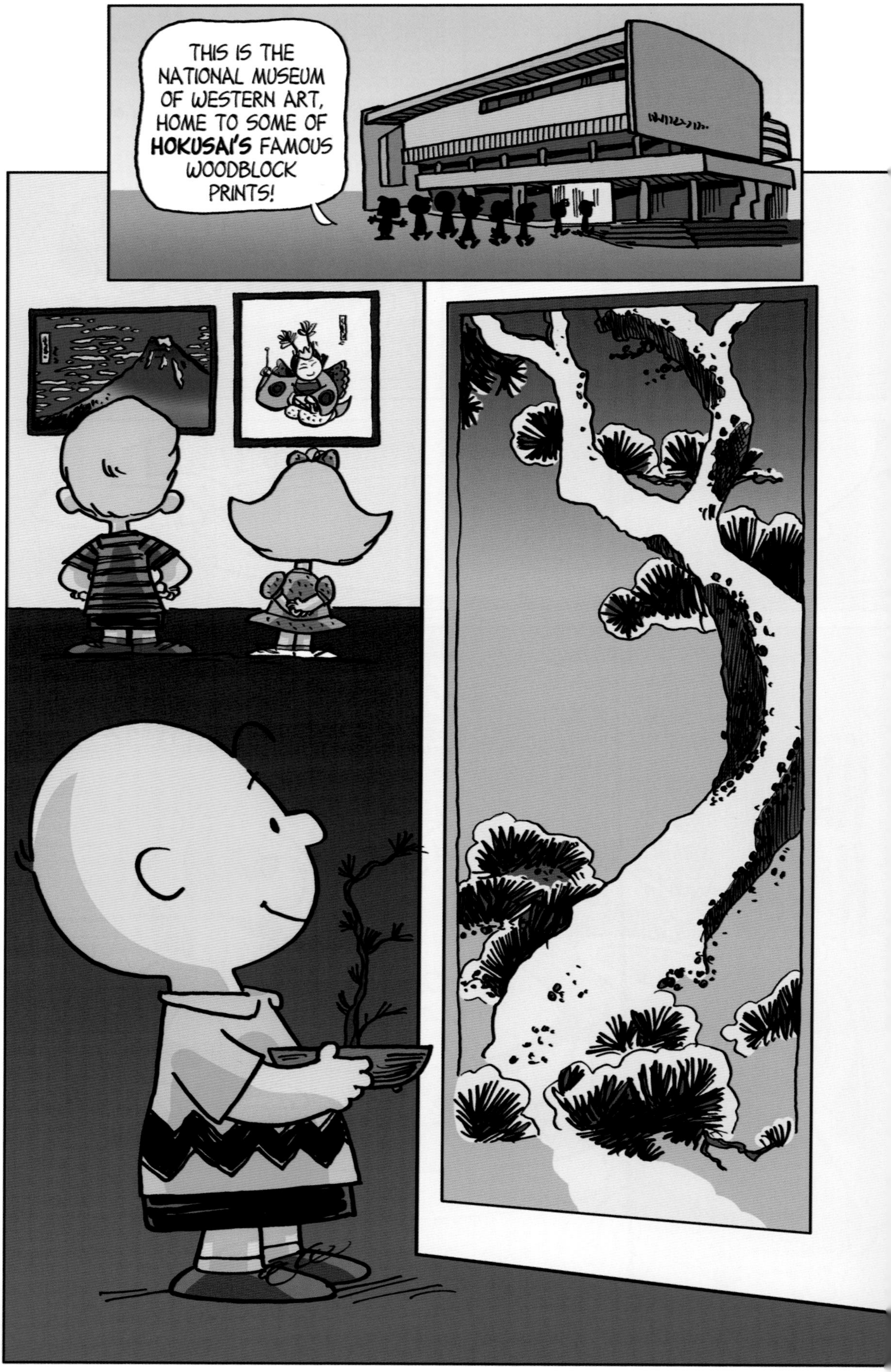
THIS IS THE NATIONAL MUSEUM OF WESTERN ART, HOME TO SOME OF **HOKUSAI'S** FAMOUS WOODBLOCK PRINTS!

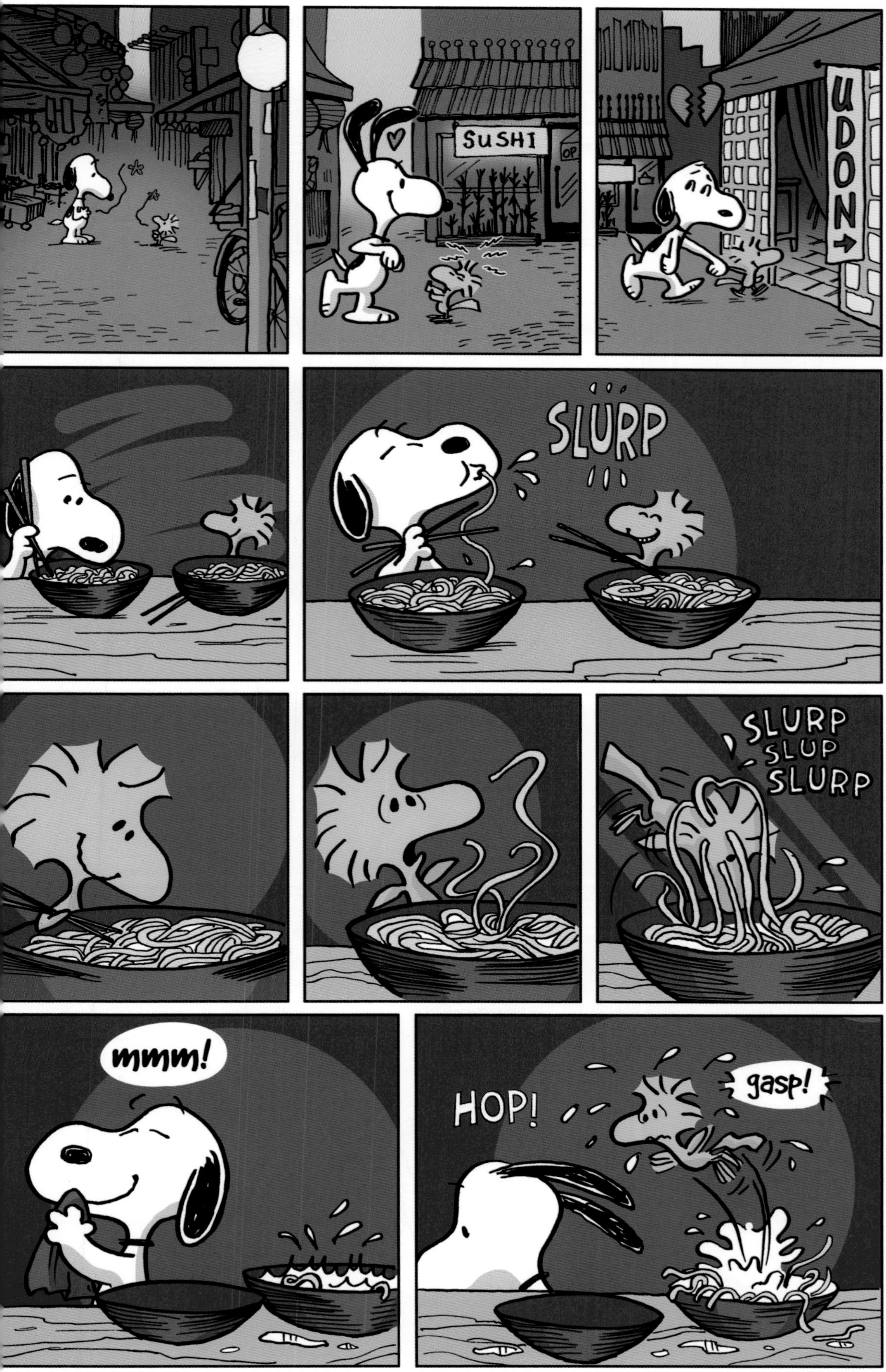
SUSHI
UDON
SLURP
SLURP
SLUP
SLURP
mmm!
HOP!
gasp!

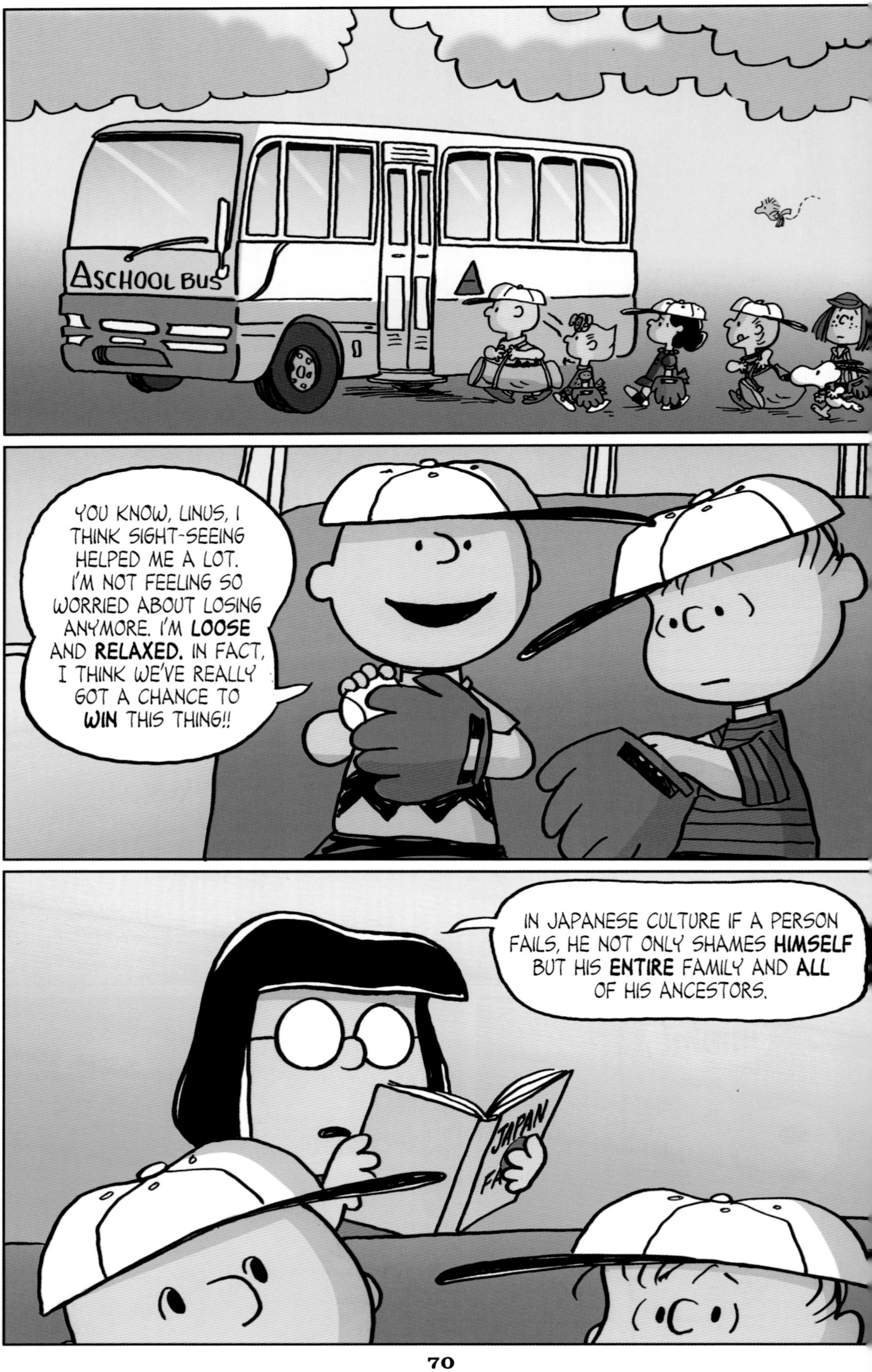
ASCHOOL BUS
YOU KNOW, LINUS, I THINK SIGHT-SEEING HELPED ME A LOT. I'M NOT FEELING SO WORRIED ABOUT LOSING ANYMORE. I'M **LOOSE** AND **RELAXED.** IN FACT, I THINK WE'VE REALLY GOT A CHANCE TO **WIN** THIS THING!!
IN JAPANESE CULTURE IF A PERSON FAILS, HE NOT ONLY SHAMES **HIMSELF** BUT HIS **ENTIRE** FAMILY AND **ALL** OF HIS ANCESTORS.
JAPAN

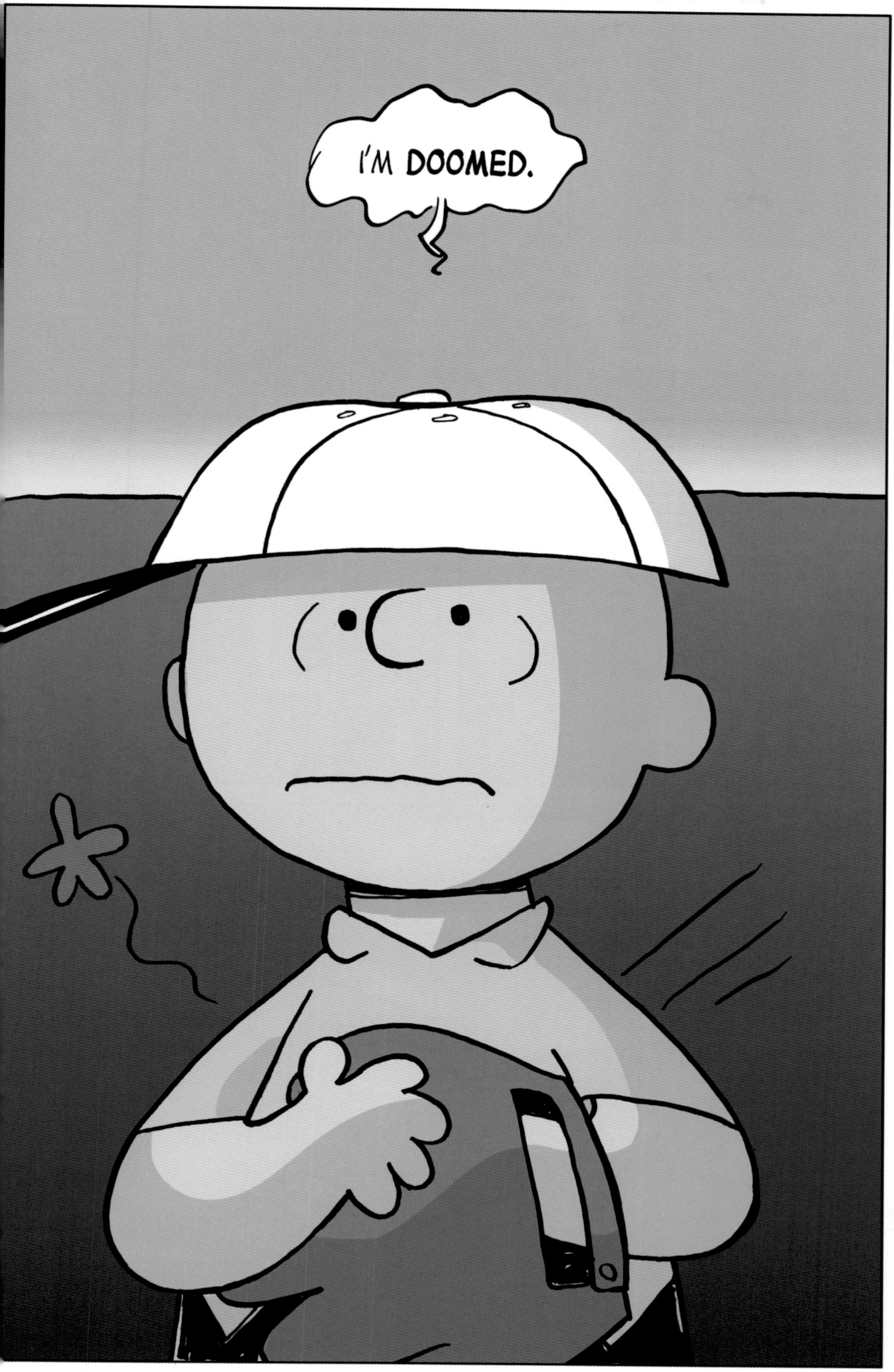
I'M DOOMED.

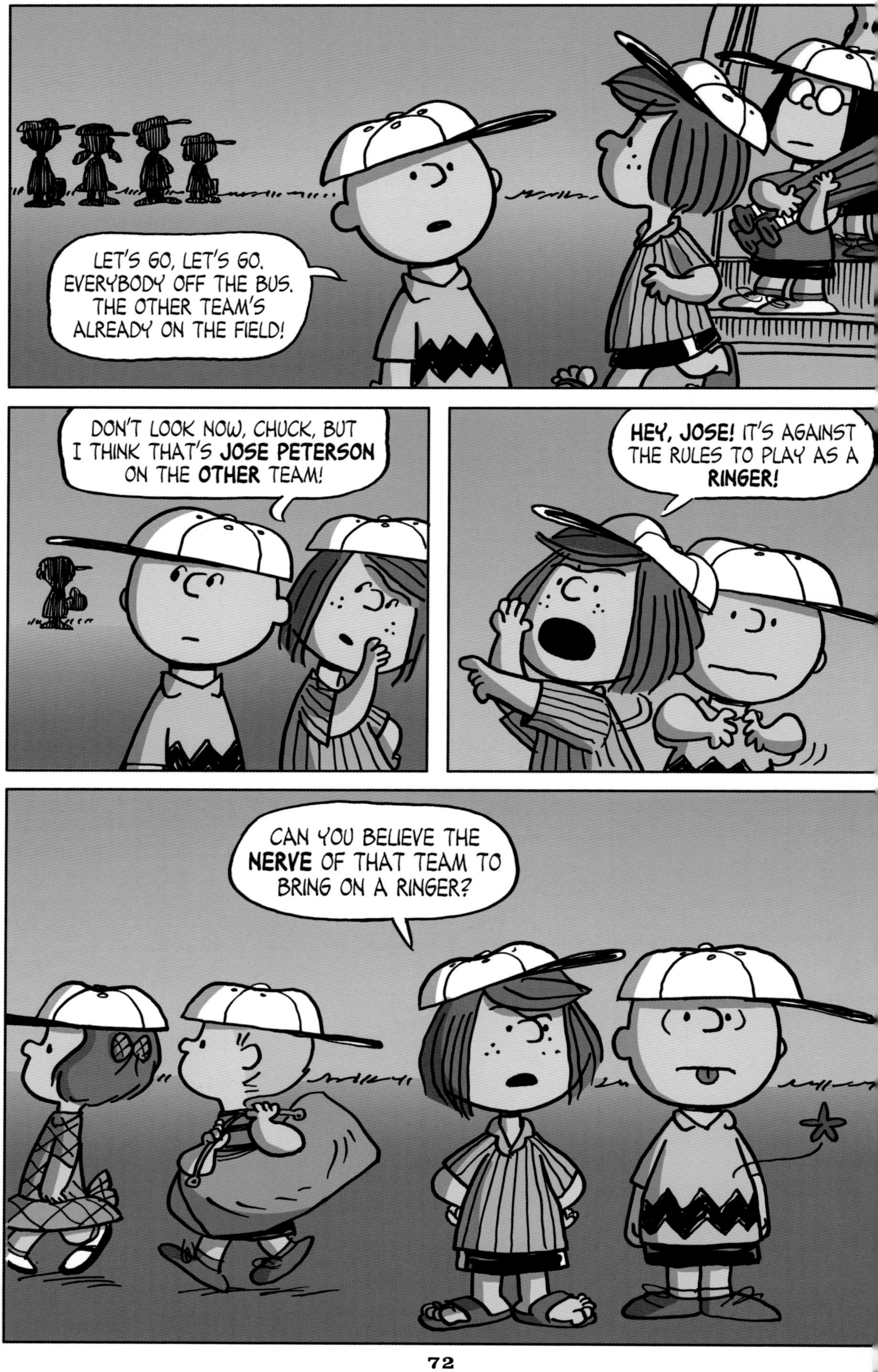
LET'S GO, LET'S GO. EVERYBODY OFF THE BUS. THE OTHER TEAM'S ALREADY ON THE FIELD!
DON'T LOOK NOW, CHUCK, BUT I THINK THAT'S **JOSE PETERSON** ON THE **OTHER** TEAM!
HEY, JOSE! IT'S AGAINST THE RULES TO PLAY AS A **RINGER!**
CAN YOU BELIEVE THE **NERVE** OF THAT TEAM TO BRING ON A RINGER?

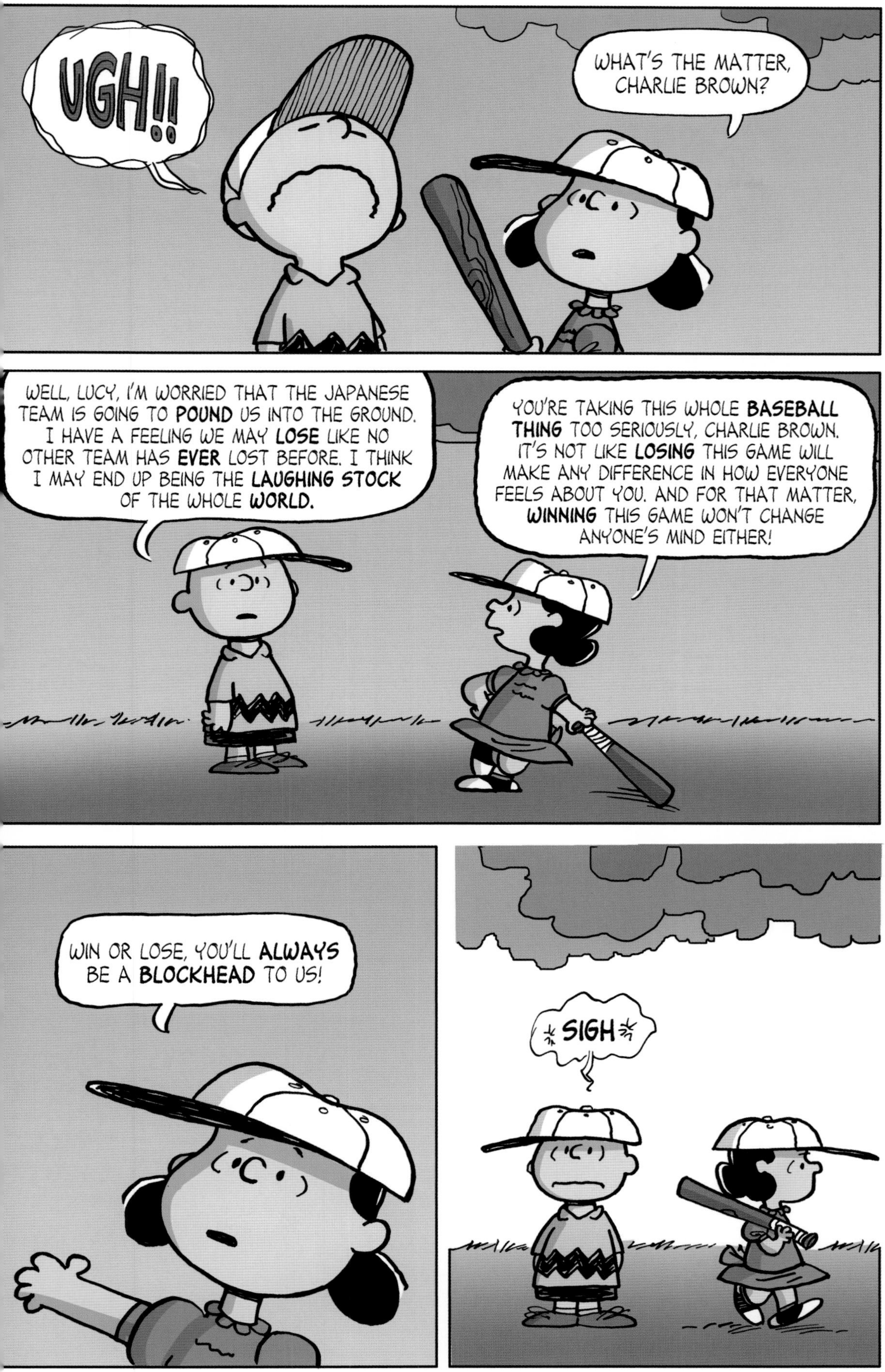
UGH!!
WHAT'S THE MATTER, CHARLIE BROWN?
WELL, LUCY, I'M WORRIED THAT THE JAPANESE TEAM IS GOING TO POUND US INTO THE GROUND. I HAVE A FEELING WE MAY LOSE LIKE NO OTHER TEAM HAS EVER LOST BEFORE. I THINK I MAY END UP BEING THE LAUGHING STOCK OF THE WHOLE WORLD.
YOU'RE TAKING THIS WHOLE BASEBALL THING TOO SERIOUSLY, CHARLIE BROWN. IT'S NOT LIKE LOSING THIS GAME WILL MAKE ANY DIFFERENCE IN HOW EVERYONE FEELS ABOUT YOU. AND FOR THAT MATTER, WINNING THIS GAME WON'T CHANGE ANYONE'S MIND EITHER!
WIN OR LOSE, YOU'LL ALWAYS BE A BLOCKHEAD TO US!
SIGH

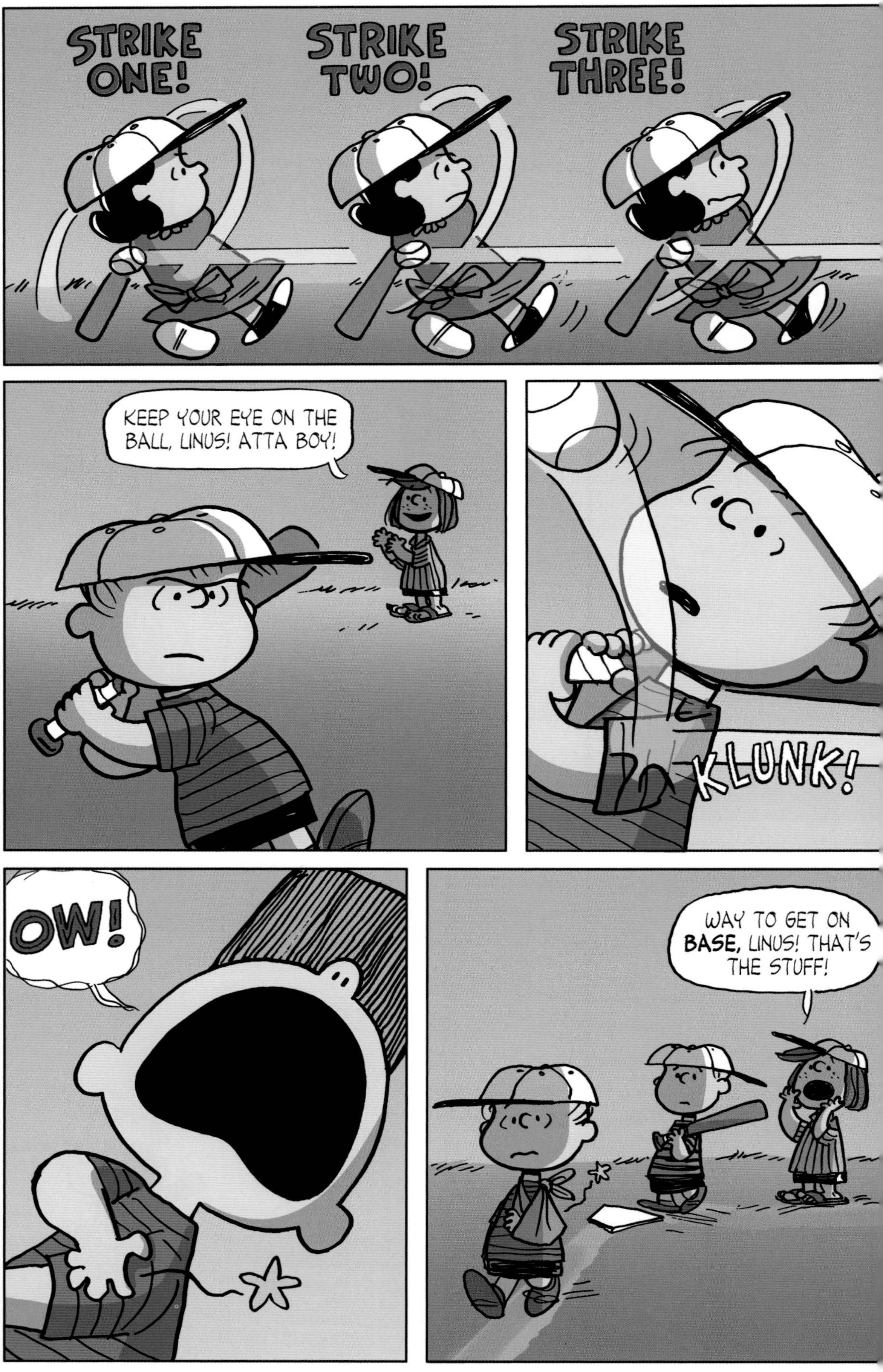
STRIKE ONE!
STRIKE TWO!
STRIKE THREE!
KEEP YOUR EYE ON THE BALL, LINUS! ATTA BOY!
KLUNK!
OW!
WAY TO GET ON BASE, LINUS! THAT'S THE STUFF!

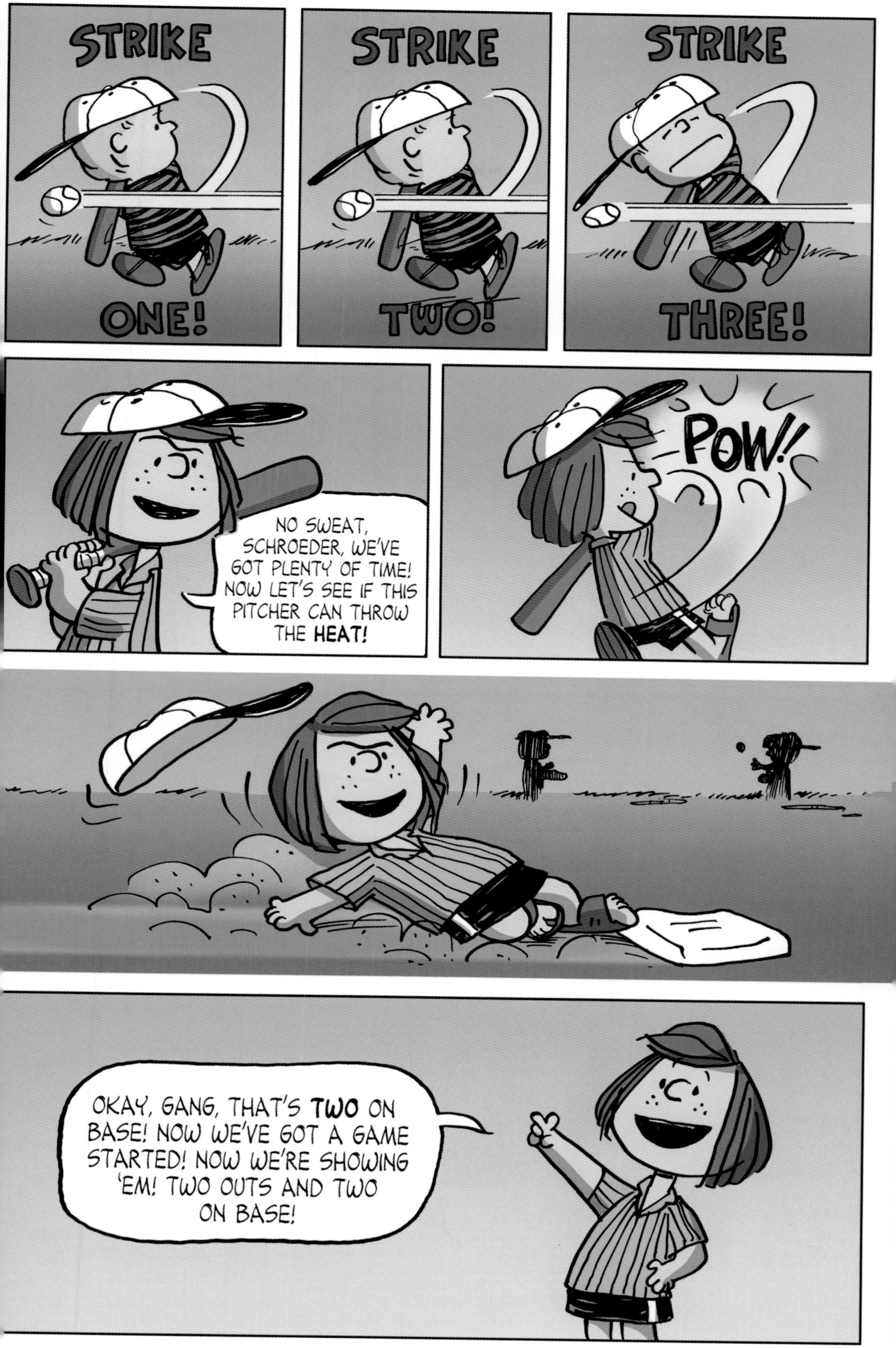

STRIKE
ONE!
STRIKE
TWO!
STRIKE
THREE!
NO SWEAT, SCHROEDER, WE'VE GOT PLENTY OF TIME! NOW LET'S SEE IF THIS PITCHER CAN THROW THE **HEAT!**
POW!
OKAY, GANG, THAT'S **TWO** ON BASE! NOW WE'VE GOT A GAME STARTED! NOW WE'RE SHOWING 'EM! TWO OUTS AND TWO ON BASE!

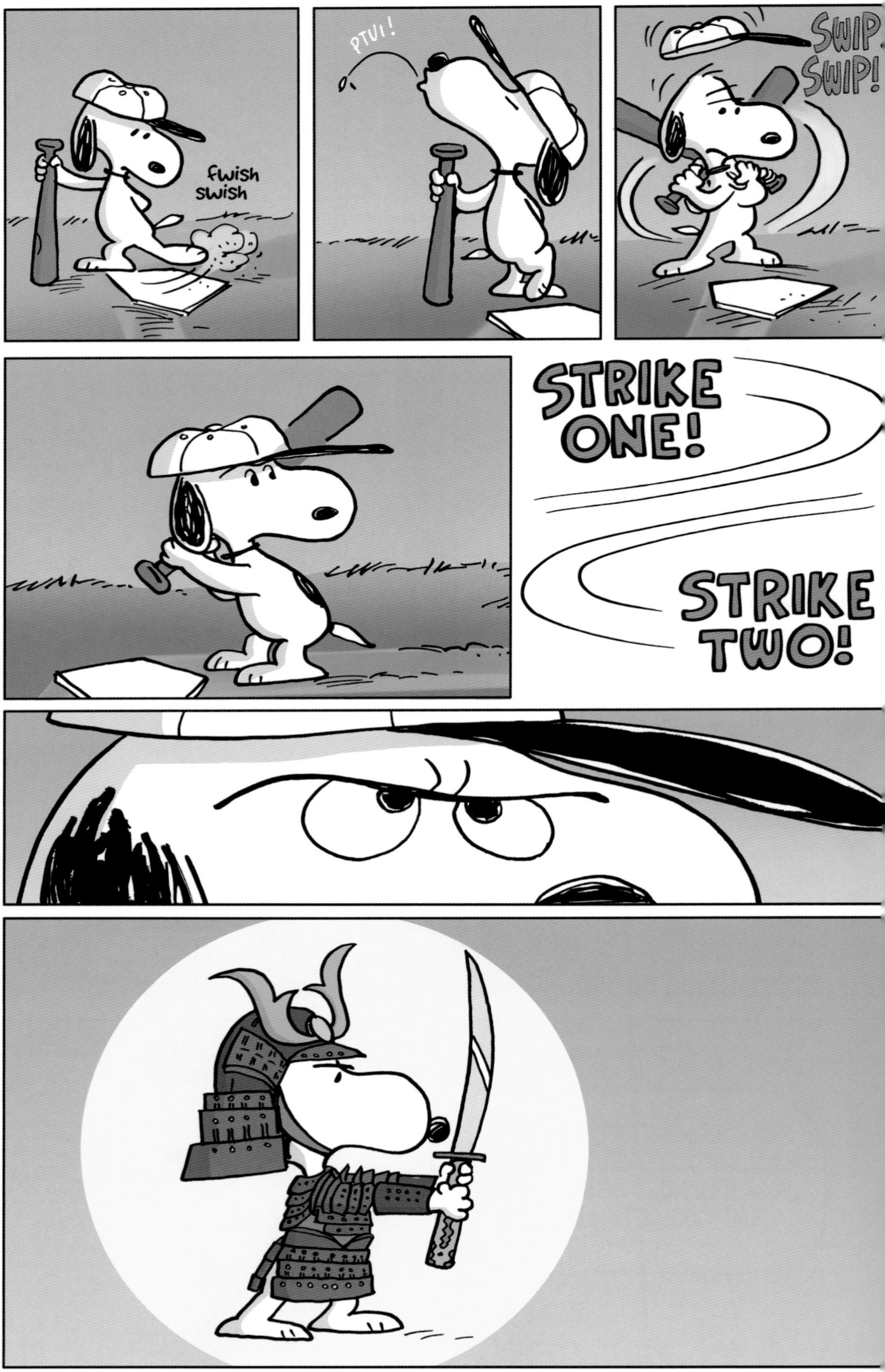
fwish
swish
PTUI!
SWIP!
SWIP!
STRIKE
ONE!
STRIKE
TWO!

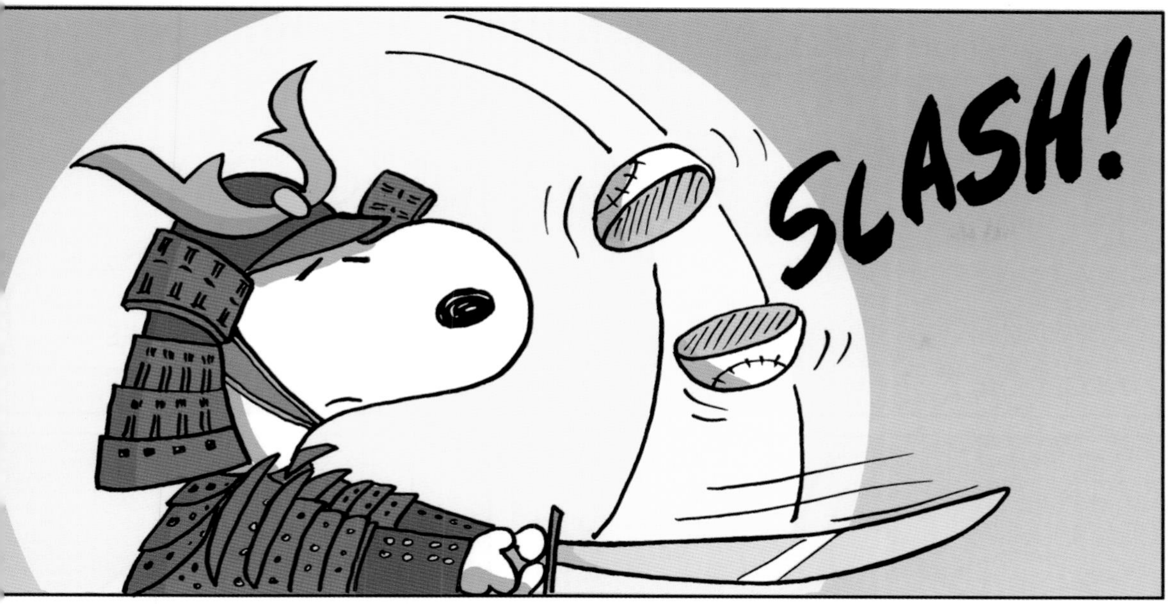
SLASH!

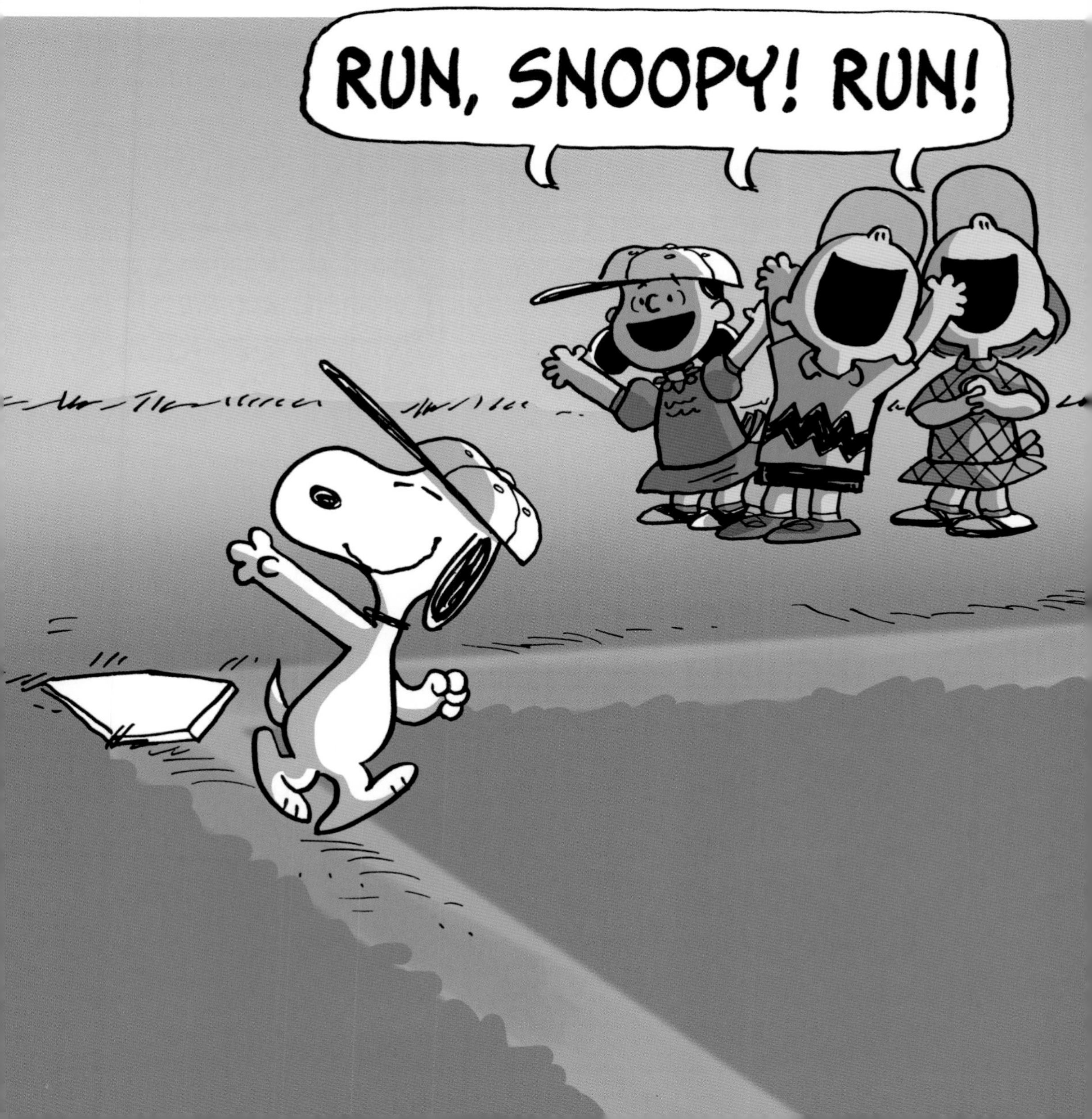
RUN, SNOOPY! RUN!

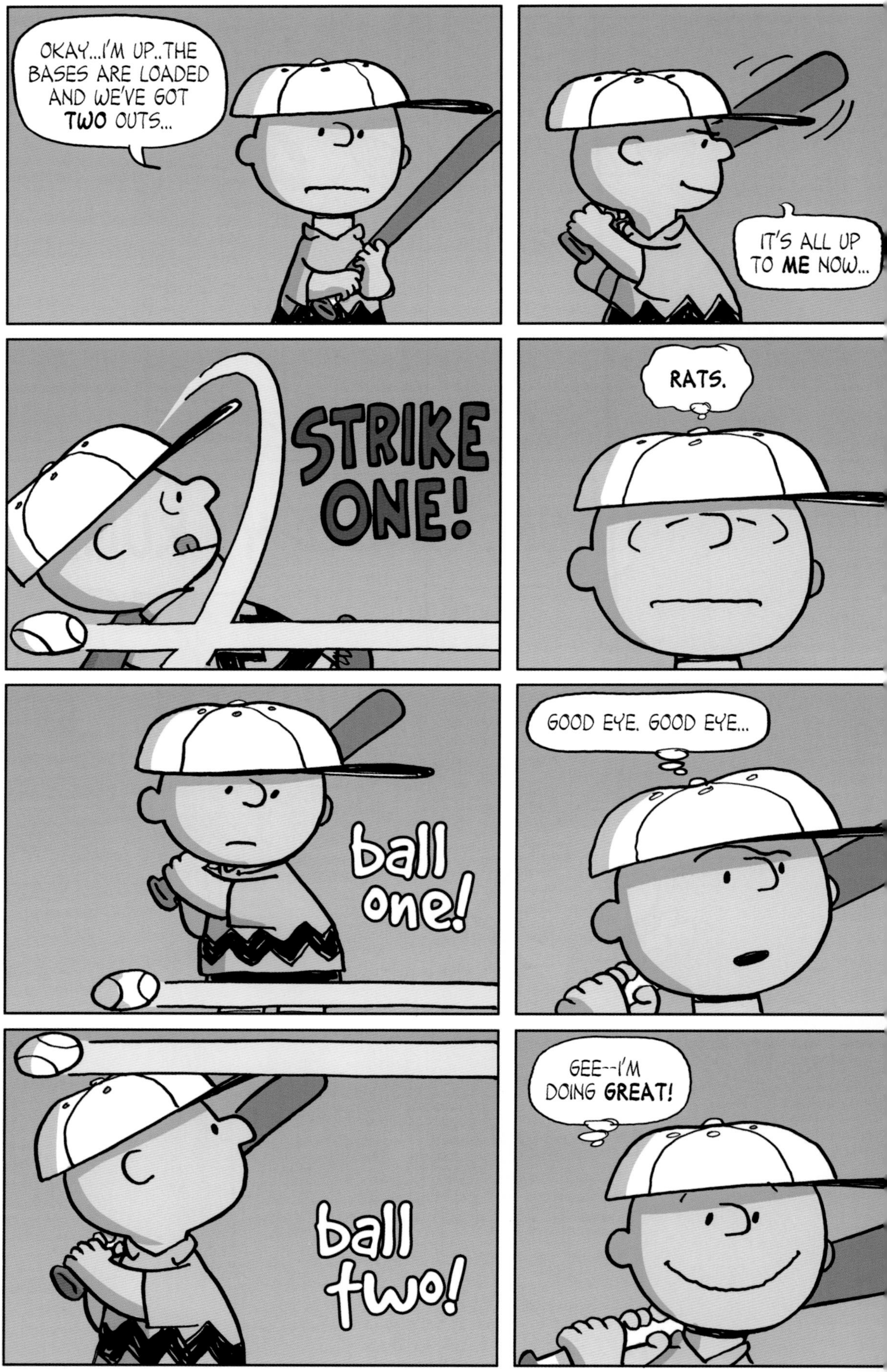
OKAY...I'M UP..THE BASES ARE LOADED AND WE'VE GOT TWO OUTS...
IT'S ALL UP TO ME NOW...
STRIKE ONE!
RATS.
ball one!
GOOD EYE. GOOD EYE...
ball two!
GEE--I'M DOING GREAT!

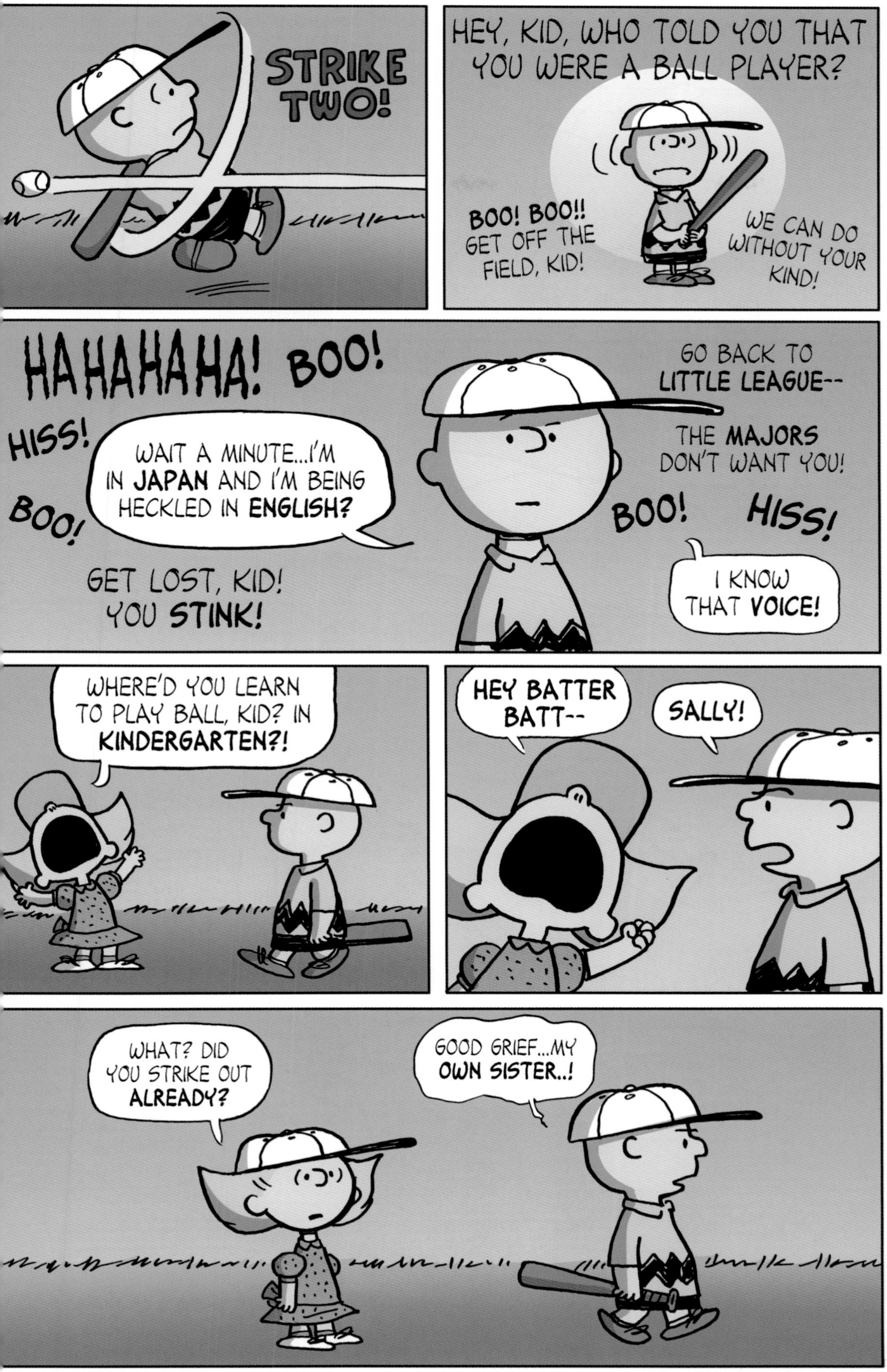
STRIKE TWO!
HEY, KID, WHO TOLD YOU THAT YOU WERE A BALL PLAYER?
BOO! BOO!! GET OFF THE FIELD, KID!
WE CAN DO WITHOUT YOUR KIND!
HAHAHAHA! BOO!
GO BACK TO LITTLE LEAGUE--
HISS!
WAIT A MINUTE...I'M IN JAPAN AND I'M BEING HECKLED IN ENGLISH?
THE MAJORS DON'T WANT YOU!
BOO!
BOO! HISS!
GET LOST, KID! YOU STINK!
I KNOW THAT VOICE!
WHERE'D YOU LEARN TO PLAY BALL, KID? IN KINDERGARTEN?!
HEY BATTER BATT--
SALLY!
WHAT? DID YOU STRIKE OUT ALREADY?
GOOD GRIEF...MY OWN SISTER..!

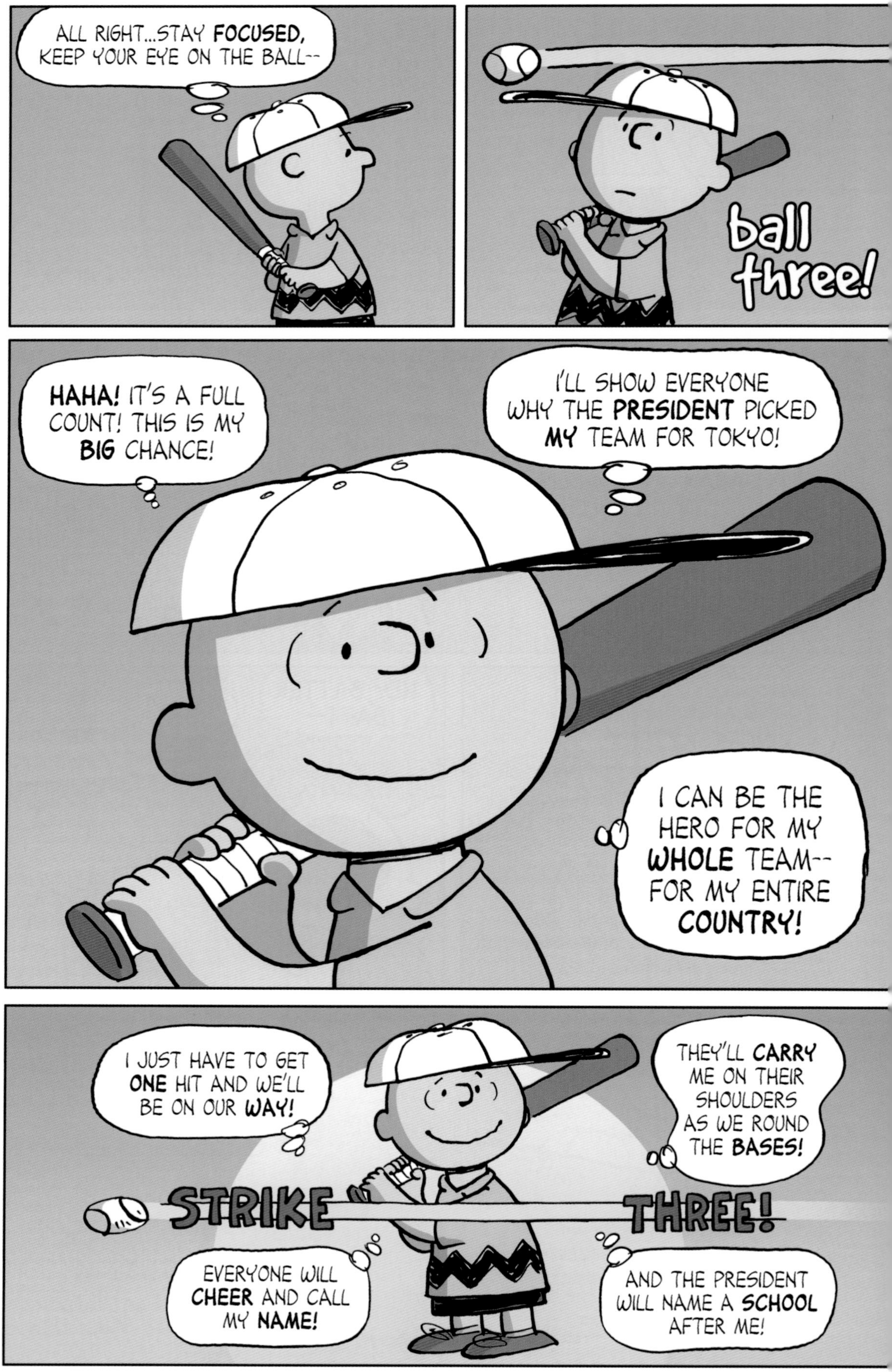
ALL RIGHT...STAY FOCUSED, KEEP YOUR EYE ON THE BALL--
ball three!
HAHA! IT'S A FULL COUNT! THIS IS MY BIG CHANCE!
I'LL SHOW EVERYONE WHY THE PRESIDENT PICKED MY TEAM FOR TOKYO!
I CAN BE THE HERO FOR MY WHOLE TEAM-- FOR MY ENTIRE COUNTRY!
I JUST HAVE TO GET ONE HIT AND WE'LL BE ON OUR WAY!
THEY'LL CARRY ME ON THEIR SHOULDERS AS WE ROUND THE BASES!
STRIKE THREE!
EVERYONE WILL CHEER AND CALL MY NAME!
AND THE PRESIDENT WILL NAME A SCHOOL AFTER ME!

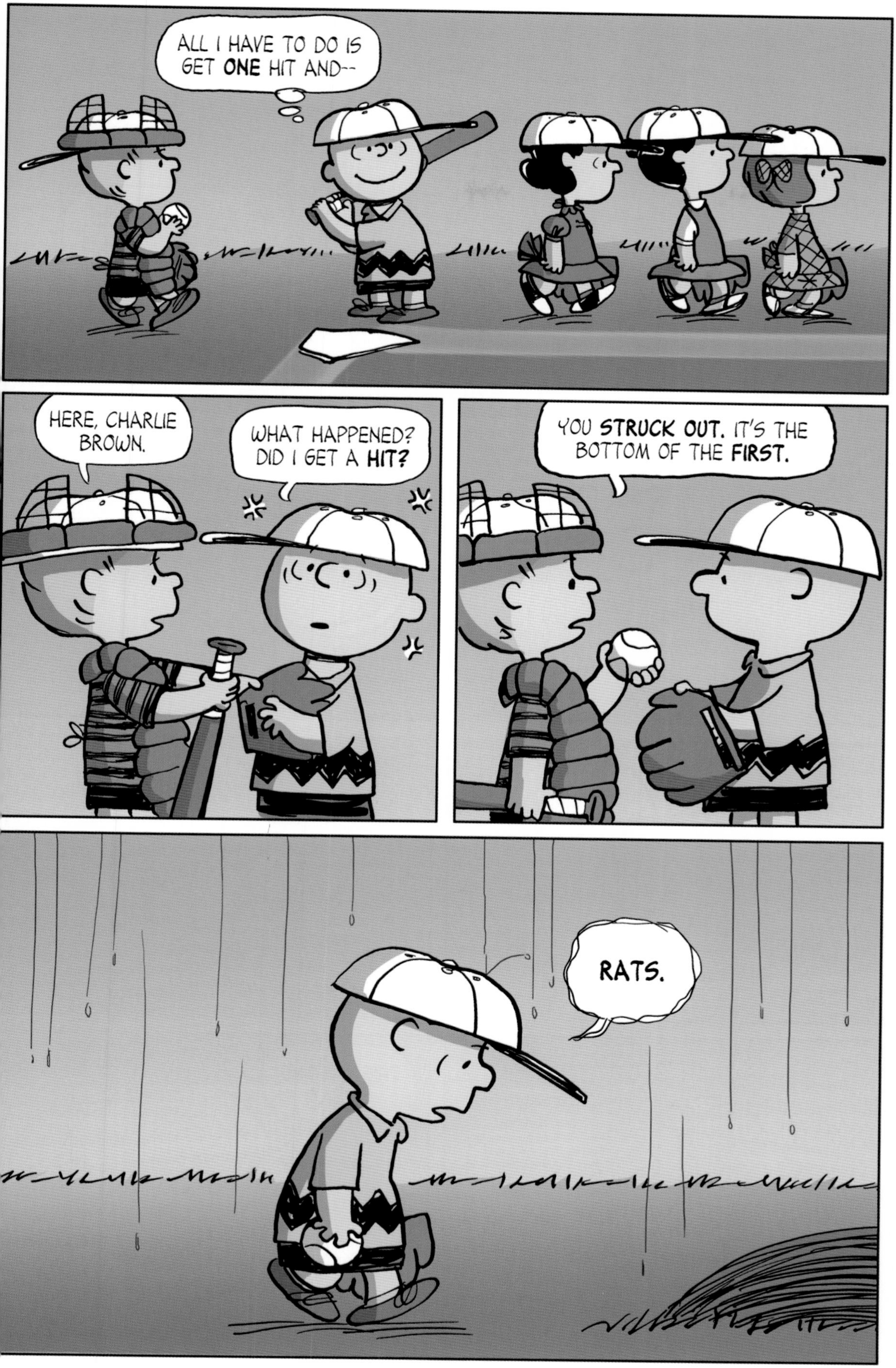
ALL I HAVE TO DO IS GET ONE HIT AND--
HERE, CHARLIE BROWN.
WHAT HAPPENED? DID I GET A HIT?
YOU STRUCK OUT. IT'S THE BOTTOM OF THE FIRST.
RATS.

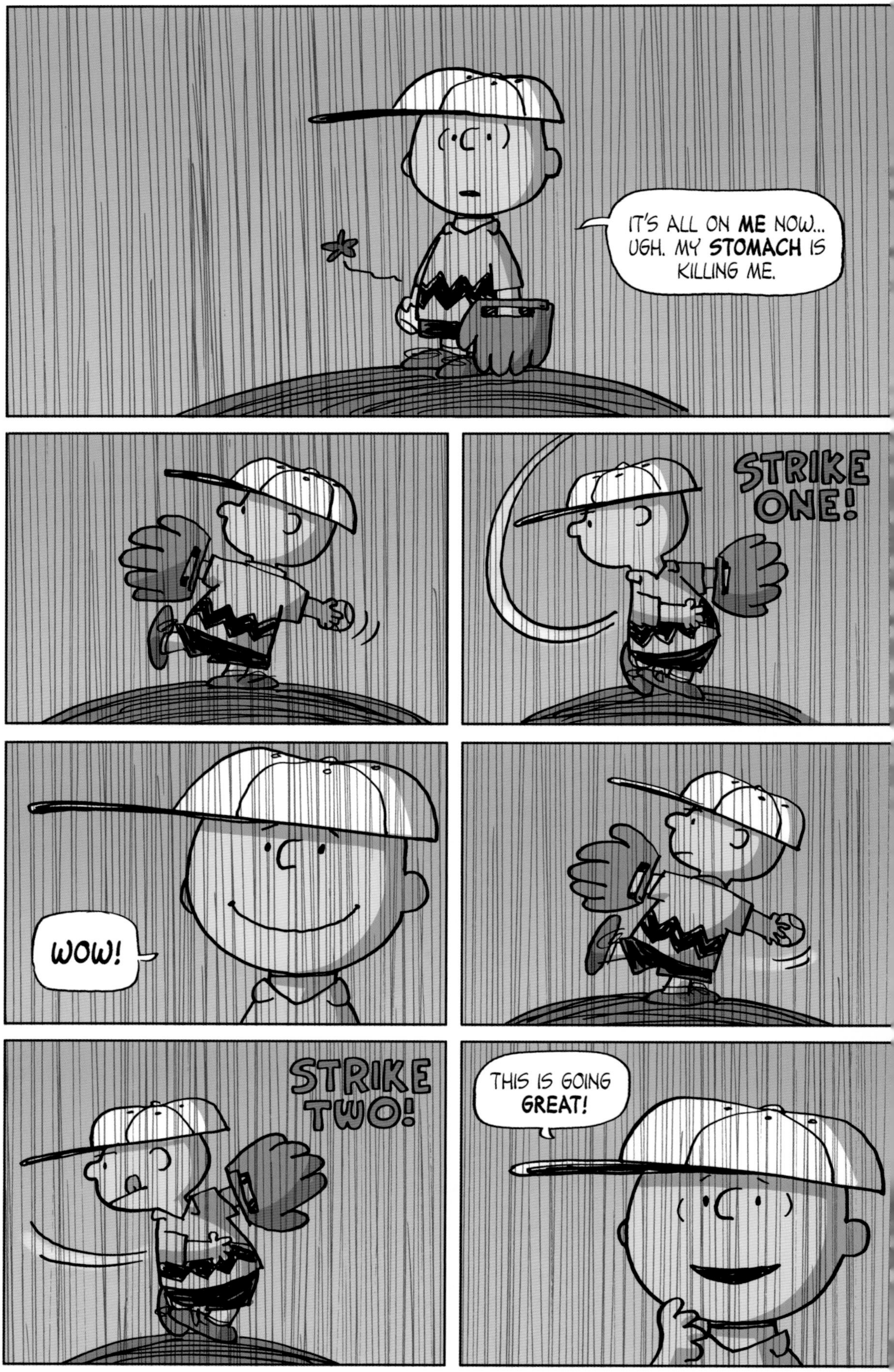
IT'S ALL ON ME NOW... UGH. MY STOMACH IS KILLING ME.
STRIKE ONE!
WOW!
STRIKE TWO!
THIS IS GOING GREAT!

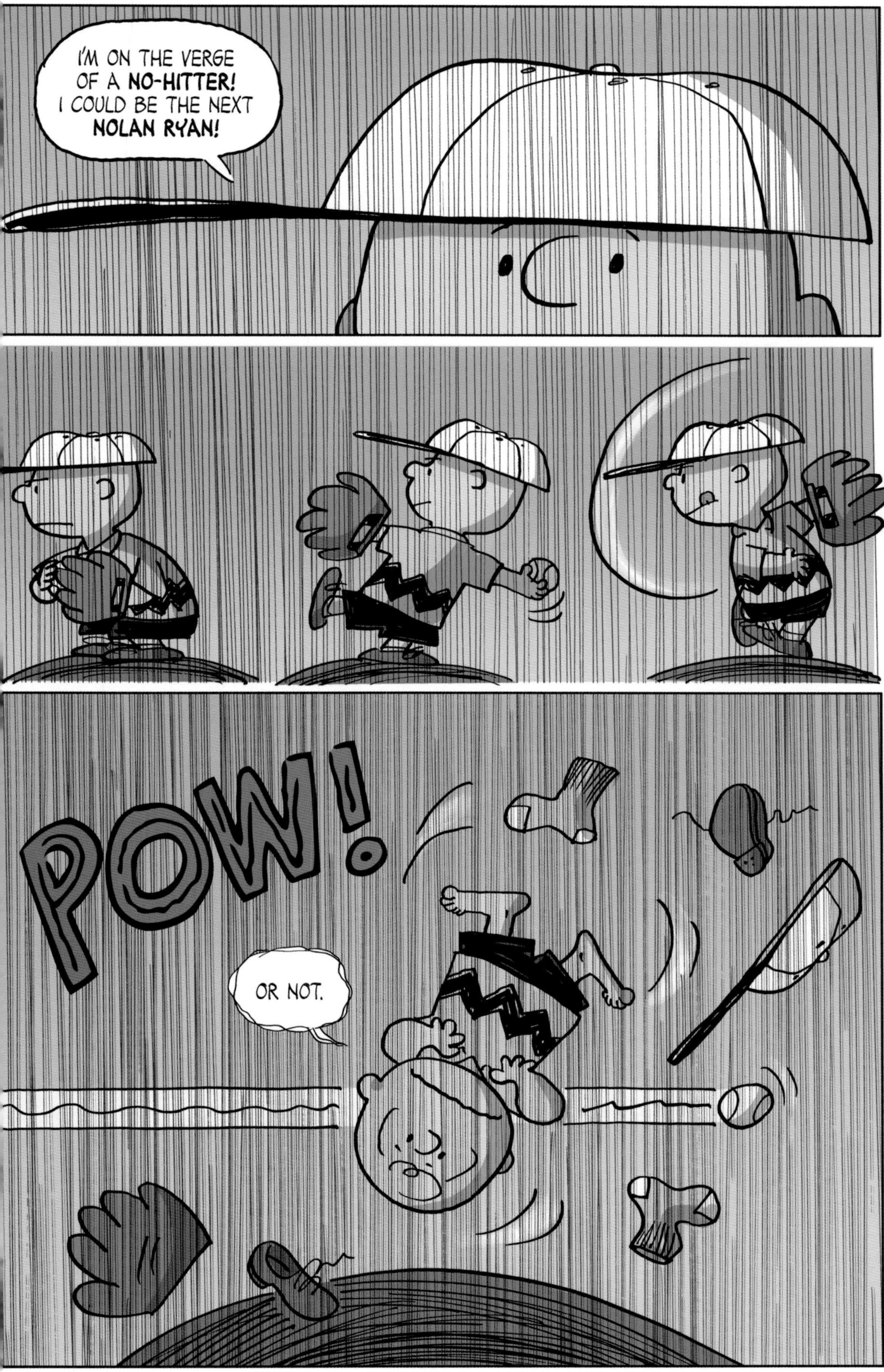
I'M ON THE VERGE OF A **NO-HITTER!** I COULD BE THE NEXT **NOLAN RYAN!**
POW!
OR NOT.

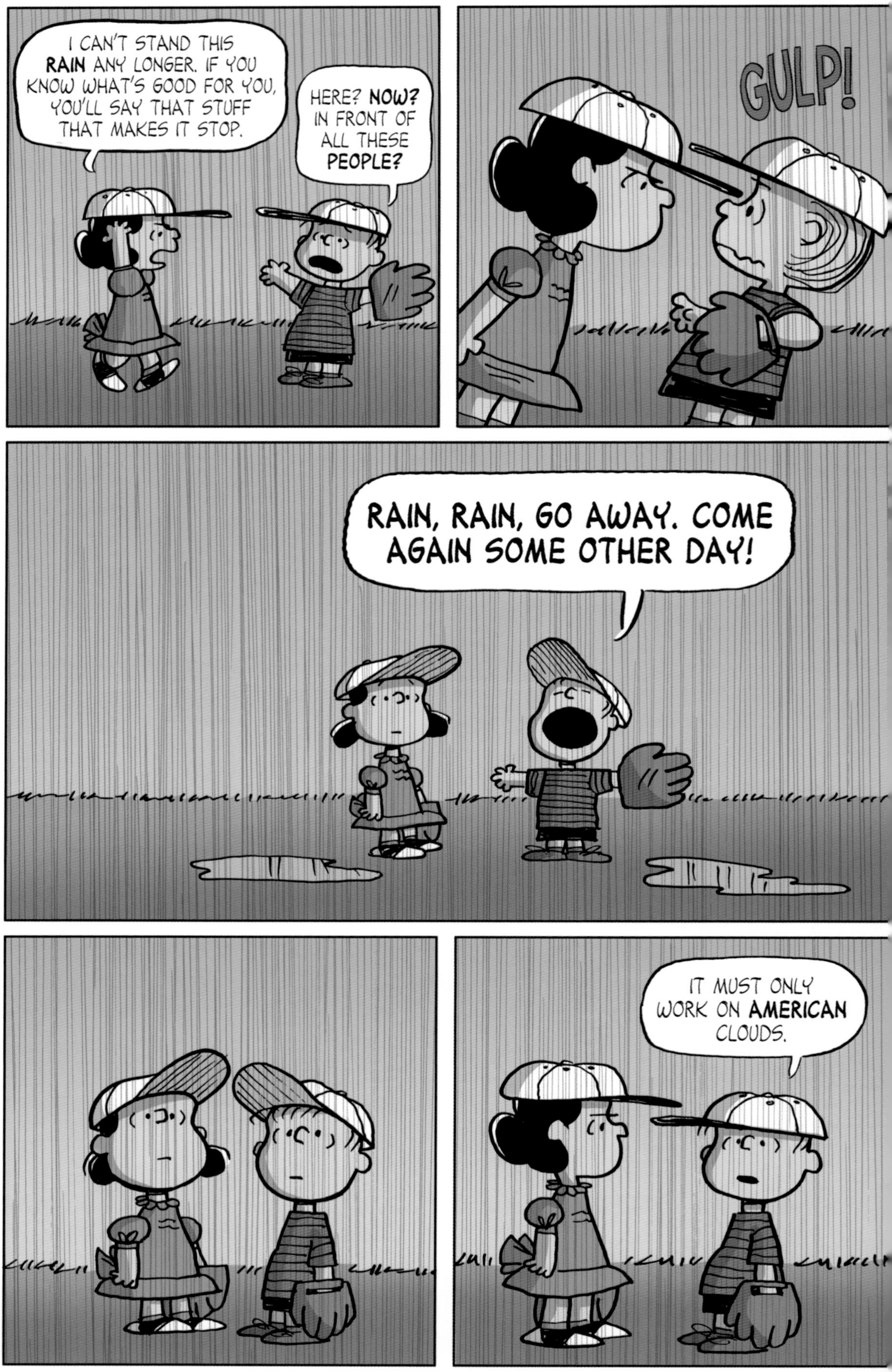
I CAN'T STAND THIS **RAIN** ANY LONGER. IF YOU KNOW WHAT'S GOOD FOR YOU, YOU'LL SAY THAT STUFF THAT MAKES IT STOP.
HERE? **NOW?** IN FRONT OF ALL THESE **PEOPLE?**
GULP!
RAIN, RAIN, GO AWAY. COME AGAIN SOME OTHER DAY!
IT MUST ONLY WORK ON **AMERICAN** CLOUDS.

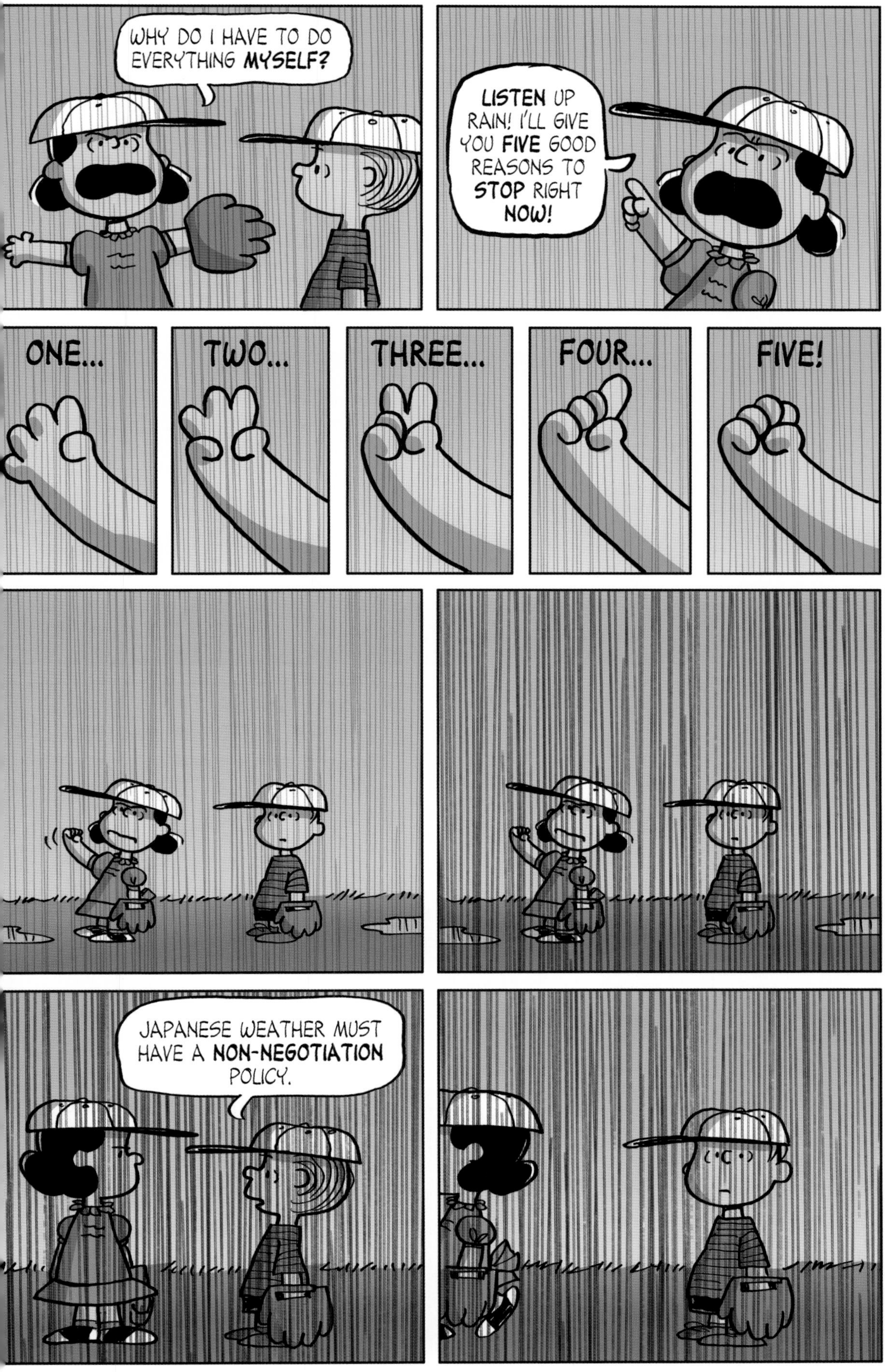
WHY DO I HAVE TO DO EVERYTHING **MYSELF?**
LISTEN UP RAIN! I'LL GIVE YOU **FIVE** GOOD REASONS TO **STOP** RIGHT **NOW!**
ONE...
TWO...
THREE...
FOUR...
FIVE!
JAPANESE WEATHER MUST HAVE A **NON-NEGOTIATION** POLICY.

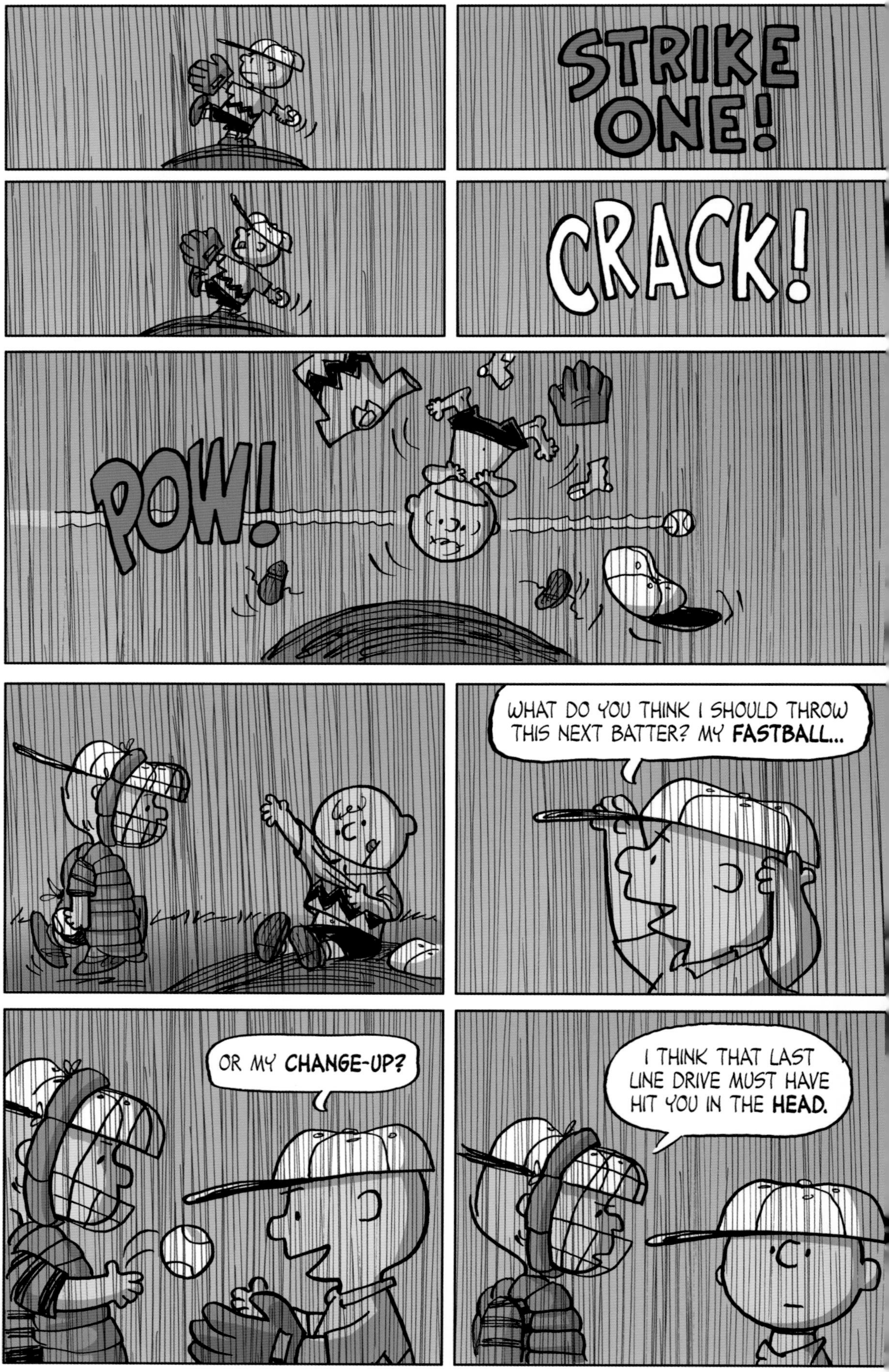
STRIKE ONE!
CRACK!
POW!
WHAT DO YOU THINK I SHOULD THROW THIS NEXT BATTER? MY **FASTBALL...**
OR MY **CHANGE-UP?**
I THINK THAT LAST LINE DRIVE MUST HAVE HIT YOU IN THE **HEAD.**

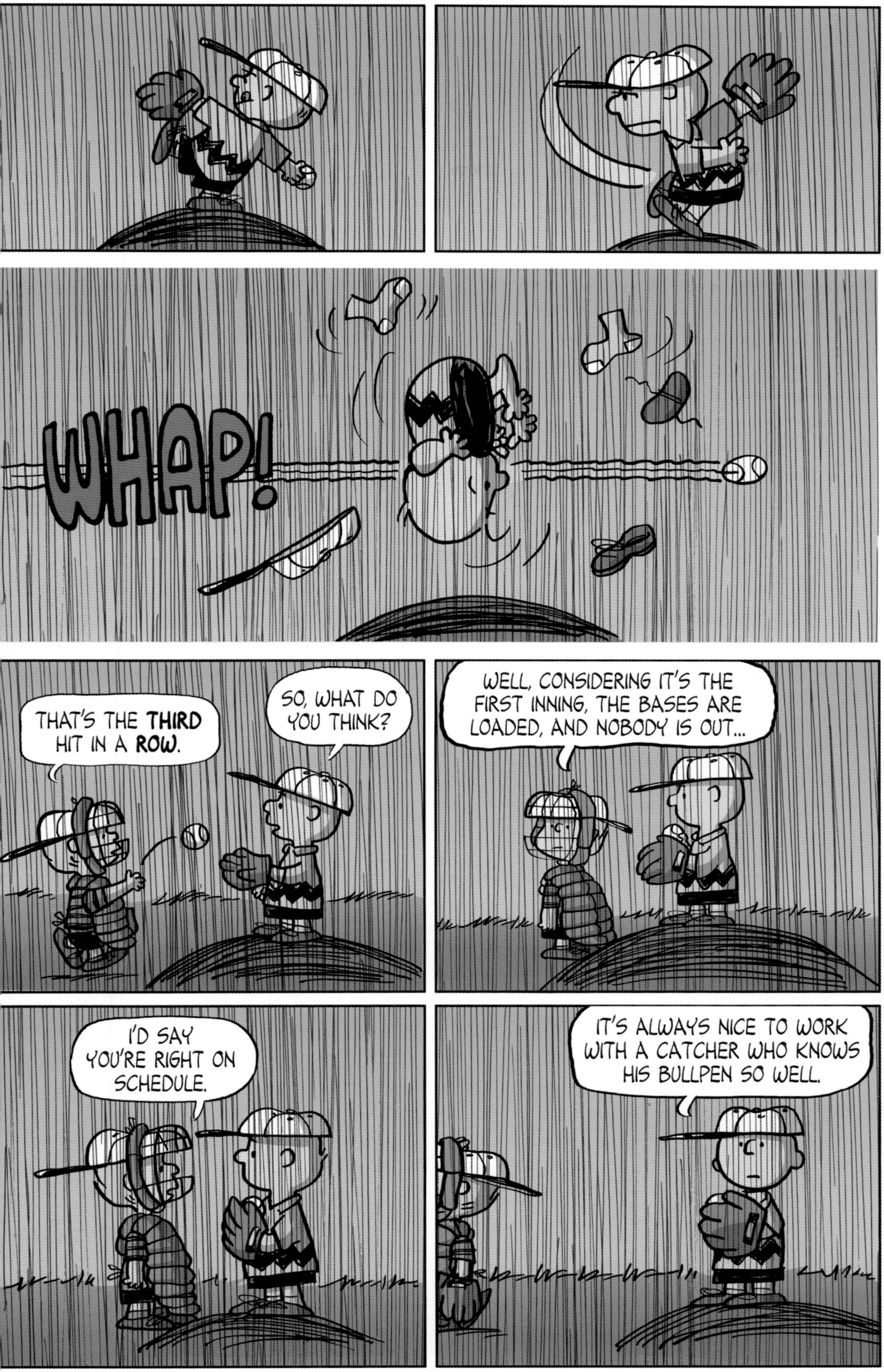
WHAP!
THAT'S THE **THIRD** HIT IN A **ROW**.
SO, WHAT DO YOU THINK?
WELL, CONSIDERING IT'S THE FIRST INNING, THE BASES ARE LOADED, AND NOBODY IS OUT...
I'D SAY YOU'RE RIGHT ON SCHEDULE.
IT'S ALWAYS NICE TO WORK WITH A CATCHER WHO KNOWS HIS BULLPEN SO WELL.

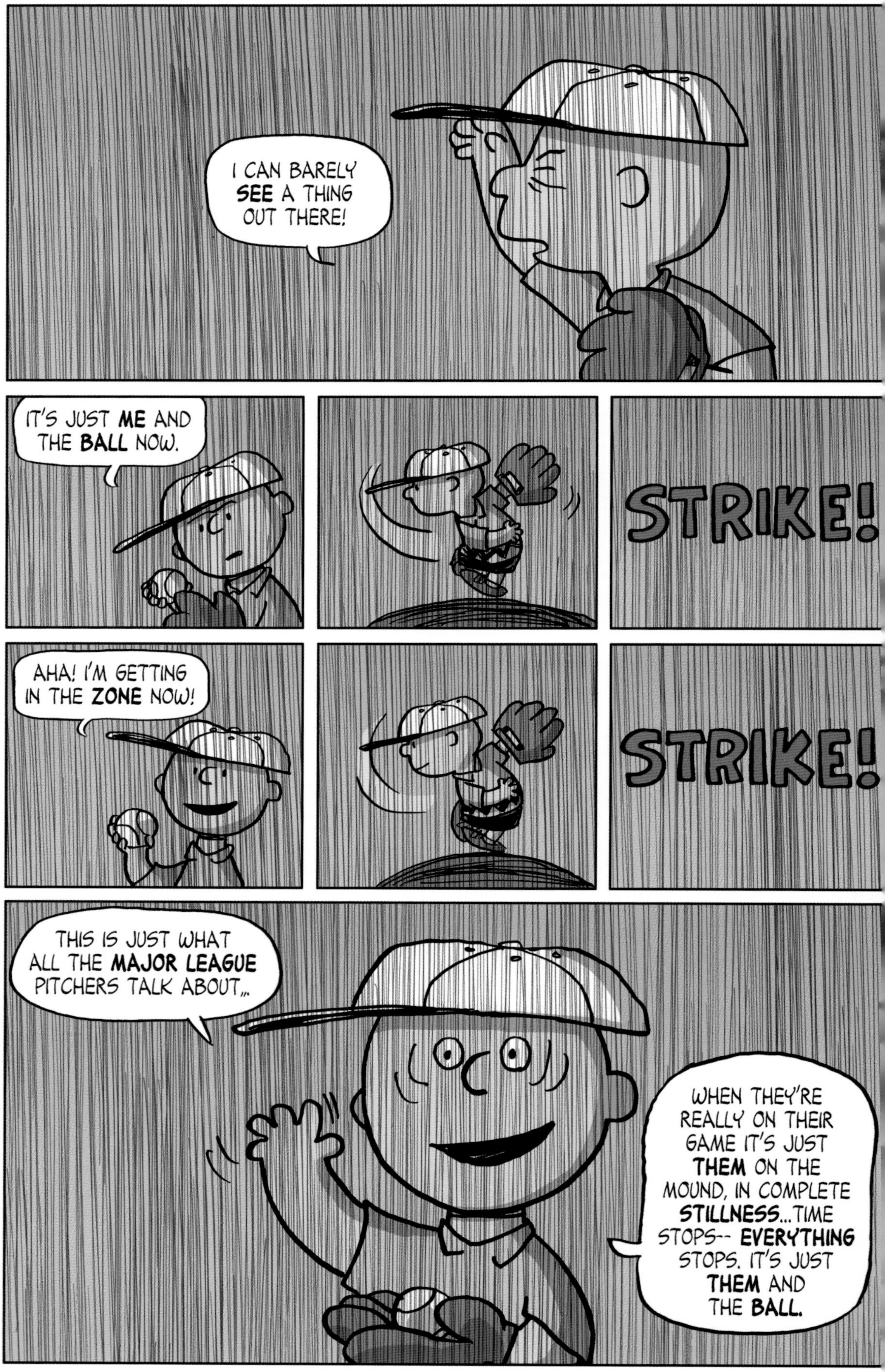
I CAN BARELY SEE A THING OUT THERE!
IT'S JUST ME AND THE BALL NOW.
STRIKE!
AHA! I'M GETTING IN THE ZONE NOW!
STRIKE!
THIS IS JUST WHAT ALL THE MAJOR LEAGUE PITCHERS TALK ABOUT...
WHEN THEY'RE REALLY ON THEIR GAME IT'S JUST THEM ON THE MOUND, IN COMPLETE STILLNESS...TIME STOPS-- EVERYTHING STOPS. IT'S JUST THEM AND THE BALL.

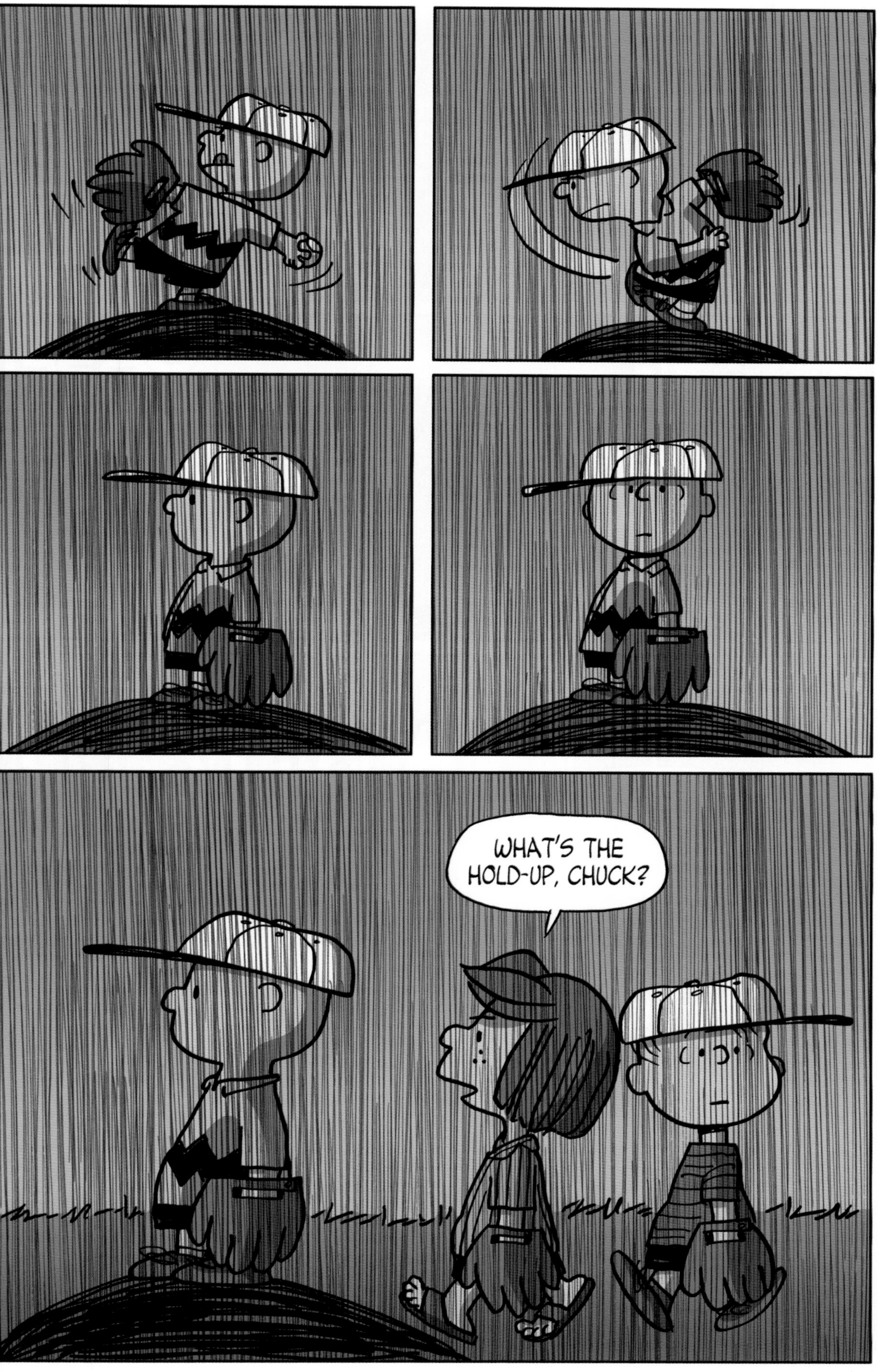
WHAT'S THE HOLD-UP, CHUCK?

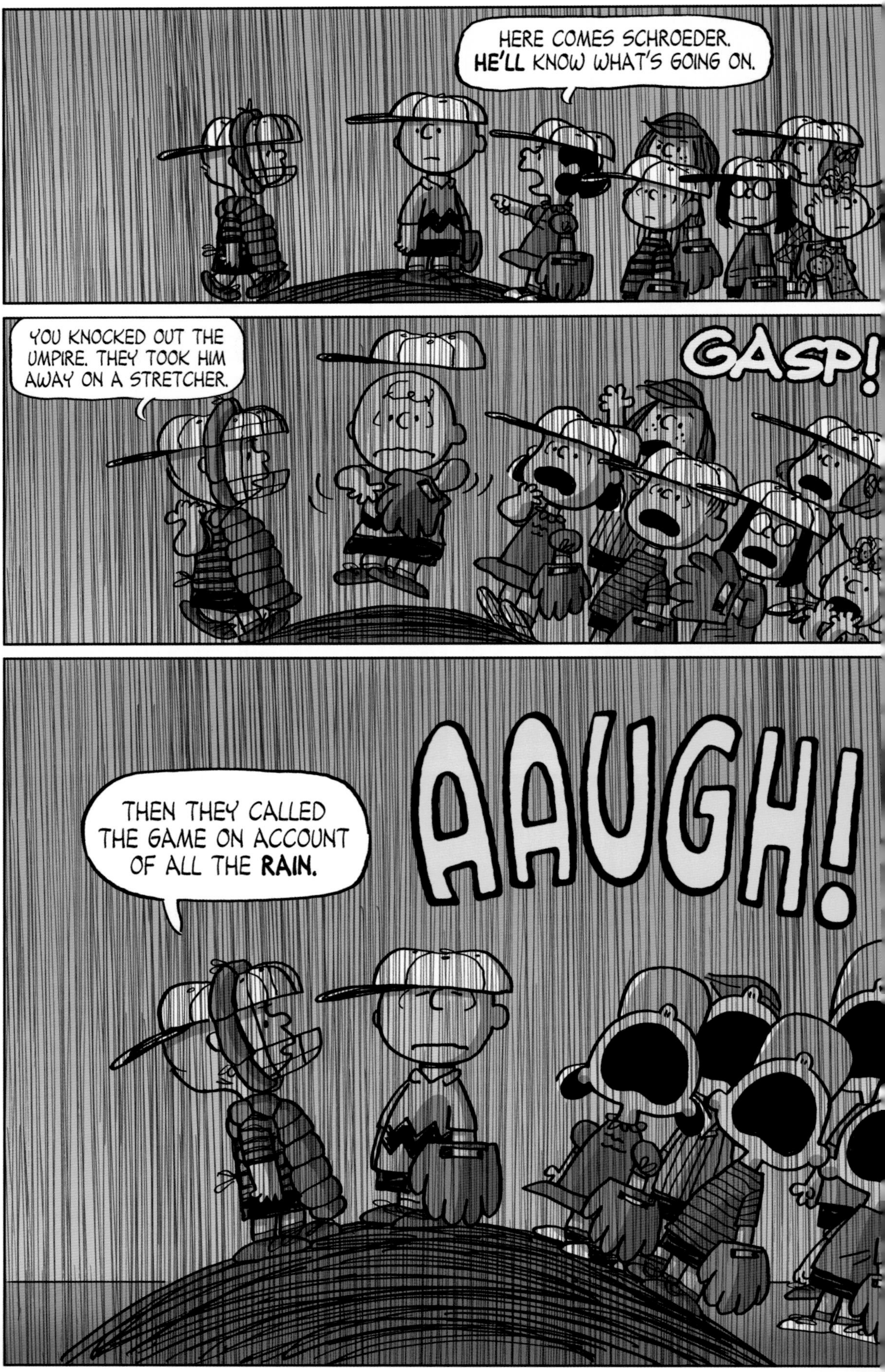
HERE COMES SCHROEDER. HE'LL KNOW WHAT'S GOING ON.
YOU KNOCKED OUT THE UMPIRE. THEY TOOK HIM AWAY ON A STRETCHER.
GASP!
THEN THEY CALLED THE GAME ON ACCOUNT OF ALL THE RAIN.
AAUGH!

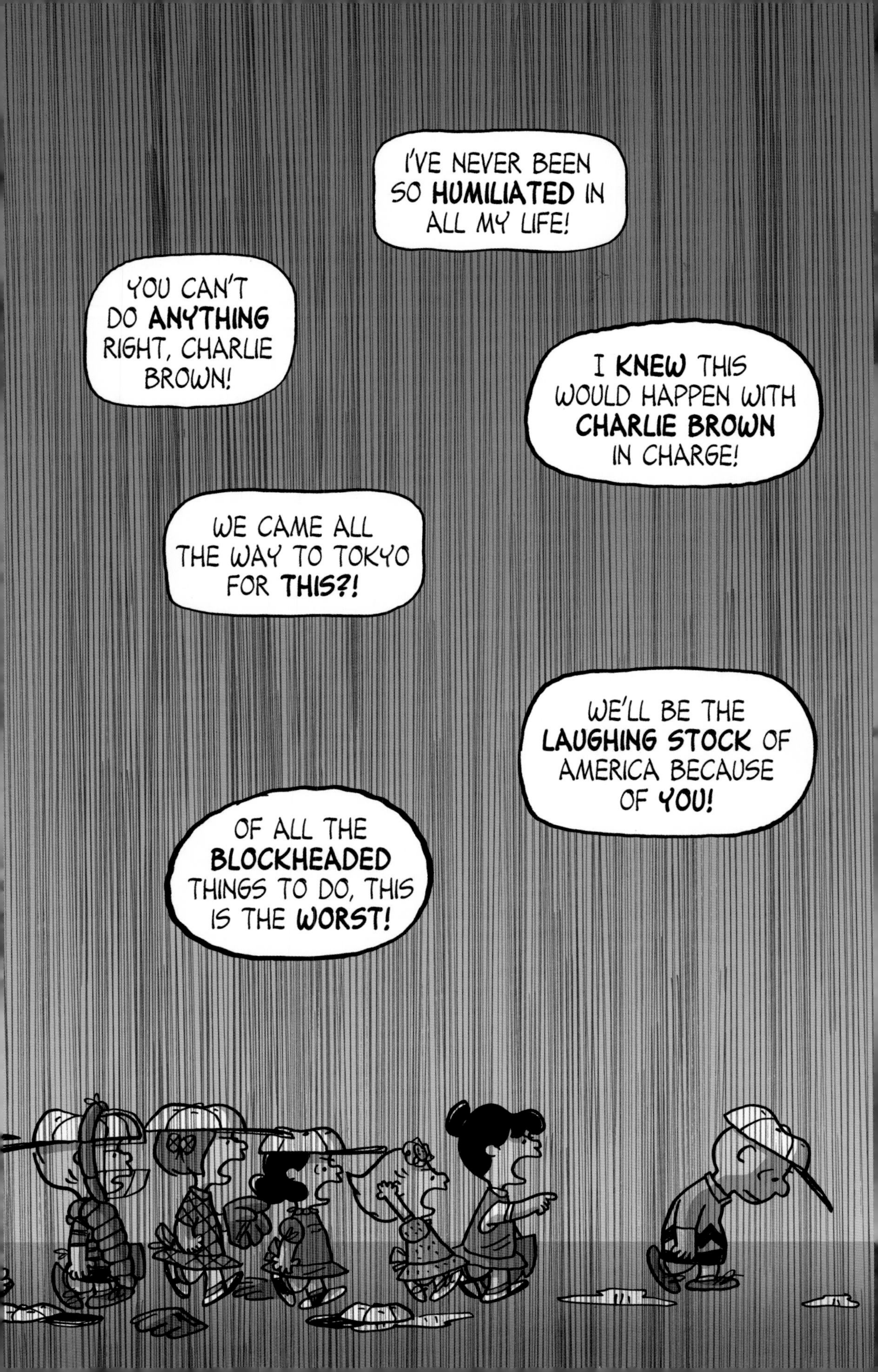
I'VE NEVER BEEN SO HUMILIATED IN ALL MY LIFE!
YOU CAN'T DO ANYTHING RIGHT, CHARLIE BROWN!
I KNEW THIS WOULD HAPPEN WITH CHARLIE BROWN IN CHARGE!
WE CAME ALL THE WAY TO TOKYO FOR THIS?!
WE'LL BE THE LAUGHING STOCK OF AMERICA BECAUSE OF YOU!
OF ALL THE BLOCKHEADED THINGS TO DO, THIS IS THE WORST!

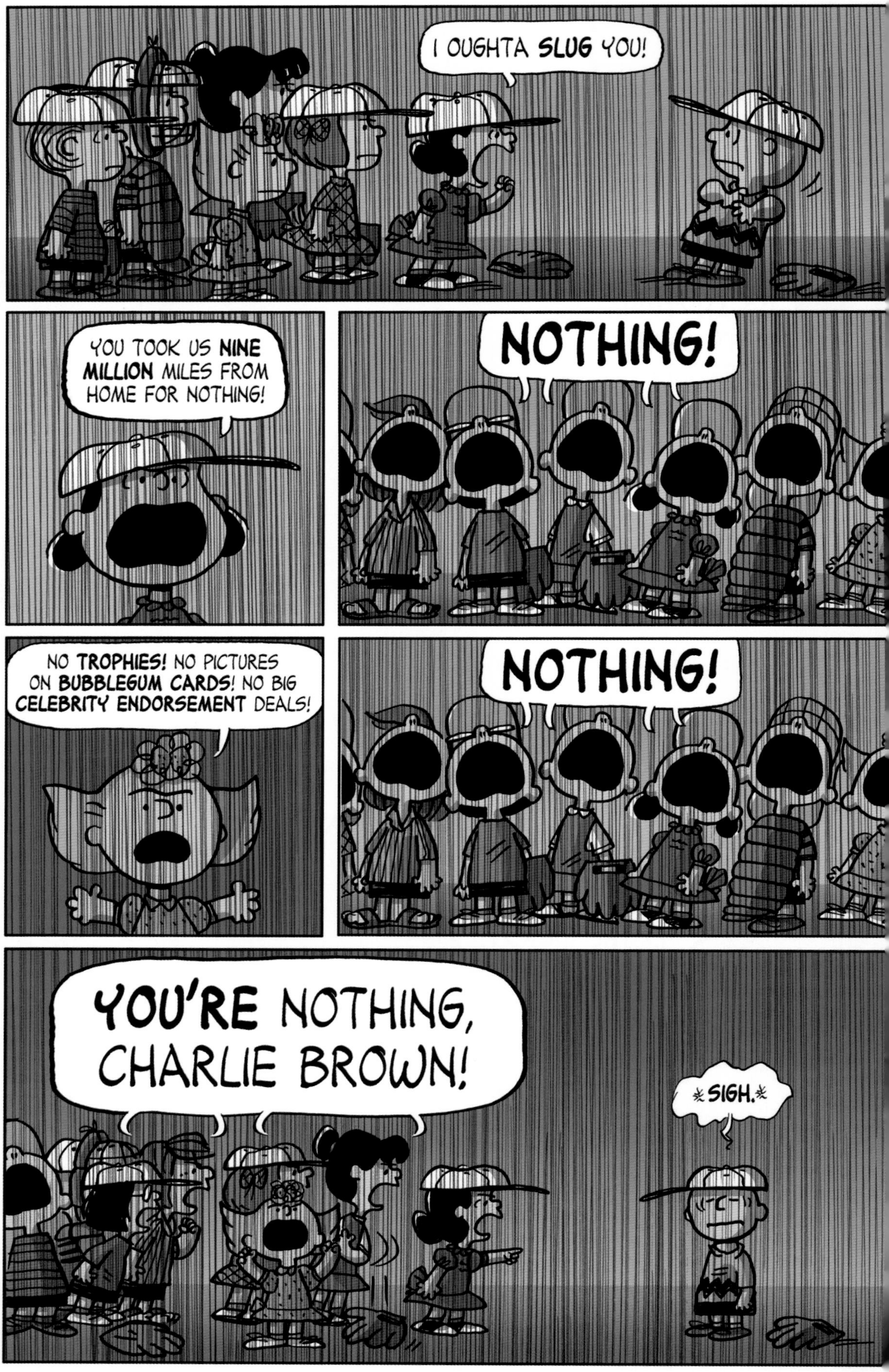

I OUGHTA SLUG YOU!
YOU TOOK US NINE MILLION MILES FROM HOME FOR NOTHING!
NOTHING!
NO TROPHIES! NO PICTURES ON BUBBLEGUM CARDS! NO BIG CELEBRITY ENDORSEMENT DEALS!
NOTHING!
YOU'RE NOTHING, CHARLIE BROWN!
SIGH.

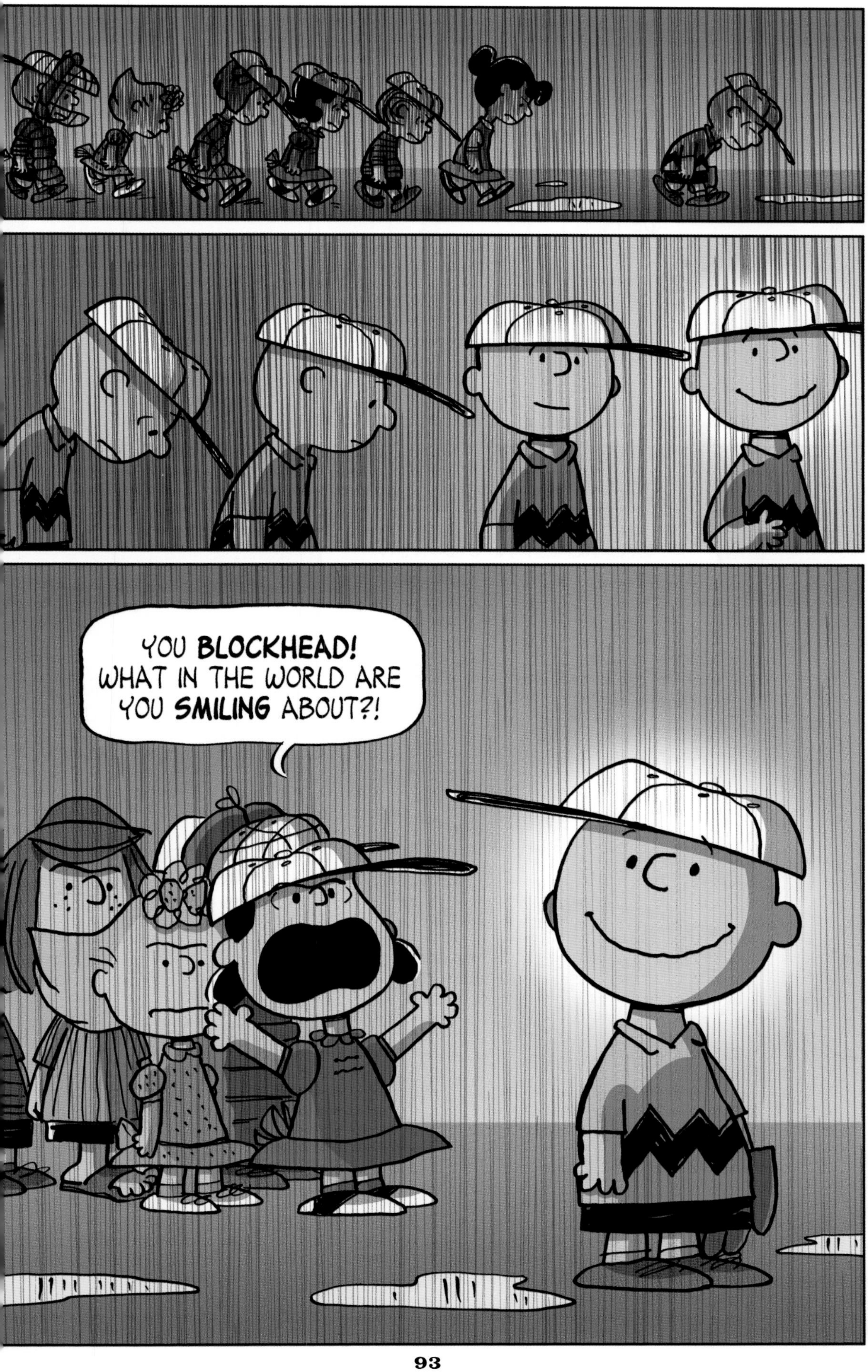
YOU BLOCKHEAD! WHAT IN THE WORLD ARE YOU SMILING ABOUT?!

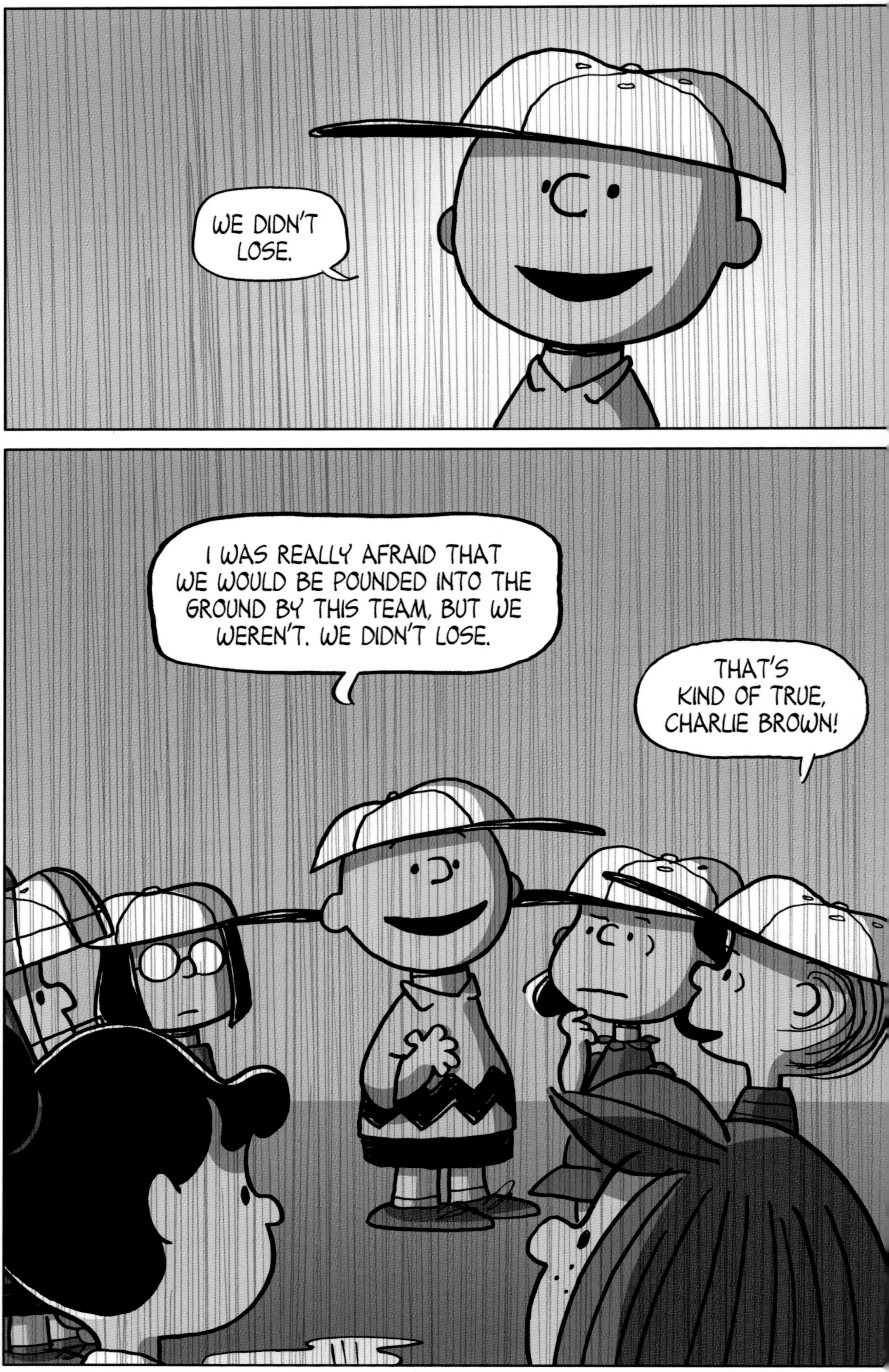
WE DIDN'T LOSE.
I WAS REALLY AFRAID THAT WE WOULD BE POUNDED INTO THE GROUND BY THIS TEAM, BUT WE WEREN'T. WE DIDN'T LOSE.
THAT'S KIND OF TRUE, CHARLIE BROWN!

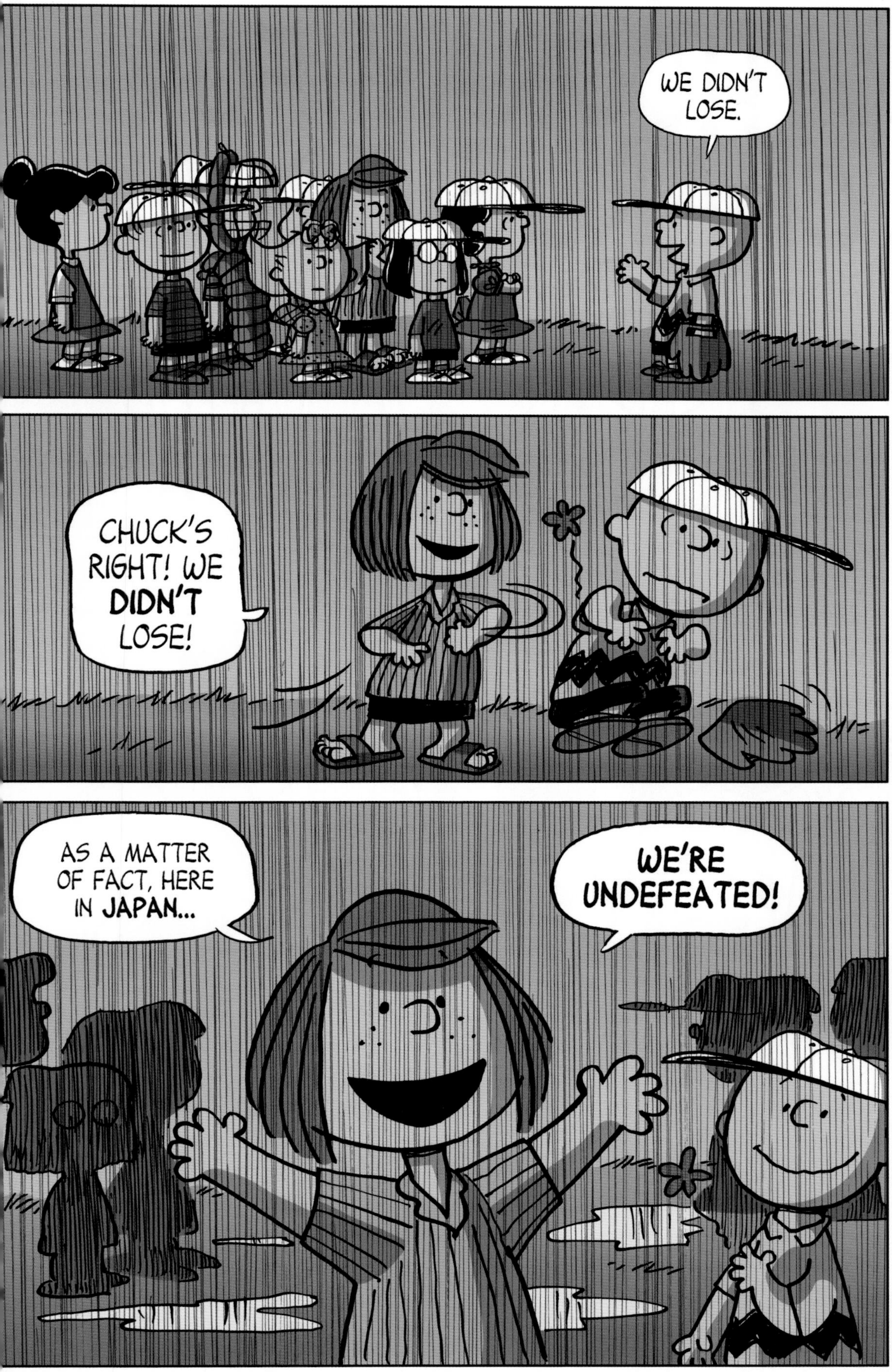
WE DIDN'T LOSE.
CHUCK'S RIGHT! WE DIDN'T LOSE!
AS A MATTER OF FACT, HERE IN JAPAN...
WE'RE UNDEFEATED!

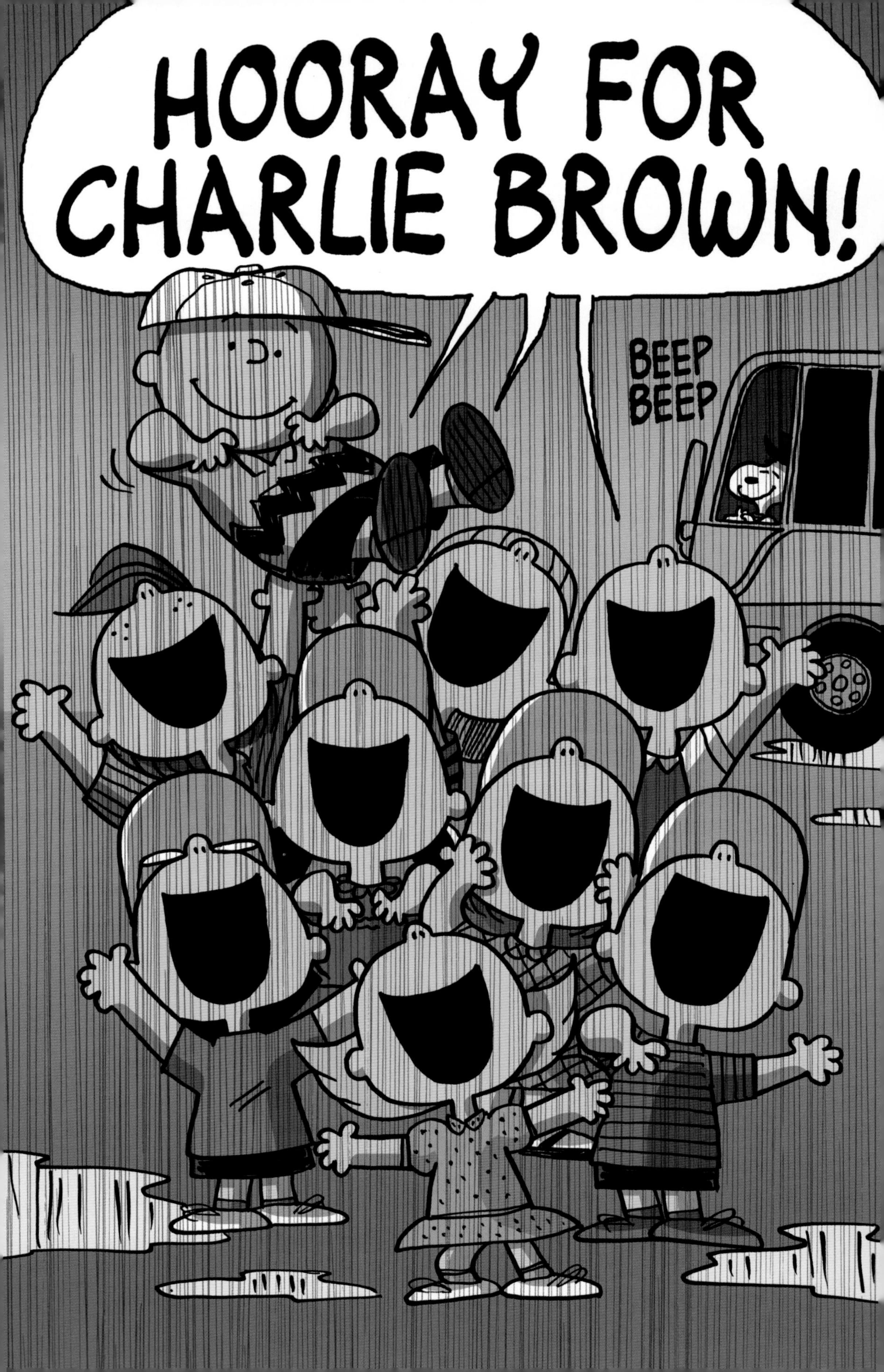
HOORAY FOR CHARLIE BROWN!
BEEP BEEP

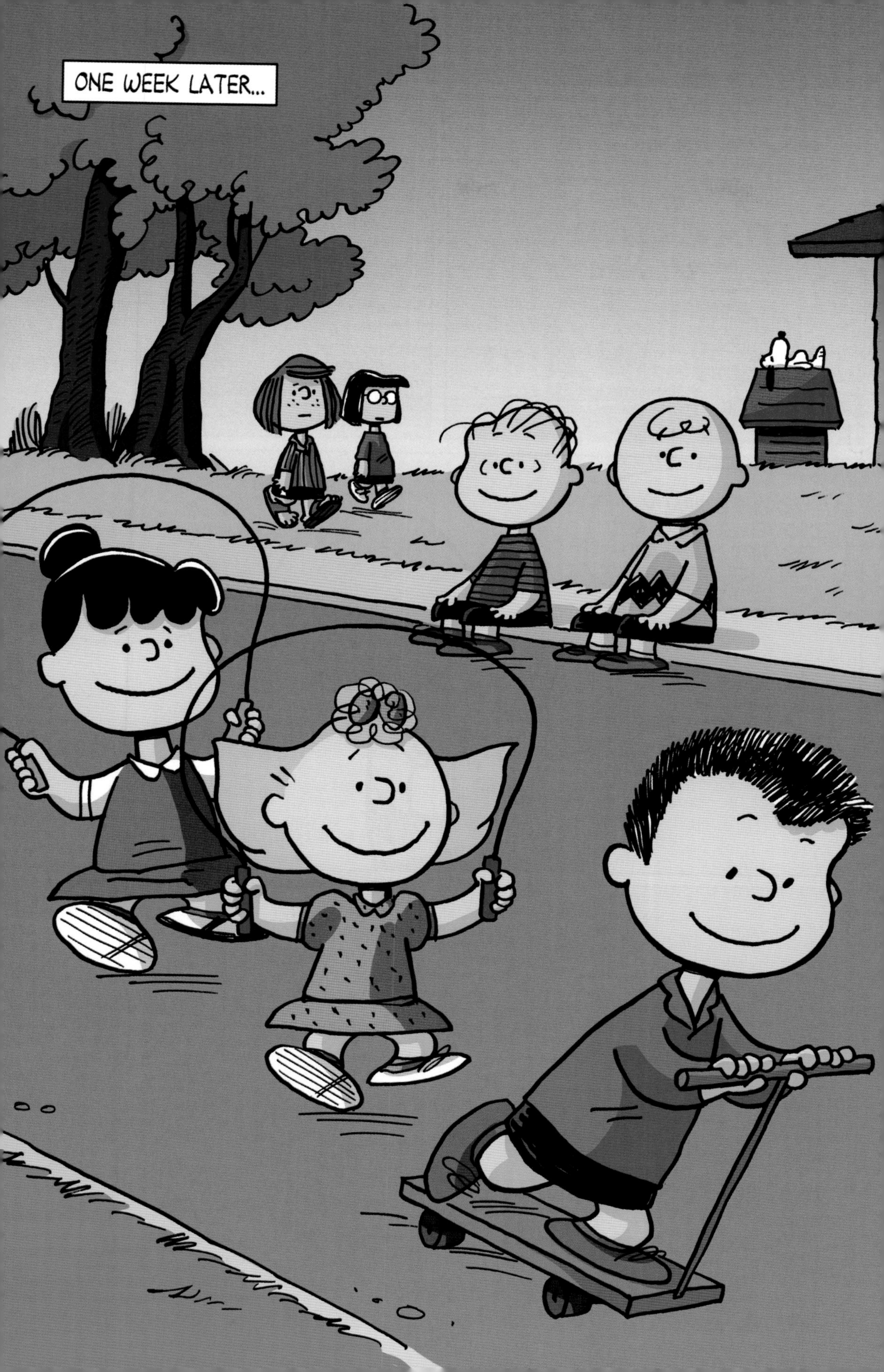
ONE WEEK LATER...

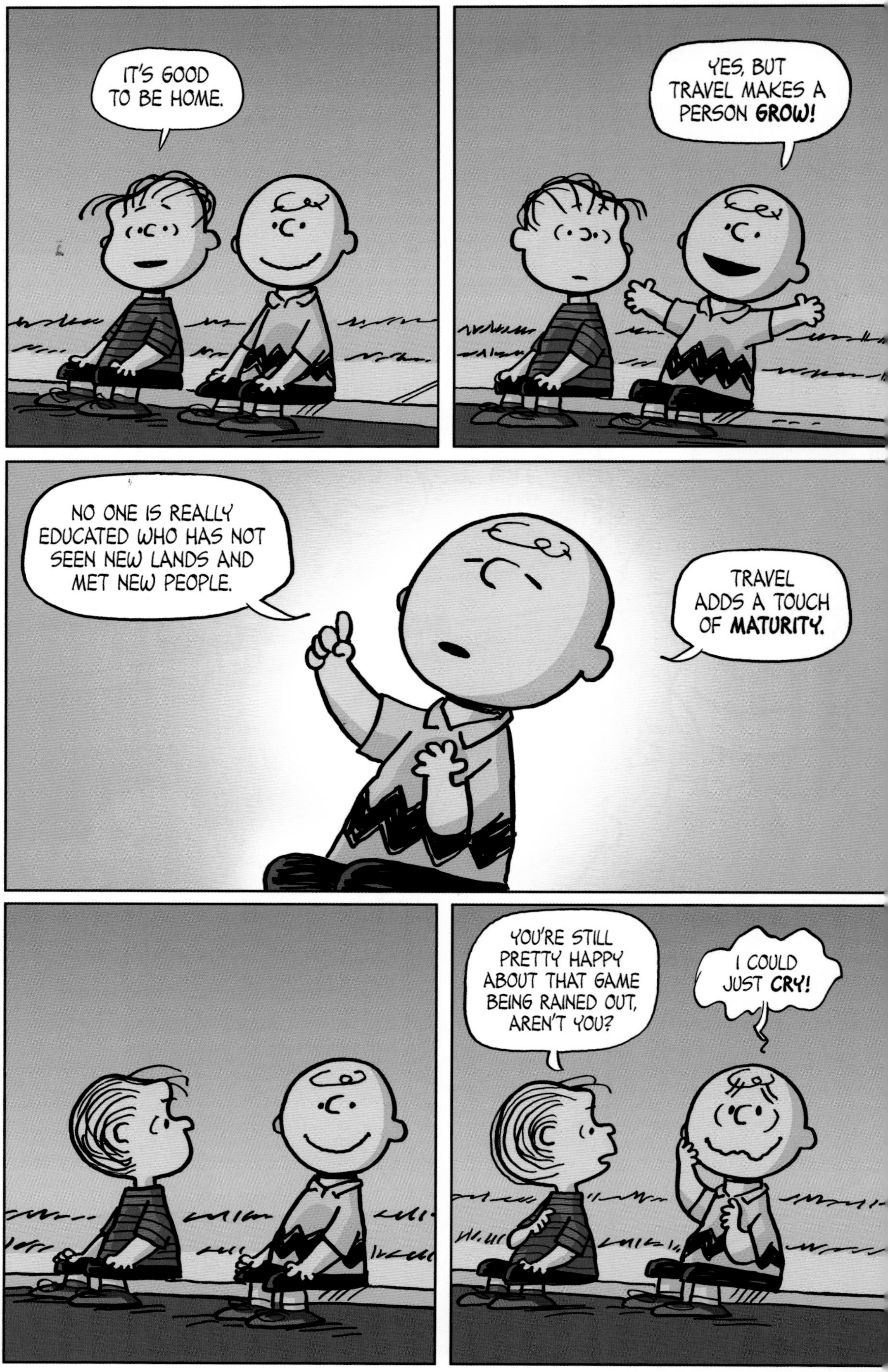
IT'S GOOD TO BE HOME.
YES, BUT TRAVEL MAKES A PERSON **GROW!**
NO ONE IS REALLY EDUCATED WHO HAS NOT SEEN NEW LANDS AND MET NEW PEOPLE.
TRAVEL ADDS A TOUCH OF **MATURITY.**
YOU'RE STILL PRETTY HAPPY ABOUT THAT GAME BEING RAINED OUT, AREN'T YOU?
I COULD JUST **CRY!**

THE END

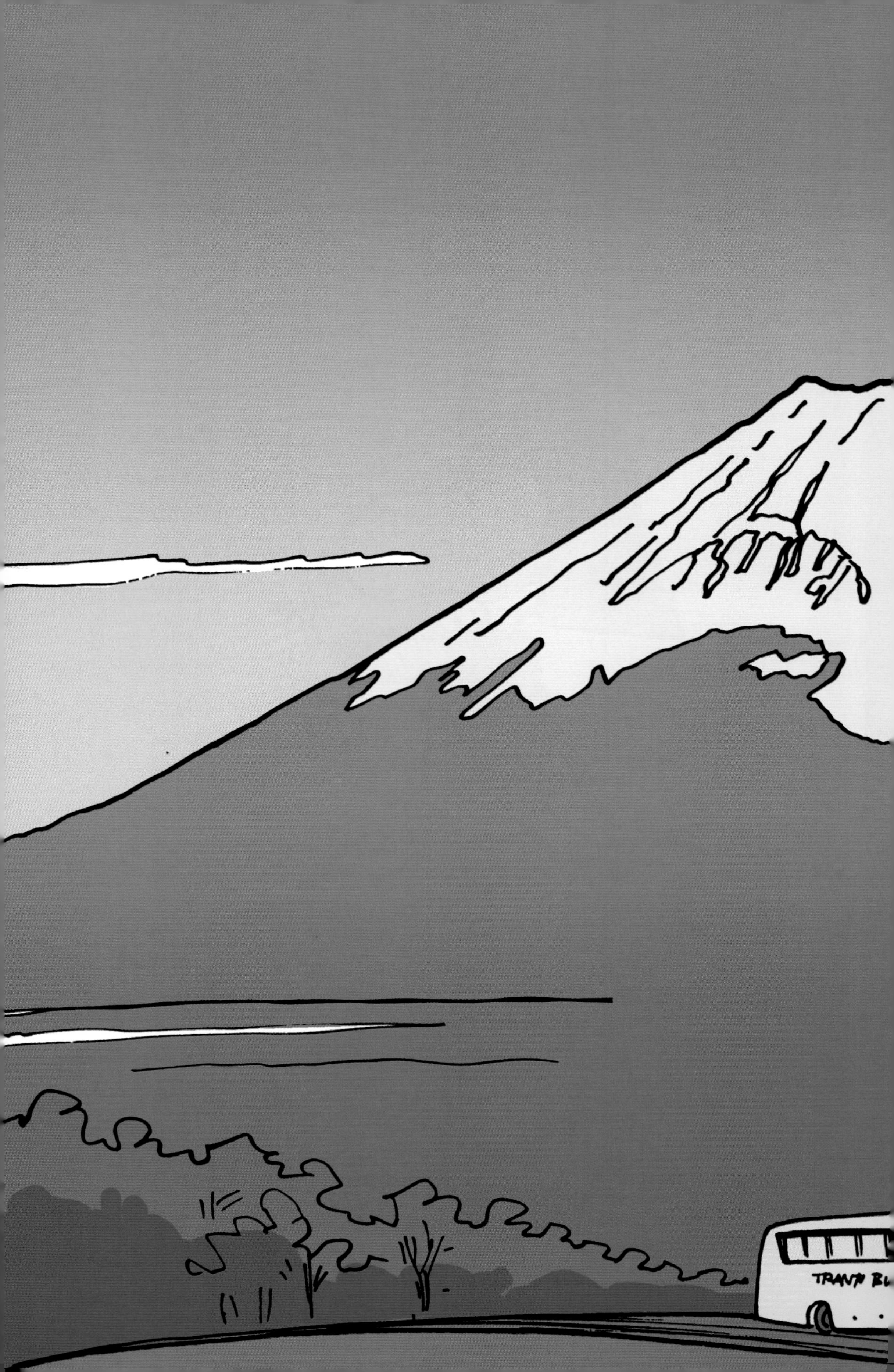

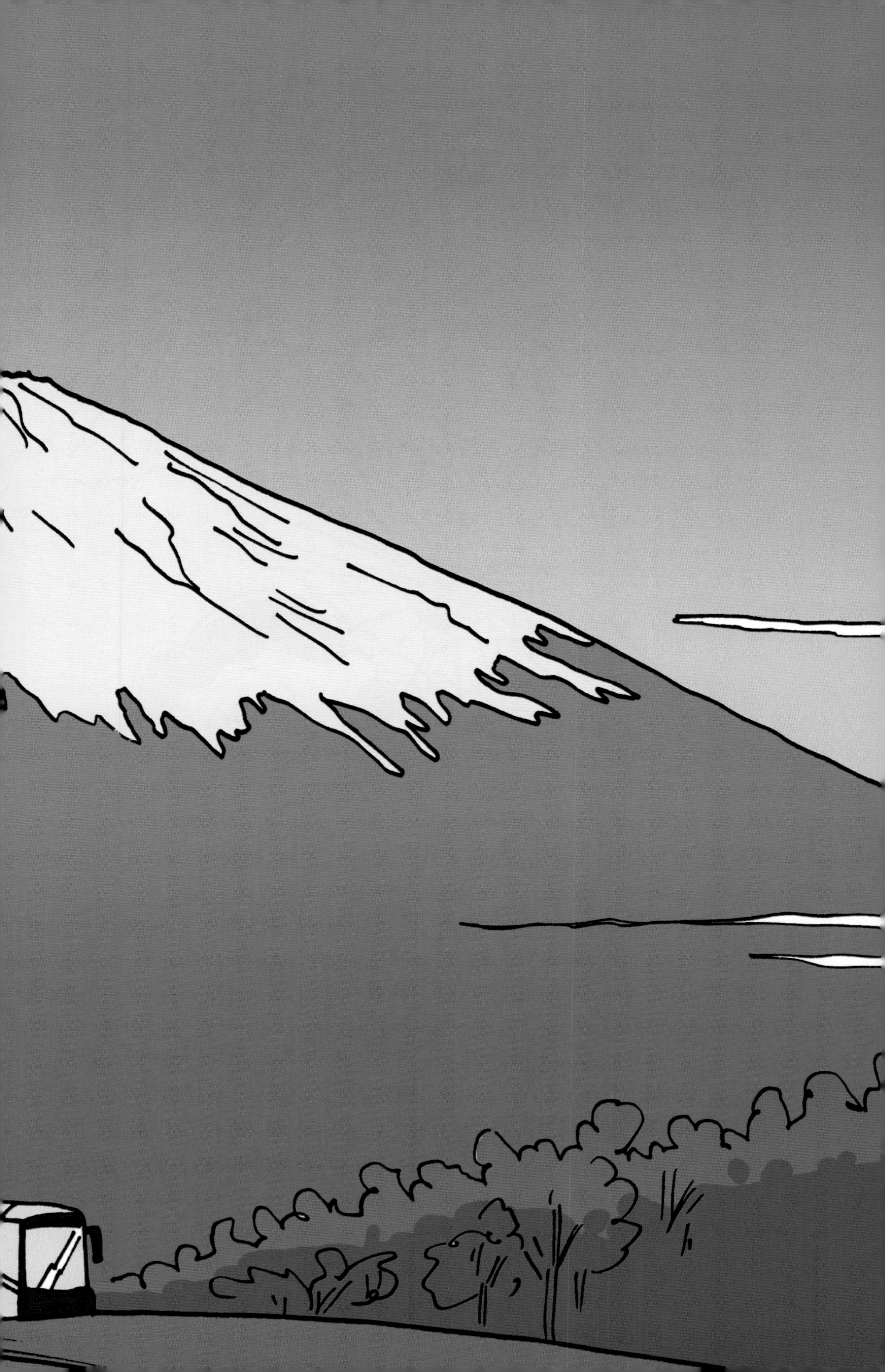

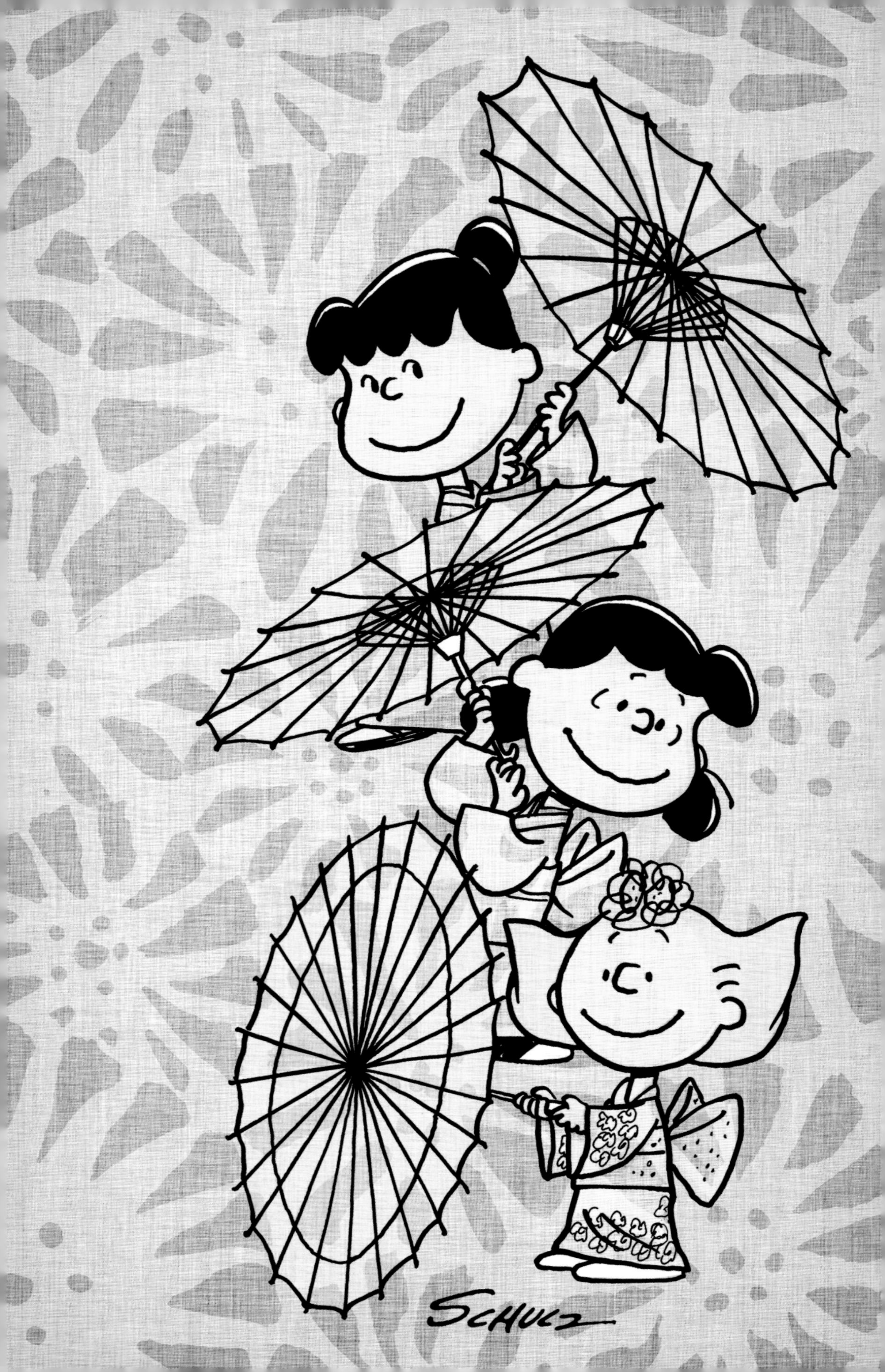
SCHULZ

BEHIND-THE-SCENES

IT'S TOKYO, CHARLIE BROWN!

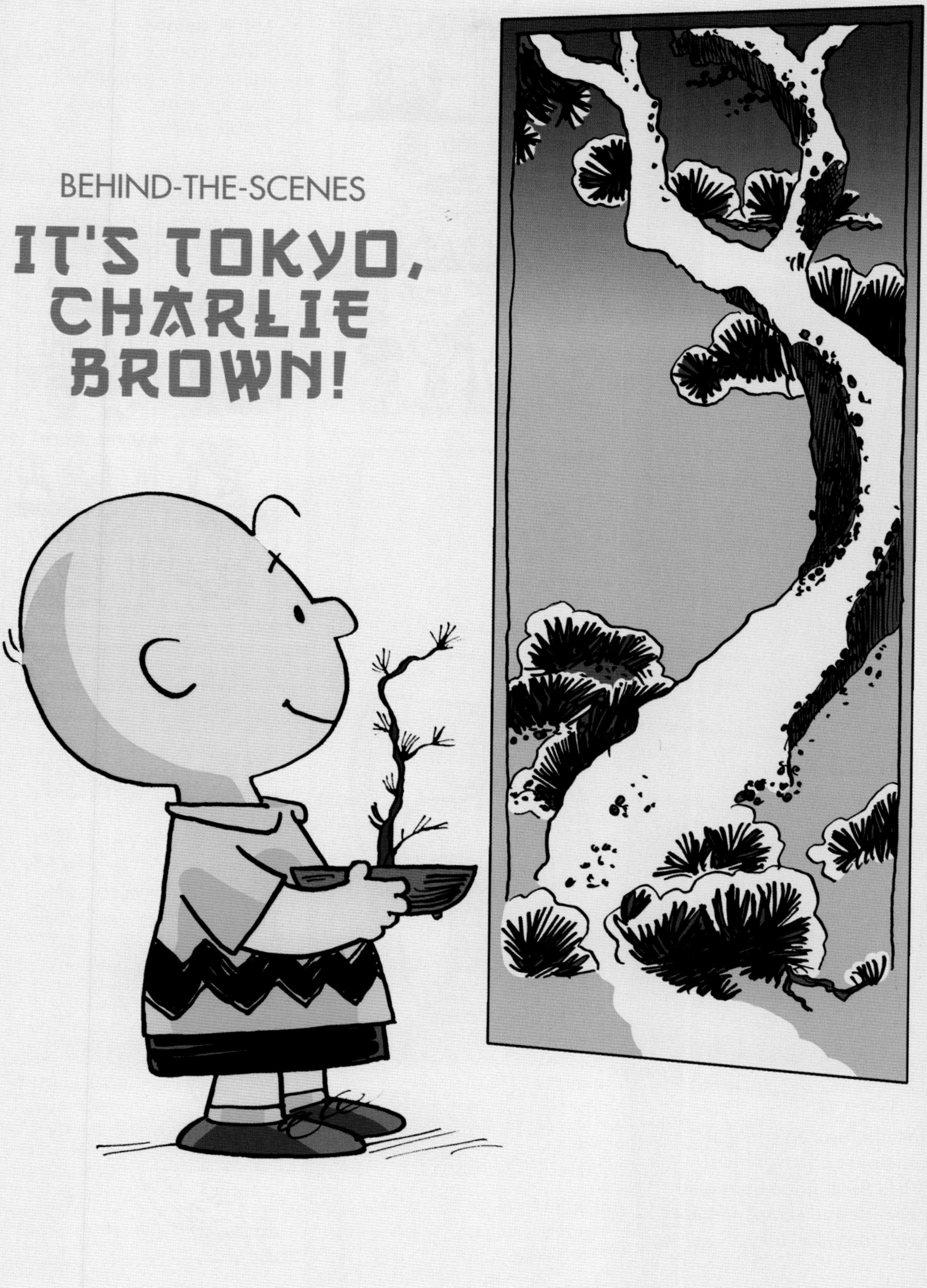

From Strip to Script...

To help ground the new story in Schulz's voice right from the start, the opening sequence of the book was largely built from original PEANUTS comic strips.

Compiled Companion draft to the roughs Jan

It's Tokyo, Charlie Brown!

Page 1 A

We start on a sunny afternoon. It's the last g
pep talk to Charlie Brown on the mound.

Schroeder

If you can get this last man out, Cha
Therefore, I would suggest you thr

Shermy has joined the conference.

Shermy

No, don't do that! Throw him a d
Most of the team is now n the mo

Gang:

How about a knuckleball?... Or a
Can you throw an upshot?... Ho

The team starts to return to their positi

Shermy,

Just strike this kid out, Charlie Brown!

Patty

What if he can't do it?

Lucy,

If he doesn't throw a strike, I say we all kick him!

Page 1B

Charlie Brown, *alone on the mound, facing the opponent,*

Either this guy gets a hit and they win, or I strike him out and we win...

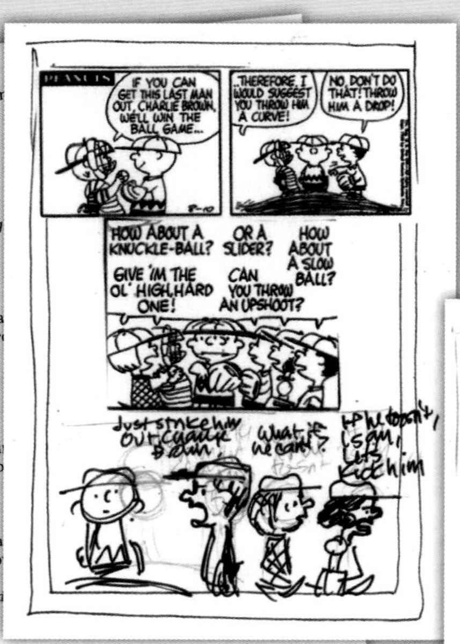

PEANUTS
IF YOU CAN GET THIS LAST MAN OUT, CHARLIE BROWN, WE'LL WIN THE BALL GAME...
...THEREFORE, I WOULD SUGGEST YOU THROW HIM A CURVE!
NO, DON'T DO THAT! THROW HIM A DROP!
HOW ABOUT A KNUCKLE-BALL?
OR A SLIDER?
HOW ABOUT A SLOW BALL?
GIVE 'IM THE OL' HIGH, HARD ONE!
CAN YOU THROW AN UPSHOOT?

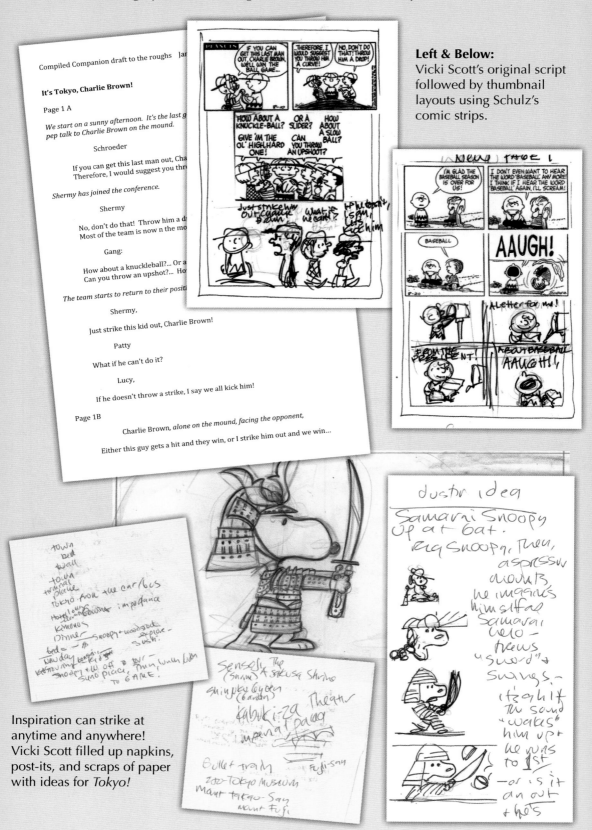

Left & Below:
Vicki Scott's original script followed by thumbnail layouts using Schulz's comic strips.

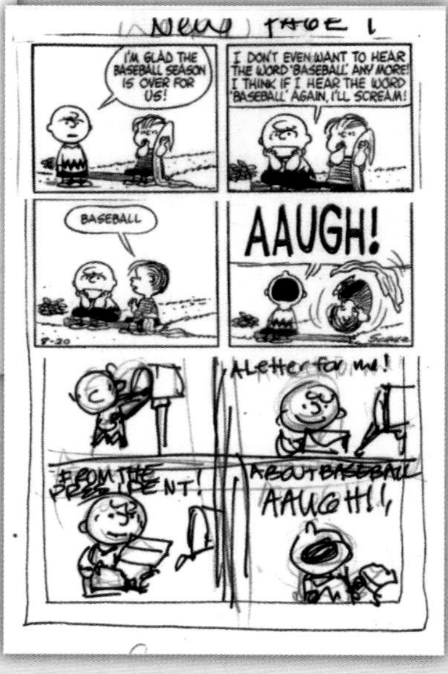

I'M GLAD THE BASEBALL SEASON IS OVER FOR US!
I DON'T EVEN WANT TO HEAR THE WORD 'BASEBALL' ANY MORE! I THINK IF I HEAR THE WORD 'BASEBALL' AGAIN, I'LL SCREAM!
BASEBALL
AAUGH!
A Letter for me!
AAUGH!

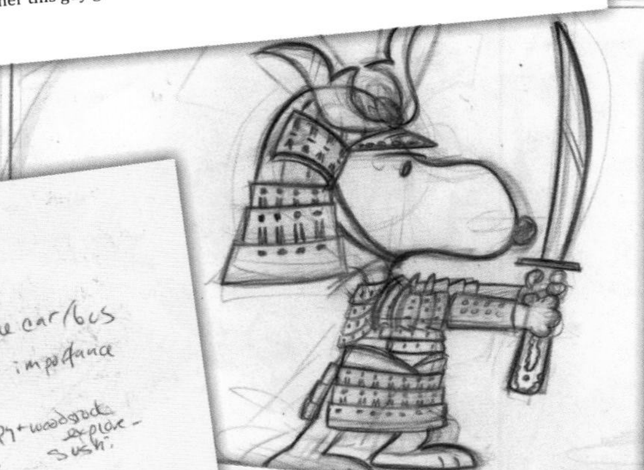

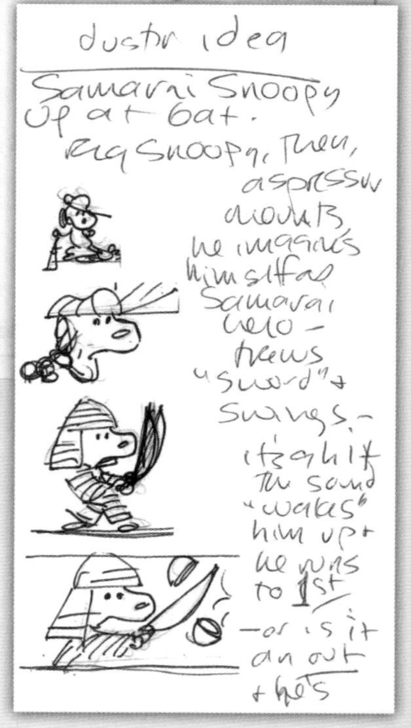

dustin idea
Samurai Snoopy up at bat.

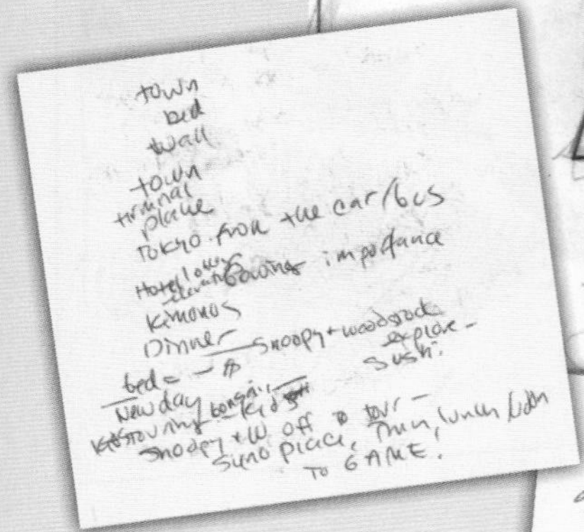

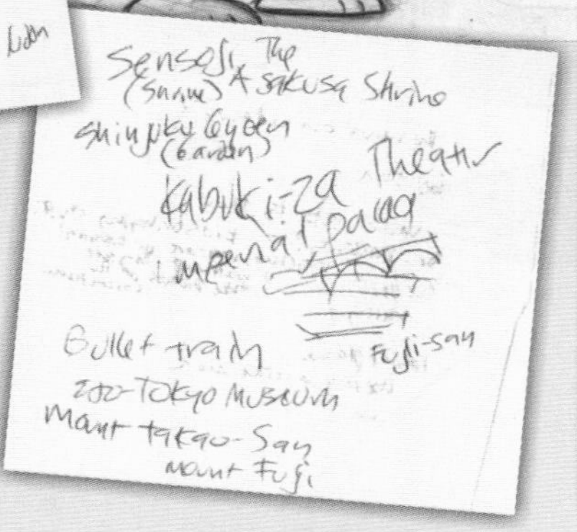

Bullet train
Mount Fuji

Inspiration can strike at anytime and anywhere! Vicki Scott filled up napkins, post-its, and scraps of paper with ideas for *Tokyo!*

Snoopy & Woodstock's Adventures in Tokyo...

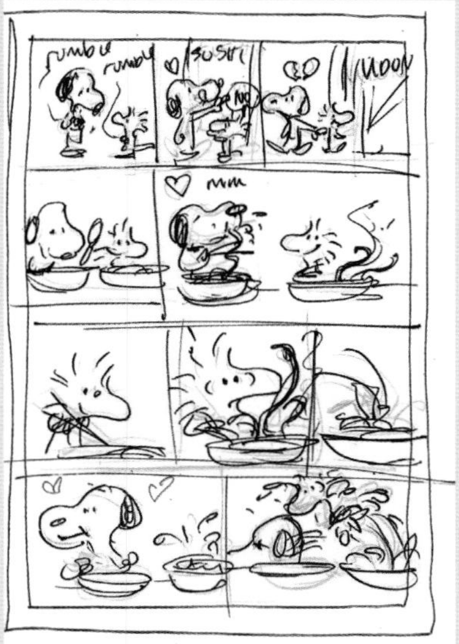
rumble rumble
SUSHI
UDON
mm

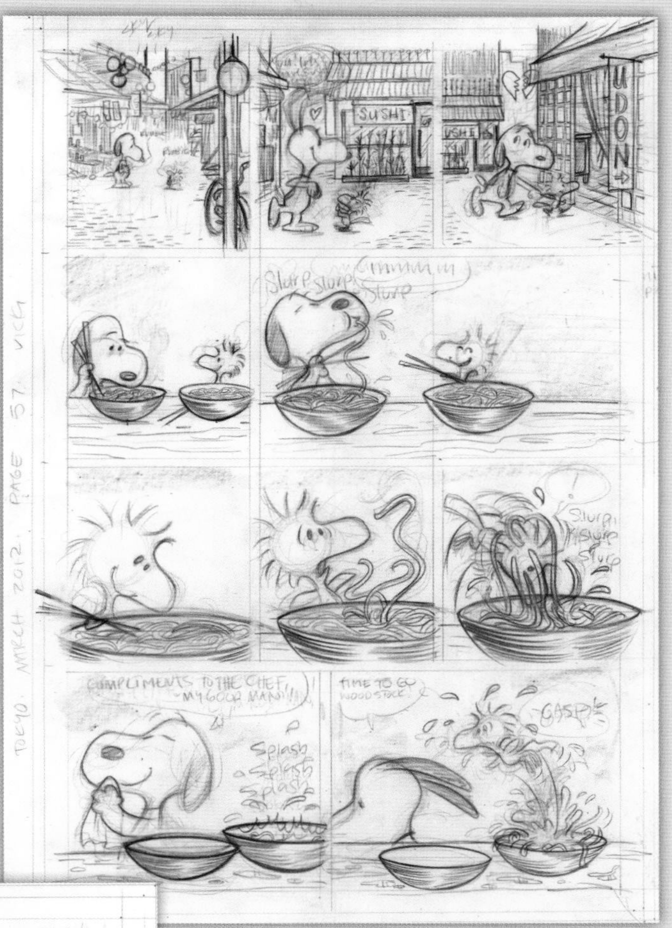
SUSHI
UDON
Slurp slurp slurp
mmmm
Slurp slurp slurp
COMPLIMENTS TO THE CHEF, MY GOOD MAN!
TIME TO GO WOODSTOCK
GASP!
Splash splash splash
TOKYO MARCH 2012 PAGE 57 VICKI

Top & right: A night on the town, thumbnails and full pencils. "It was fun to have poor little Woodstock valiantly battle his food!"
–Vicki Scott

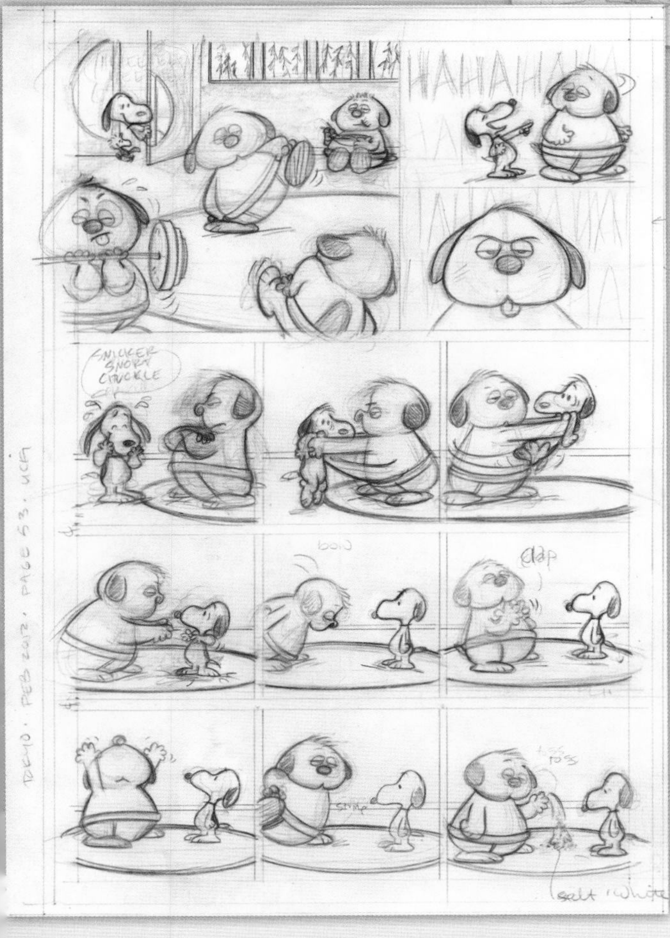
HAHAHAHA
SNICKER SNORT CHUCKLE
bow
clap
toss toss
TOKYO FEB 2012 PAGE 53 VICKI

Left & below: The sumo challenge, full pencils and thumbnails. "Snoopy's brother, Olaf was the perfect build for Snoopy's sumo wrestling opponent. It was lots of fun to draw!"
–Vicki Scott

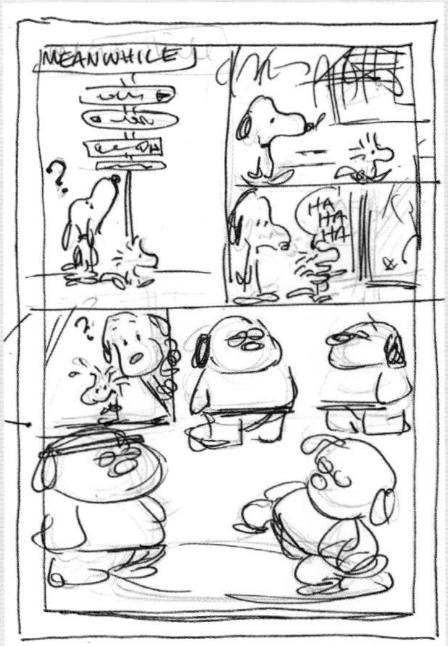
MEANWHILE
HA HA HA

Research & Reference

Believe it or not, writer and artist Vicki Scott has yet to travel to Japan, but that didn't stop her from writing a well-researched travelogue. Vicki also had help from her Schulz Studio mates, many of whom have been to Japan and supplied lots of photo reference for her. Below are the photos and the scenes they inspired for *It's Tokyo, Charlie Brown!*

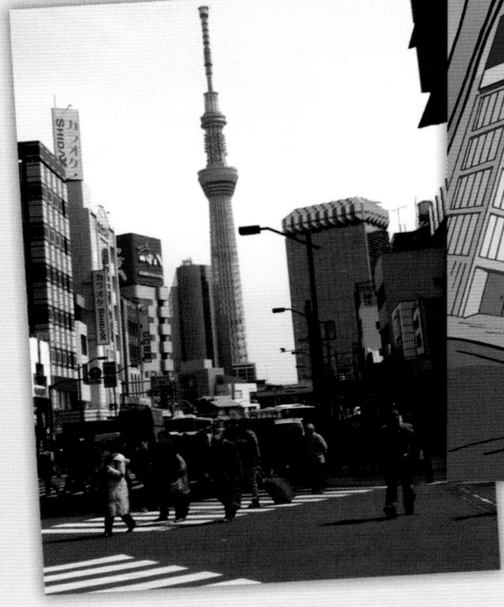

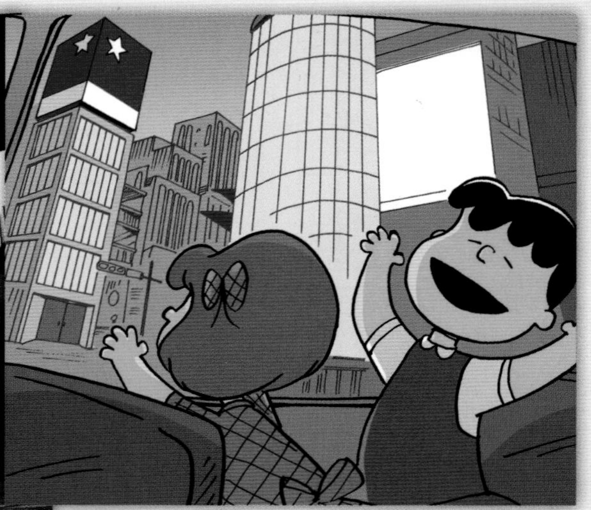

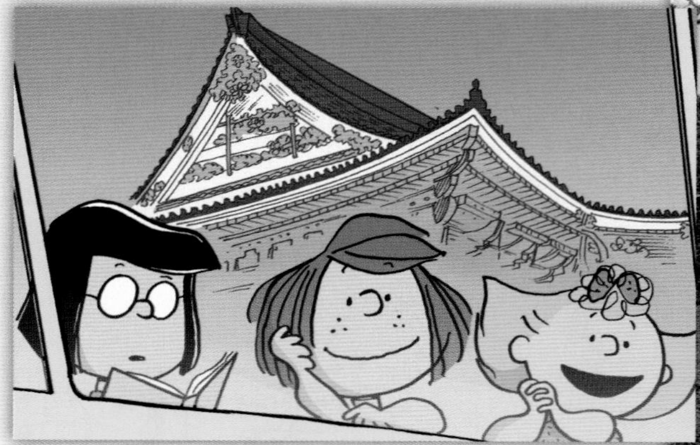

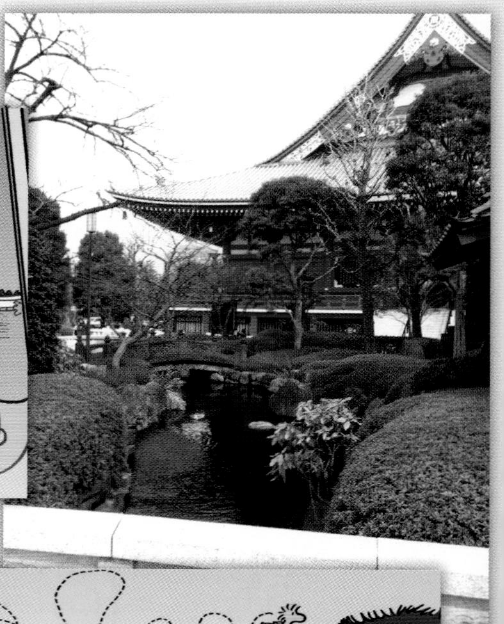

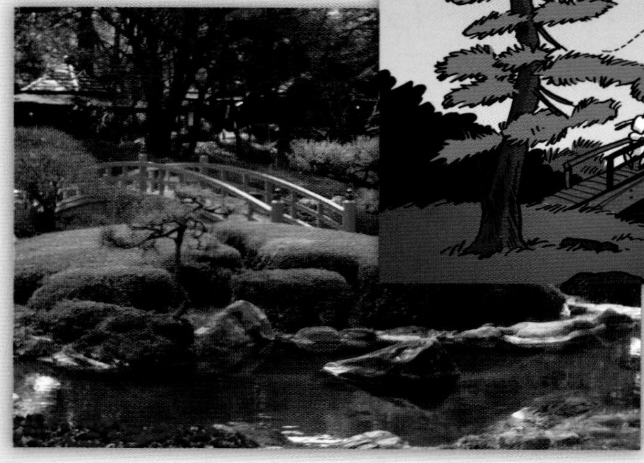

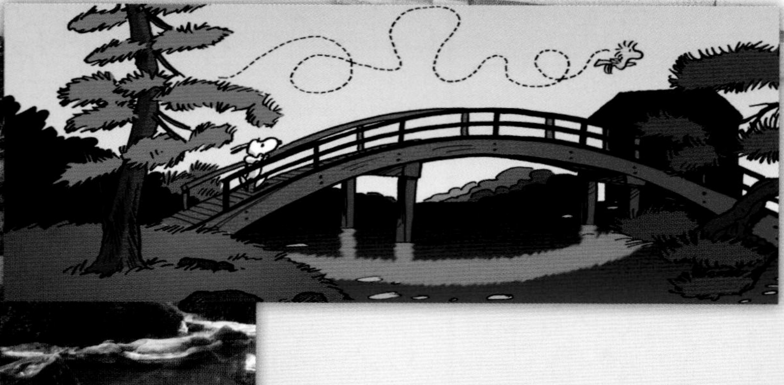

photos by Justin Thompson

Gallery

These limited edition postcards (as well as "Umbrella Girls" as seen on page 102) were created especially for the San Diego Comic-Con 2012 announcement of *It's Tokyo, Charlie Brown!*

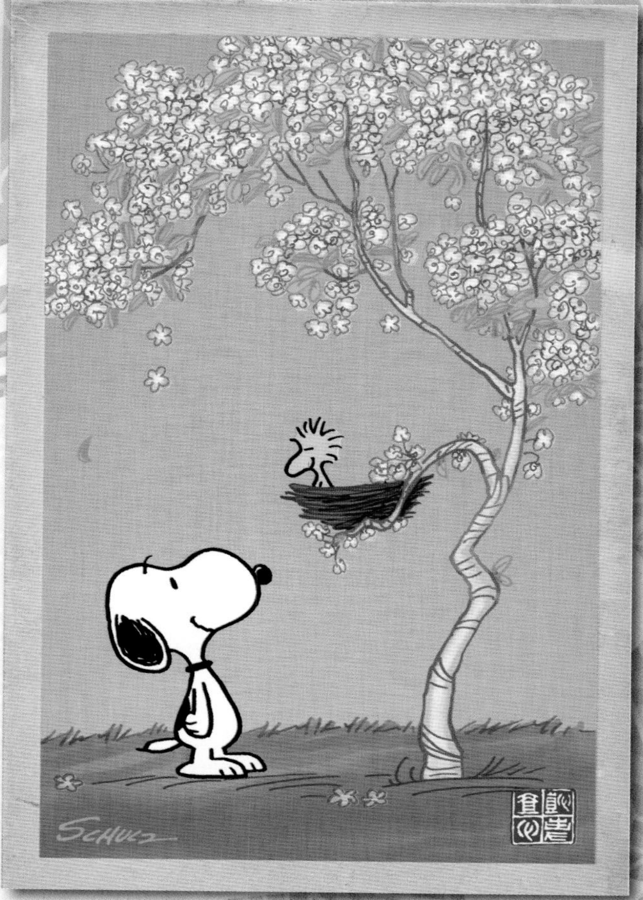
SCHULZ

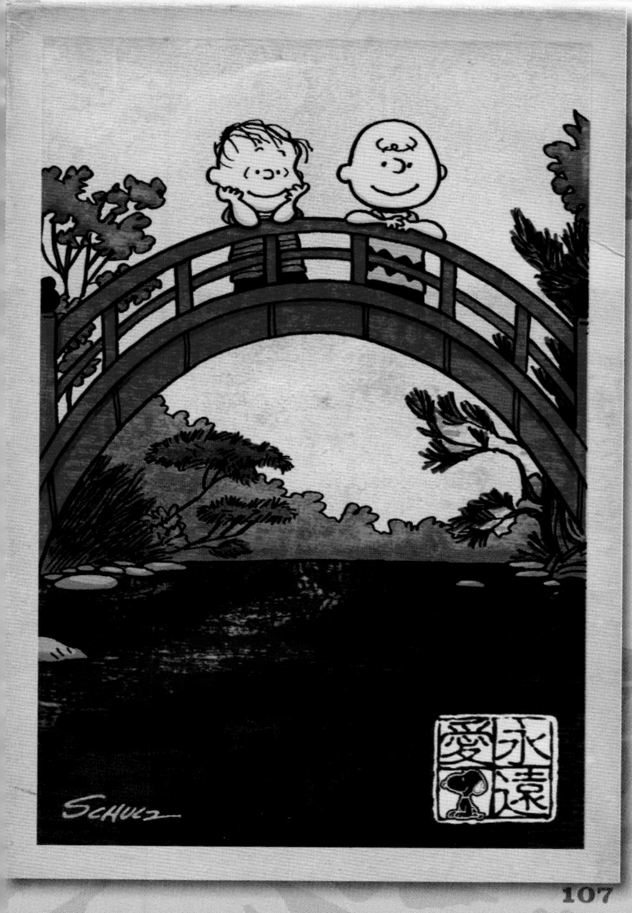
永遠
愛
SCHULZ

Conversation with the Creators, Vicki Scott and Paige Braddock

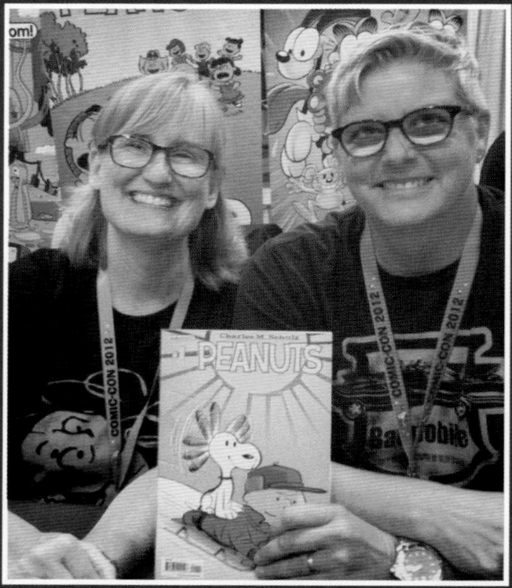
PEANUTS
COMIC-CON 2012

Photo by Evelyn Braddock

Writer and Penciller Vicki Scott (left) and inker Paige Braddock (right), pictured signing at the KaBOOM! booth at San Diego Comic Con 2012.

Where did the idea for "It's Tokyo, Charlie Brown" come from?

VS: Just after the graphic novel "Happiness is a Warm Blanket, Charlie Brown" came out, I heard that a publisher in Japan wanted to create stories that put the PEANUTS characters together with Japanese characters in original stories. Of course this was an impossible dream, as there are very clear PEANUTS rules to work within. For example, we can't invent new characters, we can't use adults, Charlie Brown can't kick the football...but I like puzzles and the idea for a new story stuck with me.

Then one day a couple of ideas crossed my mind at the same time, and suddenly I had the entire ending for the book! And the ending was exactly the device I needed to let me NOT break any of the rules. Once I got the story started, the rest of the staff here at the Schulz Studio kindly added ideas along the way. It is a very supportive and enthusiastic staff; without this creative climate, I doubt I would have come up with the initial story.

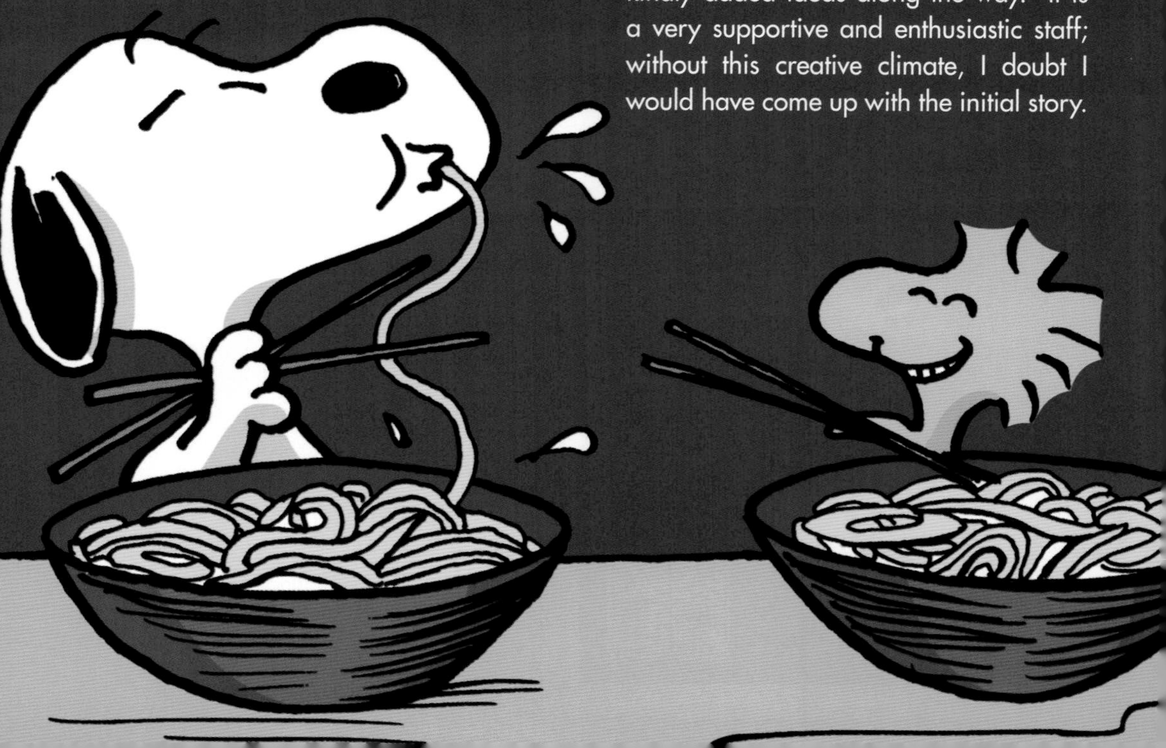

In the comic strip PEANUTS, the kids rarely ever traveled far from their neighborhood, were you worried about taking them all the way to Japan? Where did you look for inspiration and influence when crafting the story?

VS: The great thing about these characters is that whether they go across the street or around the world, they are still just themselves. Part of my aim was for the kids to interact freely with Japanese locations and experiences so I looked to the PEANUTS TV specials and movies for the way their adult-free world was presented. I tried to replace all the adults in Japan with Marcie's really good tour book!

The book is very well researched, have you been to Japan before? What kind of research did you do to make sure the locations and architecture had an authentic Japanese look & feel?

VS: I am a big fan of Japanese art and architecture (and food!). Travelling to Japan has been on my to-do list for years, but I have not been there yet. Fortunately, most of the staff here at studio has been to Tokyo, so they helped me with a lot of advice and fact-checking. Other than their stories and photos, I did my research online and with my own tour books of Japan. San Francisco's Japantown is one of my family's favorite spots as well!

Are particular PEANUTS characters or personalities that you enjoy writing and drawing more than others? What sequence did you have fun drawing the most?

VS: Gosh, I would be hard-pressed to pick a favorite character. I mostly enjoy writing conversations between them. That's when they are funniest. As far as which sequences I enjoyed drawing the most, I would have to say the two sequences where Snoopy and Woodstock dine out. It was fun to have poor little Woodstock valiantly battle his food.

How is a comic book page constructed and what tools do you use?

VS: For me, I still draw on Bristol board with pencil. And lots of erasers...so many erasers...

PB: Mr. Schulz used a very specific sort of pen to ink his comic strip-- an Esterbrook 914 radio pen. It was an old school quill pen. So it has a steel tip, called a nib, and you dip it into an ink bottle each time you want to ink a section of the artwork. The pen nib that Schulz used was discontinued a long time ago...like in the 70s and Schulz bought out their entire remaining stock. When I first started working with Schulz at the studio he gave me a box of these special pen tips and that's what I use for inking so that I can match his style.

Where do you plan on taking the PEANUTS characters next?

VS: After such a big trip, maybe they should stay closer to home for the next story. Possibly a summer camp story will be next! It's always fun to watch what happens at summer camp and how the kids all muddle through.

Charles M. Schulz once described himself as "born to draw comic strips." Born in Minneapolis, at just two days old, an uncle nicknamed him "Sparky" after the horse Spark Plug from the Barney Google comic strip, and throughout his youth, he and his father shared a Sunday morning ritual reading the funnies. After serving in the Army during World War II, Schulz's first big break came in 1947 when he sold a cartoon feature called "Li'l Folks" to the *St. Paul Pioneer Press*. In 1950, Schulz met with United Feature Syndicate, and on October 2 of that year, PEANUTS, named by the syndicate, debuted in seven newspapers. Charles Schulz died in Santa Rosa, California, in February 2000—just hours before his last original strip was to appear in Sunday papers.

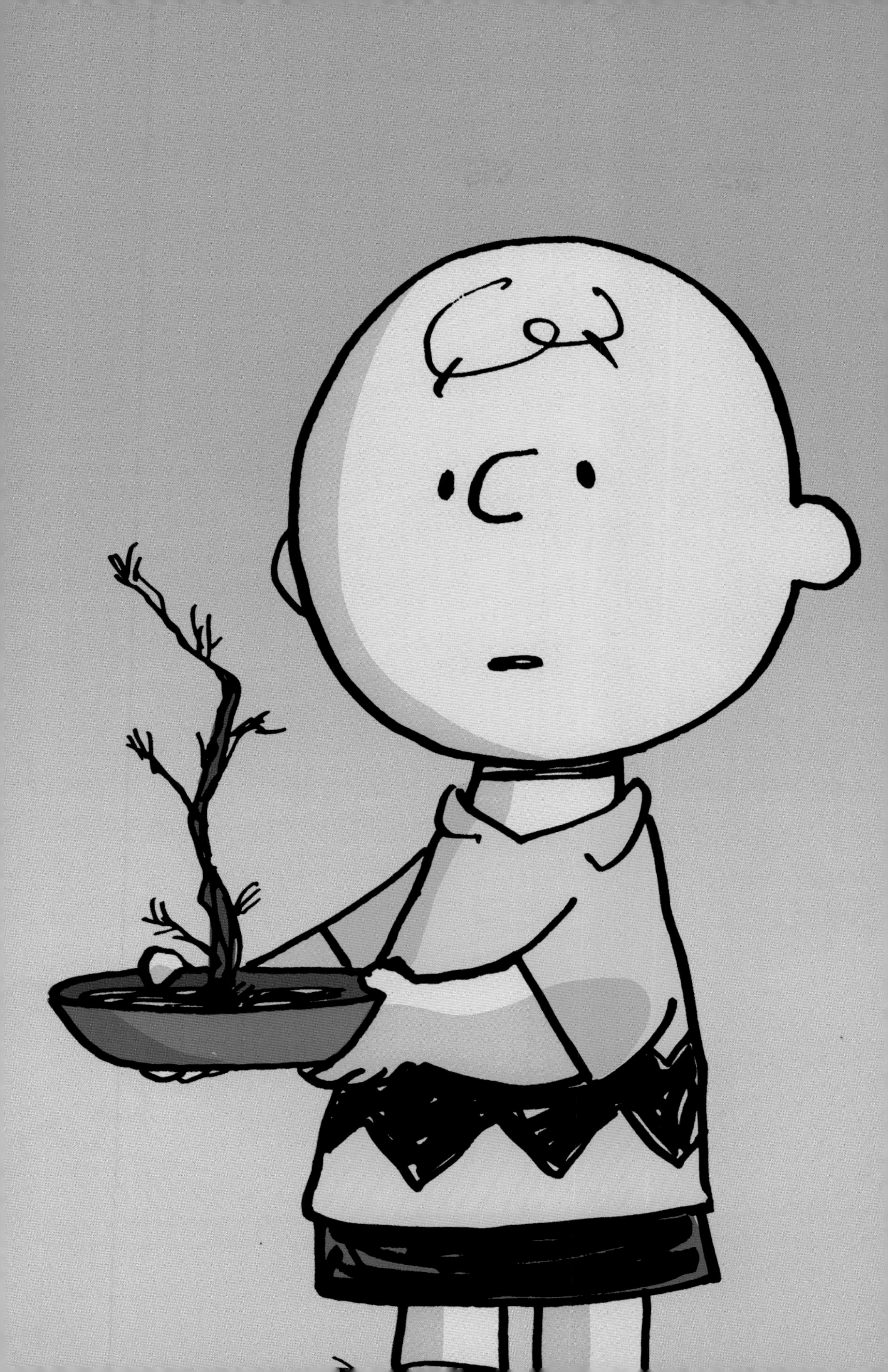

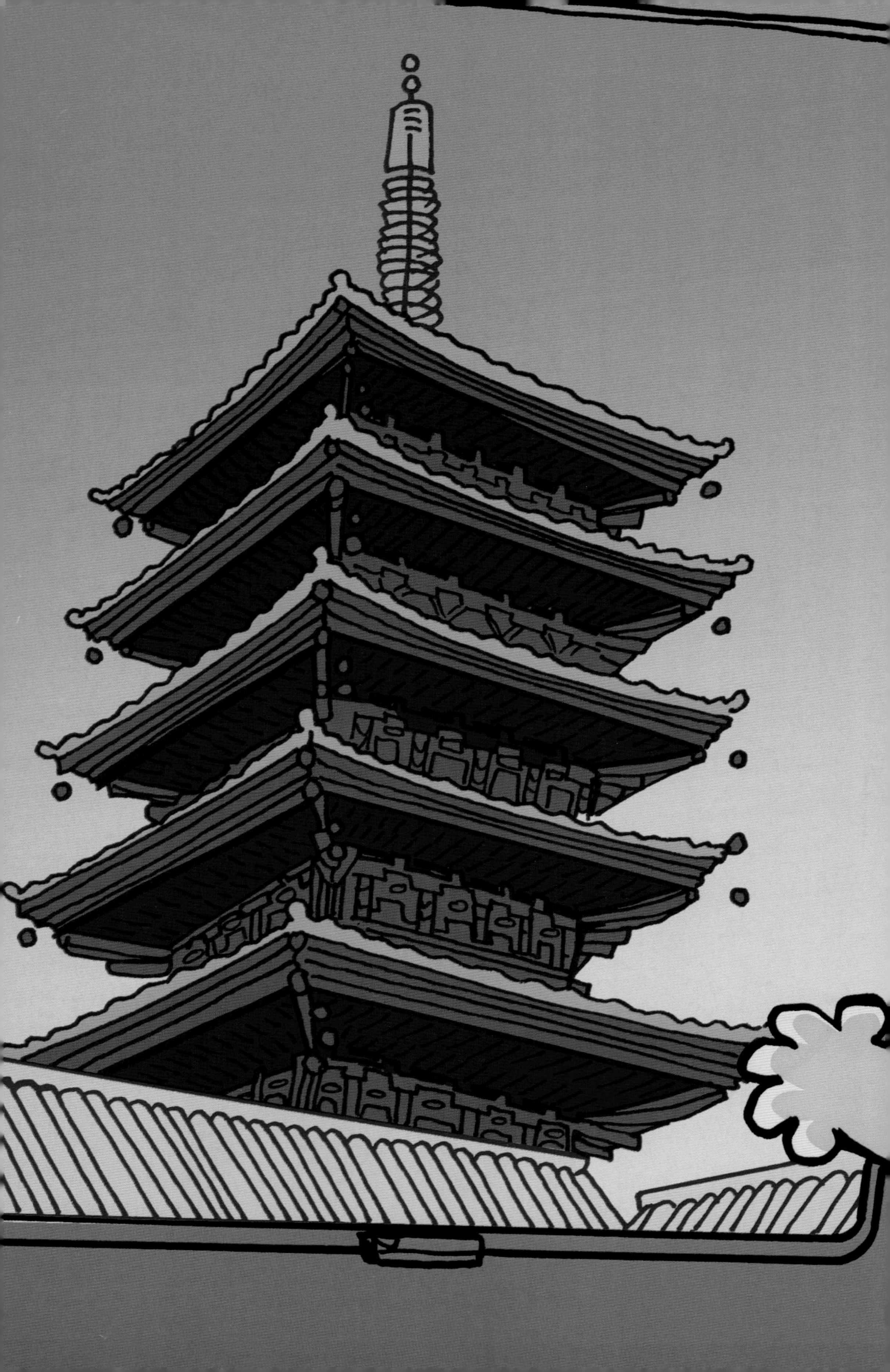